THE MONSTER'S CORNER

SELECTED WORKS BY CHRISTOPHER GOLDEN

ADULT FICTION
Joe Golem and the Drowning City [with Mike Mignola] (Coming in 2012)
Baltimore, or The Steadfast Tin Soldier and the Vampire [with Mike Mignola]
Wildwood Road
The Boys Are Back in Town
Ghosts of Albion: Accursed [with Amber Benson]
Ghosts of Albion: Witchery [with Amber Benson]
The Ferryman
Straight On 'Til Morning
Strangewood

THE SHADOW SAGA
Of Saints and Shadows
Angel Souls and Devil Hearts
Of Masques and Martyrs
The Gathering Dark
Waking Nightmares

THE VEIL
The Myth Hunters
The Borderkind
The Lost Ones

THE HIDDEN CITIES [with Tim Lebbon]
Mind the Gap
The Map of Moments
The Chamber of Ten
The Shadow Men

THE MENAGERIE [with Thomas E. Sniegoski]
The Nimble Man
Tears of the Furies
Stones Unturned
Crashing Paradise

YOUNG ADULT FICTION
The Secret Journeys of Jack London: The Wild [with Tim Lebbon]
When Rose Wakes
Soulless
Poison Ink

THE WAKING [written as Thomas Randall]
Dreams of the Dead
Spirits of the Noh
A Winter of Ghosts

OUTCAST [with Thomas E. Sniegoski]
The Un-Magician
Dragon Secrets
Ghostfire
Wurm War

ANTHOLOGIES
The New Dead
British Invasion [edited w/Tim Lebbon and James A. Moore]
Hellboy: Odd Jobs
Hellboy: Odder Jobs
Hellboy: Oddest Jobs

THE MONSTER'S CORNER

STORIES THROUGH INHUMAN EYES

Edited by Christopher Golden

Sharyn McCrumb

ST. MARTIN'S GRIFFIN

NEW YORK

VMNH
Oct. 20, 2018

THE MONSTER'S CORNER. Copyright © 2011 by Christopher Golden. All rights reserved. Printed in the United States of America. For information, address St. Martin's Press, 175 Fifth Avenue, New York, N.Y. 10010.

www.stmartins.com

Library of Congress Cataloging-in-Publication Data

The monster's corner : stories through inhuman eyes / edited by Christopher Golden.
    p. cm.
 ISBN 978-0-312-64613-4
 1. Horror tales, American.
 PS648.H6M64 2011
 813'.087380806—dc23

2011020407

First Edition: October 2011

10 9 8 7 6 5 4 3 2 1

CONTENTS

vii

Contents

THE MONSTER'S CORNER

MONSTROSITY: AN INTRODUCTION

ANYONE WHO HAS EVER READ my work, or even glanced at my Web site, will already know that I love monsters. Not in the manner of some passing fancy, the way teenagers express their—OMG—love for those shoes, that dress, this hat. Nor can my love for monsters be compared to your love of ice cream or pizza or pad thai or whatever makes you salivate. It is an enduring love. A love that comes with a deep and abiding connection, an understanding, a *knowing*.

One of my earliest childhood memories is of sitting on the back porch of my house on Fox Hill Road in Framingham, Massachusetts, with the little black-and-white TV my mother sometimes had on in the kitchen and watching *Frankenstein* for the first time. I might have been seven. When the monster finds a moment of joy with the little girl by the lake, laughing with her and tossing flower petals into the water until she is the only flower remaining to be plucked and cast . . .

Wow.

The moment terrified me and broke my heart, all at the same time. The monster didn't know any better. He didn't understand the world into which he had been thrust. He had been created with the power to do so much damage, to inflict so much brutality, and yet all he wanted was peace and laughter. When the monster is shown walking into the village with the dead girl in his arms and the villagers react with horror and hatred, the tragedy is complete.

I cried that day. I'm sure I cried in horror and in fear, but I know that my tears also sprang from my sadness for this creature whose monstrosity is no fault of his own.

In the years that followed, I developed a love for all kinds of monsters, thanks in large part to a television landscape that included *Creature Double Feature* and local programmers who filled their airwaves with Japanese giant monster movies, 1950s atomic nightmares, Hammer horror classics, and others in that vein. But it wasn't just the movies. My favorite Bugs Bunny cartoons always had monsters in them. When I started reading comic books—or, rather, buying them on my own—I gravitated toward the wonderful horror comics Marvel published in the 1970s.

While there are monsters who are simply that and nothing more, who are truly evil and alien, there are so many more that inspired me to think and feel. The 1976 remake of *King Kong,* with Jeff Bridges, might not be very good (hey, I was nine, cut me some slack), but when Kong died at the end, it broke my heart. Even as an adult, when I watch the 1933 original, it touches me.

The Tomb of Dracula, the finest of the Marvel horror comics, gave us a Lord of Vampires who was terrifyingly evil, and yet astonishingly human and sympathetic as written by Marv

Wolfman and drawn by Gene Colan. His behavior was monstrous, and yet readers could not help but *feel* for him.

As my literary interests grew, I found myself gravitating toward such portrayals of monstrosity again and again. I read Mary Shelley's *Frankenstein* at last, and finally realized something that I had known in my heart for years by that time—the monster was the hero. The monster was the protagonist. Though the story might be structured otherwise, the language and characterization made it an inescapable truth.

This epiphany opened up a whole new way for me to see these stories. Godzilla, of course, was widely misunderstood. Magneto might be the X-Men's greatest nemesis, and his methods wrong, but he believed in his cause—believed he was doing the right thing for his people.

In college, I wrote more than one paper dissecting my favorite film, *Blade Runner,* examining the *Frankenstein*-like moral structure of Ridley Scott's masterpiece. When it came time to write a term paper on *Moby-Dick,* there could be no other choice for me than to write an essay titled "In Favor of the Whale." Though the novel is structured to make Ahab the protagonist, everything about Melville's language tells us that the opposite is true.

Monsters and monstrosity. Both subjects fascinate me. So much of what we write on those topics is about how we view ourselves, and about the things we fear in ourselves and in others. We want understanding for our own behavior, for the ugliness or otherness we see in ourselves. Like H. P. Lovecraft's outsider or Billy Joel's stranger (not Camus's stranger—that guy's an asshole), we exist in a world that either does not notice us, or does not notice the *us* we believe ourselves to be, or which we hope will never notice the *us* that we fear will not find acceptance in the world. Who are we? What are we? Will others understand?

Back to *Blade Runner.* Roy Batty tells his creator that he has done terrible things, but "nothing the god of bio-mechanics wouldn't let you in heaven for."

Monstrosity is about how we define each other and how we define ourselves. It's about what we see in the mirror and what we fear others will see. And, at its most basic, it is also about the disturbing truth that we do not know what it is in the minds of others, that the woman next to you in line at the bank or the man dressed as Santa at the mall may view the world and humanity and morality very differently from the way that you do.

Now, let's talk about reality for a moment. There are monsters, and then there are monsters. There are real killers who go on rampages that leave people dead and others wounded and destroy the lives and the hopes of so many. These are the real monsters, and there are others in our world. My understanding of and sympathy for monsters does not extend to these real-life horrors. It is reserved for the Beast who is misunderstood, whose noble intentions are wrongly perceived by so many, but who, if he is fortunate, finds understanding in the eyes of a Beauty.

Let's be clear about the line between fiction and reality in my philosophy of monsters. Andrew Vachss, novelist and warrior for the rights of children, once wrote—and I paraphrase—that you can have sympathy for how the monster became the monster without having sympathy for the monster itself. You can sympathize with the child whose experiences forged him into a soulless killer, but once he becomes a monster, sympathy ends.

Got that? Good.

Back to fiction, and my love of fictional monsters.

When I conceived of this anthology, it was with the same love of monstrosity that I described above. I knew that many other writers shared my love for such stories. Once again, as in *The New Dead,* I cast the net wide, luring in contributors from all genres, knowing that such variety would produce a wealth of different approaches to the subject matter. I talked about *Frankenstein* and *Moby-Dick,* and they got it, every last one of them. They understood that, even in the case of a monster who wants to eat us or stomp us or deceive us, sympathy is all in your point of view. Professor X wants mutants to live in peace with humans. Magneto thinks that humans are likely to exterminate mutants if mutants don't get rid of humans first. You could make an argument that neither of them is wrong.

Stephen King once wrote—and again I'm paraphrasing—that the way we identify monsters is by collective agreement. "I'm okay, you're okay, but eww, look at that." I'm fairly certain the thing we're pointing to, the thing that makes us scowl in disgust, is pointing back with the same look of revulsion. It's all a matter of perspective. Eew, look at that. Eew, look at *us.*

Which brings us right back to the outsider, and the mirror. What we hide. What we fear in others and ourselves. Monstrosity.

The contributors to this anthology took up the challenge

admirably. I had only a few rules. Number one, no vampires and no zombies. You can find more than enough of that elsewhere, and they're too easy as go-to monsters. Number two, I discouraged human monsters, although you'll notice that a couple of them slipped in here. Number three, the stories had to be original, though I broke that rule, too. One of the stories was published in a small press anthology that sold about a hundred copies before it appeared here. If you're one of the hundred people who've read it before . . . sshhh. I won't tell anyone if you don't.

The results are wonderful. In the following pages there are stories of fear and stories of heartbreak. There are stories of madness and stories of humor. There are philosophical musings and cruel twists of fate. There are man-eating plants, and even a little sympathy for the devil.

Come, then, and look at things from a new perspective. See the world through inhuman eyes.

Join me in *The Monster's Corner.*

THE AWKWARD AGE

by David Liss

PETE ALWAYS BELIEVED that he and Roberta had done everything they could do, but they'd been doing everything they could for so long that the urgency had long since slipped away, leaving nothing behind but familiarity. It was one of those situations that looked pretty much awful from the outside but was just everyday life to those inside.

So it was a surprise more confusing than pleasant when the phone rang one weekday night and Pete found himself talking to a woman with one of those congenial San Antonio accents that bespoke social fluidity and comfortable wealth. "Is this Neil's dad? Hi. This is Mason's mom." Which is to say, *my* mother. I'm Mason. And I know you won't be happy when you find out how exactly I knew so much about Pete's life, his take on things, what went on in that fucked-up head of his. You are not going to like it, but I promise to tell you. Only not yet. For now, you are going to have to trust me, which is a lot to ask, I know. But people do trust me. I guess I have one of those faces.

* * *

Back to their phone conversation. Pete knew of no child named Mason, so the call caught him off guard. Mason's mother, Cindy, whom Pete immediately recognized from her voice as a particular kind of San Antonio woman—a blond, ponytailed, lacquered—wanted to invite Neil to sleep over with Mason on Friday night. There were some calls across the house, some quick checking of schedules, and the thing was arranged. Just like that. Not until it was all over did Pete cajole Neil away from his computer long enough to answer some rudimentary questions about Mason, who was, by definition, remarkable simply for being Neil's friend.

It was not Pete's fault that he had no idea how to communicate with his son. Not really. On his best day, Neil was impossible to talk to, and this conversation turned out to be even more difficult than most. Neil had been a withdrawn kid when they'd lived in San Diego, and Pete had hoped their move to San Antonio two years ago would give him a chance to open up, to reinvent his life, but it hadn't. He remained the same. Quiet without being moody. Withdrawn without being sullen. Alone without being lonely.

What little attention Neil had for his father evaporated the minute my name was mentioned, and he instantly retreated to the far reaches of his bed, tucked his receding chin into his too-large T-shirt, and mostly nodded yes or shook his head no or shrugged that he didn't know. Pete—who was tall, broad in the shoulders, fit from a regular and moderately punishing gym routine—felt like a menacing ogre, and he couldn't find it within himself to press on with the interrogation. He finally opted for a strategic retreat rather than continue to embarrass his son or do anything that might somehow endanger the sleepover.

Roberta, the lady of the house, made her own foray into Neil Land, but emerged with no more success. "I didn't want him to feel so uncomfortable that he'd cancel," she said later that night as they lay in bed. She was reading a mystery that she'd read a jillion times before. Roberta loved to reread books. Some of her favorites she'd read twenty times or more, which Pete would have considered less absurd if she were reading Proust or Joyce, but these were books by Janet Evanovich or John Grisham, books that hardly warranted a single skim, let alone dozens of attentive reads. Some years ago Pete had found this habit endearing, but now he thought it silly, even embarrassing.

"It's weird," Pete said. He was leafing through the *New Yorker*, not reading much of anything. "He's getting kind of old for sleepovers, don't you think? I'm worried there might be some kind of gay component to this. Or pre-gay."

"You think this is a pre-gay sleepover?" asked Roberta.

Pete set down his magazine. "I'm saying it's odd. I mean, I don't care if he's gay. I'd celebrate him being gay."

"Like with a coming-out party?" Roberta asked. "Our neighbors would love that."

"At least he would be enthusiastic about something. I just want him to be who he is instead of . . ." But Pete did not finish the sentence, because the only possible way to finish it was *nothing*, which was, to his own great shame, how he had come to think of Neil: as a walking depository of nothingness.

Neil always been that way; even as a baby he'd been detached, uninterested, unnaturally calm. Pete and Roberta had done all the right things, gone to all the right doctors, had all the right tests. The results were always the same. There was nothing wrong with Neil. He had no developmental issues; he was nowhere on the autism scale. He was intelligent and responsive, but he didn't care for people. That was who he had always been.

"You should simply enjoy the fact that he has a friend," Roberta told him.

A few minutes later, when she turned out her light, Pete vaguely considered rolling over toward Roberta, who remained very attractive for a woman of forty-seven—pretty, slim, the gray in her hair sexy in a Disney villainess kind of way—but he didn't know if he exactly wanted to have sex. The last three or four—yes, it was exactly four—times he'd made advances, Roberta had rejected him, and he didn't know if he was up for the emotional trauma of five in a row. He might be awake half the night, pondering this rejection, wondering what it meant for their eighteen-year-old marriage. Alternatively, she might be interested, and he wasn't entirely sure that would be a good thing either. In theory sex seemed like an excellent idea, but even at its most rushed it was a time-consuming business, and it was already after midnight. He had work to finish in the morning. Did he want to have sex, or did he want to have *had* sex already so not having sex could be something he didn't have to ponder? As he turned over these ideas, Roberta began to snore in a low, grumbling rhythm and the decision was made for him.

It turned out that Roberta could not take Neil over to my house on Friday night. She was the program director of an oldies radio station, and a crisis had exploded across station management with shocking urgency. The station's popular morning DJ announced he'd received a lucrative offer from a station in Baltimore, and Roberta had to attend an emergency meeting about how to confront this offer. Pete, who telecommuted as a software engineer for the database company he'd been with in San Diego, had the flexible schedule, and he was the one who picked up all the parenting slack. On the way to my house, Neil slouched in the front seat, playing with the satellite radio, settling on some kind of shrill dirge-like music that left Pete feeling both anxious and depressed.

"What's this Mason like?" Pete attempted.

Neil shrugged and then attempted to retract his mass of curly brown hair into his chest cavity. "Okay, I guess."

"Yeah? What do you two like to do together?"

"I don't know. Nothing."

At a stop sign, Pete took a moment to look at his slight, pale, gaunt specter of a son. "Is he also into computer games?"

"Who?" asked Neil with complete sincerity.

"Who do you think?" Pete sighed with frustration. "Mason."

Neil didn't respond, but his silence was not of the furtive or guilty kind, and Neil was already drifting off into the blank space he so much preferred to conversation. Pete decided to let the matter go.

Mason's family, which is to say my family, lived in one of those massive old Alamo Heights houses on one of those winding old streets near the dam. It was the kind of house, inhabited by the kind of people, that made Pete feel small and insignificant and destined to be an outsider in San Antonio. Here was land money, oil money, cattle money. Here were people who surrounded themselves with uniformed Mexicans and felt no discomfort in wielding their complete authority over them, comfortable giving out orders in their competent Spanish. They were the sort of people who, when they heard Pete was a software engineer, would say, "I think that's great!" as if to announce that they were okay with Pete's curious little career. They were accepting of his meaningless toil. They were willing to put a happy face on his inexplicable lack of riches. Mason's family's immodest weal made any interest in Neil even more inexplicable. Pete steadied his nerve as he pulled into our circular driveway, and Neil grabbed his bag and was out the door before Pete had unbuckled his seat belt.

Cindy was precisely what Pete expected—pretty and faded, slim, blond, ponytailed, tennis outfit as casual attire, too much makeup, certainly some minor plastic surgery, possibly something major. He felt like he needed a translator when talking to women like this.

"Those kids," she said, looking toward the house, where the silhouettes of two figures were visible on the other side of the curtains. They stood there, still, bodies at odd angles, surely listening to the adults.

After Pete shook her hand and uttered a few awkward words of introduction, Cindy pressed on with her breathless and insincere enthusiasm. "I am just so glad Mason met Neil. I know he's been a good friend, and Mason's had such a hard time this year. Fourteen is such an awkward age, don't you think?"

Pete agreed because he supposed, from talking to parents who had kids Neil's age, that they had difficulties he and Roberta did not—drama and romance and hormones and emotions. Slammed doors and unfinished homework and asserting dominance. Pete had heard about these things. Also, agreeing seemed to be the best way to keep the conversation to a minimum, and more than anything else, Pete wanted to be in his car and driving away. After answering Cindy's questions about what Neil liked to eat and how late was absolutely too late to stay up, Pete was soon free to retreat to his Accord and return home.

Later, Roberta was angry with Pete for not going inside the house, getting a sense of what the family was like—they didn't even know if Cindy was married. Pete hadn't noticed if she wore a ring. He hadn't figured out a way to meet Mason, to lay eyes on the first friend Neil had made in years. Roberta's irritation bordered on genuine anger.

Pete didn't have the energy to defend himself. If he had, the discussion might have turned into a real argument, but as far as he could tell, he had done nothing wrong. He could hardly have forced his way into the house. He offered to call over there, but Roberta did not want to embarrass Neil in front of his only friend, so she managed to keep her curiosity under control. When Neil was safely returned home at the promised time the next morning, it was apparent there was nothing to worry about. That Neil would not describe his night as anything other than *fine* and *okay* in itself raised no red flags. That was Neil.

Roberta wanted to reciprocate as quickly a possible, both to show their appreciation and so they could have the chance to meet this elusive Mason, so the following Friday evening Cindy's Escalade pulled into their driveway, and Pete watched from the window as my mother emerged, followed by a figure with long dark hair and dressed entirely in black. The first thing Pete noticed was that I had girlish hair—a long, straight tumble of darkness with two elevated purple pigtails. Then he noticed that I was wearing leggings and a skirt. It took a few seconds for Pete to put all the pieces together and realize that his fourteen-year-old son was having a sleepover with a girl. Or was it a cross-dresser? No, it was definitely a girl.

It was not Pete's first encounter with Texas girls with ridiculous names, androgynous only because they were not first names at all. Nevertheless he'd assumed—of course he'd assumed—that someone named Mason would be a boy. Masonry was masculine work, after all. Now both Pete and Roberta were so paralyzed by surprise and awkwardness, they could not even begin to imagine how they ought to act. There was no precedent, no guidelines. They stood, mouths open, eyes wide, while an uninvited girl walked up their driveway followed by her blond, attractive mother, whose prettiness diminished in the wake of her daughter's presence. Charisma radiated from Mason like radioactive waves. Pete saw at once that this was not just a girl. Mason was something special.

So, yes, he noticed me right away. Unlike small and androgynous Neil, I was neither scrawny nor underdeveloped. I was a full head taller than Neil, broad in the shoulder, and respectably stacked for a girl my age. I wore a long black skirt, black boots, and a gauzy blouse that showed off enough cleavage to make a point, but not so much as to venture into whore territory. Despite the dyed black hair and the excessive makeup, neither of which Pete was inclined to find particularly appealing, I had his full attention.

"I can't thank you enough for having Mason over," Cindy said, keys still in hand. She looked, as if with longing, at her Escalade. "Y'all are so nice."

"It's the least we could do. After you had our *son* sleep

over with your *daughter*," Roberta said, emphasizing the gendered nouns in case this aspect of the situation had somehow escaped Cindy's notice.

"Y'all are so nice," Cindy said again. "And I *love* your house!"

"Are there any . . ." Roberta waved her hand in the air and then, noticing what she was doing, stopped. "Are there any special rules you want us to enforce."

I looked at Cindy and she looked away. "No," said Cindy, who after a moment remembered her smile. "I trust y'all."

With Cindy retreating to her car, Pete and Roberta hurried into a huddle as they attempted to formulate a strategy, but things quickly devolved into Roberta berating Pete for not having discovered last weekend that Mason was a girl. Roberta wanted to find some excuse for sending the girl home, but Pete wouldn't allow it. It would be enough for her to sleep in the guest room. He did not want the girl to sleep in Neil's bedroom, but he certainly didn't want her to go. For Neil's sake, he told himself, and at that point he wasn't even lying.

Pete would not have thought of himself as the kind of man who would become fixated on a fourteen-year-old girl, but let's look at the facts a little more closely. First of all, the girl in question did not look fourteen. That has to count for something. An uninterested party would think I was sixteen, maybe even eighteen. It's not the most dignified thing in the world for a forty-five-year-old man to fall for an eighteen-year-old girl, but it is hardly pedophilia. I looked like a woman, not a girl, so while we are certainly entitled to think of Pete as a perv, we are not necessarily obligated to do so.

Secondly, I went after him. Maybe. That *is* what happened, isn't it? At times he was so sure, but other times—well, it was complicated, wasn't it? As the more mature of the two of us, he ought to have found it within himself to be wise and dignified and refuse to enter into some kind of fucked-up relationship because the girl wanted to or seemed to want to or whatever it was that was going on. All of that is surely true, and yet I went after him, almost certainly, and he enjoyed it too much to find the will to resist.

Pete certainly had no way of preparing himself for what was coming. It began as nothing more than an awkward social situation that would someday turn into the kind of funny story you tell after a little too much to drink. I disappeared with Neil into his bedroom, where we did whatever it was we did—Pete certainly had no idea what was going on in there, and he didn't want to humiliate his son by having a peek—until dinner, when we emerged looking neither entirely guilty or innocent. We sat at the table, where we were presented with Roberta's chicken enchiladas, and Pete tried not to avoid looking at me, because that would be rude, but to avoid looking at me too much, because that would be rude, too. Mainly he kept sneaking glances, trying to remember if I was quite as striking, quite as interesting and pretty and magnetic as he recalled me being when he was looking elsewhere. And I was. You'd better believe it.

Over dinner Pete kept staring longingly at a distant wine rack, but he and Roberta—mostly Roberta—had decided not to model drinking in front of the children. Behind the decision was an unspoken need to set clear, strict, puritanical boundaries. Uncorking a wine might just be the first step to an untamed, drunken bacchanal. Mason's mere presence in their home that night was an assault upon the fortress of propriety, so cracks in the walls could not be tolerated. Consequently, Pete made do. Roberta, meanwhile, made a valiant and highly laudable effort to make conversation about normal things—which classes Neil and I shared, what subjects I liked best, what kind of after-school activities I enjoyed. I grant her points for her careful navigation away from questions that might have embarrassed Neil, such as which friends we had in common, what it was we liked to do together, or what, precisely, my interest might have been in a boy whose parents had come—really through no fault of their own—to regard him as something of a ghost.

Questions directed at Neil lost momentum and died. There was no inquiry that could not be satisfied with a shrug or nod or shake of the head. Both parents tried, and both failed. When I talked, I found ways to include him that did not involve any actual response from him, and I knew he would be grateful.

Roberta gave up on directing questions at Neil and focused on me. "So tell us, Mason, what kinds of after-school activities do you do?"

I did not give her the kind of withering glance that any self-respecting goth girl would launch at a parent floundering this badly. Instead, I smiled broadly, waving my fork around for emphasis as I told her about my hours logged on the school literary journal. "I," I assured her, "am a poetess."

Pete liked the way I talked. He liked the youthful exuberance and brazen self-confidence, all laced with the most subtle hint of self-effacing irony. As dinner went on, Pete regarded me less as a child and more as a person, less as a curious invader and more as an interesting, even welcome, intervention into his musty routine. That was what led Pete to ask more interesting questions, because he believed I could handle it, because he believed the answers would be illuminating. He wasn't a parent passing judgment on the peculiarities of the younger generation. He wanted to know. "I'm interested in your, I guess, style, Mason."

"Pete!" Roberta objected.

"I don't think I'm being rude," said Pete. "Mason knows that she dresses in a particular way, and she knows it is going to attract attention. It's not offensive to ask you about it, is it?"

"Of course not." I smiled at both of them. "If you dress in a way that makes people stare, you should be prepared to discuss it."

"Is it some sort of a music thing?" Pete asked. "Are you dressing like a singer? Like, I don't know, Marilyn Manson?"

"Who?" I asked. "Oh, yeah. My mom used to listen to him, I think. I don't mean that in a bad way. I like oldies, but my look isn't about music."

"Is it about *Twilight*?" asked Pete. "Are you into vampires?"

"I'm not a vampire, Pete," I said.

"I'd never suggest you were," he said, feeling a little chastised, and feeling it was deserved. He realized he had veered into the condescending, and wished to correct course. "Of course not."

"Some people are," I told him as I picked at a piece of chicken. "Some people like to pretend they are, and some people actually are. But I'm not."

"We know you're not, honey," said Roberta.

"I'm a ghoul," I said.

This kind of pronouncement can bring a conversation to a halt, but I had confidence I could get things moving again. Neil chewed on obliviously. Roberta looked at Pete, as though begging for some kind of lifeline. Pete grabbed for the goblet of wine he wished were by his placemat.

"Oh," said Roberta at last. "That's so interesting."

Pete sucked in his breath, came to terms with the lack of wine, and chose to valiantly march into the battle. "Is there a difference?" He met my gaze for the first time, holding on to it, and he smiled. I smiled in return, and he knew he was having fun now. He wasn't teasing me. He wasn't interested in humiliating me or showing me up. He told himself he was treating me like any guest. In fact, he was flirting with me. "Isn't ghoul just a kind of generic term, and maybe vampire is, I don't know, a subset of ghoul? All vampires are ghouls but only some ghouls are vampires. Like squares and rectangles."

"It's a common mistake," I told him, careful to sound amused as well. I was also flirting. "Really, there's no reason to be embarrassed. But no vampires are ghouls. Different things. Vampires suck the blood of the living. Ghouls survive off the flesh of the dead. And, to a lesser extent, disillusionment."

"Is this appropriate dinner conversation?" Roberta asked.

"Don't we all eat the flesh of the dead?' asked Pete, holding up a piece of chicken on his fork.

Across the table, Neil sawed a piece of enchilada in half with his knife and fork.

I met Pete's gaze, firm and steady, and showed him my best,

full-toothed, red-lipped smile. "Indeed we do. But," I added, "a ghoul prefers to eat uncooked human flesh."

"I really don't think we should be talking about this," said Roberta, "but what a wonderful imagination you have."

They made up the guest room for me. "We're not comfortable with the two of you sharing a room together," Roberta said. "You understand, don't you, Neil?"

He shrugged. "I guess. Whatever."

Pete stared at his son in undisguised disappointment. A charming, sexy, unconventional girl was sleeping over at his house. Surely this was the time to rouse himself from his torpor. Surely this was something worth fighting for, but Neil glanced at his cuticles and jabbed at the carpet with the tip of his sneaker.

They let us stay up playing video games until eleven, and then it was lights out. The guest room had its own bathroom, so I disappeared inside but did not get undressed. I turned out my light, and by midnight the rest of the house was dark. I waited, not certain what Pete would do, but I knew a thing or two about desire and longing, and I'd placed my bets. A little after one in the morning, I saw a light go on in the kitchen. I heard the shuffle of feet, the low murmur of the TV, and the distinctive popping of a cork. Pete decided he would have that wine after all. I waited until I thought he'd have had time for a glass and then went out, still fully dressed, still fully made up, looking fresh, rested, impossibly unrumpled. He was sitting at the kitchen table, wearing a white T-shirt and cotton shorts, watching a black-and-white movie on the TV, with a bottle of wine and a glass in front of him. And he was glad to see me. Maybe even relieved. He didn't know himself.

"Where do you keep the wineglasses?" I asked.

He paused for a moment, and somewhere in his reptile brain a thousand possibilities played out, a thousand choices presented themselves, but there were really only two, and he chose between them without taking a moment to seriously consider the alternative. He looked at my lips, red as blood and glistening from a fresh application of lipstick, and gestured toward one of the cabinets. I took a glass, sat down across from him, and poured. I swirled my glass, took a sip, and then looked at the label.

"So, what?" he asked. "You're some kind of bad girl?"

"I like wine," I said. "I prefer old-world reds. You know, big Italian wines, especially anything from Piedmont, but this is pretty good for a California cab." I took another sip and met his gaze, enjoying astonishment and pleasure, enjoying the distant thrum of gears turning in his mind. "Define 'bad girl.'"

"Come on," he said. "What are you doing with Neil? You are a beautiful young girl and Neil is . . . You know."

I leaned forward, letting my top sag just enough to improve his view. "Tell me."

"There's nothing wrong with him," Pete said, staring into my face because he dared not look down my top. "He's just a loner. He doesn't have a lot of friends. You must know that. Before you, he didn't seem to have any friends, and he didn't seem to mind. As near as I can tell, the other kids don't pick on him. They hardly even notice him. When we have conferences at school, his teachers need a minute to go through his file, as if they're trying to remember who he is. Christ, sometimes I come home and see him and remember that I have a son."

"And you're telling this to his only friend?"

"It's crazy," admitted Pete. "I guess I wonder if maybe you know him, really know him, in some way that Roberta and I don't. Maybe you can tell me something." He finished off his glass and poured himself another one. After a moment's thought, he refilled mine. "I'm sorry. You must be uncomfortable."

"No," I said. "I appreciate that you talk to me like I'm a peer. You don't talk down to me. You expect me to get things. And I do. I get a lot of things."

"You seem very mature. For a ghoul."

"Gotta respect the ghoul," I said.

"Human flesh," he said.

I smiled. "And disillusionment."

"Tasty," he said.

"You'd be surprised." I met his gaze and held it until he looked away. Then I said, "So, we can be friends, right? We can hang out?"

"Come on." He leaned away from the table, creating more space between us, not because that's what he wanted to do, but because it was what he thought he ought to do. He liked the idea of being my friend. He liked the idea of hanging out with me. He hated that he liked the idea, but he liked it all the same.

"No," I said. "You come on."

"How exactly is that going to work? You're in middle school, and you think we can just hang out? I'm forty-five years old," he said, wanting, more than anything else, to hear that it didn't matter.

"Forty-five," I said. "Now *that* is an awkward age."

* * *

I let the better part of a week go by, but on Thursday I called him on his cell phone, right after school, a good couple of hours before Roberta would be home. "Engineer any good software today?"

"How did you get this number?" he asked.

"I found it in Neil's phone," I told him. "I was snooping. I'm very curious."

"Right," he said. "I was about to run some errands. You're lucky to catch me."

"I *am* lucky to catch you," I agreed.

"So, Mason," he said. "Can I do something for you?"

"What do you have in mind?"

There was a pause. "I mean, are you calling for a reason?"

"Do I need a big reason? I thought we were going to be friends."

"Mason, this is weird," he said.

"I know. Right?"

Another pause. "I just don't think this is a good idea."

"Are you going to give me a lot of crap about age difference? Are you really that shallow? Because I don't think you are. I enjoy your company and you enjoy mine, and there is no reason why we can't be friends other than the fact that, on some abstract level, you think it can be interpreted as weird. And maybe that's true. Maybe, in general, it *is* weird for a person as old and feeble and decayed as you to be friends with a bright young fountain of potential like me, but the question is, do you think it is always weird? Do you think it is weird in this particular instance?"

"Wow," he said. "Have you been practicing that?"

"It just came out, but it sounded awesome, right? I know! I was totally on a roll!"

He laughed. "You make a convincing case."

"Good, so I'm at home, my mom is not. Why don't you come over. I'm about to watch this old movie, *Showgirls*? Have you ever seen it? It's about strippers or something, and it's supposed to be so terrible that it's awesome." I gave him a few seconds to consider all this. "Join me?"

He took a few seconds himself. "I can't. I have, uh, errands."

Is there a way to interpret an invitation to watch a semipornographic film in an empty house as anything other than a come-on? Pete worked hard to find another explanation, because the most obvious one seemed so improbable—and so very much what he wanted—that he found it impossible to accept. Mason did not understand what she was doing. Mason was naive. Mason was so incredibly not interested in Pete that she viewed him as essentially sexless, which meant there was no erotic component in watching a dirty movie with him. One of those things had to be true because the alternative, that sexy young Mason was into him, meant he would have to develop some kind of response. Of course he could not make a move. Any kind of sexual relationship with her was unthinkable—and a crime. If they were caught, it would mean scandal, prison, the destruction of his family. It was also adultery, and despite the chronological fatigue currently buckling the walls of his marriage, Pete loved Roberta, had never cheated on her, and didn't relish the idea of doing so.

But there were those little nagging questions. Would cheating really be that big a deal? What was cheating—what was it really? Just body parts touching, when you thought about it. Like shaking hands. In the end, what did it really mean? And what if it turned out that he fell in love with Mason? Then shouldn't he be with her? Statutory rape, as a law, made sense in most cases, but Mason was clearly no ordinary fourteen-year-old. She was a woman, and there was nothing perverted in desiring her since he desired her as a woman, not a child.

He desired her. Yes.

These thoughts ping-ponged through Pete's mind as he ran his errands, through dinner, through after-dinner television. In the middle of a show he and Roberta always liked to watch together—though they watched it only because she had a crush on one of the actors—Pete got up and went to Neil's room, knocking once, and then entering when Neil grunted his approval for entry.

Inside the room, Neil sat at his desk, using his mouse and keyboard to lead a knight on a horse across a hilly landscape.

"You have a minute?" Pete asked.

"Okay," Neil said, not looking up. "I'm supposed to meet someone from my guild in like ten minutes."

"Sure," Pete said. He sat on Neil's bed, which had been made with almost military precision. There was no junk on the floor. His books were put on their shelves in alphabetical order. There were no posters on the walls. It had never occurred to Neil that he might want to personalize his space.

"Are you still friends with Mason?" Pete asked.

"I guess," Neil said, continuing to ride his horse across the landscape. "I mean, maybe. I don't know."

25

"Do you like her? I mean, like for a girlfriend?"

"Nah."

Pete needed a moment here. There was no awkwardness in this. No embarrassment. Pete had the distinct feeling that Neil had never considered Mason as an object of desire—that now that the topic had been raised, he still didn't.

"Does she still want to hang out?" he managed.

"Not really."

"Since when?"

"Sleepover, I guess."

"And how do you feel about that?"

Neil shrugged. "I don't feel anything about it."

Pete stood up. "You don't feel anything about it? You don't have any friends, Neil. Don't you care that you don't have friends? Don't you care that this beautiful girl wants to spend time with you, that she's been—I don't know—chasing you? Haven't you noticed? Are you just going to let her get away from you without even noticing that she's there?"

Neil stared at his father with a surprise that bordered on a kind of confused alarm. "She's okay, but you know."

"Okay," Pete said. He walked toward the door, now afraid he'd raised his voice, that Roberta had heard him. He put his hand on the doorknob, turned back to Neil, and said, "Okay," again. And that was it. Neil was already back at his keyboard, piloting his horse toward another figure on a horse. He tried not to think about the impossible, nonsensical, fantastical possibility that Mason had used his son to get to him. Why would she do that? Who was Pete that a fourteen-year-old girl would give a crap? Maybe Mason liked Neil for his own sake. Maybe she saw something in him that his own father simply could not, and while Pete found that thought as comforting as he did shameful, he could not make himself believe it. Even if it was the most logical explanation, it did not feel true.

Pete walked back to the TV room and sat next to Roberta, who hadn't noticed he'd been gone, let alone heard him raise his voice. Roberta watched her show, and Pete thought about what might have happened if he had watched *Showgirls* with Mason.

Wasting no time, I texted Pete just before noon the next day.

> ME: what r you up2
>
> HIM: Hi Mason. I'm working. Shouldn't you be furthering your education?
>
> ME: take me 2 lunch
>
> HIM: Wouldn't you have to miss school?
>
> ME: So not ur problem 12:15 at gas station, 1 block north of school
>
> HIM: I don't know.
>
> ME: Yes u do I'll b there

He came. Of course he came. How could he not? I'd made it so easy to say yes, so hard to say no. He picked me up in his Accord and smiled politely and did not touch me or leer at me, despite my wearing a very tight black T-shirt and short skirt in which I looked entirely like a woman and nothing like a child. I had my hair back in a ponytail, and he liked the way it looked. He liked being able to see my white neck. He liked my profile. He liked it all.

Pete had decided he would do everything he could to act as though meeting me for lunch, helping me to skip school, were the most natural thing in the world. He wore khakis and a button-down shirt, and he felt certain he looked handsome and competent, and he felt muscular and trim and ten years younger than he was, and he kept trying to forget what he was doing, how crazy and strange and dangerous it was. He wanted to enjoy the sensation of being near me, of being so close to my youth and vitality and freshness, and my near total absence of world-weariness. He didn't want to think about what any of it meant or where it would lead or how insanely and foolishly self-destructive this single act was, how it could ruin his marriage and his life and everything. He wanted to inhabit the experience, and he could not remember the last time his life offered up a moment sweet enough to deserve that kind of attention.

"Where do you want to go?" he asked.

"Someplace I can get a beer," I said.

He paused for a moment, and then decided not to be shocked or surprised or concerned. He decided to go with it. In some sense, he decided I was in charge, and he knew he was deciding that, and it was possible he even liked it. Pete was not accustomed to drinking beer in the afternoon. He might do so at a weekend party, but on a weekday, when he ought to be working—that was something that had quite literally never happened before. When you are self-employed, working entirely without supervision, it is healthiest to view midday drinking as strictly for drunks and losers, the pathetically unproductive. He knew that, and yet now that I had suggested it, Pete could not help but find the idea appealing. More than appealing. Seductive. It was a doorway to an entirely different life, and he was surprised how easy it was to decide to step through it. "What time do you have to be back?" he asked.

I pressed myself into the seat. "I don't. I don't ever have to be anywhere."

He took me to a Korean place off Walzem where we ordered barbecue and drank Japanese beer while we snatched up spicy pickles and potatoes and little tiny fish with our chopsticks. Pete hadn't known what to expect when I ordered the first round of beer, but the waiter had only nodded, not so much concealing his reaction as never having one. Maybe he was used to parents ordering drinks for their underaged children. Maybe he never doubted that I was of age. Maybe I simply had that effect on people. Certainly, Pete reflected, he'd already done things with me and for me that he never would have imagined doing, so he simply assumed the waiter was no different.

The beer turned out to be just what he needed. It didn't make the situation any less strange, but it helped him to settle in, to work up the nerve to say what needed to be said. "What exactly is up with you and Neil?"

I let the bottle of beer dangle between my thumb and index finger, swinging like a pendulum. "What do you mean?"

"Give me a break, Mason," he said, loving the feel of my name in his mouth. "You know what I mean."

"Nothing is up with me and your son," I said. "He is my

friend. I like Neil. I'm not dating him. We are not having any kind of sexual relations, if that's what you want to know. Anyhow, I have a boyfriend."

"You do?" Disappointment, followed by chastising himself for that disappointment. What possible concern of his could it be if I had a boyfriend or not? I had a boyfriend and had no interest in Pete in that way, just as he had supposed, just as he had always known. He felt utterly deflated and utterly relieved. He felt like the world was righting itself and, in the process, he was sliding off the surface and into the void.

"You don't think I could have a boyfriend? You think ghouls don't deserve love?"

"That's not what I'm saying," he said. "Of course it isn't. I'm just making conversation, I guess. Acknowledging that I heard you."

"He's older than I am," I said. "I like older guys."

This got his attention. "How much older?"

"Tenth grade."

I could see the emotions swirl across his face like the time-lapse image of a hurricane. Never had Pete felt quite so many of his forty-five years all at once, all so bitterly. He ordered us another round of beer.

"His name is Ryan," I said. "And he is so hot. God, I love him. He plays JV football, but he's not the jock type. He's really cool. You would *love* him. I can't wait for you guys to meet."

"Yeah, well, I don't know how feasible that is," he said.

"And he is so good in bed. Fuck. I know I shouldn't say things like that. I know. I'm sorry. Cindy always says I need to censor myself better, and I swear I'm working on it."

So now Pete knew. I wasn't hitting on him, he concluded. He was an absurd, self-deluding, middle-aged clown. That much was now clear, wasn't it? But then how to explain the flagrant flirting, the inviting him over to watch *Showgirls*? Could he have been so wrong about all that? How could he have misunderstood so many signals? He couldn't have, but then how could he make sense of this new development?

It would have been so easy for him to escape. He could have done it right then, and to do it he only would have had to say precisely what was on his mind. He could have asked me what I thought I was doing with him. He could have asked me why I was flirting with him and then talking about my hot boy-friend. He could have said that he found this situation very confusing and strange, and maybe the strange part he could live with, maybe he liked the strangeness. He could have said how much he enjoyed me and being near me and talking with me and drinking three or four or five beers with me in the afternoon and blowing off that work he swore he would get done that afternoon because being with me was so much bet-ter than any of that, but he could *not* deal with how confus-ing it was. He could have said that he didn't know if it was because of my youth or the generation gap or just the pecu-liarities of my personality or the fact that maybe I ought to be on meds, but clearly I did not understand the mixed signals I was sending, and he needed me to explain. That's all it would have taken. Web snapped, snare broken. It would have been so simple, but simple doesn't mean easy, and for Pete the hard-est thing would have been to say the words that banished the illusion that a beautiful, impossible, unobtainable girl desired him. So he said something else. He said, "You know what? You should feel free to be entirely yourself around me."

"I will," I lied as I took a piece of kim chi.

There were more texts. I sent him a message every day. Then two or three and then four or five times a day. I would sometimes wait an hour or two before responding to his. He always responded right away. There were more lunches with more drinks. We would sneak away, he from his home office and me from school, and we would eat and linger around the table at some obscure Asian eatery with stained linoleum floors and peeling wallpaper and delicious food—restaurants in forgotten corners of the city where no one he knew would ever go. We would get pleasantly, and never excessively, drunk. I put my hand on his arm while we talked. I hugged him hard both hello and good-bye. I pressed myself against him, and let him catch me breathing in the scent of him as though these hugs could sustain me. Those moments, he was sure, were the happiest of his life, so true and so hopeful and so full of sweetness.

Sometimes he would think that if he considered Mason, really considered her, who she was and what she said and did, then he knew he didn't really want *her*. Even in some fantasy world in which they could be together, the relationship could never last, and it wasn't because of the age difference either. It was because the things that made Mason so tantalizingly desirable were not the things on which real love was built. He knew it, and knowing it did not matter.

Roberta noticed nothing. That was the crazy thing. He kept waiting for her to say something, to discover the e-mails or the texts or smell the beer on his breath or my scent on his clothes, but she never did. He sat across from her at the dinner table, still half buzzed from lunch with his secret fourteen-year-old friend, and waited for the other shoe to drop. He cooked up explanations and excuses and narratives that would attempt to make sense of his relationship with me. But Roberta never asked or noticed, which only left Pete feeling emboldened.

And work. That was the crazy thing. Pete felt like he was in some kind of moralistic novel from the fifties, one in which his halfhearted efforts to escape from his life of quiet desperation would lead to his loud and chaotic destruction. His productivity fell off. He was sure of it, but no one at the company noticed. His superiors still sent him enthusiastic e-mails about his work. If he missed a deadline by an hour or two, no one seemed to mind, and it occurred to him that for years he'd been making himself crazy to hit deadlines no one but he cared about. Pete was crashing and burning, but no one troubled to take note. His work, his attention, his daytime sobriety weren't missed.

Pete wrote his code during the day, and then in the evening he would sit through his quiet dinners with Roberta and Neil, and then Neil would slink off to his room and he and Roberta would watch some television in which neither of them was particularly invested. They would go to the bedroom and read for a little while, and now and again they'd have satisfactory if familiar sex. That was it. That was his life. That was the sum of his existence without me, and I outweighed all of it. He would have let it all go for me if he could.

He couldn't, of course, and so he would spend long hours, awake in his bed at night, thinking that he would just need to wait until I was eighteen. Three years and seven months. That was all he would have to wait, and then Neil could go be Neil on his own. Roberta didn't want Pete around anyhow. Not really. They were just a comfortable habit now. In three years and seven months he would run away with Mason. He promised himself it would happen, and he refused to think about all the reasons why it was impossible because he knew that if he did not have me to give his life meaning, the emptiness in my wake would be unbearable. It was the one thing about me of which he was absolutely certain.

So he sent me more messages and longer messages and asked to meet with me more often. To counter this boldness, I talked incessantly about Ryan, about how much I loved him, how much I missed him when he was not around, how we had amazing sex, how I gave him a blow job for scoring a touchdown. This stuff killed him, and I could tell it did, but he would not tell me to stop, he would not ask me what I wanted with him, he would not ask why I wanted to spend time with him. Someday he would be with me, but that was an impossibly distant future. For now, it was enough that nothing change. If I were to come on to him and kiss him and that led to sex, maybe it would be hot and exciting and amazing, but next would come guilt and drama and perhaps jail, and he didn't want any of that. He didn't want to cheat on his wife and he didn't want to be the sort of person who would sleep with a fourteen-year-old girl. What he wanted was for things to be exactly the way they were, and maybe hearing about Ryan was the price he had to pay for that to happen. Maybe as long as I was in love with Ryan, and having sex with Ryan and talking about Ryan, Pete would be safe inside his insane and happy bubble.

One day, after three beers and over the remains of pad thai, I began the next phase. "How come you never invite me over to dinner anymore?" I asked.

He looked at me, and then away, and then at his food. Then he looked at me again. I was wearing a black summer dress with spaghetti straps, and it was less like clothing than a wrapping to conceal my nudity. Pete tried not to let it distract him and to focus on the task at hand. He had become used to regarding everything I said as a puzzle or a test, and he considered the best way to tackle this one. "I thought you and Neil weren't friends anymore."

"But you and I are," I said.

"So, you want to have dinner at my house? With my family?"

"Are you ashamed of me?"

It occurred to Pete that they'd never discussed what they did as secret. They never talked about it as sneaking around. Did Mason not see it that way? Did she have no idea that adults were not supposed to do things like this? While his heart hammered with the thrill of the illicit and the daring, did she regard this as just another lunch with just another friend? He did not know. He did not fucking know, and he could not stand not knowing.

"I just don't know how comfortable Roberta is around ghouls," he said.

He was trying to keep it light, and I knew it, but I chose not to take it that way. I slammed down my beer. "Why do you want to make my life into a joke?"

"Why do you want your life to be a joke? You are a bright, beautiful girl, so why do you need to pretend you are some kind of monster?"

"I was honest with you from the beginning," I said. "This is what I am. I never pretended otherwise. I am this way because of my own actions, but I don't have a choice. You are either my friend and accept me or you aren't and don't. There's no other way to see it."

"Mason, I didn't mean to upset you."

"Too late," I said, finishing my beer. "I think of my friends as people who would do anything for me."

"I would do anything for you," he said.

I snorted.

"No, really," he said, and he was pleading now, desperate that I believe him. "I would do anything for you."

"Would you kill someone for me?"

"If necessary, yes," he said.

"And if it weren't necessary?" I asked.

"This is silly," he answered.

"You're right, it is silly," I agreed. "Take me home, please."

We talked about it over a series of e-mails and texts. I apologized to him, told him I'd been tired and moody and on the rag, that he had done nothing wrong, but that was the moment things changed. I slowed it all down. I didn't respond to all his messages, and when I did respond, I waited longer than usual. I would make dates for lunch and then cancel. I left him hanging.

For Pete, these were not easy days. Things with me were not what they had been. There was no comfort to take in Roberta, who grew older and cold and remote. Neil was isolated and broken—a complete failure as a child and a monument to Pete's complete failure as a parent. All the miseries of his life began to come back into focus, now more vivid than ever for having been briefly occulted.

The more I withdrew, the more he thought about me, until he reached the point where he realized that he was thinking about me every moment of his day that he was not specifically thinking about something that required his attention. I was his default mode, his anger, his resentment, his confusion, his rage toward himself for his own inaction and hesitation and refusal to walk away from something so impossible and destructive. He would vacillate between confusion, hope, and despair, unable to make sense of anything I had ever done, anything I had ever said. Nothing in his life had given him the tools to sort out the mystery of Mason. His internal compass was like that of a plane lost in the Bermuda Triangle, the needle spinning endlessly, north every direction and none at all.

In was in this period when Pete, moping and hollow, ran into Cindy at the grocery store. Maybe he might have avoided her in the past, but now he was desperate. He would take any contact with me he could manufacture, even if it was secondhand and through my mother. She was at the deli counter as he pushed his way past, and she looked away, hoping to avoid him. Normally he would have pretended not to see her pretend not to see him and wheeled his cart right on past, but not now, now when he stood to possibly learn something about me, so he put on his best smile and pushed his cart over to her.

"Cindy, hi. It's Pete. Neil's father."

She met his false smile with one of her own. "Of course. How are you? How's Neil?"

"Oh, we're good." Pete was already tiring of the small talk, feeling it gum up his brain. "How's Mason?"

Cindy stared at him. "Oh, you know."

"No, I don't. How is she?"

"You know how it is with kids their age. It's a challenge. Especially Mason. She just hasn't been the same since her father."

"I'm sorry, I didn't know anything about this. Her father—died?"

Cindy nodded, and her eyes were moist. Pete wanted to get the hell out of there. He hated making this woman cry, but he also felt certain he was on the verge of something important. "That's when it all started, you know, with her look and every-thing. They were never close, but I was out of town when it happened. I wished she'd called the police right away or called me or something. But she didn't. That's what happened to her, you know."

"What happened to her?" Pete demanded. He didn't raise his voice, but he could feel himself getting intense.

"She was alone with the body too long and she tried—" Cindy turned away.

"She tried what?"

Cindy shook her head. "It was hard. That's all I meant. Don't tell her I told you about her father, but if it comes up, please don't let her think I told you more." She pushed her cart away.

Pete stared after her, resisting the urge to chase her, to make her tell him what she did not want to say because Pete thought he knew. He was certain he knew what I had tried to do with my father's body. What I had done with it. Pete thought he knew, and he was right.

After leaving him in this state for almost a month, I called him. "Hey, Pete."

"Hi, Mason." He tried to sound neutral, not bitter and delighted and angry and hopeful. It was just after noon on a weekday, and I heard the slur in his voice. He'd been drinking. On his own. Every day he waited for me to call or text or e-mail, and some of those days he drank.

"It's so good to hear your voice," I said. "I've missed you so much!"

He didn't want to say it. "I miss you, too." He said it anyhow. "How have you been?"

"Okay," he said. "You?"

"So busy, but listen, I need some help. Do you think you could help me? I need you to give me a ride tonight."

Hope. Yes, there was anger and hesitation and fear and confusion, but more than anything else, hope, and he was full of willingness to forgive me for everything—for teasing him and misleading him and telling him about my sex life with my sixteen-year-old boyfriend—if only I would be his friend again and let him do me a favor. "A ride where?"

"I'll tell you when I see you. Can you pick me at my house at about eleven? I'll be waiting outside."

"Listen, Mason, I don't think I can do that. It's, I don't know, crazy."

"Why?"

"Because it is, that's why. What would I tell Roberta?"

"Tell her you are doing me a favor," I said. "She *has* met me."

This was precisely the sort of thing that left him so utterly rudderless, and he needed a moment to formulate a reply. "What about your mother?" he asked. "Can't she take you?"

"My mother. Please," I said, which both ended that line of inquiry and provided absolutely no information.

There was a prolonged silence and then, finally, "I'll be there."

Where I wanted to go was the cemetery, the Jewish cemetery, because Jews did not embalm their bodies. I told him where and I told him why, and he drove me. He tried to make conversation, to keep things light, to ask what I was up to, but I was not in the mood for talking. He even asked me about Ryan in the hopes of rousing me out of my stupor, but it was of no use. "Mason, what is going on?" he asked at last.

"I'm hungry," I said.

"Then let's go out to eat," he said, excited. There would be food and drink and we would have a little too much and I would touch his arm when I talked and he would feel light and giddy and young and full of potential and he would forget how unhappy he was.

"Not that kind of hungry. I need to eat real food. There was a funeral today. There'll be something fresh."

"Mason," he began.

"I told you," I said. "I told you the first time we met what I was. I know you didn't want to listen, you didn't want to believe, but it is part of who I am, and I have to eat. If I don't, I will die. Is that what you want?"

"Let me take you home," he said, putting a hand on my arm, daring to initiate touching for the first time, to thrill at the feel of my skin, of my warm flesh, of the roundness of my arm. He loved me. He really did. "You need some sleep, and you'll be fine."

I jerked away from his grip. "Are you my friend or aren't you?"

"You know I am," he said.

"Then come with me. Help me, and if you want, you can join me."

"Join you?"

"Take my hand. You can be like I am."

He stared at me. "Are you quoting Blue Oyster Cult?"

"I'm alluding to Blue Oyster Cult," I said. "It's not the same thing. But I am also offering us a way to be together."

"Why me?" he said. "Why did you choose me?"

We all have our blind spots and our weaknesses, and this was mine. This was the question to which I'd never formulated a response, and I should have known it was coming. I should have seen it as inevitable, but I slipped up, and now I had to think on my feet. I could not hesitate. I could not appear to be fabricating something, and so I told him the truth. "I saw you at school, picking up Neil, and you were what I wanted. I knew you were. You were like a perfectly ripe piece of fruit ready for picking. And so I picked you. Now you are mine, if you want to be."

He stared at me, daring to hope that what I said was true, that I could somehow make him something else, that he could walk away from his life and have a reason, a necessity, to become something else. Even if it meant becoming a monster, was it worth it? Was becoming something unspeakable too high a price to pay for becoming something new? Pete had already had a taste of what it would be like to live outside the realm of the acceptable, he had desired the forbidden, he had flirted with becoming an outcast, and all of those things had seemed wonderful and welcoming and sweet, and that was why he followed me into the graveyard.

I stared at him hard, daring him to turn away from me. "You said you'd do anything for me. You said that. Did you mean it?"

He nodded.

"Then it's time to show me."

Of all the things he did that night, following me inside was the hardest. To enter a graveyard at night was a thing so strange, so against every instinct, that it made the rest that much easier. We trudged across the vast expanse of markers and monuments. The air was warm and pleasant, and the half-moon provided us with just enough light. Somewhere in the far distance, the cemetery's lone security guard sat in his little room, watching his little television, oblivious to our trespass.

I'd scouted ahead, so I knew where to find the fresh grave with its loose soil and the shovel sticking out like a toothpick in a plate of hors d'oeuvres.

"Dig," I told him.

He stared at me. "You want me to dig up a grave? Why?"

I smiled. "Because you want to know what's at the bottom. You've always wanted to know, haven't you? What do I want with you? What am I after? There's only one way to find out."

He looked at me, unable to believe he was here, in this graveyard, truly considering something so insane as digging up a dead body. "You could simply tell me," he said.

I shook my head, sympathetically, not at all unkindly. "No," I said. "That's not how it works. There's only one way to find out. You can dig, or you can never know."

That was why he picked up the shovel and thrust the blade into the loose soil. That was why he worked with calm, steady, untiring effort while I sat on a nearby gravestone and painted my fingernails black.

When the grave was dug and the coffin was open, it was his turn to watch, and he did watch. He looked on while I ate. I did not need to remove my clothes, but I did that for him, to give him something to consider, to ponder, to enjoy while I engaged in an activity that he must at first find revolting, and later find something else entirely. And when I'd had my fill, I took the shovel and removed the top of the corpse's skull and handed him a beautiful cut of the freshly dead and yeasty-smelling brain. I stood before him naked, my breasts streaked with dirt and blood, holding the flesh out to him like a supplicant making an offering to her god, and he took it and bit into it and his knees became weak.

"Wow," he said, dropping down onto the grass as he chewed thoughtfully. "It's amazing. I can—I know what she was feeling, I know what she thought, how she made sense of things. I know what it was to be her."

I stood there and looked at him and smiled. "I know," I said, "that's how it works. You just know."

I watched. I watched him know what it was like to be that deep inside someone's head, to understand a stranger's life with intimate certainty. I looked at him and smiled, and wiped my mouth with the back of my naked arm. Pete had been

amusing, and he'd been useful, but I could see it might get tiring soon enough. And when it did, well, something might
happen to Pete, and then it would be time for me to find out
what he'd been thinking all this time . . .

SAINT JOHN

By Jonathan Maberry

1.

SAINT JOHN WALKED through cinders that fell like slow rain, and he found twenty-seven angels hiding behind the altar of a burning cathedral.

2.

AN HOUR BEFORE that he found a crushed and soiled rose.

He stole a wheelbarrow from a hardware store and filled it with the weapons he had collected since the plague began and wheeled it to the cathedral. Saint John sang songs in his head while he worked. He did not sing them aloud, of course. God had told him years ago to sing all of his songs of praise in the temple inside his head. He left the barrow by the curb and walked up the stone stairs. The door was ajar, the lock chopped clumsily out of the wood by an axe.

There was an explosion behind the far row of buildings, and Saint John turned and stood on the top step as golden embers fell. He tilted his head face upward, eyes closed, tongue out, smiling as he waited for a piece of ash to find him. When it did he pulled it in with the tip of his tongue and savored it. The strongest flavor was the uninspired taste of charcoal that had to melt before he could enjoy the other tastes. Ghosts of flavors. There was sweetness there, like meat. A sharpness like ammonia. The tang of acid sourness. He did not know what this ash had been. Something alive, that much was certain, but that could be as true of a tree as of a dog, a pigeon, or the postman. He wished that he could discern which, but a learned palate was an acquired thing, its subtle perceptions honed through practice, observation, consideration, and repetition. Saint John did not believe that he would have the time to sample and catalogue the many flavors and combinations of flavors of this apocalyptic feast. The fires would not last as long as his appetites.

Pity.

There was an explosion off to his left. He cocked his head and replayed the boom in his memory and then listened to the echoes as they banged off the building that surrounded the stone library. He smiled faintly. This *was* something he knew well. The blast was ordinary, not military ordnance. Probably a car gas tank rupturing from superheated gases as the vehicle burned. Semtex or C-4 each had its own unique blast signature, much like the calibers of bullets, weights of loads, and makes of guns. Each possessed a unique voice that whispered its secrets to him.

As if to reaffirm this, there was a rattle of automatic gunfire followed by three spaced shots. A military M-4 and a Glock nine. Unique in their way, but commonplace since the Fall.

The Fall . . .

The concept of it was old in his mind. Saint John had expected it, prepared for it, *known* that it was coming ever since that day when he was reborn in the blood that flowed from the thousand cuts on his father's flesh. That's when the Voice began speaking to him in his mind, telling him of the Fall that would come. That was years ago, and it was old and sacred knowledge to him. However, to the people around him, the panicked masses dwindling down to a scattered few, the Fall was immediate. It was their All, and in their panic they probably did not remember the world as it was before. Saint John was sure of that. He could see it in the eyes of everyone he met.

And yet the Fall, in societal terms, was only a few months old. A few weeks, if you start counting from the day when the offices of the CDC in Atlanta were overrun by mobs desperate for vaccines for the pandemic flu. Someone had begun a campaign on the Net saying that the CDC was hoarding stockpiles of the vaccine and selling it only to the super rich. The story was probably spurious, but the pulse of the nation had quickened to a fever pace. Atlanta had become a rallying point for protests, and the crowds surrounding the Centers for Disease Control had swelled to an ocean of angry, frightened people. Hundreds of thousands of them. Saint John had been among them; not because he believed the nonsense about the hoarded vaccines, but because the atmosphere of panic brought with it an apocalyptic flavor that he found delicious and uplifting. He was there on that Thursday morning when the temperature of the crowd had reached the boiling point. Like a field of locusts they went from sanity to insanity in the blink of an eye, and the National Guard troops were crushed under the sheer numbers. Shots were fired—shotguns loaded with beanbag rounds, Tasers, and finally bullets. Blood perfumed the air, but the crowd was in motion now, a mass mind bent on smashing down doors and walls.

In one of the last newscasts Saint John heard before the TVs all went dark, the authorities expressed fears that in an attempt to find the mythical stockpile, the mobs had crashed into labs and hot rooms and viral storage vaults, inadvertently releasing many more diseases into the population. Saint John did not know how many viral vaults had been breached, but he suspected that there were seven of them. Seven seals were broken. As the plagues spread, the riot became a constant state of being, and it was then that Saint John revealed himself and walked among the diseased and dying, the murderous and the mauled, his knives in hand, a walker following in the hoof-prints of the Horsemen.

He smiled at the thought and stretched out a hand to catch a soft piece of white ash. Then something closed out those sounds and drew Saint John's attention from the burning city back to the steps on which he stood.

A woman came running down the street, weaving and trip-ping and staggering under the weight of pain. She wore only a green T-shirt and one low-heeled shoe. Her thighs were streaked with blood. She screamed continuously in a red-raw voice. He watched her reel and stumble, but she was beyond the ability to focus her mind and muscles on the task of run-ning. It made her clumsy and slow.

"There she is!" cried a voice. Male, out of sight around the corner. Saint John took a half step back, allowing the shad-ows of the entry arch to enfold him.

A moment later two men came pelting down the street after the woman, yelling and laughing. Saint John winced at some of the things they said. One man was completely naked, his semiflaccid cock swinging and bouncing against his thighs with each step. The other, a college jock type in SpongeBob boxers and Timberlands, had the distinctive lesions of the AL3 strain of smallpox blossoming on his face.

"Here kitty, kitty," called the Jock, laughing as his words drew a flinch from the woman. Her screams faded to a choked sob.

She turned toward a parked car and ran for it. Saint John wondered what sanctuary she thought it would afford her. The windows were broken out, the tires long since slashed. But she stumbled and fell before she got within a dozen paces of it, her knees striking the asphalt hard enough to pull fresh screams from her chest. Her eyes were wild, and even though she looked briefly in Saint John's direction, it was clear that she did not see him standing in the shadows. She fell forward onto her palms and tried to crawl toward the car, but the Jock caught up with her and used his body to slam her to the ground. The Naked Man's cock was stiffening in anticipation as his companion used his knees to spread the woman's legs.

This was clearly the latest act in a play that had started hours ago. Saint John had no doubt. Intervening now could not save her. This woman was broken. If not by the rapes and abuse, then by whatever else she had lost. Whatever else had been torn from her. Family, safety, personal sanctity, perhaps even purity. Gone now, as most things were gone. What did not burn was plundered in the food riots, and what was not plundered rotted as the pathogens swept their way through

49

the dwindling herd of humanity. This woman was a corpse whose ghost was still too shocked to leave its shell. That was sad, he thought, because to linger was to experience—with whatever sense and perception remained—all of the further indignities these monsters needed to inflict so that they could convince themselves that *they* were still alive.

Saint John did not like that. There was no beauty in this setting, and suffering without beauty was disgusting. It was crass and vulgar. Artless.

"You got her?" yelled a gruff voice, and a third man emerged from the shadows. He was massive, a construct of anabolic steroids and overdeveloped muscle; he had turned himself into a freak even before time had decided that all of humanity should share in freakism. This one did not run. He swaggered slowly, his thick fingers undoing his belt buckle and zipper with the kind of deliberate calm that was itself a statement. An alpha to this small pack of dogs.

The Big Man was smiling, lips curled back from rows of white teeth. He came and stood over the woman, and it seemed to Saint John that he was so into this moment that he did not blink. He grinned and grinned, and never flinched when bombs went off in the next street. He let his trousers drop and grabbed for his crotch, massaging hardness despite the limitations of steroids and other drugs. Saint John knew this type. If he could not rape he would brutalize, and it was all the same to men of his kind; his actions were completely unconnected to sex. Pain was the pathway to ecstasy for him.

Saint John knew that, and understood it from a height that gave him a much clearer perspective.

The Big Man pushed the smaller Naked Man out of the way and pawed at the woman, driving more screams from her.

Saint John stepped down. A single step, but it was his first movement, and the three men had not noticed him any more than had the woman.

Saint John took a second slow step, and the kneeling man looked up and snarled. "Fuck off! This whore is ours."

Ah, and that is how worlds turn. On a word or phrase. Ill chosen and ill timed.

This whore is ours.

This whore.

Whore.

Saint John sighed. Such an unfortunate choice of words. Few words were less welcome to his ears. Not even the tough Aryan Brothers in the cell block had used that word around him—not after his first week in the Supermax. One of them had, but their surviving members passed warnings down the line, to big stripes and little fish. Even though the word was tattooed on Saint John's own flesh in blue letters on his back, with an arrow pointing down between his shoulder blades to his buttocks. Burned there ages ago by an ex-con friend of his father's; the act performed back when Saint John was the child Johnnie. Burned into him with a Bic pen, a lighter, and a pin while the boy who was not yet Saint John lay stretched out and bound with duct tape. *Whore,* it said. Branded fast while his father and the ex-con laughed and belched and spat on each letter as they waited for their dicks to get hard.

The ink had not even dried, the burns had not yet stopped singing their white-hot song, when his father had shoved the tattoo artist aside to show why he had wanted those words put there. The tattoo artist had gone next. And then the other men. A pig roast, they had called it. Friends of his father's. Men who shared the same appetites.

Men like these men.

This whore is ours.

And now these three men who crouched in the ash around the half-naked woman had conjured with that word.

Whore.

Saint John took another step.

There had been nine men back then, on the day the word had been fixed with boiling ink into his skin. The boy that he had been had survived it and the next day had fled. When he had come back in the night a month later and looked in through the window, he saw the tattoo artist burning those same letters in another child's flesh. A girl, this time. Gender had not mattered to them. They coveted what they could dominate, what they could force.

Her screams made the men laugh.

As this woman's screams made these men laugh.

Whore.

Back then, on the day when he had been marked, it was not the first time he had heard that word. Not nearly the first.

But it was the first time that another voice spoke inside his mind.

The Voice had told him to go into a sacred place inside the mansion of his thoughts. The Voice guided him there, and with each inward step the laughter and grunts of the nine men diminished until they were no more than a faint and unimportant background noise.

The Voice had guided him back to the world later, when his body had been cut loose and thrown into the corner between the fridge and the stove. It was there to tell him what to pack and when to run, and schooled him on how to live after he'd fled. It brought him back to the house on the night the men had strapped the girl down, and it spoke great secrets to him when he begged for answers.

He had done everything exactly as the Voice instructed. Saint John later understood that it was the Voice of God, and upon that realization he had begun the transformation from Johnnie to the saint. He was glowing with holy purpose when he returned to his father's farm. There were always gallons of gasoline in the barn, standing in a row beside the posthole digger, near where a machete hung from its peg. When the Voice of God spoke, the lessons were always simple, always clear. The lessons were about clarity and simplicity.

And about fire. Ahh . . . fire was such a beautiful doorway.

Saint John took another step down. The cathedral had lovely white granite steps and an archway carved with the austere faces of a hundred saints. Fellow saints, and Saint John wondered if each of them had been given the gift of the Voice. Probably. Why else would they be saints? How else could they be?

The Jock and the Naked Man looked up at Saint John. They looked up from what they were trying to do, shifting their eyes reluctantly from dirty flesh and bitten skin to this annoyance. This intrusion.

Saint John did not move with haste. Haste caused rabbit reactions, quick and defensive. He wanted to see the dog reactions. The jackal reactions. That happened best if he moved slowly, giving each of them the opportunity to make slight perceptual shifts as his personal bubble extruded outward and pushed against the outer edges of their self-confidence. It was very much like subtly shifting to stand too close to a person in a crowd—at first they think you're leaning in to hear better, to catch every drop of conversational juice, but then they notice that you do not lean away when they've finished speaking. That's when the hound that dwells in the middle of their brain raises its head and lifts its ears to tufted points, sniffing and smelling the wind.

First comes speculation as distances are judged and given value; then confusion as those values are ignored. Then defensive caution as the social bubble pops to demonstrate that it never really offered any protection. It was an abstract bubble after all.

Then comes alarm.

He watched for this in their eyes. The Naked Man was less focused, his eyes continually drifting down to what the Big Man was trying to do. His penis was more erect than the Big Man's, and bigger, but he was not the alpha of this pack and he knew that he would have to wait. The Naked Man licked his lips in nervous anticipation.

The Jock was the one who looked up at the stranger descending the steps and briefly smiled. Maybe he thought that this newcomer wanted to join in and he was preparing a stinging rebuke. Maybe it was an uneasy smile. Maybe it was a smile that would include an invitation to be the fourth car in this train.

The Naked Man flicked a glance up, then down at the woman, and back up to Saint John. For a moment there was a fragment of shame in his eyes for what he was doing. Not for the woman or her humanity, but for his own participation in something they all clearly knew was wrong. Anarchy did not yet completely own this man's soul.

Saint John marked that one in his mind. A flicker of remorse in the presence of continued action was not a saving grace. It spoke to understanding, and complicity here was proof of corruption. A man like this would not initiate a rape, but he would always go where a door was opened. There had been men like him on the night that ugly word had been burned onto Johnnie's skin. One of them had even whispered, "I'm sorry," as he had hunkered over and thrust. Saint John had spent a lot of time with him later on.

The Naked Man looked away. He was a loose-lipped slobbering buffoon. No muscle tone, skin like a mushroom. White and spongy.

It was the Jock who first realized the danger. As Saint John descended another step toward the screaming thing over which the men crouched, the Jock's inner hound finally came to point.

"Hey—jackass," he snarled, "what the hell are you doing? I told you to fuck off."

Saint John smiled. "You must stop this and go your way," he said. "Man's hand was not fashioned by God to lay waste to that which the Lord has made."

The Jock stared for a two-count and then burst out laughing. "Who the fuck are you supposed to be? Church isn't until Sunday, dumbass."

The Big Man paused to punch the woman in the thigh, angry that he was having so much trouble getting hard enough to penetrate her.

Saint John descended one final step. Now he stood above the tableau. The woman's dirty blond hair cobwebbed the asphalt.

"It *is* Sunday," murmured Saint John, but the reply was lost beneath the woman's screams. Saint John wore white bedsheets as clothes, the material lashed to his limbs and torso with strips of white tape on which he had written crucial passages of scripture. Not from the Bible, but new scripture the Voice had spoken to him. The sheets were tattered now from all that had happened since the city had begun to burn, and the tatters floated on the hot breeze, like streamers of pale seaweed in a sluggish tide.

The Jock was still in dog mind, bolstered by the presence of the pack and the alpha. The others were, too.

Saint John wanted to laugh, to kiss each of them for that ignorance. It was as delightful as it was false. So entertaining.

But he did not laugh. Instead he cast his face into the beatific smile he wore at such moments. Like Leonardo's model, his smile was a tiny curl of the lip that promised secrets but not answers. He spread his hands high and wide. He had long arms and longer fingers tipped with nails that had each been painted a different shade of night gray.

The Jock nudged the Big Man, pack dog alerting the alpha to the possibility of something wrong. When the Big Man looked up, the smaller man bent and tried to kiss the woman. Even to Saint John such a kiss was strange and awkward. Obscene.

The Big Man growled deep in his chest as he saw Saint John standing there with his arms outstretched.

A ripple of explosions troubled the air close by, and the three men looked over their shoulders. Even the woman looked.

That amazed Saint John because he could not imagine in what way the destruction implied by those blasts could possibly matter to any of them. How could anything beyond the confines of this moment matter to them? Were these men in particular too stupid to grasp the importance of *now*?

Apparently so.

One by one they turned back to Saint John.

The Jock said, "Fuck off, you little faggot."

"Get your own," said the Naked Man.

The Big Man could not be bothered to pay a moment's further attention to the interruption. It's why he had a pack. Instead he glared down. "Lay still, you bitch."

Saint John caught a flicker of movement, and he looked across the street to see a fourth man standing by the corner. He was a shifty, nervous little thing. Clearly a junkie or a drunk suffering through DTs. He shifted from foot to foot and grabbed his crotch, but he didn't cross the street. He was either too afraid of the three more aggressive pack members, or he had not yet crossed the line that separated social depravity from personal destruction. The man caught Saint John looking and immediately whipped his hand away from his crotch. He stood there, staring back, mouth open like a silent ghost.

The three men surrounding the woman laughed and told her the things they were going to do, and told her how much she would like it. And the penalties that would be imposed if she did *not* like it.

The predictability of this drama, and the triteness of the dialogue, began to wear on Saint John. He lowered his arms and said, "Let me share with you."

They all laughed, confirming that they were too stupid to understand what was going on.

"Let me share," repeated Saint John as he reached into the folds of his blowing white clothes and brought out his toys. They gleamed in the smoke-stained firelight. They were small and elegant, each polished to such a perfect shine that they seemed to trail sparks as he once more brought his hands out to his sides. A delicate blade extended the reach of each hand as he stood cruciform on the step above them.

The Jock and the Naked Man stared in awakening horror as everything froze into a bubble of time in which they all floated. The woman lay supine, her mouth strained open to cry out for mercy from a God who most of the survivors of the plague believed was either dead or mad. The Big Man knelt between her thighs in a mockery of a supplicant. On either side of him crouched the Naked Man and the Jock, their hands pressing the woman's wrists to the ground as above them an angel spread its glittering wings.

Saint John stepped down onto the pavement, and two steps brought him to the curb. The Jock could have reached up to strike him. But he was unable to move. In his mind the pack was gone, transforming him from predator to prey.

"Thy will be done," whispered Saint John, and a sob of joy escaped his throat as his arms folded like wings and the knives flashed a crisscross before him. Rubies of hot blood splattered the steps and his clothes and his face as veins opened to his touch. Before the Big Man could look up again, Saint John swept his arms back and forth, each movement ending in a delicate flick of his artistic wrists.

The Big Man finally looked up as blood slapped him across the face. Saint John appeared not to have moved, his arms held out to his sides. But on either side of him the members of the Big Man's pack sagged to the ground in disjointed piles.

Saint John watched the man's eyes, saw the whole play of drama. The brutal lust and frustration crumbled to reveal shock. Then there was that golden sweet moment when the Big Man looked into the eyes of the cruciform saint and saw the only thing more terrible and powerful than the portrait of himself as postapocalyptic alpha that he had hung inside his own mind. Here was the sublime Omega.

"No," the Big Man said. Not a plea, merely a denial. This was not part of his world, not before or after the Fall. He had survived the plague, God damn it; he had fought through the riots and the slaughters. He had become more powerful than death itself, and he expected to rule this corner of Hell until the End of Days.

Yet the Omega stood above him, and the pack lay drowning in their own blood. So fast. So fast.

The Big Man tried to fight.

But before he could close his fists he had no eyes. Then no hands. No face.

No breath.

The Big Man's mind held on to the last word he had spoken. *No.*

Then he had no thoughts and the darkness took him.

3.

ACROSS THE STREET the nervous little junkie was backing away, one hand clamped to his mouth, the other still clutching at his crotch. When he reached the corner he whirled and ran. Saint John did not give chase. If the little junkie and these dead men had friends, and if those friends came here, then there would be more offerings to God. If it happened that the offering included his own life, then so be it. Many saints before him had died in similar ways, and there would be no disgrace in it.

Saint John turned suddenly, aware that he was being watched. He looked up the stairs to the church. The doors stood ajar, and the faces of saints and angels watched him. Stone saints from the carvings around the arch.

But the angel faces? They watched from the open doorway. Cherubim and seraphim, hovering in the darkness. Saint John lifted a hand to them, but they were gone when he blinked.

Saint John wiped blood from his eyes.

Still gone. There were only shadows in the doorway. He nodded. That was okay. It was not the first time something had been there one moment and not the next. It happened to him more and more.

Even so, he let his gaze linger for a moment longer before turning away.

"Angels," he said softly, surprised and pleased. He had only ever dreamed of angels before. Now they were here on earth, with him. And that was good.

4.

THE WOMAN LAY CURLED in pain, drenched in the blood of the three monsters who had hurt her, her faced locked into a grimace; but the scream that had boiled up from her chest was caged behind clenched teeth.

She stared at Saint John. Not at his knives, because even in her horror she understood that they were merely extensions of the weapon that was this man.

Saint John took a step toward her. Blood dripped from his face onto his chest.

"God," she whispered. "Please . . . God."

Red splattered onto the cracked asphalt.

The saint knelt, doing it slowly, bending at ankle and knee and waist like a dancer, everything controlled and beautiful. The woman watched with eyes that were haunted by lies and broken promises. If she had possessed the strength, her muscles would have tensed for flight; but instead there was a weary acceptance that she was always going to be an unwilling participant in the ugly dramas of men.

Saint John bent forward and placed the knives on the edge of the curb with the handles toward her. Inches from her outstretched hands. Dead men lay on either side of her, but she watched this, darting quick glances from the bloody steel to Saint John's dark eyes.

He sat back on his heels, letting his weight settle. The movement was demonstrably nonaggressive, and he watched her process it.

"What . . . what do you want?" she asked weakly.

He said nothing.

"Are you going to hurt me, too?"

"Hurt you?"

She jerked her head toward the dead men. "Like them. Like all the others."

"Others?" echoed Saint John softly. "Other men attacked you?"

A cold tear broke from the corner of one eye. She was not a pretty woman. Bruises, battering, and blood had transformed her into a sexless lump. The animals who lay around her had wanted her because of some image in their minds, not because she fit their idea of sexual perfection. She was the victim of smash-and-grab opportunism, and that was as diminishing as being the tool by which men satisfied their need to demonstrate control.

"How many men?" asked Saint John.

"Just today?" she asked, and tried to screw a crooked smile into place. Gallows humor.

Embers still fell like gentle stars. Both of them looked up to see burning fragments peel off of the roof of the cathedral. The cathedral itself would be burning soon. Sparks floated down like cherry blossoms on an April morning.

The woman looked down and slowly pulled together the shreds of the T-shirt. There was not enough of it to cover her nakedness, but the attempt was eloquent.

"You won't hurt me, too, mister," she said softly, almost shyly, "will you?"

"No," he said, and he was surprised to find that his mouth was dry.

"Will you . . . let me go with you?" It was an absurd question, but he understood why she asked it.

He shook his head. "I'm not a good companion."

"You helped me."

Helped, she had said. Not *saved.* The difference was a thorn in his heart, and he hated that he had allowed himself to care.

He said nothing, however. It would be impossible to explain.

The woman crawled away from the dead men and huddled behind a corner of the car. "What's your name?"

"What's yours?" he countered. He prayed that it would not be something symbolic. Not Eve or Mary or—

"Rose," she said. "My name's Rose."

"Just Rose?"

She shrugged. "Last names really matter anymore?" She coughed and spat some blood onto the street.

"Rose," he said, and nodded. Rose was a good name. Simple and safe. Without obligations.

"What's yours?"

She asked it as he rose to stand in a hot breeze. The sheets he had wrapped around his body flapped in the wind.

"Does that matter?" he asked with a smile.

"You saved my life."

"I ended theirs. There's a difference."

"Not to me. You saved my life. They'd have raped me again and made me do stuff, and then they would have killed me. The big one? He'd have killed me for sure. I saw him stomp another waitress to death 'cause she didn't want to give him a blow job. She kept screaming, kept crying out for her mother."

"Her mother didn't come?"

Rose shook her head. "Her mom's back in Detroit. Probably dead, too. No . . . Big Jack got tired of Donna fighting back

63

and just started kicking her. It didn't make no sense. He'd have worn her down eventually. They had us for almost a week, so I know."

Saint John closed his eyes for a moment. *A week.*

Rose said, "I've seen what happened with other women. There's only so long you can fight before you'll do whatever they want." She wiped a tear from her eye. "Donna was just nineteen, you know? Her boyfriend was in Afghanistan when the lights went out. He's probably dead. Everybody's dead."

"You said everybody gives in. You kept running. Kept fighting."

Rose looked away. "I got nothing left. These pricks . . . this was all I had. They won."

"No," he said softly. "You have life."

She cocked an eye at him. " 'Cause of you."

Saint John wanted to turn, to look up and see if the angels were still watching from the shadowy doorway, but he did not. Angels were shy creatures at the best of times, and he did not want to frighten them off. If "frighten" was a word that could be used here. He wasn't sure and would have to ponder it later.

When he noticed the woman studying him, he asked, "Would you have given in? Stopped fighting them, I mean?"

"Probably. If I did they would have treated me better. Given me food. Maybe let me wash up once in a while."

"Would that have been a life?"

Rose looked up at the embers and then slowly shook her head. "Don't listen to me, mister. They gave me some pills to make me more attractive. No—that wasn't the word. What is it when you cooperate?"

"'Tractable'?"

"Yeah."

"They gave you pills?"

"Yeah. I can feel them kicking in now. Oxycontin, I think. All the edges are getting a little fuzzy."

Saint John gestured to the knives. "Do you want these?"

She looked at the bloody blades. Embers like hot gold fell sizzling into the lake of blood that surrounded the three dead men.

Rose shook her head.

"Are you sure?" he asked.

A nod.

"These men," he said gently, "there will be others like them. As bad or worse. There are packs of them running like dogs."

"I know."

"Then take the blades."

"No."

"Take one."

"No."

They sat and regarded the things that comprised and defined their relationship. The embers and the smoke. The blood and the blades. The living and the dead.

"Not everyone's gone bad," she said.

"No?"

She managed a dirty smile. One tooth was freshly chipped, and blood was caked around her nostrils. "There are guys like you out here."

"No," he whispered. "There is no one like me out here."

They watched the embers fall.

After a while, she said, "You came and saved me."

"It was someone else's moment to die," he said, but she did not understand what that meant.

"You saved me," she insisted, and her voice had begun to take on a slurred, dreamy quality. The drugs, he realized. "You're an angel. A saint."

He said nothing.

"I prayed and God sent you."

Saint John recoiled from her words. He felt strangely exposed, as if it were he and not this woman who was naked.

Then he felt the eyes on him again. Saints and angels from the doorway.

He stood. "Wait here for a few seconds."

"Where are you going?" she asked with a fuzzy voice.

"Just around the corner. I'll be right back, and in the meantime the angels will watch over you."

"Angels?"

"Many of them."

Her eyes drifted closed. "Angels. That's nice."

Saint John hurried to the corner and around it to a side street filled with looted shops. He did not linger to shop carefully; instead he took the first clothes he could find. A black tracksuit made from some shiny synthetic material, with double red racing stripes and a logo from a company that no longer existed. There were no sneakers left, but he found rubber aqua shoes of the kind snorkelers and surfers used. No underwear, no medicine. The last item he selected was a golf club. A seven iron. He smiled, pleased. Seven was God's number.

With the clothes folded under one arm and the seven iron over his shoulder, Saint John left the store, stepping over the rotting bodies of two looters who had been shot in the head.

It was impossible to say whether they had been killed by the police or other looters, and even if that information had been known, Saint John doubted that there was anyone still alive who cared. Certainly he did not.

He rounded the corner and stopped.

The woman—Rose, he reminded himself, her name was Rose—was gone.

Saint John set the clothes and the golf club down and ran the rest of the way, the streamers of his bedsheet clothes flapping behind him. The three dead men were there. His wheelbarrow of weapons was there. She was not.

Saint John looked for her for almost half an hour, but he could not find her.

As he walked back to the cathedral he found that he was sad. Saint John was rarely sad, and almost never sad in relation to a person. Yet, dusty and crumpled as she was, Rose had touched him. She had been honest with him, of that he was certain.

Now she was gone. He wished her well, and when he realized that he did, he paused and smiled bemusedly at the falling embers. It was such an odd thought for him. Alien, but not unwelcome.

"Rose," he said aloud.

5.

SAINT JOHN GATHERED up the weapons—knives, a club made from a length of black pipe, a wrench caked with blood— and carried them up the stairs to the church. There were guns in the wheelbarrow, and even a samurai sword that the former owner had not known how to properly use. Saint John had obliged him with a demonstration. The wheelbarrow was heavy with them; it had been a fruitful week. He carried them, an armload at a time, into the church, counting out his ritual prayers with each slow step. He wanted to get everything right; there was no need for haste, though. This was the end of the world, after all. To whom would haste matter? Inattention to details, however, could have a profound effect. Saints and angels were watching.

With his first armload hugged to his chest, he stood on the top step. The faces of the saints regarded him, and shadows cast by flickering flames played across their mouths so that it seemed as if they spoke, whispering secrets. Some of them Saint John understood; some were still mysteries to him.

He did not see the faces of the angels. The open doorway was a dark mouth, but it was filled with empty shadows, and so he entered with his armload of weapons. He paused in the narthex and looked down the long aisle that ran from the west doorway behind him all the way to the altar at the eastern wall.

The cathedral was vast, with vaulted ceilings that rose high into the darkness. The arches were revealed only by stray slices of firelight through the broken stained glass windows, and in this light the lines of stone looked like bones. Saint John walked to the center aisle and stopped by the last row of pews, bowed reverently, and then walked without haste through the vast nave toward the altar table.

"I bring gifts," he said. His voice was soft, but the acoustics of the cathedral peeled that cover away to reveal the power within, sending the three words booming to the ceiling.

As he walked to the altar the weapons clanked musically, like the tinkle of Christmas bells. He stopped at the edge of the broad carved silver altar table and laid his offering in the center. Then, taking great care, he arranged the blades and hammers and brass knuckles in a wide arc, the blades pointed toward the rear wall, pointing to the base of the giant crucifix that hung on the eastern wall. Jesus, bleeding and triumphant, hung from nails. Saint John knew the secret story of this man. Jesus had not died to wash away the sins of monsters like Saint John's father. No, he had allowed his body to be scourged and pierced as part of the ritual of purification, then he had ascended through the pain into godhood. Saint John marveled that so many people over so many years had missed the whole point of that story.

Once the knives were arranged—seventeen in this armload—and the rest of the weapons, Saint John bowed and headed outside for more.

It was on his second trip into the church that he noticed the footprints on the sidewalk. Small feet. A woman. Rose? Surely hers, but there were other prints; much smaller and many of them. They were pressed into the thin film of fine ash that had begun to settle over everything. Delicate steps.

Angel feet?

Saint John stood for a moment, his arms filled with blood-stained weapons, contemplating the footprints. Then he went inside.

However, he paused once more as he approached the altar table.

On his previous trip he had placed seventeen knives on this very table, arranged by size and type, from a machete to hunting knives and steak knives to a lovely little skinning knife with which he had whiled away an evening last week. There were not seventeen knives now.

Now there were two. Only the long machete and an unwieldy Gurkha knife remained. The brass knuckles and clubs and guns were still there. Fifteen knives, though, were gone.

Saint John considered this as he laid his second armload down on the altar. He did not for a moment believe that he had only imagined bringing in those knives. Many material things in his perception were of dubious reality, but never blades. They were anchors in his world, not fantasies. The flying saucers he sometimes saw . . . those, he knew, were fantasies. Knives? Impossible.

Nor did he believe that someone—perhaps the little junkie—had snuck in here and stolen the knives.

He was considering possibilities and probabilities when he heard a soft sound. Barely a sound at all. More of a suggestion, like the sound shadows make when they fall to the ground as the moon dances across the sky. Soft like that.

He cocked his head to listen. The cathedral was empty and still.

Were demons moving silently between the pews? Had demons come to take his knives?

Saint John was suddenly very afraid.

Could demons materialize enough to be able to like a piece of metal? Before this moment he would have been certain of the answer to that question, but now he wasn't so sure. The knives were gone.

Had the demons made the footprints in the ash? Were the demons here in the church, maybe preparing to hunt him with his own knives? Had the Fall of man made the demons bolder? Had it given them more power? Had it, in fact, kicked open the door between Hell and Earth?

These were terrifying thoughts, and Saint John whirled, drawing two knives from sheaths concealed beneath the white rags that covered his thighs.

"This is the house of God!" he yelled into the dusty shadows. "You may not be here!"

He heard the soft sounds again. Louder this time, and more of them. A scuffle of invisible feet moving in the shadows behind the screen that separated the altar from the choir's chancel. The sounds were stealthy, of that Saint John was certain.

The fact of their stealthy nature injected a dose of calm into his veins. Stealth was a quality of caution, of fear. Predators are stealthy for fear of chasing off the prey they need to sustain their lives. Prey is stealthy to avoid being attacked. For both, fear was the key.

Fear, even in a terrible predator, revealed the presence of weakness. Of vulnerability. An invulnerable demon would not fear anything.

You are a saint, whispered the Voice inside his mind.

A saint. He nodded to himself. A saint in a church.

Saint John felt the fear in his heart recede. Not completely, but enough for strength to flood into his hands from the knives he held; and from his hands to his arms and the muscles in his chest, and to the furnace of his heart.

He could feel his mouth twist in contempt. He raised his arms to his sides, the blades appearing to spark with fire as they caught stray bits of light from the fires burning beyond the broken stained glass windows.

71

"I am Saint John of the Ashes," he cried in his booming voice. *"Exorcizo te, immundissime spiritus . . . in nomine Domini nostri Jesu Christi!"*

A figure stepped out from behind the screen. He was dressed in filthy rags and held one of Saint John's gleaming knives in his fist.

"Go away!" said the figure.

Saint John had begun to smile, but his smile faltered and then fell from his lips.

If this was a demon, then it was a demon wearing the disguise of a cherub. The fist that was wrapped around the knife was barely large enough to encircle the handle. Its face was round-cheeked but hollow-eyed, dusted with dirt and soot, dried snot around the nostrils, tear tracks in the grime. And upon the shoulder of the T-shirt he wore was a single bloody handprint. A child's handprint.

The cherub pointed the knife at Saint John.

"Go away!" he said again. His voice was small and high, but there was so much raw power in it that Saint John was almost inclined to take a backward step. But he did not.

He asked, "Who are you to tell me to leave my father's house?"

The cherub's eyes were blue and filled with a fascinating complexity of emotions. His body trembled, perhaps with hunger or with sickness from one of the plagues; or fear. Or, Saint John considered, with rage barely contained.

This was surely no demon. He held a sanctified blade in a way that showed he understood its nature and purpose; and yet he appeared in the face and form of a child of perhaps eight. Or . . . seven?

That would be exciting.

That would be wonderful, perhaps miraculous; and Saint John was now convinced that he was in the presence of the miraculous. Or on its precipice.

Saint John took a step forward. The cherub—or child, if it was only that—held his ground, but he raised his knife a few inches higher, pointing it at Saint John's face and giving it a meaningful shake. He held the knife well. Not perfectly, but with instinct.

"I'm not messing," said the cherub. "Go away."

Saint John was close enough to kill this child. He had the reach and the knives; but he merely smiled.

"Why should I leave?"

"This is *our* house."

Ah. *Our.* A slip.

Saint John thought of the scuffle of footprints in the ash. And of fifteen missing knives.

"This is my father's house," Saint John said. "This is the house of God."

"You don't live here," insisted the boy.

"I do."

In truth Saint John had never been inside this particular church before, but that didn't matter. A church was a church was a church, and he was a saint after all.

"Who's there?" said another voice. A woman's voice. Vague and dreamy and slurry. Saint John smiled.

"Rose . . . ?"

There was a stirring behind the screen and the hushed whispering of many voices. More than a dozen, perhaps many more. Male and female, and all tiny except for Rose. Shadows

73

moved behind the screen, and then Rose stepped out. She wore a choir robe that was clean and lovely in tones of purple and gold; but her face was still dirty and bloody and puffed.

"You're real?" she asked as she stared at Saint John. "I thought I dreamed you."

"Perhaps you have," said Saint John, and he wondered for a moment if he, too, was dreaming, or if he was a character in this woman's dream. "I am sometimes only a dream."

Her face flickered with confusion. The drugs the men had given her held sway over her; however, she kept coming back to focus. Saint John knew and recognized that as the habit of someone who was often under the influence and practiced at functioning through it.

"Are these your kids?"

As she asked that, more of the cherubs came out from behind the screen. Many of them carried knives. *His* knives. The cherubs were tiny, the youngest in diapers, the oldest the same age as the blue-eyed boy who still pointed his knife at Saint John's face.

Saint John counted them. Twenty-six. The firelight from outside threw their shadows against the wall, and their shadows were much larger. Did the shadows have wings? Saint John could not be sure.

"Go away!" growled the lead boy. "Or I'll hurt you."

"Hey," slurred Rose, "be nice!"

"He's one of *them*!"

Rose's eyes cleared for a moment. She studied Saint John and his knives; then she shook her head. "No, kid . . . *he* isn't. He's the one who saved me. I prayed to God and He sent him to save me."

The lead boy's eyes faltered, and he flicked a glance at Rose. In that moment of inattention Saint John could have cut the child's throat or cut the tendons of the hand holding the knife. He could have dropped one of his own knives and used his hand to pluck the knife from the boy.

He did none of those things.

Instead he waited, letting the boy figure it out and come to a decision. Allowing the boy his strength. The boy refocused on Saint John, and his eyes hardened. "Where'd they take Tommy?"

"I don't know who Tommy is."

"You took him. Where'd you take him?"

The other children buzzed when Tommy's name was mentioned, and now their eyes focused on Saint John. He saw tiny fists tighten around knife handles; and the sight filled him with great love for these children. Such beautiful rage. They were ready to use those knives. How strange and wonderful that was. How rare.

How like him; like the boy he had been when *whore* was burned onto his back and he had first listened to the Voice and heard the song of the blade.

"I do not know anyone named Tommy," he said. "I have never seen any of you before, except Rose, and I met her only a few minutes ago."

"Bull!" the lead boy snapped.

"Shhh," said Saint John. He took a half step forward, almost within the child's striking range. "Listen to me."

The boy's eyes drifted down, and Saint John could see that he was assessing the new distance between them. So bright a child. When his eyes came back up, the truth was there. He knew that he was in range of Saint John's blades and over-matched by his reach. Even so, he did not lower his knife—and it was *his* now. He had claimed it by right of justice, and Saint John was fine with that.

So Saint John lowered his own knives. He slid them one at a time into their thigh sheaths and stood apparently unarmed and vulnerable in front of this cherub. He saw the child's eyes sharpen as he realized the implication of this, the threat unspoken behind the sham of vulnerability. Most adults would never see that. Only someone graced by the Sight could see that.

The boy hears the Voice, thought Saint John.

"Tell me who you are," he said, "and tell me what happened to Tommy."

6.

THE LEAD BOY told the story.

They were orphans. They lived with four hundred other children at St. Mary's Home for Children.

Mary. Ah. That name stabbed Saint John through the heart. *Her* name. His mother. Long gone. First victim of his father. She had tried to protect her son from the devil in their home. She had survived a hundred beatings, but not the hundred and first. A blood clot. Mary.

Mother of the savior.

Saint John already knew where this was going. He wasn't sure he liked it, though.

The boy said that a line of buses set out from St. Mary's two weeks ago, heading for a government shelter here in the city. There was a riot, fires. Gunshots. The driver was killed. The nuns were dragged off the bus. The boy did not possess the vocabulary or the years to understand or express what had happened to the nuns. He said that men did "bathroom stuff" to them. His eyes faltered and shifted away, but it was enough of an explanation for Saint John. He had been raped for the first time when he was younger than this boy. He knew every euphemism for it that existed in human language, and some spoken only in the language of the damned.

While the men were fighting with the nuns, this boy opened the back door of the bus and made the rest of the kids run. There had been forty-four of them on his bus. Last night there were only twenty-seven. Tommy had been playing on the steps of the church this morning, and men had come to take him away.

They heard him screaming all the way down the block and around the corner.

"Describe the men who took him," said Saint John. The boy did. Most of them were strangers. Two of the men fit the descriptions of the Jock and the Big Man.

Rose was fighting to stay awake, but when she heard those descriptions she jerked erect. "That's the same assholes who—"

Saint John nodded. "Tell me where they kept you, sweet Rose."

"Why?" she demanded. "The kid's gone."

"No!" yelled the lead boy. Others did, too. A few of the younger ones began to cry. "I'm gonna get him back!"

Saint John shook his head. "No," he said. "You won't. You'll stay here and guard your flock."

The boy glared at him. There was real fire in the boy's eyes; Saint John could feel the heat on his skin. It pleased him. It was like being a stranger in a strange land and unexpectedly meeting someone from your own small and very distant town. He had not expected to see that blaze here at the curtain call of the human experience.

"Tell me your name," said the saint.

"Peter."

Saint John closed his eyes and sighed. He smiled and nodded to himself. When he opened his eyes, Peter was still glaring at him.

"I am going to find Tommy," said Saint John, "and bring him back here."

Rose snaked a hand out and grabbed his wrist. "Christ, are you nuts? They'll fucking slaughter you. There are like ten or twelve of those assholes over there."

Saint John said nothing, and his smile did not waiver.

Rose finally told him where the gang lived and where they "played." Saint John nodded. To Peter he said, "Stay here. Stay silent. Stay hidden."

"You can't tell me what to do."

"No. I can only tell you how to stay alive."

Peter scowled. "You're gonna get killed. You're gonna leave us like the nuns did and the driver did."

Saint John could feel the weight of the knives hidden in his clothes. He said, "Doubt me now, Peter. Believe me when I return."

And he left.

7.

THERE WERE SIXTEEN MEN at the hotel that had been converted into a lair for rabid dogs. Sixteen men on three floors.

Saint John drew his knives and went in among them.

Sixteen men were not enough.

The skinny junkie was one of them. He was on the third floor, sleeping in a bed with a woman who was handcuffed to the metal bed frame. Her skin was covered with cigarette burns. Saint John revealed great secrets to the little junkie. And to the others. For some of them it was very fast—a blur of silver and then red surprise. For a few it was a fight, and there were two Saint John might have admired under other circumstances. But not here and not now.

Saint John painted the walls with them. He opened doorways for them and sent them through into new experiences. He took the longest with the two men who were in the room with Tommy. They were the last ones he found. So sad for them that circumstance gave Saint John time to share so many of his secrets. The boy was unconscious throughout, and that was good; though Saint John wished that Peter could have been here to serve as witness. That child, of all of them, would probably understand and appreciate the purity of it all.

Saint John left the adult captives with keys and weapons and an open door. He set a fire in the flesh of the dead men and on the beds where the women and this body had been. As he walked away the building ignited into a towering mass of yellow flames.

Saint John carried Tommy in his arms. Halfway to the church the child's eyes opened. He beat at the saint with feeble fists.

"N—no . . ." the boy whimpered.

"No," agreed Saint John. "And never again."

The boy realized that he was wrapped in a clean blanket, and when he looked into Saint John's eyes he began to cry. He tried to speak but could manage no further words. In truth there was no lexicon of such experiences that was fit for human tongues. Saint John knew that from those days with his own father and those vile, grunting men. The look the saint shared with the boy was eloquent enough.

Saint John bent and whispered to him. "It was a dream, Tommy, but that dream is over. Peter and your other friends are waiting."

When he reached the square where the cathedral sat, Saint John saw that the fire on the roof had failed to take hold. The tiles smoldered, but the church would not burn. Not tonight.

The fire of the burning hotel lit the night, and as he walked, Saint John could see the other cherubs—the angels—and the dusty Rose standing in the doorway of the church, surrounded by the arch of caved saints, and every face was turned toward him.

Peter broke from the others and ran down the steps and across the street. He was crying, but he still held his knife, and he held it well. With power and love. Saint John approved of both.

Rose came, too; wobbling and unsteady, but with passion. Her face glowed with a strange light, and she reached out to take Tommy from Saint John. Her brow was wrinkled with confusion.

"Why?" she demanded.

There was no way to explain it to her. Not now. She would understand in time, or she would not.

Rose turned, shaking her head, and carried Tommy toward the church as the other angels flocked around her.

It left Saint John and Peter standing in the middle of the street. They watched the others until they vanished into the shadows, then turned and watched the glow of fire in the sky. Finally they turned to face each other. Peter slowly held out the knife, handle first, toward Saint John.

Saint John was covered with blood from head to toes. He had a few bruises and cuts on his face and hands. He sank down into a squat and studied the boy.

"No," he said, pushing the offered knife back. "It looks good in your hand."

The boy nodded. "You didn't answer the lady," he said. "She asked you why you went and got Tommy."

"No," Saint John agreed. "Do you need me to explain it to you?"

Peter looked down at the knife and at the blood on Saint John's face, and then met his eyes. The moment stretched around them as embers fell from the sky. In the distance there were screams and the rattle of automatic gunfire.

"No," said Peter. Saint John knew that this boy might even have tried to get Tommy back himself. He would have died, of course, and they both knew it. Peter was still too young. But he would have tried very well, in ways the men in that building would not have expected. The boy would not have died alone.

Saint John nodded his unspoken approval.

They smiled at each other. Together they crossed the street

and mounted the stairs and stood on the top step, watching the city die. There were fires in a dozen places.

"It's pretty," said Peter.

"It's beautiful," said Saint John.

The boy considered. He nodded.

The golden embers floated down around them.

RUE

by Lauren Groff

THE GIRLS SLIP IN AT NIGHT. I see the ravages in the morn-ing, the bald patches in the tansy, the yarrow mowed in swaths. Vervain and pennyroyal, feverfew and sage, ginger, lemon balm, parsley. A tincture or tisane of any of these, and the white bellies of the girls stay smooth, scrubbed from inside out. It is true: Secretly I planned my gardens for these girls. After the Ministers seized the country and remade it in God's name, I could be hanged in the gibbets for my garden; I could be laser-flayed for the powers of my plants. But the girls only talk be-tween themselves, and steal, and in any case they are too quick for me. They watch my house for movement, or listen for the slide and drag of my bad leg. When I know they are there, I stand and clump over to the door as quietly as I can. But in the sudden crack of light that falls into the garden, a girl is always leaping, a white doe, over my stone fence.

Tonight, I hear another one out in the darkness. I pause the movie I am watching and move silently through the house and onto the warm lawn. I can come close enough to catch this girl's arm: She is either stupid or her ears are too stuffed with panic to hear. She spins under my grip and I see her broad, triangular face turned to dumpling in terror, the pillowcase in her hands stuffed with rue.

I know this girl. She is the long-legged one who breathes her wet breath onto her desk. Then she makes a brush of her red hair and paints the moisture into designs that fade as she draws them. The boys find this behavior mysterious. I find it gross. Her *essais* in my class are trite beyond belief, not to mention ungrammatical.

I know why you're here, I say.

She blinks and her eyes fill with tears. Two waning moons are reflected in them. Don't tell, she whispers. Don't call the Ministers.

I shrug: I must, I say. It is illegal, what you are doing. You will go to prison and maybe die there. Or one of the work camps, if you are lucky.

Oh, she says. Madame. Please. I'll do anything.

She looks me deep in the face, trying not to look away. Anything, she says, and reaches out a hand and makes an attempt at a caress. I watch her hand near my bicep and falter, then fade away. She can't look at me.

Not that, I say, drily. But there is something.

On her face, the hope flares briefly like an ember. Then, under the wash of my words, under all that I require of her, the hope extinguishes. She hangs her head. When she nods, the moons fall from her eyes and break on the ground.

Days pass, and my own waiting grows inside me, a pulsing, moving creature in this desiccated body. All day in my classes,

I read from Perrault, leaving a crumb-trail, but not a soul is clever enough to pick it up. I show them films I have found online, *À bout de souffle*, *Les enfants du paradis*. Blasphemy is not blasphemy, it seems, when it is in another language. Also, the students don't understand enough to complain.

When the bell rings, during the interclass prayers, I see how the red-haired girl bulges against her uniform. She notices I notice and startles and pales.

Now I wait for her in a thigh-high sea of Queen Anne's lace in the dark. Here she trudges, at last, through the gate. If she thinks I don't notice the flash of mute stubbornness when I reach out to guide her into my house, the pure donkey of her, she is wrong.

The dogs come as I had thought they would, but I had washed her trace from my path with the hose, then dragged her dress full of rocks down to the river and threw it in. All day, we hear the poor dogs bay on the riverbank, and when the Village Ministers come knocking at the door, the girl is safely hidden in the garret, and I am fishing my underclothes from a great pot on the stove.

It is forbidden for men to look upon a woman's private things, not that the Ministers would want to see my translucent monstrosities. With some pleasantries in French that they only half-remember from my classes and say to please me, they bow away.

At last, the girl and I are alone.

I carry on at the school as if all were normal, as if the girl weren't at home swelling in my absence. I make the chicory coffee, because I am the one who does it best, and listen to the bloodless criticism of the government in the grunts of the other teachers when they read the State News before First Prayer. Too frightened to make more definite criticisms, too weak to hold it all inside, these pasty, pale creatures call themselves my colleagues.

I carry on. *Un, deux, trois* for the elementary, *Demain, dès l'aube* for the high school. A subtext of gossip goes on under my nose. When one is ugly enough, one can feign ignorance with great success. I hear the whispered theories about the girl, who in her absence has become an unlikely Jeanne d'Arc: They say she has rebelled against the Ministers' strict regime, has fled into the mountains with the anarchists. One can almost see her as these hopeful children do, rushing down from the mountains, swords in both hands, her long red hair licking in the wind. Not even the boys who knew the depth of her badness suspect where she truly is: on my couch watching Gospel shows on the television, eating my rich egg custards, my baked bread, my raspberry jam.

Day and night, the blinds are closed, the house set far from the road. And yet one day I come home to hear her high, clear soprano dazzling all the way to the gate, and clump inside, hiss and spit at her like an angry cat.

After that, she is silent. Her skin, unsunned, turns mushroom. Only her long red hair gleams, still glorious, in the darkness of the house.

I hate you, she whispers over my roasted chicken one night.

I pretend to not hear.

I hate you, she says, louder.

Such gratitude. I slap her.

She holds her hand to her cheek, bloodred in the shape of my hand.

Without me, I say, the Ministers would have you. And where would you be? As soon as the baby came, you'd be dead.

No, she says. I'd have made the boy marry me. I'd be free.

I smile at her, not unkindly. Which boy? I say, and the rest of her skin goes as ruddy as her cheek and she holds my eye for one beat, two. Then she bows her head and salts her meat with her tears.

The time comes. I must gag the girl to keep her screams inside her. I call in sick to work, pinching my nose to pretend sinus trouble, and the secretary is startled: Twenty-five years, and I have never been ill once. And then the bustling, the kettles of hot water, the sheets torn to stanch the blood, the rust spreading across my mattress. I play my parents' Chopin records loudly to cover the girl's muffled pain. All day and into the night, we struggle, the girl and I, Jacob and angel. Sweat paints the air.

The girl rips, it seems, in two, and the baby, a waxy livid thing, bawls in my hands. It is a girl with fat folds and curlicues of red hair all over her body. Her eyes open and they are chips of the sky.

I feel myself floating out of the twisted body I call my own when I look at this creature, more beautiful than anything I have seen. This child of mine.

When I look up, dazzled, the girl on the bed is reaching out her arms, her face hungry. Please, she says, and I put the child in her arms.

Oh, she says. Oh, she's so beautiful. The infant nuzzles her breast, slides her little face to the nipple, tries to latch on. The girl says, weeping, Oh, my baby.

I snatch the infant back. My baby, I say.

No, the girl says. The donkey has risen again in her, kicking, and surprises me. She sits up against the headboard, though it clearly pains her, though she has not stopped bleeding, and levels a finger at me. Give my baby to me.

A demand? I say. You are in no position to demand. All I have to do is call the Ministers, and off you go. You wouldn't survive a year in the work camps, you know.

The girl's stupid face has turned into a fist. Whatever the Ministers do to me, she says softly, will be nothing compared to what they will do to you. For a long, horrible moment, this gives me pause. Even idiots, at times, can stumble on truth.

But. One could never have survived the purges I survived in my own youth without being canny. Survived; not unharmed. My leg twisted when they sliced my Achilles tendon, my womb twisted with forced use. I scrubbed potatoes in the rebels' kitchen, reciting poetry in Romance languages, keeping fresh my Ph.D. in comparative literature. I spent the bad nights on my back translating the poems into English. Such ugliness as mine has been earned.

I played along with the girl. For two days, as she became peremptory, demanding food and help, picking up the telephone threateningly when I even neared the baby, I pretended fear. And then on the third night, I slipped some ground passionflower into her tea. Passionflower, with its variegated petals, with its good, black heart. Her face closed like a letter. She slept and slept.

The infant also drank the passionflower in her mother's milk and slept for over twenty-four hours. This was fortunate, for by the time the child woke I had ridden my bicycle through the night and the day and the night again, with her bound to my back like an extra hump. By the time she began to stir, I had abandoned the bicycle and was on the train.

I had made a giant bottle in the station, and as the infant was struggling to wake, I put the nipple in her mouth and she sucked and sucked her hunger away.

Now she looks at me, sated, clean, lulled by the quick flash of the very fast train over the countryside, and I smile down to her. I imagine her mother in my bed, just now awakening in her own pain and mess, slowly lifting a hand to her lovely pale face. She winces, I imagine, at the light through the curtains, parted for the first time in so many months. The sun falls on the empty bassinet beside her, and the silence in the house becomes an accusation.

A man in a business suit looks at us over today's State News and smiles. Grandmother? he asks, and I smile back. Godmother, I say. He says the required response: Blessed be the Godparents, though there is a glint of interest when he looks at my twisted old body. Godparents are normally young and hale, able to raise the children if anything goes awry for the parents, if they are denounced and deported, if the Ministers find deviance in them at all.

I must be the most unlikely Godmother this man has ever seen.

I am the most unlikely mother, I know, that's a certainty.

And so we slide, quiet and calm, into the city by the sea.

The afternoon of our arrival I buy a house on a path lost through thickets of dune-weeds, a high-gabled antique with wind-battered gray boards. The Realtor tells me hesitantly that the house is so cheap because it has been on the market for years and years, and has been on the market because it is haunted. I laugh, and the baby makes a little birdlike coo in response.

Ghosts, I say, do not bother us.

It is isolated, she says. Five miles from any store.

We require no company, I say.

Where the house is, the ocean is too rough against the rocks to sunbathe, she says. And even if you were to go swimming, the riptide will take you out to sea in a blink.

Do I look like the beachgoing type? I snap bitterly, and her eyes slant away. Then I say more calmly, We will take it.

If the Realtor is surprised to see me count out the money bill by bill, she doesn't show it. She hands me the key. I will have a boy bicycle groceries up to you today, she offers. It is a courtesy we show to all our buyers. I smile at her, and take a few minutes to write out a list of things I need. Her eyes widen when she scans it, but she swallows and nods, and I can feel her relief cracking when I finally leave the room.

The boys arrive after I have opened all the doors and windows and the strong sea wind is carrying the dust out the door. I have scrubbed the kitchen tiles to their original white, and have swept and washed the bedroom where the baby and I will sleep.

The seven boys stop their bicycles, exhausted, at the porch. They carry up the wooden crates and put them in the hall, their sweat dripping on the floorboards. The baby gurgles, and one handsome blond boy with eyes the pale of sage stops to smile into her face. I tip them all generously, and they ride off into the dusk, down the hill again into the city.

I close the door. I intend for those boys to be the last males ever to step foot into this house. I say it aloud to say it at all. My words hang in the air, then chime back to me, silvery and quick. The ghosts approve.

After a quick supper and bottle, I take the baby out to the back of the house, where the garden ends at a cliff's edge. Stars pulse over the last red line of sunset. I hold the child up to show her all this vast beauty, to let her feel the night wind, full of spray.

This is happiness, my girl, I say aloud, and find myself laughing for the first time in years. The baby sticks out her tiny pink tongue and licks the salt from the air.

It takes until the baby's head stops wobbling on her neck for her name to come to me. When it does, I cannot believe it took so long. The herbs her mother was plucking that night when I stopped her in my garden; what I feel growing furiously in the world we left behind, a building storm of the birthmother's wrath and sorrow.

Rue, I say, smiling. A cousin of rouge; my well-chosen road. I say to the baby who blinks and focuses, My daughter, your name is Rue.

* * *

I scan the State News every day until I find the notice about a runaway returned home to our old village; I think of Rue's mother's body slowly healing in my cottage, the girl eating my food until there was no more to eat, then waiting it out another week until hunger drove her home.

It goes on to say that she was in the public stocks for a week; and I think of the neck-polished wood on the little dais in front of the Library. How it would smell of accumulated sweat and shame and rain in the pores of the wood.

She will be sent to a work camp for a few months, it says, in light of the complications of her case; and I think of the girl cracking rocks, picturing each rock my ravished face.

I shiver. But then I put my hand on the baby's back. Her breathing, in and out, calms me. It plays between the sound of the waves, echo or source: and who would be so foolish as to try to tell the difference?

The wind turns icy. My bicycle slips over the road under my body when I try to ride it, and I fear for Rue in the little seat behind me. I stay in the house and order groceries by telephone. When the man puts them on the porch, he picks up an envelope of cash. It is such a smooth transaction, and I have come to fear the glances of strangers so, the feeling that everywhere I turn in the world I have Rue's mother's eyes upon me, that I continue the practice into the spring when the winds quiet and bring the sweet perfumes of washed-up seaweed and cherries in bloom. I stop taking the State News. If the world hums and clanks and grinds its machinery elsewhere, I don't know or care. The baby grows, sits up, grins. Her hair on her skin is a smooth, soft pelt that I love to rub my cheek against. Her hair on her head is the color of the world seen through a glass of wine. I speak to her in French and this is the language she first learns. She speaks falteringly, then lispingly, then clearly. *Maman,* she calls me. The white kitten that showed up on our porch hungry one morning, its pink mouth open in a jagged bawl, she names Milou after a comic-book dog. Soon, she is chattering away in the pretty dresses I make for her, my little French canary. Like this, the old language becomes another wall I build between the world and my daughter, keeping us apart.

Some days my daughter is mermaid, some days she is water. We walk slowly beyond our rocks to a calmer stretch of the beach and she crouches beside the tide pools, watching the creatures within. *Regarde, maman,* she cries, and points her finger down. I see the dazzle of the miniature world, the urchins the color of pumpkin flesh. The translucent crabs threaten their claws at my girl like tiny skeptics damning the gods. Her own head is framed against the wintry sky, reframed within its thick crowns of red braid. My old blood warms, watching her, my little girl in tights, her jacket clenched over frozen hands. So beautiful, with her mother's face and hair, and my quickness in her eyes.

Our days are sweet and short. She falls asleep in my lap, as I read to her. And underlining it all is the other mother's fury, which I feel ever nearing, ever darkening, defining our life the way shadows give definition to the day. That she will come is the one thing I know about the future, and the only thing I fear.

Seasons pass, however, with the calm of heaven. We are fond company, the cat on our laps, the good meals in our bellies culled, mostly, from our own beautiful garden, the books delivered and devoured. As we listen to the surf each night, I comb out her hair. Sometimes we play with it: It becomes tent, and I crouch beneath its scalpy smell; I heap it over my face and it becomes my own hair and we laugh at how ridiculous it is against my wizened face; I bind my wrists with it, and it takes her some work to free me. She is gentle and sleeps deeply. Raised on sweets and sea air and literature, Rue walks through dreams the way she walks through rooms.

But today she crouches in last year's swimsuit, peering again at her old friends in the tide pool, and I see how tight the suit has become on her body. She is bigger, her hips and chest, her lips suddenly abloom. I stand, agitated, shaking, saying, Oh-oh-oh. She runs over as fast as she can: Her hair is so very heavy she can't run fast or far, normally, but she does her best to help me. She asks if I am cold, and I nod, yes I am, mute. There is something wrong with my body. I cannot stop shaking; my lips can't form words.

Rue murmurs as she helps me over the suddenly steep and long path to home, and brushes my own sparse hair from my face until I am soothed asleep.

Something has shifted. My leg clumps harder on the ground, and words come with more difficulty into my mouth. Rue takes the harder cleaning, though it must hurt her neck with all its heavy hair to support when she scrubs the floors the way she scrubs, with low grunts that remind me of something I'd rather not remember. Once in a while, I see her hair resting on the windowsills, as if to quietly steal some relief. I tell her what we need and she writes the lists: My hands shake so, my writing is illegible. I still call the orders in, and she listens with a strange look on her face: I have never taught her English, and before was careful to keep her from hearing this other language. But when it is too difficult, and the man on the other end loses his patience, Rue takes the telephone from my hand and in her lisping accent tries hard to replicate my sounds. She does well, and I am proud, but there are some comical mistakes. Instead of cherries one day, we get cheese; instead of batteries, we get tweezers. But one thing I never, never let her do is to take the envelope of money out to the porch. No matter how long it takes me and how many breaks I must take on the way to the door, I am the one to risk the delivery boy. I keep my own treasure tucked away inside, as she was tucked inside me those many years before I had ever met her, or her mother, my tiny seed waiting for the right moment to bloom.

It is somehow winter again. I stand in the widow's walk as the morning dawns on the sea and watch a man cupping a cigarette in his palm beyond the dunes. What hair he has is golden, but there's a pink patch of bald at its heart. Yet he is not old. His limbs are vigorous when he shakes them, and he wears the droopy clothing the delivery boys all wear these days. He scans the windows of the house carefully, so carefully that I in my black dress behind the balustrade above the house am camouflaged, no more than a mushroom. Even from here I can see his eyes are the soft green of sage. He flicks his cigarette into the weeds. Idiot, I mutter: He could start a fire. He doesn't: At least not one I can see. He sees nothing, and the wind grows colder and he hefts one leg over the seat of his bicycle and glides away.

My limbs are full of furious energy: I have told Rue that we will make ourselves an entire set of all-new clothing, how fun! We are ripping the seams of our frocks, fairy trifles based on patterns from my faraway childhood, all swim camps and cotillions and unremembered Easter dresses. She is laughing as she rips, the excitement of destroying filling her like bloodlust. I need to keep her occupied, away from the windows; I need to think. She has rickrack in her hair and grosgrain looped over her shoulders, and even like this, silly and childish, she is a goddess.

We are laughing. Yet I smell smoke. By the time I make it to the window, however, the boy or man, or the boy-man, of the outside is gone, and only my fury remains.

Rue is so enraptured with our project that I never see her go outside, even once, even when I plead to go to our swimming hole. But now she sits frowning over a skirt she is making, and when I look at it, I feel the frown begin to spread across my face, too. There are embroidered holes in the sides and frills in the front. It is a most ugly and excessive article, an indecent thing to even look upon.

I demand to know where she could have gotten this idea: I do know that my girl is dreamy, but there is no fire to her imagination to make it dazzle in such a direction.

Rue blushes, but shrugs. She shows me a magazine she says she found under the apple tree outside, and in it I see such horrid concoctions, such stupid, bright, strange-looking people, such horrible words that if the Ministers saw it, they would kill on sight whoever was reading it. I throw the magazine down as if it has bitten me. Rue looks at me sideways and asks what it is about the world outside that I hate so. I want to tell her about everything: the rebels who methodically destroyed me, the Ministers who imprisoned us in rules, and my own old and twisted body, my hideous jail. But I look at my daughter, whom I have worked hard to keep innocent of such things, and bite my tongue. I kiss her on the musky part of her hair, and take the magazine outside and hurl it off the cliffs, into the pounding sea.

I am extra vigilant. With great effort from my body, I wait until Rue sleeps at night and steal down the hill. With rocks I lug in a wheelbarrow, I divert a stream so the path is cut off, and the delivery boys must abandon their bikes on the far side and walk the last uphill mile in wet shoes. I can hear the slop of their footsteps from afar and am ready for them far from the house, holding their pay with my trembling hand.

At night, I hold Rue's head in my lap while she reads her novel, and scratch her warm scalp, and watch her. Finally she puts down her book and sighs and asks what the matter is.

I cannot help myself. I watch myself lose control, I watch in horror as I blurt in French: If you left me, I would die, I say.

It is not a consolation that she sits up, her whole face an Ô. Under her breath she asks me where she would go. And now I see it and my dismay makes me ill: A spark from my own fevered brain has just landed in her, is now lighting her up.

* * *

Once her face was a window and now it is a door, always slamming shut. She disappears, and when I call for her in the old house, the ghosts maaa like old sheep in reply, taunting me. Mornings, she smells of grass and night. I lock her into her room, and she takes off the hinges with a screwdriver. I tempt her inside with cakes and creams, but she eats the salty, hard plums from the trees out back with a twist on her lips. I cry, but she only watches me, gone hard.

I blink, it seems, and Rue is gone. The house is decrepit without her, the windows shattering one by one under the gusts, the roof shedding shingles the way I am shedding teeth.

I saw her coming, the original mother, but never knew which direction she would take: I had feared the dark and angry force of her all these years, building with every day we were distant, one sudden day erupting. I imagined her stealing my daughter from me the way I first stole her away, carrying her bodily away. I had imagined the mother marching up the hill, grown mighty with age, and carrying the girl off like a wee infant in her arms, trailing Rue's braids in the dust.

I always thought that I would grab on to those braids and ride them, down the hill, into the town, I would tie myself into them so that when they went away in the train, they would float me like a kite behind them.

But I have known for decades that the mother is probably dead. Has been, for some time. And I should have guessed that where the mother would show herself would be in my daughter's blood. The one thing I couldn't give her. Though I would have. I would.

Those nights when poetry would not do it for me, I lay in

the pounding of my pain, under the cold rain in the mountains as the men came in, and every moment I made myself blank, and promised myself a daughter.

And now I kneel in the little nest of braids shorn from my daughter's head with her own hands, and wait for this old, crooked body to leave me be.

I wait. In my hunger, in my thirst, the courtship rises to me with the vividness of childhood dreams. I see it as it must have happened: the first words as he emerged from behind the pear tree, that strange beast, this man. He was unintelligible to the girl, and the sounds in his mouth put such fear in her heart, all she could do, this first time, was run. All night, though, he kept stepping from behind the pear, and by the morning her body trembled with wanting to see him. Then, slower, he coaxed her out. They met at night. It took no time. One kiss and Rue's mother awoke in her blood, the sexy young beast. It didn't matter that those two children didn't understand one another. Anyone would look upon my Rue and want her. And girls like Rue—too trusting, too pulsing, too unlike me in the end—never really need words in this grand world, at all.

I wait for the house to topple off the cliff, the defeated house with its defeated ghosts. And I see her in the world, shorn, feeling so light, freed from her hair, her battered house, her heavy old me, that she feels weightless in her beautiful young body, as if with one leap she would flutter into the air, my daughter turned bird.

SUCCUMB

by John McIlveen

OPEN YOUR EYES.

Yes. That's right, baby.

Oh, I startled you . . . even though I'm using my sexy voice. Sorry. Do you like it, though? Even Marilyn Monroe couldn't purr like this.

Let you go? Why? What would that accomplish? Besides, honey, you *don't* want me to let you go.

Don't fight. Save your energy. I don't want you to waste it. I'm going to want every bit of it.

Here, let me turn the light on. Yeah, that's better. The soft lighting is nice, you little Romeo, you. *Very* romantic.

Hmmm. I'm not what you expected, am I? I can see you're confused, but I can feel something under me that says you're not exactly put off, either. I am quite the looker, aren't I?

Who am I?

You don't know? Odd, you've mentioned me often enough.

No? Well, maybe it'd be better if you asked *what* I am. Ooohh, furrowed brow. Okay, here's a little hint; in Latin my name means "To Lie Under," and that's exactly what you're doing now.

To lie under.

Another thing I am is . . . I am exactly what you would want for your ultimate fantasy.

No reason to be shy, just admit it. I know what you look at on the Internet; I've seen what you like. You store the images in hidden folders, blondes, brunettes, redheads, so many pictures . . . Thousands. Dominatrix, gay, eighteen and older . . .

. . . under eighteen.

Oh, don't worry about me! *I'm* not the Judge.

But I do know what turns you on. Long hair turns you on; long red hair *really* turns you on. The redder the better, isn't that what you write, Mister i-1-2-do-U at livemail-dot-net? And hey, you're in luck! I have both, long and red!

How's this? Is this red enough for you? No dye jobs here. This fire is all me.

Come on, feel it.

Yeah, I know, I'm kneeling on your arms. That's what happens when you're saddled and straddled. Here, feel it on your face, then. Do you like how it feels? Oh, I think you do. I just felt Mr. Happy jump up and nudge my ass.

Here, feel my . . .

. . . you're looking at my tits.

It's all right. Take your time and enjoy the view. I'll tell you what, this black leather is so confining, let me unzip, that way you can feel them, too.

Oh yeah, your hands. Well, you really don't need them right now. Let's just reposition them down here a bit. Look at that, perfect for holding my ass.

Now tell me, aren't these the breasts you like best? D-cup. Dee for delectable? No silicone, no saline, just soft, perky pleasure. Feel it on your face? Hmmm. You like it playful, don't you?

Oh! You're a nipple man! Can't refuse, can you? Oh, and you like to bite, you devil! I love the teeth. Oh yeah, a little harder, that makes me want to . . . I want to grind . . . in.

Can you feel my heat? I feel yours, even through leather. Undo the snaps. Can you feel them, right where I'm hottest? That's right, open them. Oh, huh, oh, that's good. Use your fingers in . . . me. Ohhh . . . do you feel that?

Wet.

Wet helps when . . . it's time to . . . slide you in . . . slooooo-wwwly.

So hot.

Hmmm, I think you like it, you certainly like something. Is it the heat, the intense fiery . . . or is it when I squeeze you like this . . .

Wait. Slow down, not so fast, baby. It isn't time yet. Just settle down and feel me on you, around you.

Mmmm, you like it when I bite your ear; when I whisper?

Let me tell you a secret. I'm going to fuck you like you've never been fucked before. Wow, the way you just grew inside me . . . throbbing. You want that, don't you?

All right, here's another secret. I'm going to fuck you . . . to death.

Yeah, that's right, and you won't even try to stop me. I'm going to rip you inside out, and you're going to beg for more.

Awww, you're dwindling. Not a problem, I'll give you a

special little *clench* from inside me . . . and I can grip you tighter than any human hand.

See? You're back with me . . . completely. Aren't you, preacher man?

Oh, you're surprised that I know who you are, Mister Holy? At least that's what you tell them, your followers.

No, you can't pull away.

Try.

See? Not once I have a hold on you. Not when I can make you feel this good. I own you. Feel me milking you, massaging you from inside me, like little tongues licking you all over.

If your herd only knew you, your mindless minions. If they knew your sins and your weaknesses, all the ones you have always blamed on me. All the lonely wives you used, the clueless little boys, the whores, the needy runaways, all of them your toys.

Now you're my toy . . . my toy to ride.

You called me *the seductress*. You even told them you met me face-to-face and defeated me. You had no clue. You took me for granted. You saw me as a joke and you didn't believe. I thought you were a man of faith.

Well, here I am, and it seems . . . I'm winning. I'm sucking the life from you, and you can't resist.

Hold me to you. Hold on to me while I kill you. That's good. Good little preacher. Hold me tighter and wrap your arms around me.

Can you feel them? Feel the wings?

What? You're disgusted? But you can't let go, can you?

Do you feel your soul being torn from you? Isn't it amazing

how giving up your life feels so much like pleasure, how giving up your soul seems like ecstasy?

You're dying, holy man. I grind into you faster and faster, but what if I . . . were . . . to . . . stop?

Stopping will save your life. But you can't stop; can you? Even when I stop, you keep going.

Even when I reveal myself, when I lose the flesh, you can't resist. Oh, the terror in your eyes, it's delicious . . . and that, my dear, that's what turns me on.

Beg. Let me hear you beg and I'll finish you, you dog.

Good, very good. Keep begging.

But I'm going to play awhile. I'm going to bring you to the edge, and then ease off, again and again. I'm going to dangle you over the cliff until the need to release guts you and nearly drives you mad.

And again . . .

Again . . .

Now let it go. Feel it leave you. Feel it being torn from you, like a thousand rusty blades slashing inside of you, yet you still buck and thrust deeper into me, so willing to die.

So willing to be possessed.

So willing to *succumb*.

And now . . .

I have you.

Roll over, preacher.

Roll over and hold your wife. She'll be pleased to know you reached out to her in your final moments, even though she knows you've never loved her. She'll be pleased to know that you had nothing else to reach for.

And all that is left is for me to kiss you . . .
A soul kiss . . .
And a breath . . .
Good-bye.

TORN STITCHES, SHATTERED GLASS

by Kevin J. Anderson

A TINY SILVER NEEDLE, sharp point. My large fingers had grown nimble over years of practice and delicate concentration, and I could glide the moistened end of the thread through the needle's eye on the first try, then pull the strand tight. I completed the first stitches, neat ones, no excuse for clumsy black sutures such as a mortician would use after an autopsy.

The needle dipped into the end of the torn arm socket, then emerged, and I pulled the strong thread through, binding the detached arm to the shoulder. I immediately saw that I should have used white thread, because it would have been less conspicuous. I made certain the ends were neatly aligned and continued my stitching.

I sat in my dim tailor shop in the ghetto of Ingolstadt. Some called the place cramped; I found it cozy. I was accepted here, though I wasn't Jewish—what religion would accept someone like me? The people welcomed outsiders, understood them, and did not ask awkward, probing questions. It was 1938, and I'd been here for many years. I did not look forward to the day when I'd have to move on again.

I finished stitching around the stump of the arm, then snapped off the thread after tying a solid knot. I turned toward the little girl with rich brown hair and a bright mind who sat watching me. I handed back her repaired rag doll. "There, little Rachel—all fixed." I propped up the doll, moving both arms with my fingers. "She doesn't hurt."

Rachel Schulmann was far wiser than she appeared. "She doesn't hurt because she's just a doll, Franck." The child sounded as if she needed to explain to me. "She's *made,* not real."

"Of course."

In their insular ghetto, the Jews had been suspicious of me at first—a large man with rough features and a scarred face, like a boxer who had lost too many fights. I kept to myself, showing no warmth or friendship, but posing no threat. I was tired of running, and I had almost given up on humanity because of how people hated things they didn't understand, how they despised strangers and vented their anger by lighting torches, grabbing pitchforks. But here in the Ingolstadt ghetto, I was patient, helpful, with few needs or ambitions. I became a tailor because I liked to stitch things together, making certain the pieces fit. Ironic, that.

As Rachel took the doll from me, my sleeve accidentally slid up my arm. Normally, I chose to wear bulky jackets with thick cuffs, but now the girl's eyes widened as she saw the line that encircled my wrist, the still-prominent scars from the old sutures where the hand had been attached—someone else's hand, someone else's wrist, the first two pieces in becoming *me.*

"Does that hurt?" she asked, more fascinated than frightened.

I gave her a quick, reassuring shake of my head. "No, child. It's just the way I'm made."

Now that the important work was done—repairing the girl's doll—I could turn to the other work she'd brought me. Her father, the rabbi, had sent his jacket, a dark old suit that had been carefully but inexpertly patched many times over the years. Given a few days, I could have fixed flaws that the rabbi or his wife pretended not to see, tightened the stitches, trimmed the frayed cuffs and collar. But the damage was more severe, more disturbing. As soon as I looked at the torn fabric at the shoulder, the mud stains, the dried blood, I recalled what had happened. No one could keep secrets here in the ghetto.

The Nazis—three of them—had beaten Rabbi Schulmann in the streets. Laughing, they had pushed him down into the mud, and he had not challenged them, had not cursed them— but he had retained his dignity. Unwise. When the Schutz-staffel district officer, Schein, and two members of his Staffeln decided that the rabbi did not look sufficiently humiliated, they knocked him into the gutter and pummeled him with nightsticks. Some of the people gasped and moaned, helpless, while others watched in horror. Rabbi Schulmann cringed, accepting the blows, and soon enough Staffelführer Schein and his two thugs grew tired of their sport and departed.

"They attack us because we're different," the rabbi said aloud to the stunned people who rushed to help him. "To them, we're easy targets." He was bruised and bleeding, and they helped him to a doctor.

I had watched part of the incident from behind the smeared glass windows of my tailor shop. The Jews pretended that bad things didn't happen. They cleaned up all sign of the incident, erased any marks the Nazis left, as if that were the way to survive.

Now I had the rabbi's damaged and stained jacket. I inspected it, poked my thick fingers through the tear, studied the dried blood. My dark lips formed a smile. "Tell your father I can fix this, Rachel. I promise it will be as good as new by tomorrow evening."

"Thank you, Franck." She pulled her doll close to her chest. "When you bring it over, my mother and father would like you to join us for dinner. Tomorrow night?"

"I'd be happy to." I was genuinely pleased. The people rarely invited me into their homes.

Outside, in the street, I watched the Jews nailing boards across their shopwindows, which had been shattered the previous day when Schein and his entire Staffeln of ten men had hurled bricks at any business they didn't like—an accountant, a piano teacher, a baker. I knew the shopkeepers had already placed orders with a glassmaker in the city, wanting to repair the windows as quickly as possible. Within a day, the ghetto street would look just as it always had—until the next time. But inner scars did not go away so easily.

How could I not be angry?

As Rachel went to the door to leave my shop, she paused in fear. I heard the rumble of a staff car drive down the street and placed a warning hand on the girl's shoulder, holding her there to make certain she didn't run out in full view.

Staffelführer Schein sat in the back of the staff car as his driver cruised slowly down the street; he glared as the people ducked into doorways or drew the shades of their windows.

The staff car rolled by, wafting silence along the shops like a hushed breath.

"Why have they come back?" Rachel whispered.

"Because they like you to be afraid, child."

We watched as the Nazis drove out of sight, but they caused no damage . . . today.

Ingolstadt was still a small city, far from the rest of the war, with an insignificant Jewish quarter, which made Schein and the few men in his Staffeln all the more desperate for attention. But they wouldn't get it from me. I had learned long ago not to draw attention to myself if I wished to survive.

When the typical noises began to reappear in the street and people emerged from their shops with a nervous sigh, I let the girl run back to her parents. "Tell your father I'll bring the jacket tomorrow night."

In the past century, much had changed in Ingolstadt.

Because I hadn't come alive the way a normal person did, neither did I age or die as a normal man would. Most children have only dim memories of their early childhood, but I can remember the vivid flood of images and sensations from the moment I opened my dull yellow eyes on the table, surrounded by lightning, to see the face of Victor Frankenstein, my creator . . . my father . . . the man who was so horrified by *me* that he had cast me out.

Victor hated me because I was different, even though he had made me that way. What choice did I have but to hate him in return?

In a hundred years, the people of Ingolstadt had done their best to forget, or at least to pretend ignorance of, the history of their town. The ancient castle was gone, torn down stone by stone at the turn of the twentieth century. The old mill had burned long ago, then been rebuilt, only to be abandoned again. It was now an ancient wreck on the hill above the town.

I had traveled the world, gone to the frozen ends of the earth in pursuit of Victor, where I'd strangled him aboard a ship in an icy sea. It should have been my vengeance, my victory, after I'd leapt overboard to drift away on a detached ice floe, but I had learned much since then.

Now I had come back home to the small German city that was my birthplace. My Jewish neighbors accepted me without asking too many questions, sometimes looking at me with pity, sometimes with a hard swallow and dry throat, as they saw my scars, my lumpish features. But I have done nothing to make them fear me. I was no longer the vengeful clumsy monster, but rather just someone trying to fit in. For a while, I felt I had a chance . . . but then the polical situation had grown worse, the Nazis came to power on a wave of blame and fear, and I didn't think they would let anyone live peaceably and unnoticed.

After the girl was gone, I took the rabbi's jacket and used gentle strokes of a bristle brush to clean the mud; I blotted with chemicals to soak out the bloodstains. Then, with tiny perfect stitches, I began to repair the damage.

I toiled all night long by lantern light, and I had the rabbi's jacket cleaned, repaired, and even pressed well before sunup. But I couldn't allow myself to do things that were *too* mysterious. If I did my work too quickly, too perfectly, there might be stories about me dabbling in dark magic, being a secret outcast sorcerer hiding in the ghetto of Ingolstadt. Rumors are easy things to start.

Since the Nazis openly blame the Jews for every perceived crime, one would think the people here in the ghetto would not be so quick to cast suspicions themselves, but it is part of the way humans are made, scars they don't even see inside themselves.

Because I don't need sleep—one of the gifts that Victor forgot to include when he gave me my life, like a missed stitch—I sat up and read the newspapers until dawn, when I would be able to venture into the streets again without looking like a fearsome, hulking shadow.

I had one paper from Berlin, one from Salzburg, and even a weekly Yiddish edition (though my grasp of the language was still uncertain). The date was November 9, 1938, and the political situation in Germany was grim. By reading the slanted stories, I could sense a brewing storm on the horizon—a storm that would not bring the spark of life, like the one that had reanimated me, but rather destruction. All of Germany—maybe even all of Europe—seemed to be full of peasants carrying torches, looking for a target. . . .

When the ghetto began to bustle in the morning, I helped an old silversmith across the street rehang a splintered door that the Nazis had damaged during their previous escapade, and he was grateful for my help. I had little else to do, a pair of trousers to alter, a few buttons to reattach. I walked the length of the ghetto, without any particular aim. A dark cloud seemed to hang over the people, as if they knew something terrible was about to happen, but they pretended it was just another day.

That evening I brought the repaired jacket to the rabbi's house, which was adjacent to the synagogue, and also carried a sack with four apples I had purchased from the cart on the corner. Rachel was delighted to see me, and the rabbi thanked me for my help. He tried on his repaired jacket, pronounced it perfect.

His face looked as battered and discolored as mine had once appeared, the purple bruises from his recent beating now turning yellow at the edges. When he caught me looking at them, he said, "They will heal. We must give thanks that no greater harm was done. They have had their fun. Staffelführer Schein and his men are like angry unruly children."

The rabbi's wife was furious on his behalf. "And you think because you let them beat you that they'll be satisfied now?"

"What would you have me do?" the rabbi said in frustration.

Rachel quickly held up her doll, smiling at me. "Could you make me another one, Franck? You're so good at stitching."

"Rachel, that's not a polite request to make," her father admonished.

My dark lips formed a smile. "But a perfectly reasonable one, Rabbi. I may have some scraps of old cloth left and a few rags. Would you like me to make a husband for your stitched-together woman?"

"Yes, please."

She had no idea how much that thought hurt me. If Victor had done that one thing for me, we would never have needed to become enemies. But Victor Frankenstein was a terrible man. And the peasants called *me* inhuman!

Frau Schulmann had made a fine meal with whatever was available. She even simmered the apples I had brought with a pinch of cinnamon and some sugar.

After we ate, the rabbi invited me to smoke a pipe with him as we listened to the world news on the radio. After the tubes had warmed up, he tuned to the strongest radio station, which was playing Wagner. The rabbi sat back contentedly, puffing smoke.

I felt relaxed, remembering another old man, a blind man alone in a cottage who had befriended me and taught me many things, showing me the kind side of the human heart for the first time. I missed that blind old man; I'd seen too few people like him in all of my years.

When the radio announcer read the news in a terse voice, the rabbi and I both listened. Tensions in Germany were already strained. Many Jews, feeling displaced and victimized, had already fled the country if they had the means to do so. They lost their homes, their wealth. They tried to find someplace to hide.

But today the situation grew much worse. In Paris, a German diplomat had been assassinated by a Polish Jew, a young man incensed by how the Nazis were persecuting his people. The assassin had been driven to violence out of despair and help-lessness, but as I listened to the angry news announcer, I knew that the young man's actions would only aggravate the situa-tion for the Jews. In fact, I was certain things would rapidly get worse. The announcer added at the end, as if it were a foregone conclusion: "Investigators are certain this is part of a much larger Jewish plot to overthrow the government."

Rabbi Schulmann turned gray and shook his head. "Oh, no." He uttered a quick prayer. "This is just the excuse the Nazis have wanted for a long time."

From the kitchen where she washed the dishes, his wife looked at him with wide eyes, frightened by the news. Rachel played with her doll in the room, and she surprised us again with her perceptiveness. "Are we in danger, Papa? Will the bad men come hurt you again?"

Rabbi Schulmann heaved a long sigh, pained by what he had to admit to his daughter. "We must pray it won't happen, my dear."

The girl was grim and serious. "We should have a golem to protect us, just like in Prague. Then we can be safe."

"That's just a story, child," Rabbi Schulmann said.

But the girl was indignant. "You said it was a *true* story."

The rabbi looked up at me with weary eyes, explaining, "It is a frightening tale, my friend—a good tale, but I can't guarantee its veracity. In Prague in 1580, Rabbi Loew fashioned a large and powerful being out of clay, a *golem,* to protect our community from a Jew-hating priest who incited hatred among the Christians. When the mob came to the ghetto, Rabbi Loew's golem stood strong and protected the Jews, preventing a pogrom. But then the golem ran amok, threatening innocents, causing great damage. Rabbi Loew was forced to remove the spark of life, rendering the golem lifeless again." He turned to his daughter. "It is meant to be a lesson."

"I still think we need our own golem," said Rachel. "But without the last part of the story."

Outside, we heard growling engines, screams, gunfire . . . then laughter accompanied by the sounds of shattering glass.

* * *

Fires began to start. Staffelführer Schein rode imperiously in his staff car with two of his men, flanked by two more Staffeln on motorcycles. His men threw rocks and bricks, smashing every intact window on the street. When some of the shop-keepers and families ran out, begging them to stop, the Nazis threw rocks at them instead.

The old silversmith whom I had helped flailed his hands and stood in front of the door we had just repaired. One of the Staffeln grinned, hefted a broken brick, and hurled it with deadly aim, smashing the center of the silversmith's forehead. He collapsed, surely dead.

The men fired their rifles into the air, but I was sure they would choose other targets soon. When the rotund baker shook his fist and cursed them, the Staffelführer turned in his seat in the staff car, raised his Luger, and shot the baker in the chest.

"Burn the synagogue," Schein ordered. "That's where they plot against us!" His men tossed kerosene lanterns against the synagogue door, smashed more windows.

Rachel ran into the street, crying, screaming in her little-girl voice for the Nazis to stop. The terrified rabbi grabbed her and pulled her back, but she'd already drawn the Nazis' attention. They spotted, and recognized, the man they had beaten only days earlier.

"Please don't hurt her!" Rabbi Schulmann cried, but the Nazis raised their guns.

I had seen mob hatred before, had faced it and barely sur-vived. The Nazis were destructive and dangerous, more orga-nized than unruly town peasants and capable of causing far more damage. I would have preferred to stay in my tailor shop and not get involved; that would have been the smart thing to do.

I may be large, I may look ungainly, my hands and limbs stitched together from mismatched parts, but Victor had done his work well, and I could move with predatory speed and power. I lunged forward to place myself in front of the rabbi and Rachel.

The Nazis opened fire.

I felt the impact of three rifle bullets and a much smaller caliber handgun bullet. My chest caught the deadly projectiles, preventing them from harming anyone else. The hot bullets damaged skin and muscles, but my body had already been dead once and would not so easily be brought back to death.

The Nazis had fired first. Now it was my turn.

Paying no heed to the spreading fires, the astonished crowd, or the arrogant sneer on the Nazi faces, I was upon the nearest SS man. I grabbed his rifle and yanked it free with such force that three of his fingers snapped; I heard a sickening pop as his shoulder dislocated.

I brought the butt of the rifle down so hard in the center of his face that it caved in his skull, just like the old silversmith's. Then I swung the rifle sideways and shattered the spine of a second man.

I charged over to the two Staffeln who were now scrambling off their motorcycles. With one hand on each, I grabbed them by the lip of their helmets, yanked them up—I think one neck broke instantly. The other soldier flailed and thrashed, but I slammed them down to the street. Then I picked up one of the motorcycles, raised it high over my head, and brought it down onto them, crushing both. In moments, I had dispatched all the Staffeln, none of whom had a chance to fire another shot.

Last was Staffelführer Schein. He stared at me with round eyes and gaping mouth. I think he had shot his Luger at me several times, but I hadn't even felt the bullets. I grabbed the pistol and the hand that held it, and turned the weapon. I meant to bend Schein's arm at the elbow, but bent the middle of his wrist instead. It didn't matter. I jammed the Luger's hot barrel up under his chin and crushed my fingers around the trigger, firing off another shot that went through the top of his head.

Only fifteen seconds had passed.

Though the fires continued to burn in the synagogue and chunks of broken glass fell out of the smashed windows, the silence around me seemed deafening. I turned. There were several bullet holes in my own garments, but they could be easily repaired with a few neat stitches.

What I could not fix, though, was the fear and horror with which Rabbi Schulmann and his people now regarded *me*.

"What have you done?" the rabbi asked softly.

"Saved you." How else could I respond?

"Maybe . . . maybe not." The rabbi shook his head, as if paralyzed by a nightmare. "What are you?"

Now my own hiding of the truth, my own erasure of my unnatural past, was laid bare before them. They saw my ugliness, saw the scars, and quickly classified me as "not one of us." Even though I had helped them, stood against their enemies, saved them from the attack of these monsters, they regarded me with fear. Even Rachel.

"He's the golem," she said.

"You killed the Nazis," said the rabbi. "Now they'll come back for us and take their vengeance tenfold. They will retaliate, kill us all."

I knew, though, that Ingolstadt had only a small Nazi garrison, a minimal presence, and I had killed all of them. It would take days, perhaps as much as a week, before the district leader began to wonder what had happened to Schein and his men. We would have time . . . if the people let me.

I glanced up at the murky dark sky. There was no moon tonight. I had to hope that the other citizens of Ingolstadt wouldn't take it upon themselves to attack the Jewish quarter in retaliation for the news of the recent assassination.

"I have an idea," I said. "We will need blankets to cover them." As if they were no more significant than the doll I had repaired for Rachel, I picked up the dead Nazis and tossed them into the staff car, piling them like cordwood. "We can dispose of the bodies, get rid of the car and motorcycles. No one ever has to know."

"We all know," the rabbi said.

"And you'll be alive to know it." I looked down at Staffelführer Schein, who lay atop the pile of bodies. He reminded me too much of how Victor had looked after I'd strangled him up in the frozen sea. I felt no satisfaction, no relief, barely even a sense of justice.

Frau Schulmann was sobbing, as were several others in the street. Finally, some went to fight the spreading fires and save the synagogue. Others went to tend to the bodies of those the Nazis had killed.

"This will get much worse for us," the rabbi said, his voice hollow. "If you were a real golem, I could remove the bit of scripture that reanimated you, the spark of life." He shook his head. "But I don't have that power. I don't know where you come from. I can only ask you to go away and leave us alone. We don't want you here—you're too dangerous."

The Jews were afraid of me, but at least they didn't have pitchforks and torches. I would do them one last favor, then I would be gone to find someplace up in the rugged mountains.

I looked once more at Rachel, but the little girl did not look back at me. Her rag doll had fallen onto the street.

I gathered every remnant of Staffelführer Schein and his men, then drove away in the staff car, out of Ingolstadt and up the rutted dirt road that led to the abandoned, creaking mill, where winds whistled through broken windows. I piled the bodies inside the old mill, then set fire to the old structure. I do not like dangerous, unpredictable fire, but this brought more satisfaction than terror. As the windmill blazed into the dark sky, it seemed very appropriate to me—a different sort of ending. This time, *I* had torched the place, winning my own victory against superstition, prejudice, and fear. Even though it would never end there . . .

I set off in the staff car, driving away into the rugged mountains, far from Ingolstadt. I intended never to return—although I had said the same thing a century before.

Hours later, when the car was nearly out of gas, I found a pull-off by a steep cliffside, tossed the motorcycles off the cliff, and pushed the empty vehicle over, where it tumbled off into the darkness. Even if the wreckage was eventually found, no one would ever know the answers.

Still feeling no pain from where I'd been shot, no weariness despite the labors of the night, I trudged up into the empty high valleys and isolated crags. I didn't care about the cold glaciers or windswept basins. I just needed to find a place where I would be alone . . . where I belonged.

RATTLER AND THE MOTHMAN

by Sharyn McCrumb

I'M NOT GOING TO SAY that he didn't look dangerous, because he did.

Now, I don't hold with talking to dead people, though it seems I have to do it often enough. And worse, besides.

You'd think that holing up out in the woods like I do, living on Dr Pepper and Twinkies, would give me more peace and quiet than John ever saw. *(That there's a biblical reference, which slides right past most people nowadays. There's a lot wrong with life in the twenty-first century, which is why I took to the woods in the first place, but in a world where the Dalai Lama is on Twitter, I don't reckon there's much hope for any of us Shamen—New People's word—to get let alone.)*

My favorite neighbors are the ones that fly south for the winter, or else hibernate in a cave until spring. They're never a bit of trouble, but unfortunately in the warmer months, the woods tend to fill up with varmints. There's some idiot a ways down the road who fancies himself an independent filmmaker, which means he has no money and can't spell. Anyhow, he's been going around trying to recruit the locals to

work for free in his magnum opus, *Haints in Hillbilly Holler.*
Said I'd be a natural. I told him I'd rather be dragged backward
through a briar patch, which he took to mean "Maybe." He is
from Florida, and doesn't speak the local dialect very well.
From what he said about his movie, I can see that he plans to
trot out every old stereotype in the book and make everybody
in these mountains look like ignorant savages, just to juice up
his cheesy horror flick. He ought to play the monster himself.
Typecasting.

And I'm always getting tomfool backpackers traipsing out
here, asking me for something to cure what ails them, which
is mostly boredom and too much civilization, from what I
can tell.

If they're polite fellers, and in genuine distress, I give them
sweet tea with sassafras; and if they're arrogant *turistas* who
sneer at my shack and snicker at my accent when they think
I'm not noticing—why, I give them a dose of laxative, whether
they need one or not. They're just irritating, but when you've
had to listen to lectures on string theory from a Cherokee
ravenmocker, and stand under cold iron to get rid of the night
riders, why, you get a little short on patience with the common and garden variety of idiot: the kind that wear Sierra
Club sweatshirts and use poison ivy leaves for toilet paper.

Things do tend to simmer down a bit of an evening. I reckon
those suburban hikers are afraid they can't see the snakes un-
derfoot in the twilight, so they go off to wherever it is that
L.L.Bean-wearing, cell-phone-toting, vegan-and-mineral-water
pioneers go when it's time to turn in.

That's when I drag an old wooden kitchen chair out into
the yard, take out a jug that *ain't* tea and sassafras, and start

counting the stars. There's a deal more of them out here than there are in city skies, and usually I have the rest of the evening to sit back and commune with them all by my lonesome. But on that particular night, before it got dark enough for the stars, and I was just watching the bats overhead, circling the tree-tops and chasing bugs, I saw something up there, hanging in the dark sky, in the distance between the ridge and the moun-taintop. At first I thought it was one of them bats, until I calcu-lated in my head how far away it had to be, and that told me that the thing was closer in size to a hang glider than it was to a bat—except that it wasn't a hang glider, either, because its wings were moving.

I turned that straight chair around so that I could keep an eye on that flying thing until I could figure out what it was I was seeing. My money, if I had any, would have been on the merry pranksters from the nearest air force base, because the film-maker couldn't even afford a paper airplane. The word around here is that the pilots like to fly their newest experimental air-craft low along the ridges to scare the bejesus out of any locals who happen to be watching. I was wrong about that, though.

Just for the heck of it, I reached around for my lantern, lit it, and waved it slowly, side to side while I faced that flying thing. I hoped it would come close enough to give me a better look at it. Sure enough, after a second or two, it noticed my signal, because it seemed to wobble for a moment in midair, and then it commenced to fly straight for me. I set down the lantern and waited for my visitor to arrive.

It didn't take long. First it circled the treetops around my cabin, same as the bats were doing, only instead of eating bugs, it was checking me out, maybe looking to see if I was armed with more than a lantern.

I wasn't.

Most of the dangerous things that hunt me up in these woods wouldn't even slow down for a firearm, and the ones that would—the bears and the bobcats—generally don't want trouble any more than I do, so we maintain a judicious neutrality. I'm generally polite to the others—the Cherokee gods and such—though I can't say that I care overmuch for their company.

The thing was coming closer. It looked like a big shadow, blotting out the night sky, and then it swooped down below the treetops, and when I got a better look, I was staring into a pair of red eyes that looked like the running lights on an airplane—except they blinked a time or two. They sat there in a shadowy face that I would have paid more attention to if I hadn't been sidetracked by the fifteen-foot leathery wings stretching out behind him and flapping slowly as he set himself down in the grass a few feet away from my chair.

In the faint glow of the lantern light, I could see him more clearly now. He was roughly human shaped, standing upright on long legs that ended in bird claws. Those red eyes flashed and glowed, seeming to take in everything around him. They were set far apart, on the outer edges of a round face with a sharp beak of a nose and a lipless mouth that made me think of a cave entrance: just a way into darkness. I was wondering if he had teeth, and not particularly eager to find out.

The whole cast of his countenance would cause you to think "insect," by way of classification, except that his expression and bearing said that there was somebody home. He was a lot smarter than a housefly. You could tell.

His body was covered with a fine fluff, (gray or blue—I couldn't tell in the dim light)—that might have been fur or the sort of downy feathers you see on baby birds. I could have reached out and stroked him to find out which it was, if I'd wanted to.

But I didn't want to.

Still keeping those burning eyes trained on me, he folded his wings up against his back, and lowered himself ceremoniously onto a sycamore log that I keep moss-free and weeded, in case I get company. While I had been watching him draw a bead on me, swoop down, and make himself comfortable on the log, my mind had been flipping through possibilities. The Cherokee in these parts told tales of a giant fire-breathing wasp named Ulagu that burned all the trees off Roan Mountain, so that they never grew back. The summit of that mountain is treeless to this day, with nothing bigger than rhododendron bushes growing there. Nobody knows why. Scientists call such bare mountains "balds," but that's a classification, not an explanation, so I guess a giant wasp is as good an answer as any. I didn't think this was him, though. Those old stories made the wasp out to be a lot bigger than my seven-foot visitor here, and not much to speak of in the brains department, so I had ruled out Ulagu. That only left one possible candidate, and, as unlikely as it was for him to drop by, I figured he had.

"Good evening," I said, giving the creature a cordial nod, while I sized him up some more, trying to think of something polite to say to someone maybe seven feet tall, and covered with duck down.

He inclined his head in my direction, and I took that for a gesture of greeting. The silence stretched on some more, so finally I said, "I didn't expect to see you here."

It was hard to tell anything about his emotions from that Halloween mask face of his, but I swear I think he looked pleased when I said that. He got up and let out a little shriek, sort of an owl-noise, and stomped one of those big chicken feet of his in the dust. Then he stretched out those leathery fifteen-foot wings to their full length in order to impress me even more, so I added, "Nope. I certainly did not expect to see you here. *You being from West Virginia and all.*"

Well, that stuck in his craw. He blinked in mid-preening and looked down at me, and then his wings started folding back of their own accord. You could tell that he'd have been a lot happier if I'd gibbered and cowered at the sight of him, but there's been worse things in my yard than him, and I wouldn't give him the satisfaction of thinking he had impressed me.

"I would greet you by name to be neighborly, but I don't think they went so far as to give you an official name up there in West Virginia, did they? And I don't believe they ever figured out that you already had a name that you picked up somewhere else. In that other range of mountains where you've been seen now and again, I believe they call you Garuda, don't they?"

When I said that, those red eyes of his blinked half a dozen times, and he started looking around the yard, as if he expected people to jump out of the bushes and tackle him. I couldn't think of anybody that would want to try, but I just kept smiling pleasantly at him, while he made up his mind about what to do next.

Finally, in a guttural voice with an accent I couldn't place, he said, "There are many garudas. It is not a name."

He droned on for a while about the four garuda kings, and about the great cities of the garuda, and their eternal enemies the nagas, which, as far as I could tell, were either snakes or dragons, but apparently the garudas' mission in life was to kill nagas. He claimed he could get so big that his wingspan would be twelve hundred miles wide, and that with one flap of those wings he could dry up the sea. He offered to demonstrate, but since Tennessee is within twelve hundred miles of the ocean, I thought it best to decline the offer.

I shrugged. "Well, maybe garuda isn't a given name, then. I thought it had more of a ring to it than Mothman, but that's just a personal preference."

He just went on staring, so I said, "You are that particular garuda, though, aren't you? The one in West Virginia that they called Mothman?"

It had been about two hundred miles north of here, as the . . . well, *moth* . . . flies. Back in the late 1960s, as I recall, two young couples had spotted a hawklike creature out in a rural area near an abandoned military facility outside Point Pleasant, West Virginia. The thing had scared the bejesus out of them. They even claimed he flew after their speeding car. But aside from a few evening appearances to frighten the locals, he hadn't really done any harm. Not so much as a chicken went missing anywhere that could be blamed on him. But then, in December of '67 something terrible did happen. And he got blamed for that quick enough, which is human nature, I suppose, to single out the different one and then ascribe all the bad luck to his existence. Of course, they might have been right. Given the powers he claimed he had, he would certainly be capable of wreaking any amount of havoc. I was trying to think of a polite way to introduce the topic, without—you know—ruffling his feathers.

"The Mothman, yes," the creature said, nodding his head slowly up and down. "I was called that once. They searched for me for many days then. But we can change. Change size. Change shape. Some garudas can take on the aspect of a human."

I eyed him thoughtfully. "You haven't quite got the hang of that yet, have you?"

He shrugged—at least I think that's what it was. Then he leaned forward and locked eyes with me, and he seemed to wait for a minute as if he was listening to something far off. "You don't mind this visit from me," he said slowly, stating a fact. Then he cocked his head and waited some more. "You are not afraid of me, not like other people are. You like your solitude—yes . . . understandable. But you would mind even more having some ordinary human intrude upon you here—a hiker perhaps, or a tourist. You prefer me to them."

Well, you can't argue with a creature who tunes in to minds as if they were radio stations, so I just nodded and sat back, wondering what it was he had come about. He wasn't ready to tell me, though, and after the silence had stretched on for a couple of minutes, I said, "You know, you scared people pretty bad back in the sixties in West Virginia, appearing in the dark in front of their cars, and peeking in the windows of a house. They're still talking about it."

He grunted.

"Somebody even came through here one time wearing a Mothman T-shirt. I reckon you're as close as West Virginia has ever come to having a dragon."

He growled deep in his throat, and those big leathery wings of his rustled some. "I . . . am . . . not a *naga*!"

"No, no. No offense. Easy there, big guy." If you think ambassadors have a tough job, you should try having diplomatic relations with a supernatural being. "I just meant that you were out of the ordinary for the area. They're not used to big scary things with wings."

"I was there before they were."

I nodded, not the least bit surprised. "Thought that might be the case," I said. "Seems to me I heard a Shawnee tale or two that you'd fit into pretty well."

"The old ones. Yes. They understood me better than these people there now."

"Well, I expect that was because folks back then just accepted the evidence of their own senses, whereas people today are always having to filter their reality through science textbooks and conventional wisdom and whatever the journalists are selling this month, which is just another name for the lies everybody believes."

He ignored that last sally. Apparently, he wasn't up to debating the politics of culture, or else, after the first few millennia, it just becomes monotonous. He said, "I was there already. I was there before the people. When I first knew the place, the land was covered by a warm shallow sea."

I nodded. "I'd heard that. A few million years back, wasn't it? Most of the continent was underwater back then. I know coal was formed from the ferns around that time. Bet there were dinosaurs poking around in the shallows of those ancient seas."

His eyes flashed again, and he hissed, "Nagas!"

"Well . . . I suppose . . . to stretch a point." Dragons, dinosaurs . . . it was all a question of semantics, I reckon. Or maybe we all just see what we expect to see. "But they're all gone now."

The eyes glowed red again, and he said, with something like satisfaction warming his voice, "All gone. Yes. I killed them."

"You—" I remembered I was talking to a deity of sorts, and that his experience of time and reality was not the same as mine. Anyhow, I wasn't going to out-and-out call him a liar. I've had so much practice being polite to city-slicker trail bunnies that putting up with an ancient winged monster was a piece of cake. Anyhow, his tales were less outlandish than some of theirs. "Killed them yourself, did you?"

His wings fluttered a little. "I told you. When I attain my full size, and beat my wings, I can dry up the sea."

"Yes, you did mention that. I reckon that would do it. I'll take your word for it. So you dried up that shallow sea that was covering West Virginia, and then you killed off the nagas that were left?"

He nodded. "Then I rested for a great stretch of time. Things were quiet."

We lapsed into a companionable silence while I mulled over this new theory of dinosaur extinction. I didn't think there would be any use mentioning it up at the university, though. I didn't have any letters after my name, so I wasn't even allowed to have an opinion. Besides, the truth is just what everybody already believes, and this wouldn't fit into their game plan even a little bit.

After a few more minutes of companionable silence, another thought struck me. "How come you stayed around after you had destroyed all the nagas?"

"I required a long rest after such a great battle."

"A few million years, huh? That's how I feel when I've cooked a whole kettle full of stew and then tried to eat it all. Makes me want to sleep for days. You ate them, didn't you? The nagas? All of them?"

He grunted. "As many as I could. I spit their bones into the mud."

"Yeah. I think we found them."

"Then I went back to the other oceans, where there are other garudas. Time passed there. We built cities, and fought other nagas. But one day I returned to the land where the shallow sea had been. And when I arrived, there were new minds in the land where the seas had been. Minds like yours."

"That would have been the Shawnee, I expect. I think we're distantly related." And if he had left in the late Pleistocene and returned with the Shawnee, that had been one heck of a long nap, followed by an extended visit to Asia, between wiping out the dinosaurs and turning up again in West Virginia maybe three thousand years ago. But, like I said, he may not experience time the way we do, and I wasn't up to talking metaphysics with him—not sober, anyhow. I had a jug of moonshine under the sink, and it crossed my mind to offer him some of it, but he looked like he might turn out to be a mean drunk, so I thought better of it.

"Shawnee . . ." He was tasting the word, or maybe trying

to set up a chord in his memory. I wondered where he had been lately.

"Yes, I expect you remember them. They were quiet folks, living with the land, before the current occupants arrived and started paving roads through the forests and cutting off mountaintops to get to the coal."

He nodded slowly, as if he were summoning up the memory from a long way off. "I remember them. That was a peaceful time. The creatures who inhabit a garuda's land become as children to us, and from time to time we try to listen to their wishes, and to please them."

I didn't much like the sound of that. It seemed to me that there was a lot of room for misunderstanding between a group of simple country people and a giant winged creature who lived outside time. I'd be careful what I wished for around him.

"Can you read exactly what people are thinking?" I asked, belatedly cautious.

He considered it. "I can hear your mind better than most. Perhaps it is the solitude of the woods, with no other minds nearby, but I think it is more."

I nodded. I figured that whatever made me able to talk to the dead, and have other equally irritating experiences, had probably upped the broadcast signal of my thought waves. I didn't consider it a blessing.

"But although I hear you . . . I do not often hear the single thoughts of one of your kind. Your minds are too small for me to see within, and you live for such a little time. But sometimes when a great many minds are all wishing for the same thing, their thoughts become strong enough to reach me."

"Uh-huh." I didn't appreciate that remark about little

minds, but I decided to let it go. "Did the first people here wish for anything in particular?"

"Long ago they feared monsters in their land, and as a gift to the people I killed them all."

I had a pretty good idea of what those monsters would have been: saber-toothed tigers, American lions, mastodons—and with all my heart I wish he had left them alone, but it was about ten thousand years too late to quibble about it now. I tried to keep my voice steady. "Did they ever wish for anything else?"

He nodded. "Strange new people came into their land. Not so many at first . . . Just enough to build a fort out of dead trees and clear some land by the great river to grow crops. The forest people knew that if all went well with these people, many more would come. They wished them gone."

I only remembered it because it had happened in Shawnee territory, which is a particular interest of mine. In 1775, just before the American Revolution got going, George Washington himself had sent a group of settlers out to colonize some land he owned at the very end of what was then Virginia. The future president bought up some land grants from veterans of the French and Indian War until he had accumulated about thirty-five thousand acres out there, right on the Kanawha River, in addition to all the other territory he owned farther east. He personally selected that land, and planted some oak trees there, so I reckon he liked the look of it, but somebody should have told him that the Shawnee name for the Kanawha River is Keninsheka, the River of Evil Spirits.

I took a long look at my visitor sitting on the log there in front of my cabin. I guess the Shawnee were acquainted with him, all right.

Washington figured on setting up his own little colony out there in the back of beyond, so he sent James Cleveland and William Stevens out there leading a collection of families into the wilderness to start a settlement, and, sure enough, they built houses, and cleared enough land for fields and orchards, and things seemed to be going along pretty well. But then the Revolutionary War broke out, and nobody had time to worry about a little group of settlers on the other side of the mountains. George Washington got busy. You know how it is.

So from Bunker Hill to Yorktown, everybody just went on with the war, and left those colonists out on the Kanawha to fend for themselves, and the next time anybody had any spare time to check on them, they discovered that the entire settlement had vanished. I mean: *gone.* No skeletons in the tall grass around the derelict cabins; no forwarding address carved on a nearby tree—nothing.

People have always blamed the Shawnee for the disappearance of Washington's West Virginia colony, and I thought that still might be the case, but I was beginning to think that they didn't do it in the usual way: attacking the fort and killing the inhabitants and burning the village. No . . . I think the Shawnee just . . . *wished* them gone.

The garuda was nodding. Apparently, he had been tuning in to my thoughts again, which saved a lot of backstory and chitchat, and made him a tolerable companion, except that I thought he might be a dangerous friend to have. At least when you say things out loud, you can be sure that people heard what you intended to say. Or maybe not, what with semantics and all. *(Tourists think that people who live in the woods are ignorant, but you have a lot more time to read if you don't have to commute.)*

"The Shawnee wished the colonists would leave, didn't they? All of them wished that, as hard as they could, all at once?"

"This is so. And they made offerings to me and sent up prayers. I liked that. I thought perhaps these beings in their wooden walls were nagas in another form, and so I saved my forest people from them. I made them gone."

I wondered where he had spit the bones that time.

"And then you took a nap for a hundred and ninety years or so?"

"A short sleep, yes, but when I awoke again my lands had changed. There were still forests and mountains, but now there were many minds, and many wooden walls. Great cities."

"Did you like the new people?"

"They loved the land. Because of that, they belonged. They had forgotten me, though. So I appeared once or twice to remind them who guarded their land."

"Yeah. They noticed." I thought about the terrified young couple in Mason County, West Virginia, who had reported seeing a huge birdlike creature chasing their car down a country road. Or the ones who lived near the abandoned army facility who had caught him on the porch, peeking in the windows. I'm sure that prayers and offerings to the creature were the last things on their minds.

"They did not understand my presence. I thought to do a great deed for them so that they would know who I was."

"So you looked around for some nagas, I bet?" I had begun to see that garudas were really very limited in the miracle-working department. They couldn't—or wouldn't—make you rich, or improve your health, or clean up the polluted air. All they were good for was killing. As guardians go, West Virginia could do better, but it did make me thankful that the garuda hadn't picked Washington, D.C., to call home. The wishes of the folks there would make your hair curl.

"Okay, tell me about the bridge," I said. That's almost all anybody remembers about Mothman: that in December 1967 he was seen in the vicinity of the Silver Bridge at Point Pleasant, and that a short time later, the bridge collapsed, killing forty-six unfortunate people whose cars had been crossing over it at the time.

"It was a small gesture," said Mothman.

Well, I guess it was, compared to wiping out dinosaurs and sending the Ice Age mammals into extinction, but I was still wondering why he'd pick on a bridge.

He heard my question in his head. "Because . . . that bridge led to a land of nagas."

Oh. Right. Sure, it did. *Ohio.*

He nodded. "I felt the same thing in the minds of these people that I had known in the old ones of the forest: the wishing away of an enemy."

I expect he did hear a lot of exasperation in there. West Virginians get pretty tired of the sneering jokes Ohioans tell about them, and they highly resent their overlooking the physicists and the millionaires, and thinking that the place is composed of rustic poor people. The worst, though, is when those well-meaning, fluff-brained do-gooders in Ohio load up all their old clothes in a van and go barging across the river into West Virginia to inflict charity on people who mostly don't want or need it. I think I'd rather live across the Kanawha from nagas, myself.

Mothman was nodding. "Just so," he said. "But my new children were helpless to destroy that enemy, and so I did a small thing for them. I did not destroy all of their tormentors, because these new people did not show the proper respect for me. But I let them see my power."

"How's that working out for you?"

After a long pause, the garuda said, "They turned away from me. I will not help them again. Or perhaps I will give the creatures in this land one last chance. Is there some enemy that threatens my people here? I could remind them again who guards this land."

I thought about it, and to be honest, I was spoiled for choice. Who would I like to see attacked by Mothman? The mountaintop removal people? The retired snowbirds holed up in their new gated communities, gentrifying the mountains with million-dollar "log cabins"? The oxycodone pushers who prey on the poor in spirit?

I was tempted, but I didn't want quite that much havoc on my karma, and I reckon garudas are all about karma. So I leaned in real close to the red-eyed creature, and said, "Over in the next holler, there's a feller making a movie about monsters.

"I think you should audition."

BIG MAN

by David Moody

IT WAS LIKE SOMETHING out of one of those black-and-white 1950s B movies he used to avidly watch when he was a kid: the army spread out in a wide arc across the land to defend the city, lying in wait for "it" to attack. Major Hawkins used to love those movies. Although the reality looked almost the same and the last few days certainly seemed to have followed a similar script, it *felt* completely different. This, he reminded himself, was real. This was war.

This wasn't the Cold War U.S. of the movies; it was midwinter, and he was positioned southwest of a rain-soaked Birmingham, almost slap bang in the center of the United Kingdom. But the differences didn't end there. He wasn't an actor playing the part of a square-jawed hero, he was a trained soldier who had a job to do. He was no rank-and-file trooper, either. Today he was the highest-ranking officer out in the field, or, to put it another way, the highest-ranking officer whose neck was on the line. His superiors were a safe distance away, watching the situation unfold on TV screens from the safety of bunker-bound leather chairs.

Roger Corman, Samuel Z. Arkoff, and the others had actually got a lot right in their quaint old movies. *The Amazing Colossal Man, War of the Colossal Beast, Attack of the 50 Foot Woman*—their monsters' stories always followed a familiar path: an unexpected and unintentional genesis, the wanton death and destruction that inevitably followed, the brief and fruitless search for a solution . . . but there was another facet to this story, one the movies always glossed over. Many people had died, crushed by the beast or dismembered in a fit of unstoppable rage. Property had been destroyed, millions of pounds' worth of damage caused already, maybe even billions. And they weren't standing here waiting to face a stop-motion puppet or a stuntman in a rubber suit now; this was a genuine, bona fide creature: a foul aberration that had once been human but was now anything but; a hideous, deformed monstrosity that, unless it could be stopped, would just keep growing and keep killing. The pressure on Hawkins's shoulders was intense. The implications were terrifying.

Glen Chambers—the poor bastard at the very center of this unbelievable chain of events—had, until a few days ago, been a faceless nobody: a father of one, known only to his family, a handful of friends, and his work colleagues. Hawkins could have passed him in the street a hundred times and not given him a second glance. But now he had to force himself to forget that this monster had once been a man, and instead focus on the carnage and unspeakably evil acts the creature was responsible for. No one could be expected to remain sane under the torturous circumstances Chambers had endured, and it could even be argued that he was as innocent as any of his victims, but the undisputable fact remained: Regardless of intent or blame, the aberration had to be stopped.

Major Hawkins had first become involved after the initial attack at the clinic. The people there had done all they could to help Chambers, keeping him sedated and under observation while they searched for a way to reverse the effects of the accident and stop his body growing and distorting. And how had he repaid their kindness and concern? By killing more than thirty innocent people in a wild frenzy and reducing the entire facility to rubble, that was how. Then the cowardly bastard had gone into hiding until there were no longer any buildings big enough for him to hide inside.

The attack on Shrewsbury had ratcheted up the seriousness of the situation to another level, the sheer amount of damage and the number of needless deaths making it clear that destroying the aberration quickly was of the utmost importance. This was a threat the likes of which had never been experienced before. Men, women, and children were needlessly massacred, their bodies crushed or torn limb from limb. The streets were filled with rubble and blood.

The Chambers creature had attacked the picturesque town without provocation, decimating its historic buildings and killing hundreds of innocent bystanders. Even then, when it had had its fill of carnage there, it moved on and the bloodshed continued unabated. They'd tracked the beast halfway across the country, following the trail of devastation it left in its wake. The foul monstrosity had spared nothing and no one. Even livestock grazing in farmers' fields hadn't escaped the monster's reach. Hundreds of dismembered animal corpses lay scattered for miles around.

But what was it doing now?

The creature, for all its incredible (and still increasing) size, had temporarily managed to evade detection. They knew it was close, but its exact location remained a mystery. There was no need to hunt it out; Hawkins was certain it would run out of places to hide and would have no option but to reveal itself eventually, and when it did his troops would be ready. They'd be resorting to Corman/Arkoff tactics to try to kill the creature: Hit it with everything you've got, and keep firing until either you've run out of ammo or the monster has been blown to hell and back. And then, if the dust settles and the hideous thing still manages to crawl out of the smoke and haze unscathed, you call in the big boys. A nuclear strike was an absolute last resort, but Hawkins knew the powers-that-be would sanction it if they had to (after all, it was less of a big deal from where they were sitting in their bunkers). Tens of thousands would die, maybe hundreds of thousands, but if the creature couldn't be stopped, what would happen then? No one would be safe anywhere. In the space of less than a week Glen Chambers had gone from being a faceless nobody to the greatest single threat to the survival of the human race. An indiscriminate, remorseless butcher.

Major Hawkins tried to distract himself from worst-case-scenario thoughts of uncomfortably close nuclear explosions by recalling B movie clichés and trying to find an alternative solution to the crisis. He almost laughed out loud when he considered the ridiculous and yet faintly possible notion that this thing might do a King Kong on him and head for higher ground. Imagine that, he thought, his mind swapping biplanes and the Empire State Building for a squadron of Harrier jet fighters and the Blackpool Tower . . .

"Sir!"

"What is it, Rayner?" Hawkins asked quickly, doing all he could to hide the fact that he'd been daydreaming from the young officer.

"We've found it."

The aberration that was Glen Chambers crouched in the shadows of the cave, shivering with cold, sobbing to himself and hiding from the rest of the world. He hurt, every stretched nerve and elongated muscle in his body aching. He'd squashed his huge, still-growing bulk into a space that was becoming tighter by the hour, and he knew it wouldn't be long before he'd have to move. It was inevitable, but he wanted to stay in here for as long as he was able. There had been helicopters flying around just now. They probably already knew where he was.

Earlier, just before he'd found this cave, he'd stopped to drink from a lake and had caught sight of his reflection in the water. What he'd seen staring back at him had been both heartbreaking and terrifying. In the movies, enormous monsters like this were just perfectly scaled-up versions of normal people, but not him. Since the accident he'd continued to grow, every part of his body constantly increasing in mass, but at wildly different rates. His skull was swollen and heavy now, almost the size of a small car, one eye twice the size of the other, as big as a dinner plate. Clumps of hair had fallen out while other strands had grown lank and long and tough as wire. Glen had punched the water to make his image disappear, and then held his fist up and stared at it in disbelief; a distended, tumorous mass with a thumb twice the length of any of his fingers. And his skin! He hated more than anything what was happening to his skin. Its pigmentation remained, but it had become thick and coarse, almost elephantine, and the bulges of his massive body were now covered in sweat-filled folds and creases of flesh. The only thing, to his chagrin, that still seemed to function as it always had was his brain. It was ironic: Physically he'd become something else entirely—something unspeakably horrific—but inside he was still Glen Chambers. Grotesquely deformed and impossibly sized, he now bore only the faintest physical similarity to the person he'd been just a few short days ago. But emotionally, very little had changed. Same memories. Same attachments. Same pain.

Glen's vast stomach howled with hunger. He ate almost continually, but such was the speed of his rapid growth that his hunger was never completely satisfied. He reached down and picked up the body of a sheep with one hand, then bit it in half and forced himself to chew down, gagging on the bone and blood and wool in his mouth.

His arched back was beginning to press against the roof of the cave. Time to go before he became trapped. He crawled out into the afternoon rain and crouched still. *I don't want to move,* he thought, *because when I move, people die. None of this is my fault, but I'm the one they'll blame.*

If there is a god, please let him bring an end to this nightmare.

Glen strode through the darkness, feeling neither the cold nor the rain as he pushed on through the fields around the Malvern Hills. He'd spent a lot of time here before, good times before the bad with Della and her father, and being here again was unexpectedly painful. His stomach screamed for food again and he caught a bolting horse between his hands, snapping its neck with a flick of the wrist before biting down and taking a chunk out of its muscled body. He hated the destruction he caused with each footstep, but what else could he do? It would only get worse as he continued to grow. The effort of lifting his bulk and keeping moving was increasing, and for a while he stopped and sat on the ground and rested against the side of British Camp, the largest of the hills, relieved that, for a short time at least, he wasn't the largest thing visible. The size of the hill allowed him to feel temporarily small and insignificant again.

Why had this happened to him?

Much as he'd tried to forget, he still vividly remembered every detail of what had happened. He remembered the accident—the piercing light and those screaming, high-pitched radiation alarm sirens—then the disorientation when he'd first woken up in the clinic. It had been like he'd been trapped in one of those old Quatermass movies his dad used to watch. But in those films the guy being quarantined had always been a hero—an astronaut or genius scientist—not anyone like him. He just cleaned the damn labs, for Christ's sake. He wasn't one of the scientists, he just worked for them.

They'd kept him pumped full of drugs for a time, trying to suppress the metamorphosis, studying him from a distance through windows and from behind one-way mirrors, none of them daring to get too close. But there had come a time when the medicines and anesthetics no longer had any effect, and when they finally wore off, the pain had been unbearable. He realized he'd outgrown the hospital bed and had crushed it under his massively increased weight. He was more than twice his normal size already, rapidly filling the room, and he'd become claustrophobic and had panicked. He wanted to ask to see his son, Ash, but his mouth suddenly didn't work the way it used to and words were hard to form. He tried to get up but there wasn't enough room to stand, and when he tried to open the window blinds and look out he instead punched his clumsy hand through the glass. The people behind the mirrors started screaming at him to stop and lie still, but that just made him even more afraid. He shoved at an outside wall until it collapsed, then scrambled out through the hole he'd made. He stood there in the early morning light, completely nude, almost four meters tall, and he fell when he first tried to run away on legs of suddenly unequal length. They blocked his way with trucks, and he thought they were going to hurt him. He'd only wanted to move them out of his way, but he'd over-reacted and had killed several of the security men, not yet appreciating the incredible strength of his distended frame, popping their skulls like bubble wrap.

He'd taken shelter in a derelict warehouse for a while—the only place he'd found that was large enough to hide inside. He lay on the floor, coiled around the inside of the building, and for a time he sat and listened to a homeless guy who, out of his mind with drink and drugs, had thought Glen was a hallucination. Now Glen leaned back against the hillside, crushing trees like twigs behind him, and remembered their one-sided conversation (he'd only been able to listen, not speak). Like the blind man in that old Frankenstein film, the drunk hadn't judged him or run from him in fear, but by the morning he was dead, crushed by Glen, who'd doubled in size in his sleep. Woken by the sounds of the warehouse being surrounded, he'd destroyed the building trying to escape and had literally stepped over the small military force that had been posted there to flush him out and recapture him. In the confusion of gunfire and brick dust he stumbled away toward the town of Shrewsbury, another place he'd known well, avoiding the roads and following the meandering route of the River Severn across the land.

Christ, he bitterly regretted reaching that beautiful, historic town, and his swollen, racing heart sank when he remembered what had happened there. Still not used to his inordinate rate of growth (would he ever get used to it?) and the constantly changing dimensions of his disfigured body, he'd stumbled about like a drunken giant, every massive footstep causing more and more damage. He'd crashed into ancient buildings, demolishing them as he'd tried to avoid cars and pedestrians, unintentionally obliterating the places he'd known and loved with Della and Ash. He'd killed innocent people, too, as he'd tried to get away from the town to avoid causing more devastation, and their screams of terror and pain had hurt more than anything else. He'd never intended for any of this to happen, but the final straw had been when he'd lifted his foot to step over what remained of a partially demolished row of houses and had seen a child's pram squashed flat on the pavement where he'd been standing. Had he killed the baby? He hadn't waited to find out. Instead he loped off as quickly as he was able, his ears ringing with the sounds of mayhem he'd caused.

In the shadows of the hills, Glen lifted his heavy head toward the early evening sky and sobbed, the noise filling the air like thunder. *With every hour I am becoming less a man and more a monster,* he thought. *I may not have long. If I'm going to do this, I have to do it now.*

They'd assumed he might come back to this place eventually, that he'd want Della and the rest of her family to suffer as he had. It was the ideal location from which to launch an attack on the creature—exposed, out in the middle of nowhere, away from centers of population—and a squadron of Hawkins's men had been deployed to take the monster out. They took up arms as the aberration's vast, lumbering shape appeared on the darkening horizon, still recognizably that of a man, but only just. Orders were screamed down the chain of command, and a barrage of gunfire was launched as it approached. Bullets and mortars just bounced off its scaly skin, barely having any impact at all. Incensed, the creature destroyed many of its attackers and marched on, leaving the dead and dying scattered across the land.

And then, as the last rays of evening sunlight trickled across the world below him, it found what it had been looking for: Della's father's house. The beast strode toward the isolated building, ignoring the last few scurrying, antlike men and women attacking and retreating under its feet. It swung a massive, clumsy hand at the waist-high roof of the house, brushing the slates, joists, and supports away with a casual slap, trying to peer inside through the dust and early evening gloom. And when it saw that the top floor was empty, it simply ripped that away, too, taking the building apart layer by layer, kneeling on the roadside (crushing another eight men) and looking down into the building like a petulant child tearing apart a doll's house, looking for a precious lost toy.

* * *

They weren't there. The house was empty. Disconsolate, Glen stood up and kicked what was left of the building away, watching the debris scatter for almost a mile.

Way below him, a final few soldiers regrouped and launched another attack. They were the very least of his concerns now; irritating and unfortunate, nothing more. In temper he bent down and swept them away with a single swipe of his arm, then turned and marched onward, immediately regretting their deaths.

This was all Della's fault. If it hadn't been for her he'd never have been in this desperate position. Did she even realize that? Did she know she was to blame? Surely she must have had some inkling? If it hadn't been for them splitting up and her making him sell the house, this would never have happened. If she'd just talked to him sooner, let him know how she was feeling, let him know how unhappy she was . . . She said he should have guessed, that she'd tried to tell him enough times, but what did she think he was, a bloody psychic?

It was Della's fault it had all gone wrong, and jumping into bed with her bloody therapist had been the final nail in the coffin—the full-stop at the end of the very last sentence of their relationship—but he accepted it had been his own bloody foolish pride that had subsequently exacerbated the situation. He'd wanted to do everything he possibly could to support his son, but when Cresswell earned more money in a month than he did in a year, he realized he'd made a rod for his own back. His pigheaded solution was to work harder and harder, to the point where money became his focus, not Ash. It wasn't Glen's fault he hadn't been blessed with the brains Anthony Cresswell had, or that he hadn't been fortunate enough to share the same privileged, silver-spoon upbringing as the man who'd taken his place in Della's bed. Ash didn't even like him, he knew that for a fact. *He told me himself.*

Glen had been desperate to prove his worth and not let his son down, and that was why he'd agreed to take part in the trial (that and an undeniable desire to bulk himself up and become physically more of a man than he ever had been before—he'd certainly achieved that now). It was perfectly safe and legal, they'd told him as he signed the consent forms, a controlled trial of a new muscle-building compound for athletes. All the top performers will be using it this time next year, they'd said: twice the effect, a quarter the cost, absolutely no risk . . . Maybe they'd been right about that, because he'd been taking it for a while and, other than the weight gain and a little occasional nausea, there hadn't been any noticeable side effects. It had almost certainly been the radiation from the accident that had caused the change—either that or a combination of the two. But even the accident had been Della's fault in part. If she hadn't got the courts involved and been so anal about the times he was supposed to pick Ash up and drop him back, then he wouldn't have been rushing to get his work finished on time, and he wouldn't have left the safety off when he was supposed to—

A sudden, piercing whoosh and a sharp stabbing pain interrupted his thoughts as a mortar wedged itself in a fold of leathery skin halfway down his bare back, then detonated. Glen howled with pain, his rumbling screams filling the air for miles around, shattering windows and causing panic.

Concentrate, he ordered himself, standing up as straight as he could and stretching back over his shoulder with an elongated arm, flicking away the remains of the missile with over-grown nails. Several more explosions echoed around his head—blasts that would once have killed him but were now almost insignificant. He spiraled around, sweeping more soldiers out of the way with one arm as if he were clearing them off a table, then moved forward into the brief pocket of space and marched on. *What do I do now?* He tried to remember what happened next in the movies. Was this the point where they'd drop a nuke or something equally final on him? Try to gas him, perhaps? Should he just give up now, or maybe head out into the sea and disappear like Godzilla? He wished an even bigger monster would appear on the horizon: his own Mothra or King Ghidorah, perhaps. He could fight them and defeat them and save the world and let Ash see that his daddy wasn't an evil creature now, just misunderstood. He tried to imagine the fatherly monologue that that fucker Cresswell would deliver to his son tonight: "Your father was once a good man, Ash, but good people sometimes turn bad, and he had to be destroyed . . ."

He had to find Della and Ash. In the distance up ahead now lay the city of Birmingham—a gray scar covered in thousands of twinkling lights, buried deep in the midst of oceans of green—and he began to walk toward it, breaking into a lolloping, sloping run as he gradually picked up speed, his heart thumping too fast.

Home. I have to try to get home.

The city, he quickly decided, was his safest option—perhaps his only remaining option. Surrounded by millions of people, the military wouldn't dare risk using weapons of mass destruction on him there, and those same people would become hostages by default. His presence alone would be enough of a threat to force the authorities to do what he wanted.

The beast marched across the land, leaving a trail of devastation and deep, dinosaur-sized footsteps in its wake. In its shadow the population scattered in fear, running for cover but knowing that nowhere was safe anymore. Distances that took them hours to cover could be cleared in minutes by the aberration that towered over all of them. And as it neared Birmingham and the density of the population around it gradually increased, so did the level of carnage it caused. Knowing that the city was clearly a target, the authorities tried hopelessly to evacuate the panicking masses, but getting away was impossible. In no time at all every major road was blocked solid with traffic, and the monster simply kicked its way through the constant traffic jams without a care. It destroyed a reservoir in a fit of rage, stamping on a dam and flooding acres of heavily populated streets. A hospital was demolished when it tripped and fell, hundreds of patients and staff killed in a heartbeat. Scores of schools, homes, and other buildings were obliterated; untold numbers of people wiped out by the remorseless, blood-crazed behemoth.

A large section of the city center had, at least, been partially cleared as people who fled in terror mixed with those unaware of the approaching threat who were heading home from work. In a last-ditch attempt to divert the creature, Major Hawkins launched an aerial attack.

The first fighter planes raced toward their target and fired, their munitions barely even registering on the monster's tough, leathery skin. More through luck than judgment, it flashed an enormous hand at one of the planes and caught its wing with the tips of its longest two fingers, sending it into a sudden, spiraling free fall from which it would never recover. The pilot ejected—too small for the behemoth to see or care about—and as his parachute opened, he drifted down behind the grotesque man-monster, studying the stretches and folds and impossible angles of the horrific beast as he fell from the sky.

Several other jets met with a similar fate, as did a tank that was unwittingly crushed under the monster's foot like an empty soda can as it continued to approach the center of town. It marched between massive office buildings, at eye level with their high roofs, knocking one of them over as if it were made of cardboard. How many people were still in there, Hawkins wondered from a distance. How many more are going to die?

An iconic shopping center was destroyed in seconds, rubble raining down over the suburbs, severed electrical connections and small explosions lighting up the scene like camera flashes. A historic cathedral that had proudly stood for hundreds of years, wiped out in minutes. The destruction was apparently without end.

Major Hawkins readied himself to make the call he'd been dreading and consign the monster, the city, and hundreds of thousands of people to a white-hot nuclear fate. He watched the beast in the distance, his mouth dry and his pulse racing. Around him his soldiers stood their ground, nervously waiting to engage despite knowing now that their weapons were useless. Some turned and ran, desperate to get away before either the aberration attacked or they were wiped out by whatever godawful weapons the powers-that-be were forced to resort to using.

Hawkins paused when the creature's ex-wife burst into his truck and demanded to speak to him. The scientists and the generals had failed to come up with anything useful. She convinced him to hear her out before he did anything he'd regret. Goddammit, he thought as he listened to her, this was just like something from one of those bloody movies he couldn't get out of his head. "Let me see him," she'd pleaded. "Just let me try to talk to him."

What harm could it do when so much had already been lost? It had to be worth a try. The intensity of the aberration's attacks were increasing, more lives lost with every second. Hawkins was running out of options.

Glen didn't know which way to turn. *Where do I go now?* He was still deep in the heart of the city and, to his horror, had leveled much of it. If he bent down and squinted into the confusion below he could see the full extent of the damage he'd caused. He'd taken out a loan for a car six months ago, and it had been his pride and joy. Today he'd destroyed thousands of vehicles—all of them belonging to someone like him. He'd demolished homes like the one he'd once shared with Della and Ash. Worst of all were the bodies. He hadn't wanted to hurt anyone. How would he have felt if this had happened to someone else and Ash had been killed in the fallout? Glen lifted his head and roared with pain, the volume of his pitiful cry shattering the last few remaining windows and causing numerous already badly damaged buildings to collapse.

Let this be over.
My body hurts.
Please let this stop.

* * *

Surrounded by soldiers, Della walked through the parkland, Cresswell chasing after her. Ash held the doctor's hand, his constant sobbing audible even over the sounds of distant fighting.

"You can't do this," Cresswell protested. "Della, listen to me!"

"No, Anthony, you listen to me," she said, turning back to face him. "If there's anything of Glen left inside that thing, then he'll listen to me."

"I won't let you."

"You can't stop me."

With that she turned and walked on, her armed guard forming a protective bubble around her, leading her out toward the expanse of grassland they were trying to direct the creature toward. She could see his outline in the distance now, a huge black shadow towering over the tombstone ruins of the city. High overhead a phalanx of helicopters flew out toward the monster in formation, each of them focusing a searchlight on the ground below. She waited nervously for them to return, wrapping her arms around herself to keep out the cold.

It happened with surprising speed and ease. The creature seemed to be distracted by the helicopters, and it immediately moved toward them, perhaps realizing that, as they hadn't attacked, their intentions were peaceful. Della's heart began to thump in time with its massive footsteps as it neared, and she caught her breath when it seemed to lose its footing for a moment. It lashed out and swatted one of the choppers as if it were a nuisance fly, knocking it into its nearest neighbor and sending both of them crashing down to the ground in a ball of metal and swollen flame. How many people died just then, she wondered. How many more died when the wreckage hit the ground? How many people has Glen killed?

The aberration moved closer, coming clearly into view now, illuminated by the remaining helicopters, which soared higher until they were out of its massive reach. Della looked up at it in disbelief, stunned by the size of the damn thing, and also by the fact that despite the huge level of deformation, she could still clearly see that it was Glen. Its immense frame was grossly misshapen, but there was something about the shape of its mouth and the way it held its head that she recognized; the jawline that both he and Ash had, the color of those eyes . . .

When the creature saw the soldiers around its feet, it leaned down and roared. Della thought it sounded like a cry for help rather than an attacking scream, but the military clearly thought otherwise. One of the troopers nearest to her raised his rifle, and the monster picked him up between two enormous fingers and tossed him away. She watched the body fly through the air and hit a tree, and cringed when she heard a sharp cracking sound—either the tree trunk or the soldier's bones. The monster roared again, and this time its force was such that she was blown off her feet. Another soldier rushed to help her up. She got to her feet and shook him off, then ran out toward the creature.

"Glen!" she yelled. "Glen, it's me, Della."

The aberration went to swipe her out of the way, but stopped. It lowered its huge head and stared at her. Then, after a pause of a few seconds that felt like forever, it leaned back and crashed down onto its backside, the force of impact like an earthquake. Della's armed guard held back, more out of fear than anything else, though what difference a couple of meters would make was debatable in the circumstances.

"I just want to know why, Glen," she said, still walking closer, not sure whether it could hear or understand her. "All those people killed, and for what? I know you must have been scared, in pain even, but why . . . ?"

The monster stared at her, eyes squinting, trying to focus, massive pupils dilating and constricting. Then it lifted its head to the skies and roared louder than ever.

On the ground a single figure ran through the trees. Cresswell weaved around the soldiers who stood frozen to the spot, staring up at the massive creature, and grabbed Della.

"Come with me, Della," he said, trying to drag her away. "That's not Glen anymore. Damn thing can't understand you. Stay here and it'll kill you. You've got Ash and me to think about and—"

He stopped talking when he realized the Chambers creature was looking straight at him, glowering down. He began to back away, cowering in fear, but there was no escape. A single massive hand wrapped around him and tightened, its grip so strong that every scrap of oxygen was forced from his body. The monster lifted him up and held its arm back as if it were about to throw the doctor into the distance.

"Dad! Dad, don't!"

Glen stopped.

Had he just imagined that? For a second he swore he'd heard Ash's voice, but how could it have been? He pulled his long arm back again, ready to hurl Cresswell out of his life forever. Out of all of their lives . . .

"No, Dad, please."

Glen looked down and saw his son standing in front of him. And suddenly, nothing else mattered. He stretched out and dropped Cresswell far enough away not to have to think about him, then carefully moved Della and the remaining soldiers out of the way, too. Ash stood in front of his dad, completely alone and looking impossibly small.

"*Hello, Big Man,*" Glen wanted to say but couldn't. "*I'm sorry, Ash, I didn't mean for any of this to happen. I didn't want anyone to get hurt.*"

"You okay, Dad?"

"*Not really,*" he didn't say as he gently picked his son up and held him close to his face. Ash sat down cross-legged on the palm of his father's hand.

"I've been worried about you."

"*Me too, Ash.*"

"They've been saying all kinds of things about you," Ash said, pausing to choose his next words carefully. Glen's heart seemed to pause, too. "But I don't believe them. I mean, I know you *are* a monster now, anyone can see that, but I know you didn't want to be one. I don't think you wanted to hurt them all. I kept trying to tell the man that you didn't mean for any of it to happen. I told him to try and imagine how you must be feeling. You're big and strong and everything, but I bet you're scared."

"*I am.*"

"I said they should leave you alone. I said they should find you somewhere big to rest, maybe build a big house or something like that, then let the doctors work out how they're going to get you back to normal again."

"I don't think that's going to happen, sunshine. I think it's too late now."

"I miss you, Dad. I've been really scared."

"I've missed you, too."

"They said you were coming back here to kill everyone, and I told them that was crap. I said you were coming to see me. Was I right, Dad?"

"You were right, son. I just wanted to see you again. Just one more time . . ."

Glen Chambers sat in the park with his son in his hand and listened to him talking until his massively engorged, broken heart could no longer keep him alive.

RAKSHASI

by Kelley Armstrong

FOR TWO HUNDRED YEARS, I have done penance for my crimes as a human. After twenty, I had saved more lives than I had taken. After fifty, I had helped more people than I had wronged. I understand that my punishment should not end with an even accounting. Yet now, after two hundred years, that balance has long passed equilibrium. And I have come to realize that this life is no different than my old one. If I want something, I cannot rely on others to provide it.

I waited in the car while Jonathan checked the house. Jonathan. There is something ridiculous about calling your master by his given name. It's an affectation of the modern age. In the early years, I was to refer to them as *Master* or *Isha*. When the family moved West, it became *Sir*, then *Mr. Roy*.

My current master does not particularly care for this familiarity. He pretends otherwise, but the fact that I must refer to him by his full name, where his wife and others use "Jon," says much.

He called my cell phone.

"Amrita?" he said, as if someone else might be answering my phone. My name is not Amrita. My name is not important. Or, perhaps, too important. I have never given it to my masters. They call me Amrita, the eternal one.

"The coast is clear." He paused. "I mean—"

"I understand American idiom very well," I said. "I have been living here since before you were born."

He mumbled something unintelligible, then gave me my instructions, as if I hadn't been doing this, too, since before he was born.

I got out of the car and headed for the house.

As Jonathan promised, there was an open window on the second floor. I found a quiet place away from the road, then shifted to my secondary form: a raven. Fly to the bedroom window. Squeeze through. Shift back.

There wasn't even an alarm on the window to alert the occupant to my intrusion. Quite disappointing. These jobs always are. I long for the old days, when I would do bloody battle against power-mad English sahibs and crazed Kshatriyas. Then came the murderers and whoremasters, the Mob, the drug dealers. It was the last that made the Roys rethink their strategy. On the streets, drug dealers always came with well-armed friends. I may be immortal, but I can be injured, and while my personal comfort is not a concern, my income-earning potential is. They tried targeting the dealers at home, but there they were often surrounded by relative innocents. So, in this last decade, the Roys have concentrated on a new source of evil. A dull, weak, mewling source that bores me immeasurably. But my opinion, like my comfort, is of little consequence.

I took a moment to primp in the mirror. I am eternally young. Beautiful, too. More beautiful than when I was alive, which was not to say I was ugly then, but when I look in the mirror now, I imagine what my husband, Daman, would say. Imagine his smile. His laugh. His kiss. I have not seen him in two hundred years, yet when I primp for my target, it is still Daman I ready myself for.

I found the target—Morrison—in the study, talking on his speakerphone while working on his laptop. I moved into the doorway. Leaned against it. Smiled.

He stopped talking. Stopped typing. Stared.

Then, "Bill? I'll call you back."

He snapped his laptop shut. "How'd you get in here?"

"My name is Amrita. I am a surprise. From a very pleased client."

I slid forward, gaze fixed on his. For another moment he stared, before remembering himself.

"But how did you get—?"

"I would not be much of a surprise if I rang your front bell, would I?" I glanced back at the door. "I trust we are alone?" Jonathan said no one else was in the house, but I always checked.

"W-we are."

"Good."

I sidled over and rolled his chair away from the desk . . . and any alarms underneath or guns in the drawers.

I straddled Morrison's lap. Indecision wavered in his eyes. He was a smart man. He knew this was suspicious. And yet, as I said, I am a beautiful woman.

I put my arms around him, hands sliding down his arms, fingers entwining with his. I leaned over, lifting our hands . . .

165

then wrenched his arms back so hard he screamed. I leapt from his lap, over the back of the chair, and bound his wrists with the cord I'd used as a belt.

I have subdued lapdogs that gave me more trouble than Morrison. He fought, but I have bound warriors. He was no warrior.

Next, I tortured him for information. It was a bloodless torture. Mental pain is the most effective of all, and with the power of illusion, I can make a man believe he is being rent limb from limb, and scream with the imagined agony.

As for the information I needed, it was a simple accounting of his misdeeds: details on the financial scam that paid for this mansion. I forced him to write out those details in a confession. Then I tortured him for the combination to his home safe.

With my help, the Roys kill—sorry, *eliminate*—the basest dregs of the criminal bucket. This is their divine mission, handed down to them millennia ago, when they were granted the ability to control my kind. They seek out evil. I eliminate it. A very noble profession, but one that does not pay the bills. Finding targets, researching them, and preparing for my attack is a full-time job. So the Roys, like other isha families, also have divine permission to take what they require from their victims.

Once I had what I needed, I forced Morrison to take out his gun and shoot himself, leaving his confession on the desk and adequate compensation for his victims still in his safe.

Before he pulled the trigger, he looked at me. They always do. Seeking mercy, I suppose. But I know, better than anyone, that such sins cannot be pardoned in this life. If they are, mercy will be seen as a sign of weakness, and the perpetrator will revert to his former path once the initial scare passes.

Still, they always look at me, and they always ask the same thing.

"What are you?"

"Rakshasi," I replied, and pushed his finger on the trigger.

Rakshasi. Morrison didn't know what that meant. They never do. Even those of my own heritage rarely have more than a vague inkling of my kind, perhaps from a story told by a grandmother to frighten them into obedience.

The word means protector, which has always made me laugh. We are demon warriors, cursed to walk the earth as monsters, wreaking havoc wherever we go. Disturbers. Defilers. Devourers.

It is only after we accept the bargain of the isha that we become protectors. When we rise from our deathbed, we are met by a member of an isha family. He tells us our fate. Misery and guilt and pain, forever suffering everything that, in life, we visited upon others. Yet we can redeem ourselves. Submit to their bargain, work for them until we have repaid our debt, and we will be free.

I did not take that first offer. I doubt any rakshasi does. We are men and women of iron will and we do not cower at the first threat of adversity. I truly do not believe the isha expect agreement. Not then. They simply offer the deal, and when it is rejected they leave. Then, on every succeeding anniversary, they find us, and they offer again.

In the end, it was not the misery or guilt or pain that wore me down. It was loneliness. We are doomed to be alone as we walk the earth. I might have held out if the isha had not brought me a letter one year. A letter from Daman. He, too, had been doomed to this existence. Our crimes were shared, as had been every part of our lives from childhood.

Daman had accepted his isha's bargain, and he pleaded with me to do the same. Take the deal and we would be together again. So he had been promised. So I was promised. And so I accepted.

We returned to Jonathan's house. It is the same one I have lived in for sixty years, though Jonathan and Catherine only arrived two years ago, when he took over as isha from his uncle. I came with the house. Or, I should say, it came with me.

It was no modest home, either. For size and grandeur, it was on a scale with Morrison's mansion. There were no vows of poverty in this family of crusaders. Like the Templar Knights, they lined their pockets extravagantly with the proceeds of their good deeds, which may be part of the reason behind the switch to corporate sharks. We are in a recession. To some, that means tightening the purse strings. To others, it means seeking richer sources of income. I cannot argue with that. I felt the same way when I walked the earth as a human. But it does bear noting that if the Roys free me, they will lose this income. Which gives them little incentive to agree that I have repaid my debt.

Jonathan took me to my apartment. As cages go, it is a well-gilded one. Sleeping quarters, living area, kitchen, and bath, all lavishly furnished. The shelves are lined with books. A computer, stereo, and television are provided for my amusement. Anything I wish is mine. Anything except freedom. The walls are imbued with magic that prevents me from leaving without my isha.

Beyond a recitation of events, Jonathan and I had not spoken on the four-hour drive from Morrison's house. Every isha is different. With some, I have found something akin to friendship. Most prefer a more businesslike relationship. Jonathan takes that to the extreme, talking to me only when necessary. To engage me in conversation might lead to asking about my thoughts or feelings, which would imply that I have such things. That I am a sentient being. Best to forget that.

In my apartment, I prepared dinner. A glass of human blood. A plate of human flesh. It is what I need to survive, and my ishas provide it. At one time, they used their victims. Now, that is inconvenient. One of the isha families without a rakshasi saw a market and filled it. Jonathan orders my meals. They come in a refrigerated case, the blood in wine bottles and flesh neatly packaged and labeled as pork.

I fixed a plate of curry. I may be a cannibal, but I have retained some sense of taste. When I finished, I waited for Catherine. She gives me time after a job to eat, preferring not to visit while the scent of cooked flesh lingers in the air. As a courtesy, I cracked open the windows.

Catherine extended me a return courtesy by knocking before she entered. Most of my ishas do not—either they don't realize I may have a need for privacy or they wish to remind me of my place. Jonathan regularly "forgets" to knock, which is his way of asserting his position without challenging me. I would hold him in higher regard if he simply barged in.

"How did it go?" Catherine asked as she entered. One might presume she'd already spoken to her husband and was simply asking to be polite, but with this couple, such a level of communication was not a given.

As I told her it had been a success, I accompanied her to the living area, walking slowly to keep pace with her crutches. Catherine suffers from a crippling disease that today has a name—multiple sclerosis. In general, I'm not interested in the advances of science, but I have researched this particular ailment to help me better understand the first isha's wife who has sought my companionship.

Most wives have no knowledge of their husbands' otherworldly abilities, and thus no knowledge of me. For decades, I have been shunted in and out a side door and otherwise kept in my soundproof apartment.

Occasionally, though, the Roys take a wife from within the isha community. That is where Jonathan found Catherine. And if such a choice—not only an isha's daughter, but a cripple—helped him win his position over his brothers . . . It is not my concern.

As to what Catherine and I could possibly have in common, the answer is little, which gives us much to discuss. Catherine is endlessly fascinated with my life. To her, I am the star in some terrible yet endlessly thrilling adventure.

"Have you been doing better?" she asked as I fixed tea.

"I am surviving. We both know that I would prefer it wasn't so, but . . ." I smiled her way. "You have heard quite enough on that matter."

"I wish you could be happier, Amrita."

"I've been alive too long to be happy. I would prefer to be gone. At peace." I handed her a cup. "But, again, we've talked about this enough. It's a depressing way to spend your visits. I would prefer to talk about you and *your* happiness. Did you ask Jonathan about the trip?"

Her gaze dropped to her teacup. "He said it wasn't possible. He'd love to, but he can't take you and he can't leave his duties here."

"Oh. I had thought perhaps he would be able to take me. That the council would consider it acceptable to revisit my roots. I am sorry I mentioned it, then."

"Don't be. You know I want to see India. You make it sound so wonderful. I just hope . . ." She sipped her tea. "I hope by the time he's free of his obligation, I'm still in good enough health . . ."

Her voice trailed off. I didn't need to remind her that it was a fool's dream.

"He would like to take you," I said.

"I know."

"He would like to go himself."

"I know. But his obligation . . ."

Could be over anytime he chooses. Those were the words left unspoken. Also the words *but he does not have the strength of will to do it, to defy his family by freeing me on his own, despite the fact it is his decision to make, and the council will support it.*

"I would miss you," she blurted. "I'd miss our talks."

I smiled. "As would I. If you were free to travel, though, you would see these places for yourself, make new friends. Here, we are both prisoners."

Jonathan insists she stay in the house. He says it is for her own safety, so she can't be targeted in retaliation for our acts.

She suspects, I'm sure, that he keeps her here because it is convenient. She is as much his property as I am. Without his obligation as an excuse, she'd have more freedom, whether he liked it or not.

"Jonathan knows best," she said finally. "He will free you. I know he will. It just isn't time."

It never would be. Not if I relied on Catherine.

There were many things Daman and I agreed on, as partners in life, in love, in ambition. One was that—despite the teachings of the Brahmins—all men are created equal. Each bears within him the capacity to achieve his heart's desire. He needs only the strength of will to see it through.

Daman's story was an old one. A boy from a family rich in respect and lineage, poor in wealth and power. His family wanted him to marry a merchant's daughter with a rich dowry. Instead he chose me, a scholar's daughter, his childhood playmate. I brought something more valuable than money—intelligence, ambition, and a shared vision for what could be.

A hundred years ago, when my ishas lived in England, one saw the play *Macbeth,* and forever after that he called me Lady Macbeth. I found the allusion insulting. Macbeth was a coward, his wife a harpy. Daman did not need me to push him. Every step we took, we took as one.

In our twenty years together, we recouped everything his family had lost over the centuries. Our supporters would say that we brought stability and prosperity to the region. Our detractors would point out the trail of bodies in our wake, and the growing piles of coin in our coffers. Neither is incorrect. We did good and we did evil. We left the lands better than we found them, but at a price that was, perhaps, too steep.

I do regret the path we took. Yet if given a second chance, I would not sit in a corner, content with my lot. My ambition would merely be checked by a better appreciation for the value of human life. That appreciation has stayed my hand in this matter. Which has gotten me nowhere.

My next assignment came nearly four months later. That is typical. While one might look at the world and see plenty of wrongdoers, it is a rare one that must be culled altogether. Jonathan needs to search for a target. Then he must compile a dossier and submit it to the council, who will return elimination approval or request more information. After that comes weeks of surveillance, at which point my participation is required, my talents for illusion and shape-shifting useful.

Jonathan is supposed to assist with the surveillance work. He claims he's conducting his own elsewhere, but when I've followed, I've found him in coffee shops, flirting with serving girls or working on his novel.

He is supposed to supervise me, in case I shirk my duties and find a coffee shop of my own. I've considered it. I even have an idea for a novel. While it amuses me to think of this, I cannot do it. I enjoy the unsupervised times too much to risk them, and I do not have the personality for lounging and storytelling.

However, this time when I did my surveillance I was . . . less than forthright about my findings.

The target was yet another financier. Unlike Morrison, this one had been the subject of death threats, so he employed a bodyguard—a young man he passed off as his personal assistant.

I learned about the death threats by eavesdropping. I left

them out of the report. I discovered the assistant's true nature only by surveillance. I left that out of the report as well. My official conclusion was that this man—Garvey—was no more security conscious than the others, but that his assistant was rarely away from his side, so I would lure the young man away, then let Jonathan subdue him while I dealt with Garvey.

It went as one might expect. Separating the two had been easy enough. Such things are minor obstacles for one who has spent hundreds of years practicing the art of illusion.

I got the bodyguard upstairs, where Jonathan was waiting. Then I hurried back to Garvey.

Jonathan's cries for help came before I reached the bottom of the stairs. They alerted Garvey, as I knew they would. My job, then, was to subdue the financier before he could retrieve his gun. After that it would be safe for me to go to my isha's aid.

It took some time for me to subdue Garvey. He was unexpectedly strong. Or so I would later claim.

By the time I returned upstairs, the bodyguard had beaten Jonathan unconscious and was preparing the killing blow. I shot him with Garvey's gun. Then I left Jonathan where he lay, returned to Garvey, and carried on. This was my mission, which superseded all else, even the life of my isha.

When I was finished with Garvey—after he confessed to killing his guard, then taking his own life—I drove Jonathan to the hospital. Then I called Catherine.

"I take responsibility for this," I said to Catherine as we stood beside Jonathan's hospital bed. "My job was to protect him. I failed."

"You didn't know about the bodyguard."

"I should have. That, too, is my job. We are both to conduct a proper survey—"

"If Jon didn't find out about him, there's no reason you would."

I fell silent. Stared down at Jonathan, still unconscious after surgery to stanch the internal bleeding. I snuck looks at Catherine, searching for some sign that she would secretly have been relieved by his death. I'd seen none.

She claimed to love him. She did love him. I could still work with this.

"It's becoming so much more dangerous," I murmured. "There have always been accidents, but it is so much harder to keep an isha safe these days."

"Accidents? This—this hasn't happened before, has it?"

I kept my gaze on Jonathan.

"Amrita."

I looked up slowly, then hesitated before saying, "The council has assured me that the rate of injury on my missions is far below that of most."

"Rate of injury?" Her voice squeaked a little. "I've never heard of an isha being seriously injured. You mean things like sprained ankles and bruises, right?"

I said nothing.

"Amrita!"

Again I looked up. Again I hesitated before speaking. "There have been . . . incidents. Jonathan's great-uncle's car accident, it was . . . not an accident. That was the story the council told the family. And there have been . . . others." I hurried on. "But the risk with me is negligible, compared to others."

Which didn't reassure her in the least.

I said nothing after that. I had planted the seed. It would take time to sprout.

A week later, Jonathan was still in the hospital, recovering from his injuries. I had not yet returned to my apartment—once I entered, I wouldn't be able to leave. Catherine had to retrieve my food and drink from the refrigerator. She didn't like that, but the alternative was to sentence her only helpmate to prison until Jonathan recovered.

The day before he was due to come home, Catherine visited me in the guest room.

She entered without a word. Sat without a word. Stayed there for nearly thirty minutes without a word. Then she said, "Tell me how to release you."

We had to hurry. I could only be freed without Jonathan's consent if he was unable to give consent.

We withheld his fever medication until his temperature rose. While befuddled by fever—and a few of my illusory tricks—he parted with the combination to his safe.

I retrieved what we needed, and fingered the stacks of hundred-dollar bills, but I took none. I had no need for them.

"Are you sure this is what you want?" Catherine asked as I prepared the ritual. "They say that when a rakshasi passes to the other side, there is no afterlife. This *is* your afterlife. There'll be nothing else."

"Peace," I said. "There will be peace."

She nodded. My death was, after all, to her benefit, mean-

ing the council would not judge her or Jonathan as harshly as
if they'd freed me.

I drew the ritual circle in sand around Jonathan's bed. I lit
tiny fires in the appropriate locations. I placed a necklace
bearing one half of an amulet around my neck, and the other
around his. I recited the incantations. Endless details, etched
into my brain, the memories of my kind, as accessible as any
other aspect of my magic, but requiring Jonathan's assistance.
Or the assistance of his bodily form—hair to be burned, fingernails to be ground into powder, saliva and blood to be
mixed with that powder.

Finally, as Catherine waited anxiously, I injected myself with
the mixture. The ritual calls for it to be rubbed into an open
wound. I'd made this modernized alteration, and Catherine
had readily agreed that it seemed far less barbaric.

Next I injected Jonathan. Then I began the incantations.

Jonathan shuddered in his sleep. His mouth opened and
closed, as if gasping for air. Catherine grabbed his hand.

"What's happening?" she said.

"The bond is breaking."

Now *I* shuddered, feeling that hated bond tighten, as if in
reflexive protest. Then slowly, blessedly, it loosened.

Catherine started to gibber that something was wrong.
Jonathan wasn't breathing. Why wasn't he breathing? His
heartbeat was slowing. Why was it slowing?

I kept my eyes closed, ignoring her cries, and her tugs on
my arm, until at last the bond slid away. One last deep shud-
der and I opened my eyes to see the world as I hadn't seen it
in two hundred years. Bright and glimmering with promise.

Catherine was shrieking now. Shrieking that Jonathan's heart had stopped.

I turned toward the door. She lunged at me, crutches falling as she grabbed my shirt with both hands.

"He's dead!" she cried. "It's supposed to be you, not him. Something went wrong."

"No," I said. "Nothing went wrong."

She screamed then, an endless wail of rage and grief. I picked her up, ignoring her feeble blows and kicks, and set her gently in a chair, then leaned her crutches within reach.

She snatched them and pushed to her feet. When I tried to walk away, she managed to get in front of me.

"What have you done?" she said.

"Freed us. Both of us."

"You lied!"

"I told you what you needed to hear." I eased her aside. "I do not want annihilation. I want what I was promised—a free life. For that, I need his consent, and the council to provide the necessary tools. There is, however, a loophole. A final act of mercy from an isha to his rakshasi. On his deathbed, he may free me with his amulet and that ritual."

"I-I don't—"

"You will tell the council that is what happened here. The poison I injected is the one we've used many times on our targets, undetectable. The council will believe Jonathan unexpectedly succumbed to his injuries."

"I will not tell them—"

"Yes, you will. If not, you will be complicit in his death. And even if you manage to convince them otherwise, you will forfeit this house and all that goes with it. It is yours only if he dies and I am freed. They may contest that, but even if they do, you will have already removed the contents of his safe. I left everything for you."

That was less generous than it seemed. For years, I'd been taking extra from our targets and hiding it in my room. I would not leave unprepared. I was never unprepared.

Now that the bond was broken, there was nothing to stop me from entering and exiting my apartment, and taking all I had collected. I passed Catherine and headed for the door.

She was silent until I reached it.

"What will I do now?" she said.

I glanced back at her. "Live. I intend to."

BREEDING THE DEMONS

by Nate Kenyon

FOWLER'S PINK, chubby face glistened, and he wore the hungry-dog look of a man waiting out his obsession.

"Been here long?" Ian said.

Fowler grunted and motioned for the photographs, his eyes glazed and mouth stained red from drink. He smelled of sweat and cheap cologne. Three Bloody Marys lay drained upon the nightclub table, and Fowler had loosened his tie.

Ian slipped into the booth and put his leather portfolio on the table, enjoying making the man wait a little. But Fowler would not be denied. He grabbed the portfolio and rifled through its contents, and his breathing quickened as his eyes devoured the pictures within.

Finally he sighed and straightened his head. He removed the photos and slipped them into a plain manila envelope, which he stuck inside his jacket. "You are a fucking genius," he said.

"I had to give bribes. It's expensive—"

"Your business." Fowler waved a sausage-fingered, jeweled hand. "Keep it to yourself."

Ian shrugged. He had expected this. Fowler didn't want to

know how he did it, any more than the purchasers of a pornographic magazine wanted a detailed description of how the models were selected and positioned, lighted, and airbrushed.

"When can I have the next set?"

"I need some time. And I can't keep paying everyone off and expect to get away with it."

"Well, come up with something else, then." Fowler looked irritated that he had to offer advice. "I don't have to tell you what happens if you just stop. I'm barely keeping them satisfied as it is."

"I'll get it done as soon as I can."

"Have a new batch by the end of the week."

"The end of the *week*? How the hell am I supposed to—"

The envelope appeared as if from nowhere. It looked thick tonight; a good ten grand, if his eyes served him right. More than enough to put him back to work. At least for now.

"All right," Ian said. "End of the week."

Fowler hadn't always been that way. Ian remembered a slimmer version, eager for nothing more than his next square meal. But he catered to a very eccentric group of customers, and their money was a powerful drug. And they were insatiable. If the eyes were windows to the soul, then Fowler had been blinded long ago. It would not be long before he crossed over completely and became like those he chose to serve.

Back at his studio apartment, Ian searched for his muse among the shadows that lined his walls. He had cleared most of the central space for his work. He had kept only a bed and two ragged chairs in one corner, and installed a slightly concave sheet-metal stage with a drain in the middle of the room.

The floor he kept bare and polished in case of spatters. The large, two-story-high warehouse windows let in plenty of light when he wanted it. But for the most part he kept the monstrous blinds drawn, preferring to work by candlelight, or the dark.

One of his two walk-in freezers still held a few loose ends, but nothing spoke to him as he stood within the drifting mist. It wouldn't do to throw something together with spare parts. He had something in mind, but he needed to gather the right materials.

He stopped first at Anna's place. She lived in a brownstone overlooking the river, and the stench of industrial waste wafted up through closed windows and doors and into kitchens and bedrooms and clung to the clothes hanging in closets. But tonight the air was clear, and Anna answered his knock in nothing but a nightshirt and the black silk underwear he'd bought her for her birthday three weeks before.

"Want a drink?" she asked him as he followed her smooth, bare legs into the kitchen. "I was just going to mix up something fun."

"I'll take anything wet."

She took ice from the freezer, threw tequila and a sweet mix into a shaker, and poured liquid over misted glass. He heard a soft pop as an ice cube cracked, and took a sip through slightly tender lips.

"Business?"

"You don't want to know."

She shrugged. "You're busy. My sister's in town next week. Will you be too busy for that?" She leaned back against the counter. A slight arch in her spine outlined her nipples against the fabric of her shirt. He took a long, slow look, from blood-painted toes and shapely calves past round hips and tapered waist, up to a face that held a full Spanish mouth and almond-coffee eyes.

"God, you're something. How did I get so lucky?"

"I'm not all that much. And don't try to change the subject."

"You're the most beautiful woman I've ever seen. I'm a frog and you're a princess." He took another mouthful and held it, set the glass on the counter, and pulled her shirt up to her shoulders. She shivered as he held an ice cube in his cheek and bent his head to trace a breast with his tongue, blowing frigid air gently across puckered flesh.

Later they lay in darkness across tangled sheets. Ian's sweat trickled down into the hollow of his throat. The air smelled of sex. His lungs burned with every breath.

Anna twisted a strand of hair in long, slender fingers. "I saw ants in the kitchen today," she said. "They were marching in a line from somewhere under the fridge, up and over the counter, and carrying some dried rice from a bowl I'd left out last night. Two of them started fighting, so I squished the bigger one with my thumb. And you know what the other one did? He grabbed the dead one by the head and dragged it back down to the floor and out of sight."

"That's gross."

"I know." She sighed. "I kept wondering what he was going to do with the body. Do they eat each other or something?"

"Knock it off, will you?"

"What are we doing, Ian? We've been seeing each other for three months now. I really like you. But you shut me out. I bring up something like my sister coming for a visit and you just fuck me to shut me up."

"It isn't like that at all."

"You have secrets. Where were you tonight? I called your place, the place I've never even *seen*. I don't want to stalk you. But you're taking this mystery man thing too far. Maybe I'll lose interest." She slid a sweat-slick leg out from under his and wriggled up on one elbow to stare at him.

"It was nothing. I sold some more pictures, that's all."

"Really?" She hunched a little closer. "That's great. Can I see them?"

"Nothing to see. They're just environmental shots, boring stuff." He stood in the dark and put on his shirt and pants. *You wouldn't understand.* What an understatement. "Why don't you make a lunch date with your sister and let me know the time? Call me tomorrow."

Hours later he drove back across town, cemetery dirt clinging to his clothes and his new materials safely packed away in the rear of his van. He wondered how he slipped so easily between two worlds. A starving artist given an offer he couldn't refuse? But it had been more than that. Years ago he had held several shows in little galleries in New York, mostly mixed-media exhibitions staged by old college friends, Warhol-style trash reshaped and resold, recycled. He had never had Warhol's vision, and the public knew it. His true tendencies were darker and more disturbing.

Time after time they turned him away with little or no money in his pocket, and after a while even those few friends who

185

remained stopped lending him space. For several months he wandered, mired in depression and faced with the failure of his life's dream. He never doubted he had talent (or not for long, anyway), but it remained frustratingly coy. It spent less and less of its time with him, and he began to wonder if the struggle was worth it.

He took up work in a meat market, carving up legs of beef and lamb. There he met Fowler. Fowler introduced him to another world that existed between the seams of light and behind every dark alley and shadow. Fowler's clients were the eyes staring at you from the depths of your closet. They were the chill winds lurking at automobile accidents and behind the gaze of serial killers and madmen. Ian didn't think Fowler had understood what he was getting into at the time, any more than Ian had understood himself. But soon it was too late.

He took the old freight elevator from the back lot and lugged his stinking, soggy cargo through quiet corridors. He had to make several trips. It was late, and the building was all but deserted anyway; he had seen to that soon after he had moved in, renting the space around him whenever something opened up.

Once inside he lit several thick candles and began to pace the floor, seeking that elusive well of creativity. This would be his masterpiece. It would have to be entirely new. And it had to be raw. He would create something born from the butcher's block, an assembly of everything foul and bloody the mind could imagine. They would be astonished, amazed, excited to a frenzy of lust. And they would pay with the almighty dollar.

Ian slipped his tools from their place on the wall. This section of the huge room resembled a medieval torture chamber, a look he had purposely cultivated for mood. Unfinished brick ran dark with water stains; edges of bone-scraping steel winked and smiled from hooks. Stravinsky's *Mavra* playing softly in the background, he crouched on the giant metal basin and separated the limbs of the two recently buried corpses, a child and its mother, with blade and saw. He paid careful attention to the areas less preserved from lying in particular positions. Slime and clotted blood quickly covered his hands. He did not wear his gloves, for this would be a creation close to his heart, an intimate relation.

After he finished with them he went to his freezer for more parts. His mind danced with imaginative multiple-headed creatures, three legs and no eyes, muscle and bone outside of skin. But these were only previews of the climax of his talent. A kind of frenzy overtook him. He had the answer floating about in his head, not to hide the manipulations of the flesh, but to showcase them, emphasize every unnatural joint and union.

For this he took a coroner's needle and thick black thread, working with slippery skin and mating it to bone. A woman's breast became a truncated child's limb, a fingerless hand punching its way through exposed ribs. Eyes without lids glared upward through a membrane of stomach lining. A layer of teeth planted themselves amid a pucker of flesh. Ian sliced and hammered holes, brought flesh together and ripped it apart with a violence he had previously held in check. Layer built upon layer, both intricate and roughly sculpted visions of death.

He worked through the dawn and into the afternoon. The candles burned down to nubs. The only sign of time passing was a slight glow around his heavy blinds. He lost himself in a feverish, glittery delirium.

Finally, as night fell once again across the city beyond, he stood in aching silence and observed what had grown up out of his studio floor. Candlelight flickered upon the backs of the dead. Black thread like veins lay everywhere, up one seam and down another. Toothless mouths turned to wombs, gave birth to things unmentionable. Limbs reached up and clawed the sky in agony.

Ian retched into the drain as traces of old booze turned his insides out and left him shaking and sore. A hand wiped across his mouth left a foul-smelling, slippery trail. He stood and held the heaves in check. His camera was within easy reach. Ian fumbled for it, every pore tingling at the raw power of the thing, stomach lurching and rolling. He had never before had the feeling that he had captured what his mind had been striving to create; he had always felt empty, unfulfilled, as if somewhere along the line he had stumbled off track.

But this, this was perfect.

He took to the streets the following evening to work off the ache in his legs. He had slept like the dead for a full day and woke to a clear head. He had created something unimaginable. Pornography for the supernatural. Demons did not exactly orgasm, as he understood it. But the pictures set off an erotic reaction that was both frenzied and powerful. And the Taratcha always wanted more, however satiated they might seem at first. How he could create something that might satisfy them the next time around made his blood run cold.

Anna wouldn't have understood any of it. He had kept her from his secret so far, but it was only a matter of time before she saw something.

Then there was the matter of his immortal soul. Ian had begun to sense the changes. Driving past the scene of a car accident, he would catch himself drooling a little, wanting to stop and run his fingers through pools of blood. The visits to the morgue were swiftly becoming less businesslike and more pleasurable, the sight of those lifeless, cold-blue limbs physically exciting him. Not such an unusual reaction, he reasoned, after so much effort and time spent in the company of such things, but nonetheless it was dangerous. He had never intended this to be his life's work.

By full dark he found himself in an area of nightclubs and movie houses, neon lights blinking in and out. Twenty-four-hour peep shows beckoned from behind half-lidded windows. There were people of all sorts here, businessmen scurrying home in trench coats like roaches before the sun, hookers and transvestites, bikers, drug addicts with starved faces and bruises up their arms.

Sandwiched between a tattoo parlor and a sex-toy shop was a tiny wooden door with a sign above it that read GATE-HOUSE. Ian ducked through into a narrow stairwell that smelled of urine and followed it down into dim silence. The stairs seemed to go down much farther than they should. The last time he'd been here was almost five years ago, when he'd first grappled with the details of his craft. The Gatehouse had likely saved his life then, and now with a little luck it would give him the key to saving himself again.

The place was like an oasis between worlds. Occult objects, books, and charms crammed the walls, alongside the latest scientific texts. Drugs of all kinds helped prepare the mind for new experiences. If you sat down at the table near the back and had your fortune read you might never get up again, for this fortune was real, and as so many customers had found, reality was often painfully blunt.

"So what is it this time?" The voice came seemingly out of nowhere. "Looking for demon repellent? A little soul patching? Or are you already too far gone for that?"

"Come out where I can see you, Frost."

"Nervous, eh? Ah, you're human yet." A shadow flickered and a small, lithe form materialized from the back. It was difficult to say whether the wrinkled, hairless creature that came forward was female or male, or whether it had been hiding or simply appeared out of thin air. Ian chose to believe the latter, in both cases.

"I thought you would have come earlier," Frost said. "I imagined you were dead. You've held up well, considering." He stepped closer and peered into Ian's face. One clawlike finger reached up and traced the line of his jaw. "Though they've taken their toll on you, haven't they?"

Ian nodded. "I want out."

Frost chuckled. "We all say that."

"I mean it. I've done it for the last time."

"But you like it, don't you? Or is that what you're afraid of, that you'll become like them?"

Frost had always had an unsettling ability to find the heart of the matter. He had his feet firmly placed in both worlds. Knowing someone had been there before was an odd comfort.

"Fowler's lost already," Ian said, surprised to find his voice shaking. "He wants me to keep going as much as they do. He gets off on it now. I can't get rid of him."

"You're afraid he'll come after you? Why don't you just kill him?"

"I don't kill people. And I'm not sure he wouldn't just . . . come back."

"I see." Frost stood almost a head shorter than Ian, his skull moist and gleaming under the yellow light. There was no way of telling his age. His ears were curiously withered, and his face looked like a half-eaten apple. "He might at that. Unless you catch him."

"What do you mean?"

"You've heard of the tribes in South America that are afraid of cameras? Do you know why? They believe the camera has the ability to trap the soul. Not entirely true. But it can trap other things."

"I don't get it."

"Taratcha are creatures of the night. They live off fear, the inability to see what might be coming. If you are able to photograph one, it will remain caught on film."

"Forever?"

"Until such time as you choose to look at the prints." Frost smiled. "They can get very angry at a trick like that. I'll leave the details up to you. But it seems to me that it could be the answer you're looking for."

"Thank you, Frost."

"There's the matter of payment? Even otherworldly advice isn't free."

Ian handed over a wad of bills and turned to leave. Frost caught him at the door. "Ever wonder where things like that come from?"

"What do you mean?"

"Demons. Taratcha. The sort that you might call your customers."

"I assumed they were once like us. In Fowler's case, he's a greedy bastard. I always thought he would change completely, given the time."

"It's something to think about."

"Are there other things I should be thinking about?"

Frost shrugged. "I won't tell you everything, that wouldn't be fair. But I will tell you this: Be true to yourself. And be careful, Ian Quinn. They're closer than you think."

Closer than you think. Frost's words followed him home. Had he made an unforgivable error in judgment? Was getting rid of Fowler not the answer after all?

As he stepped around the corner near his building, a shape slipped from the shadows into the light of a streetlamp. "If I didn't know any better I'd think you were avoiding me," Anna said. She wore a white tank top and jeans that clung to her curves. She'd put her black hair up, loose strands curling down to kiss her neck. "I've been calling your cell and getting voice mail."

"I turned it off," Ian said. "Needed some sleep. And the landlord's been looking for rent and I'd rather not talk to him."

"You want to know how I found you. I knew you lived in this neighborhood and drove around a couple of blocks until I saw your van. It needs a wash." She wrinkled her nose. "*You* need a wash."

"Water's off." He shrugged. "What can I say, I'm a little behind . . ."

"Why don't you come back to my place. I can cook you something nice, get you cleaned up."

"I really should get some work done."

"We need to talk, Ian." She crossed her arms over her breasts and did not step any closer. "Come with me, please. I need to know what's going on."

Back at her apartment Anna busied herself in the kitchen while Ian stood under white-hot needles of spray, washing what felt like months of grime from his skin. He hung his head under the water and breathed slowly through his mouth. Something floated and spun in the circling pattern of drain water. He waited until the water finally turned from light gray to clear, and then he stepped onto a fluffy sage green bath mat and toweled himself until his flesh stung.

He dressed in one of Anna's oversized T-shirts and sweatpants and went into the living room while she worked in the kitchen. He took a photo album from the bookshelf, sat on the couch, and flipped through its pages. Here stood Anna as a girl with a smiling man and woman, in front of a Tudor with well-trimmed shrubs; Anna in a softball uniform; vacations with white sand beaches and cruise ships the size of small continents; a series shot against a lush mountain backdrop with another woman with similar features. They wore backpacks with sleeping bags strapped to the sides. Each shot perfectly captured a smile or look, a gesture or a thought held in someone's expression.

The smell of food made his mouth water. In the kitchen, Anna had placed a full plate of chops, rice, and beans on the wooden farmer's table. She watched him rip into the meal with a half-formed smile on her face. "It's almost morning, but I thought you needed something meaty. At least someone will eat my cooking."

"Right now, I'll eat anything."

She elbowed him in the ribs and tucked one foot under her in the chair. "So where were you coming from tonight?"

"I had to take some photos of the waterfront for a client. They're going to rebuild."

"You didn't have a camera."

"Yeah, well." He shrugged. "I was scouting the location."

"Are you seeing someone else, Ian?"

"Of course not."

"Then why won't you tell me the truth?"

"It's none of your business, Anna."

"When I've been sleeping with someone for a while I kind of expect things to move forward. I like you, Ian, you're funny, sweet, sensitive. But I don't like your secrets."

"I've got a dark side."

"I want to see that, too."

"You've got to understand something about me. My work, it's like another woman I'm in love with. I can't just let her go, and I can't share her with you. The two of you wouldn't mix."

"How do you know? Maybe that could be fun. You should try me, you might be surprised." She took a deep breath as if gathering courage. "You know what I think? You're scared of a boring life. Wife, kids, house in the suburbs. You think it's death. You think you can't have that and still do what you do. Maybe you need the darkness, depression moves you, am I right? If you were happy, you'd lose your hold on that creative muse. But what good is it to shut yourself off from everyone who loves you, just because you're afraid of what might happen?"

"It isn't like that."

"No? You tell me, then. I'm in love with you, Ian. I'm willing to take the next step. I'd like to meet that other woman. But I can't be in a relationship like this, not anymore. You let me know if you ever decide to let me in."

He had left the blinds in his apartment closed. But when he opened the door they had been pulled back, bright early morning sunlight streaming down onto the stinking flesh on his sheet-metal stage. A moment later, Fowler came strolling out from the little kitchen alcove, eyes hidden behind dark glasses. "Magnificent," he breathed. His jowls trembled with something like lust. "You've topped yourself yet again. I didn't think you had it in you."

"You son of a bitch," Ian said. "If any of them followed you here—"

"Get real." Fowler swept a hand toward the window. "It's light out, or haven't you noticed? Tends to hurt my eyes, and it makes them scream. If they want to know where you live, they'll find you without any help from me."

Ian grabbed his camera from the table. He fixed Fowler through the sticky lens, found the image of the man with his palms up, gesturing. "Hey—"

Click. The flash popped and whined; bright light painted the interior of the room. Fowler winced. "Jesus Christ, will you cut it out? Hurts my eyes . . ."

Click. Pop. Another wince and a muttered breath. Ian let the camera drop to his chest. Fowler was still there.

"What the hell did you do that for?"

"You looked good standing next to it."

"Yeah. Well, don't do it again." Fowler's eyes momentarily glowed red through the dark lenses and then faded. "You ain't so cute either, you know that? You ought to look in the mirror once in a while." He moved to the door. "Get me those prints." He stole one more glance back at the creation lying still upon the bloodied silver platform, the longing plain in his face. Ian imagined him caressing its gory flanks, leaning down to touch his lips to slippery flesh. And then he was gone.

Ian pounded a fist into his palm. Fowler was not yet a Taratcha, and would not be as easy to trap as Frost had suggested. He would have to find another way.

Late that night the solution came to him. Like most solutions born of desperation, this one came upon him by chance.

He had long since gone to bed, but sleep wouldn't come at first. He couldn't yet bring himself to disassemble his masterwork. And so it sat, alone on its altar like the remains of blood worship. Ian had begun to think of it as more than his Art, a testimony to all he had accomplished, a showcase of his talent. More than that, it was his child; and as frightened as he was with that thought, he no longer had the strength within himself to be disgusted by it.

He did not know when he slept or when exactly he awakened, but for a moment the flitting shadow shapes and crawling, tentacled dream creatures remained with him. The huge loft sat black and silent as a tomb. He lay there blinking up into the dark until his bladder forced him out of bed.

When he flicked on the bathroom light he almost screamed

at the image glaring back at him through the mirror. Heavy brows overshadowed sunken, bruised eyes with a spark of red at their centers. He flicked the light off again and stood blinking in the dark. Fowler was right. He hadn't noticed how far it had progressed. But it was a reversible transformation. It had to be.

Something nagged at his mind. It was all too easy to think of the Taratcha as simply evil given form and substance, part of an ongoing underworld war, a system of checks and balances between lightness and dark. But that alone did not give them definition. It did not make them real. Now, with the image of his own face floating like a ghost in the blackness that surrounded him, he began to understand their true essence. Creatures born from a collective unconscious. Trace memory of a human race too savage to bear the light. The monster under the bed, the spark behind a pedophile's eyes. The stuffing of a madman's brain. They were *human* creations, weren't they? And what better place for the birth of a demon than within the dark heart of an artiste?

He was almost too late. When he heard movement behind him he whirled, aware of a dim, reddish glow that wholly human eyes would never have registered. The bathroom door hung open, and from beyond it came the sound of something sliding across a slick surface.

Padding silently on bare feet he slipped around the door frame, and kept to the wall as he felt his way around the circumference of the room. His camera hung with the rest of his tools. With one motion he turned, stepped forward, and brought it to his eyes. Only then did he look at what it was he had created.

It dragged itself slowly along, tiny child arms waggling,

grasping with bony fingers at the place he had been. Seams of black thread joined and divided an endless expanse of puckered flesh, opening and closing like a thousand tiny mouths. Ends of bone poked out like porcupine quills. Eyes like white-fisted tumors bulged and rolled under skin stretched tight as a bruise. A snail's trail of dark fluid marked its path from the metal stage to the floor.

A demon's first steps. Laughter was Ian's first thought; this thing, searching blindly for *him,* its creator, whatever purpose that drove it held deep inside its bloated depths and hidden from view. What would it do if it found him? Was this patricide? Or would it welcome him with open arms?

His second thought was less defined. As the creature turned and sought him with some blind sense and a voice like a thousand shrieks filled his head, he centered the frame and pushed the trigger. White light painted the room like a flare. The shrieks reached a sudden raging crescendo as the newborn demon disappeared, and he had the fleeting sense of a forest of waving limbs, frozen in time. For a moment the doorway opened itself to him as through the camera's window he glimpsed an army of impossible creatures writhing like a mound of earthworms within a tightfisted cavern of dripping stone. Then he remembered nothing, aware only of a strange feeling of loss, his own voice repeating the same phrase over and over like the words to a forgotten ritual in the sudden silence of the loft.

I'm sorry. I didn't know.

Fowler waited for him in their regular booth. He looked up as Ian approached, and this time he could not hide the hunger in his eyes.

"Jesus, you take your goddamned time," Fowler said. His voice buzzed like a radio losing its signal. Or was it something more? The sound of a man slipping between the cracks?

"Sorry. It won't happen again, believe me."

Fowler seemed appeased by Ian's attitude. But he paused when the leather portfolio slid across the moistened table, something in Ian's own eyes making him uncertain. He sensed a change here, a new confidence and strength that made him curious. Then the hunger seemed to overwhelm everything else. Fowler's fingers touched the fold, opened it. "Wait," Ian said. "I don't want you to look at them yet."

"Why the hell not?"

"Trust me on this. Take the portfolio and bring it back to me later. You'll want to be alone."

Fowler's chubby hand shot out and grabbed Ian's forearm. The grip held a little bit of desperation in it. Fowler's fingers tightened, digging. "Ever see what the Taratcha do to a man? They're not happy with killing you. They want you to live with the pain."

Ian resisted the overpowering urge to shrug off the touch the way you might shrug off a bug. "I get it."

"If you're planning to cut out on me, think again. One word from me and you're gone. Anybody you love, gone. Get that?"

"Whatever you say."

"You know, I didn't take to your new look at first. But I gotta tell you, it's an acquired taste. Keep your chin up, as they say."

Ian remained at the table for a long time after Fowler had gone. He did not touch the thick envelope that had been left for him. He ordered a drink, then another, gathering his courage.

The feeling of loss had remained with him for the rest of that night and into the morning. He had seen something in the thing, as gruesome as it was. Some spark of recognition, some kind of empathy.

The Art was the only thing he had ever truly been good at, and yet a part of him had always been ashamed. In his younger years he had frequently been asked where the darker sides of his talent came from, and when he tried in vain to answer he would often be faced with a look of pity or even guarded mistrust. *What are you hiding,* they seemed to be saying. His only reply was that he did not know.

The dim light in the bar hurt his eyes. Ian walked to the empty bathroom, hit the switch, and stood in the dark, bent over the sink and holding the cool porcelain with both hands. Finally he looked up. The mirror over the sink revealed a face that burned with its own light. He looked inward through his mind's eye and saw a sea of writhing shapes, breeding and dividing. He imagined Fowler's trembling fingers as they slipped open the leather flap, drew out the photographs, brought them close to his face: one photo, in particular, that had trapped his newborn son.

If you are able to photograph one, it will remain caught on film, Frost had said, *until such time as you choose to look at the prints. They can get very angry at a trick like that.* He imagined the explosion of flesh as his offspring, his spawn, did the work it had been born to do, erupting from the photograph and turning its rage upon Fowler, whose death would give Ian at least a chance to start anew.

His thoughts returned to Anna, and what she had said to him the last time they had spoken. *You let me know if you ever decide to let me in.* He dug his cell phone out of his pocket and switched it on. He didn't know if he could survive when these two worlds collided, but he had to stop hiding. It was time to find out whether his two loves could coexist.

It took only a moment for Anna to answer.

SIREN SONG

A KATE SHUGAK SHORT STORY

by Dana Stabenow

. . . the Sirens, who enchant all who come near them.

—*The Odyssey,* HOMER

5.

THE WITNESS TESTIFIED in a calm, level voice, responding fully to the defense attorney's questions but making deliberate, unhurried eye contact with the jury. Each jury member would meet her eyes briefly and then swivel their heads to look at the three defendants. The woman in the witness chair could have been any one of them, twenty years on.

The defendants were Pauline, Laura, and Linda Akulurak, ages sixteen, fifteen, and twelve, respectively. They were on trial for murder in the first degree, for the killing of their pimp, Dupré Thomas Jefferson, age twenty-eight, aka Da Prez, aka John Smith a time or two. He'd had a record going back to the age of nine, beginning in grade school in Los Angeles and migrating up the west coast of North America with him through Portland and Seattle and, lastly, Anchorage. He'd been tall and handsome, with a good deal of charm he had put to use in running a stable of prostitutes.

Jefferson dead was not quite as handsome as Jefferson alive, as the bullet that had taken his life had entered the back of his head at close range and had blown off the top of his skull. He had been asleep in his own bed at the time. The murder weapon was a .357 Magnum Smith & Wesson, found next to the body with one round fired. The method had the hallmarks of a gang hit, but the prints of all three defendants had been found on the weapon, along with the prints of the deceased. The defendants' hands had been tested for gunshot residue, with inconclusive results.

The prosecution had rested the day before with an air of relief. The defense had recalled the investigating officer that morning, extracting without difficulty more evidence over time of many of Jefferson's—the defense here coughed deprecatingly—family in the house at McKinley and Alder, as well as evidence of many more sets of smudged and partial prints not belonging to the defendants on the weapon. By the time the defense had excused the officer, opportunity had been extended to fifteen people, or more, if you included Da Prez's friends, which were few, rivals, which were many, and enemies, which were legion.

The defendants followed the officer to the stand. Pauline, the eldest, was a knockout, smooth brown skin over high flat cheekbones, tilted almond eyes a deep, velvety brown, thick black hair that hung to her waist in a smooth, shining cape. She wore a dark blue shirtwaist dress with a button-down collar and long sleeves, sheer stockings, black flats, small gold hoop earrings, and the merest touch of mascara. The jury, nine of them men, watched the top button of her dress with unblinking fascination.

Laura, the middle child, wore a sequined jean jacket over a

Justin Bieber T-shirt, a short pink skirt, black-and-white striped tights reminiscent of the Cat in the Hat, and yellow patent leather wedges with four-inch cork heels. Her black hair, as long and lustrous as her older sister's, was caught up in a ponytail at the side of her head with a large powder blue plastic flower on the clasp, and she wore hot pink glitter polish on her fingernails. This time, the nine men on the jury wore indulgent smiles. For that matter, so did the three women.

Linda, the baby, favored J.Crew, a polar bear tee over cargo pants and a pair of hot pink canvas high-tops with hot pink lights in the heels that blinked hotly and pinkly with every step. Her hair, as thick and as black as her sisters', was cut in a Dutch boy, with a line of bangs falling into her eyes. A Barbie doll dressed to match was clutched in one arm. This time, all twelve members of the jury looked angry, and they weren't alone. The rumble of sympathetic outrage from the packed courtroom had the judge raising his gavel to a menacing angle until it subsided.

Pauline's testimony was unemotional, factual, almost dry, but by now everyone knew how many times she had told their story, and if anything the lack of feeling engendered more pity rather than less. When the defense attorney asked her why she and her sisters had run away to Anchorage, she told him, sparing no detail of the sexual abuse visited on all three of them by their stepfather. When the defense attorney asked her why they had turned to prostitution, she said, "Why should we give it away for free? We had enough of that at home." When the defense attorney asked her if she or her sisters had killed Da Prez, she said, "He was nice to us. We were warm and dry, and we had clean clothes. He watched out for us. Why would we kill him?"

Laura tossed her ponytail a lot. When the defense attorney asked her if she'd killed Da Prez, she said in what looked like honest indignation, "No! He was nice to us. He took us to the movies." Tears welled up in the big brown eyes she turned on the judge. "You're not going to let them send us back to *him,* are you?" The judge very nearly betrayed himself by putting out a comforting hand, and pulled it back just in time.

Linda spoke steadfastly to her Barbie doll. When the defense attorney asked her in the gentlest possible voice why she and her sisters had moved in with Jefferson, she said simply, "We were hungry. And it was cold outside." When asked if she or her sisters had shot him, she only shook her head, her little girl hands smoothing Barbie's blond curls.

The last witness for the defense was the woman testifying now, a Native Alaskan like the defendants, and from their own place, an enormous wilderness north and east of Anchorage, a place of isolated villages, few roads, and a population vastly outnumbered by the resident wildlife. Yes, she knew the girls' family. Yes, she knew the girls' parents. She told of the girls' father, drowned while fishing in Alaganik Bay six years before, and of their mother, dead in childbirth three years before. Yes, she knew the girls' stepfather, in whose custody the three girls had spent the two and a half years prior to running away, and related a litany of offenses in a list longer than the Domesday Book. When asked why such a person remained in charge of minor children, she made such an obvious effort not to cast an accusing look at the judge that everyone looked at him anyway. His expression was not reminiscent of pride in his profession.

The jury wasn't out for fifteen minutes, and they came

back in with a unanimous verdict of not guilty. The courtroom burst into applause. A smile spread across the judge's face. He didn't bother gaveling them into silence.

DFYS swept down onto the girls and enfolded them in a warm, bureaucratic embrace. The press snapped photos and updated their blogs on their smartphones. The president of a local bank posed with the girls and a very large check, which represented the donations of thousands of Alaskans, alerted to the plight of the orphans by continuous and excruciatingly detailed news coverage, including graphic details, sociological commentary, and many heartwarming photographs of the girls in their new foster home with loving and thoroughly vetted foster parents, in their new schools, and guest-judging the largest cabbage at the last Alaska State Fair.

Unnoticed, their character witness slid through the crowd to the door, where a husky-wolf mix with ears big enough to cast their own Bat-Signal waited. Next to the dog was the prosecuting attorney.

The closing doors dimmed but did not obliterate the joyous noise inside the courtroom.

"Well, Kate?" said the big man with the red hair and the food-spotted tie.

"Well what, Brendan?" she said.

He looked at the double doors that led into the courtroom. "Justice done?"

For a man who had just lost a major trial in the first segment of every television news show that evening, he looked remarkably pleased with himself.

4.

"WHAT A CIRCUS," Kate said. It was difficult to make herself heard over the din. "Who leaked?"

"I don't know," Brendan said, his face grim. He led the way through the horde of journalists, Kate following in his wake, speaking no further word until they were safe behind the door of his office. They sat and regarded each other glumly. "We'll have to try them now," he said.

Kate could not hide her dismay. "Even the twelve-year-old?"

"Come on, Kate. Maybe even especially the twelve-year-old. The NRA has everyone in Juneau by the balls, and you know their tagline as well as I do. Guns don't kill people, people do. The Brady Law didn't change that, it just ratcheted up the decibel level. They fixed it so we have to try almost anyone of almost any age who uses a firearm in the commission of a crime, and this is murder."

She thought, but didn't say, that there was a dedicated lack of enthusiasm to the prosecution's entire case. Nevertheless, Brendan was right. The district attorney's office was now firmly caught between the Scylla of public opinion and the Charybdis of political necessity, and they were going to have to trim their sails very ably indeed not to end up drowned in one or eaten alive by the other.

3.

"BELIEVE IT OR NOT, he wasn't that bad a guy," Brendan said. "We hauled him in a couple of times for assaults on johns who beat up on his girls. He protected them, avenged them when he couldn't, fed them, kept them in clean clothes, even had a GP check them out once a month. Signed the older ones up with Family Planning, if you can believe that. Paid for their abortions at a legitimate clinic. Bought condoms by the case at Costco and taught his girls how to use them."

"Even the twelve-year-old?" Kate said.

Brendan raised a hand, palm out. "I know, and you're right. I'm just saying. Da Prez wasn't the worst pimp on the street, not by a long shot."

She couldn't argue with him. Over the past year too many Alaska Native girls, runaways from abusive family situations in Bush villages, said abuse almost invariably fueled by alcohol, had wound up on the street in Anchorage. On average, one in three of them was recruited into prostitution, and once they had been groomed, most pimps regarded them strictly as a cash-producing asset all too easily replaced by the next kid off the plane.

Brendan sighed. "The kids land in Anchorage, and they're cold and they're hungry and they're lonely, and they're hanging out at the Dimond Mall begging for change, and somebody rolls up in a Hummer and promises them the moon. Hard to turn that down."

The FBI's Anchorage office had recently taken a task force into the Bush to warn the elders of the trend. "They came to Niniltna," Kate said. "The whole village turned out at the gym for their presentation."

"It's not like people in the villages haven't noticed their children have been disappearing." Brendan's mouth twisted. "And it's not like most of them don't know why." He looked up. "You know the Akuluraks?"

"Knew of them," she said. "Obviously didn't know enough."

"Come on, Kate. You can't be there for everyone."

Her bleak expression was answer enough.

2.

"THEY'RE FROM NINILTNA?" Brendan snatched up the phone. "Get Jim Chopin at the Niniltna trooper post for me, pronto."

1.

THE THIRTY-YEAR-OLD HOUSE was ranch style, built on a slab with three bedrooms and two bathrooms. Green patches of moss grew on the roof, but the blue paint on the siding was only just beginning to peel, and the grass was freshly mowed.

Inside, the fixtures and furniture were worn but clean. The living room had a large flat-screen television and a floor-to-ceiling bookshelf filled with DVDs, including every Disney film since *Snow White and the Seven Dwarfs*. There were X-Men and World of Warcraft posters on the walls, a small Lucite box full of makeup on the coffee table, and a Barbie doll on the footrest of a recliner, her blond hair spilling over the edge. There were shoes and boots in a pile by the front door and coats, hats, and mittens tossed on chairs. Doors could be glimpsed down a hallway. Behind one of the doors someone was snoring.

Two girls sat close to each other on the couch, looking up at a third who sat on the coffee table, facing them. The .357 dwarfed her right hand, but she held it competently, the butt in a firm clasp, finger outside the guard, safety on, the barrel pointed down and away. "I know it's been rough," she said. "But we all agreed it was the only way."

The little one, Linda, nodded, her expression very serious. It was Laura, the middle child, who said, hesitantly, "Can't we just run away?"

"We talked about that, Linda." Pauline nodded toward the hallway. "We don't have any money, and you know he won't let us go until men don't want us anymore." She picked up the remote and clicked on the television and flicked the channel to a local news show. The couple on-screen were attractive without being glamorous, and the woman, a brunette with long hair, had a motherly look to her. "I've been watching all the local news stations. I think this is the one."

This time Linda squirmed. "Do we really have to tell them?" she said in a small voice.

"Yes," Pauline said.

"Everything?" Linda said. She stared at her shoes. "Everything he made us do?"

"Everything Rod made us do, too?" Laura said, picking at her sparkly blue fingernail polish.

"Yes," Pauline said. She muted the sound and nodded at the screen. "There's a thing called sweeps week coming up. It measures how many people are watching every channel. It means the TV stations need lots of people to watch so they can charge more money for commercials. So they run stories they think people will watch the most."

"And you think they'll watch us?" Laura said.

"We'll make them watch us," Pauline said.

"And people will give us money?"

"Yes. We'll get a grown-up to start us a bank account, and we'll say we have no money, and everyone will send us some."

"And we'll get a real mother and father?" Linda said, still looking at her shoes.

Pauline's eyes softened. "Yes."

"Are you sure?" Laura said. "Are you sure they won't make us go back to the village? Go back to . . ."

"I'm sure," Pauline said. "But only if we tell them everything. The grown-ups will make someone take us, and"—she nodded at the screen—"those people will make everyone pay attention so they give us to someone good." She put down the remote and picked up a yellow sticky note and held it out to Laura. "Here's the number. In case it isn't on the screen when . . . you know."

"No," Linda said, looking up. "It should be me. I should call. I'm the littlest. They'll feel sorriest for me."

Pauline's eyes met Laura's. "All right," she said, and handed her sister the phone. "Don't forget, leave the TV on until they come."

She rose to her feet, the .357 held firmly at her side, and walked on steady legs down the hall.

2.

"THEY FOUND THE AKULURAK GIRLS?" Kate said, her expression lightening. "God, that's great, Auntie Balasha will be so relieved, I can't wait to . . ." Her voice trailed away.

"It's not so great," Jim said, scratching behind Mutt's ears. Mutt's tongue lolled out of her mouth, her eyes half closed in an expression of blissful idiocy. "Brendan says they killed their pimp."

"Their pimp?" Kate said. And then she said, "They killed him?"

"That's not the worst of it, Kate," he said. "Believe it or not. They say that asshole Rod Jimmieskin has been molesting them ever since their mother died. They say that's why they ran off."

3.

"ISN'T THE GANG executioner's weapon of choice usually a .22?" Kate said.

"Yeah," Brendan said, "but the girls said the .357 was always right there on the nightstand." He paused. "He trained the three of them on it, you know."

"So they said." On camera, on every channel, in every television studio in the state.

"Took them all out to the firing range. Taught them how to sight in, fire, reload. How to clean it when they came home."

"I wonder whose idea that was," Kate said.

"What do you mean?"

"I mean it's kind of funny he didn't take any of his other girls out on the firing range to practice with his personal weapon."

"The sisters were living with him," Brendan said. "His other girls had their own places. And he was engaged in a business that was not what you might call low risk. He wanted them to be able to protect themselves, is what they're saying. That's how their attorney is going to explain away the GSR. They'd been to the range the day before."

"It is a problem," Kate agreed.

He totally missed the irony. "He probably wanted them to be able to protect him, if it came to that."

"I'm sure you're right," Kate said. She read down through the case file. "Why did they call the station? Why not 911?"

"They said the television was on and the number was on the bottom of the screen."

"Was it?"

Brendan nodded. "We looked at a tape of the news. KKAK runs a daily feature where they invite viewers to call or e-mail comments. They run the number and the address at the bottom of the screen through the whole feature. Linda said it was the first number she saw after they heard the gunshot."

"Why did she call?"

"She was closest to the phone."

Kate was silent for a moment. "They didn't even run. They just sat there and waited for the cops to show. Why didn't they run?"

He gave her a quizzical look. "Aren't you testifying as a character witness for the defense, Kate?"

4.

"NOTHING PERSONAL, KATE, but you look kinda grubby," Brendan said. He sniffed. "You smell kinda grubby, too."

"Like, no showers at the mall, man," she said, pouring coffee into a foam cup.

His eyes narrowed. "Wait a minute. The mall?"

She sat across from him. "Yeah, man, like, you know, the mall."

He took a deep breath and let it out. "The Dimond Mall?"

"That'd be the one." She sipped, winced, and sipped again.

"Where Da Prez picked up the Akulurak sisters."

"Where they say he did. Funny thing."

"What?"

"Not one of the kids I talked to remembered seeing the girls there."

He digested this in silence for a moment. "Not the most reliable witnesses, mall rats."

She drank more coffee. "So I spent the better part of the last five days hanging out there, Brendan. Talked to a lot of kids, and a couple of their pimps while I was at it. One of whom offered me a job, by the way. Said some of his clients liked 'em a little long in the tooth. Kinda perverted, but, hey, he had a business, he provided product for a price, whaddya gonna do."

"Is he still living?"

"Barely." She leaned forward, empty cup dangling from one hand. "The thing is, Brendan, they've all seen the Akulurak sisters on television by now. And none of them remember seeing them at the mall. Where the sisters say they hung out for a week, fighting for leftover pizza out of Round Table's Dumpster, before Da Prez came along and made them an offer they couldn't refuse."

"Doesn't prove anything one way or another." He looked at her, puzzled. "Kate, they are already caught. They're going on trial for murder on Monday. Why pick holes in their story now? What's the point?"

She looked down at the dog, who leaned against her knee and gazed up at her with big yellow eyes. "You said he was a relatively good guy, for a pimp."

"And you said he was still a pimp."

She shrugged. "It's just interesting that fresh out of the village, first time in the big city, and the girls wind up with him."

"No," he said, "not really. It's what he does. Did. He had a farm team of girls from the villages, stashed in his house and a couple of duplexes. He had a Web site, Kate. He advertised them on the Internet as Thai and Vietnamese."

"The cops had him inside for a while about six months ago," she said. She produced a piece of paper from the hip pocket of her jeans.

He took it. It was a printout of a year-old story from the local Anchorage newspaper about an arrest for assault in the first degree made by one Dupré Thomas Jefferson, aka Da Prez. The victim was one Charles Louis Carson. Jefferson claimed he had simply been defending one Loretta Igushik, street name Sweetness. Igushik, Jefferson said, was a friend whom Carson had allegedly severely beaten in the course of a lovers' quarrel.

Brendan said, "You mean about Carson being Senator Carson's son?"

"Read down."

He read some more. "You mean the quote from the unnamed source in the investigation saying at least Da Prez made sure the johns didn't mistreat his girls?"

She stood up and hit the trash can dead center with the cup. "Swish, score, two points, big team, two points." She looked at Brendan. "Did I mention, Brendan, that the Suulutaq Mine donated a satellite dish to the Niniltna School? And a computer for every desk in every room in the building? These days, school kids in Niniltna could log on to the International Space Station if they wanted to."

5.

"WELL, KATE?" said the big man with the red hair and the food-spotted tie.

"Well what, Brendan?" Kate said.

He looked at the double doors that led into the courtroom. "Justice done?"

He was looking at the doors as if he could see through them, as if the three girls were still in sight. "Brendan," she said, "you noticed there was a majority of men on the jury, right?"

He was still watching the doors. "Huh?"

"You didn't even use up all of your peremptory challenges. Didn't you think it might be better to have a balance of the sexes on a jury for a case like this one? On a jury you wanted to swing your way?"

"Yeah," he said, unheeding. "Men. Jury. Sure."

"Yeah," she said. "What I thought. Brendan, look at me."

She had to say it again before he turned his head. "You want to sleep with Pauline," she said.

He blushed and looked furtive.

"Don't despair, you aren't alone," she said. "Every man on the jury felt the same way. So did the judge. And you all wanted to adopt Laura, and you all wanted to pick up your lance and mount your destrier and slay anyone who laid a hand on Linda. I'd bet large on every man who watched any of this on television feeling the same way. Barring that, I guess you can all write checks."

His blush subsided. "So what if we did?"

"I'm just trying to answer your question," she said.

Irresistibly, his attention returned to the doors. To them he said, "What question?"

217

"Was justice done," she said, and looked at Mutt standing next to her, ears up, yellow gaze flicking between them. For a four-footed mammal with incisors of that size, justice was pretty much summed up in a "Hurt me or mine, I eat you" ethos. Come to that, the Akulurak sisters weren't that long out of the Alaskan Bush themselves.

"What?" Brendan said.

"Never mind," Kate said.

Her words were lost in the din when the doors opened and the Akulurak sisters walked out at the head of what had all the appearances of a parade. It included most of the members of the jury.

Kate's eyes met Pauline's over the crowd as it swept by. Pauline, hand in hand with her sisters, paused for one infinitesimal moment, just long enough for Kate to get the uncomfortable feeling that she could read Pauline's mind.

What else was I supposed to do? Let Rod keep on fucking me and Laura until Linda got old enough for him? It wasn't like we got any help, from you or anybody else. We did what we had to do to get out, and then we did what we had to do to stay out. So, yeah, we chose Prez, and we killed Prez, and we lied and said somebody busted into the house and did it, and I made sure there was enough evidence that at least I would be tried, and I made sure every single filthy thing that bastard Rod and that bastard Prez made us do was in people's faces every minute of every day. Now we've got a safe place to stay and a quarter of a million dollars in a bank account, and we're good until I'm old enough to keep house for all three of us. You got a problem with any of that?

The parade swept by, still in thrall to the siren song of the three girls at its head.

Maybe Kate didn't have a problem with it. Maybe it was justice, of some kind.

"Come on, Mutt," she said. "Let's go home."

LESS OF A GIRL

by Chelsea Cain

SOPHIE SAYS NOT TO WORRY—that fourteen-year-old girls get a lot of practice cleaning up blood. She says they are experts at it. They scrub it off the crotches of their underpants, she says, and off their blue jeans. They clean it out of their bedsheets and mattress pads. They wipe stray drops off the bathroom floor, off the toilet seat, off their hands, out from under their nails. They bleed like stuck pigs, Sophie says. They hemorrhage. She says, watch a fourteen-year-old girl stand up from a chair, and half the time she'll glance behind her to make sure she hasn't left blood on the seat.

She says I should stop staring and get the paper towels.

"Under the sink," she says, "in the kitchen."

Her bedroom door is painted the color of an infected sore, and is covered with posters of actors wearing fake vampire fangs. Last year the door was yellow, and papered with pictures of horses.

It has been a long time since I've been out of the room.

I like it here, in the room. The smell of cherry lip gloss, piña-colada-scented candles, cotton-candy-scented hair spray, the

Tide laundry detergent her mother washes her sheets with, hamster pee and sawdust, an orange peel that's been rotting in the trash can under her desk for two weeks, talcum powder, and glue.

But now I can smell none of that.

Now it is sweat and blood and butchered meat.

"Paper towels," Sophie says again. She looks down at Charlotte's corpse, at the blood on the carpet, and frowns.

I reach for the doorknob and open the door to the hall.

"Don't let my mother see you," Sophie calls.

It's like walking the plank, going off the high dive.

The hallway is thirty-seven steps. Framed color photographs of Sophie and her family line the walls. Their eyes follow me. They are wearing sweater vests. They are wearing white turtle-necks. Now they are wearing denim and leaning against hay bales. Now they are lined up on the beach in front of the cold Pacific Ocean.

I am walking, but I can't hear my steps on the carpet.

Now they are dressed in holiday velvet in front of the Christmas tree. Now they are lying side by side making snow angels.

There are seventeen stairs down to the first floor.

I can see the pale blue glow of Sophie's mother's laptop. It smells like hair dye and charred wood and rotten grapes. She is sitting on the couch, with her feet up on the coffee table next to a glass of wine.

I have made a life out of moving silently, avoiding detection. I can stand against a wall so still that in the right light I am practically invisible. I am the thing you think you see at night in your room, before your eyes adjust and you decide it's just a sweater slung over the back of a chair. When your hand slips off the mattress at night, I am the creature you fear will grab it from under the bed. I am Sophie's naked, hairless twin. Her exact shape. Her budding breasts. Her skinny legs. I have her scars, her bruises.

The paper towels are under the kitchen sink. Sophie's mother buys Brawny. It's expensive. But Sophie says that her mother likes the guy on the package.

I slip the paper towels under my arm and back out of the kitchen, the ripe stink of rotten food in my nose, through the living room, past Sophie's mother's back, the blue glow of her computer, the smell of her red wine, up the seventeen stairs and down the hall to Sophie's bedroom door.

Her twin bed is against the wall in the corner. The blue floral bedspread is pulled up neatly over the pillow. Postcards and pictures torn out of magazines are taped on the wall over the headboard. The bookshelf is crammed with books and horse show trophies and a few collectible dolls that she's never been allowed to play with.

There's a sticker on her desk that she put on the outside of a drawer when she was eight and hasn't been able to get off. It's a castle, but the edges are torn where she's tried to peel it from the wood. There's another bookshelf on the other side of the room, this one lined with stuffed animals. They are grouped into families: all the bears together, all the dogs, all the cats. The pink and orange lava lamp on her bedside table oozes and glows. The ceiling is covered with glow-in-the-dark stars. There are seven empty Diet Coke cans on the dresser.

Charlotte lies dead on a polyester sleeping bag on the floor next to Sophie's bed. It is a Hannah Montana sleeping bag.

Sophie is digging out one of Charlotte's eyes with a spoon.

You know when someone is trying to pop the pit out of a not-ripe avocado? That's what it looks like.

Eyes smell like seawater and newspaper ink.

Sophie's got one hand on Charlotte's forehead and her other elbow akimbo, the spoon pressed into Charlotte's optical bone, fighting a tide of thick red ooze.

She looks up at me. "Close the door," she says.

I close the door and lock it.

The red eye slime slides down Charlotte's cheek. Sophie has zipped the sleeping bag halfway up, so that Charlotte is tucked in, like this is a sleepover. Hannah Montana smiles happily.

The spoon makes a wet squishing sound.

The swollen flesh of Charlotte's tongue sits limply between her braces. Dark bruises, dotted with broken blood vessels, encircle her neck and lower jaw. Her head is tucked back, chin up, so that the jagged wound across her throat is pulled wide, a crevice of bloody tissue and fat. Her hair, still blond from summer, is a bird's nest, crusted with blood.

I stay by the door.

There's a slurp and a pop, and then Sophie has Charlotte's eyeball in her hand and she's pulling and twisting because the optical nerve is still tethering the thing to Charlotte's brain, and then, snap, the eyeball comes loose. Sophie lifts it up and holds it out to me like she's found a particularly interesting shell, the eye soft and red, shredded nerves dangling from it, and Sophie says, "Eat it."

I meekly show her the Brawny. "Maybe we should clean up first?" I suggest.

Sophie shakes her head, almost sadly, and presses her cupped hand toward me. "You're so pale," she says. Her fingernails are painted with purple glittery polish.

"I'm not hungry," I say.

"Hand me that," she says. "I'm going to get the other one." She is pointing to the ceramic dish on her beside table. It's shaped like a cupcake. The frosting part is the lid. It has a red cherry ball on top and fake rainbow sprinkles. The cupcake is where Sophie keeps her treasures: two baby teeth, the head of the small plastic boy who used to live in her dollhouse, a 1935 penny, a rock, a piece of a broken cup, a Matchbox car she found underwater in the Gulf of Mexico on vacation. I hand her the cupcake and she dumps the contents out on the floor. They bounce and skid out of sight, the teeth, the penny, the car. Sophie drops Charlotte's eye inside the cupcake.

"What did you think this was going to be like?" Sophie asks me.

I don't say anything.

She frowns again and lifts her eyebrows. "I want us to be friends forever," she says.

She looks so sincere. And hurt. I have rejected her offering, that blue, blue eye. Now I feel like a monster.

"Fine," I say.

I pluck the eyeball out of the cupcake and put it in my mouth and roll it around a little. It's still warm and slippery with metallic-tasting blood. When I bite down it pops inside my mouth, releasing a sweet sugary gel that coats my tongue and slides down my throat.

A warm light tickles down the length of my arms.

I lick my lips.

"See?" Sophie says. Her eyes shine and she digs the spoon into her friend's other eye socket.

Squish.

My stomach churns.

I move Sophie's hand away and squat over Charlotte's face and I tongue her dead eye, working it loose, sucking on it, chewing on the lid, the tiny eyelashes between my teeth, until it slips into my mouth and then, panting, I chew through the nerve fibers, slurp out the blood, and swallow. The warm fluid of her fills my mouth and runs down my throat.

I can feel Sophie watching me, so I slip my fingers deep into Charlotte's eye socket, hook them under the bone, and pull until I hear her skull crack. Her head changes shape as the bone gives way, less of a girl now than meat. It's easier that way.

I try to eat quickly. The splinter of bone, the chewy knot of her tongue, the dry hay of her hair, her flesh and fat and clothes. My mouth stings from the metal of her blood, the sharp bits of her.

She is young and comes apart easily. Fat from muscle. Muscle from bone. Cartilage and connective tissue. Blood and spinal fluid and mucus.

I devour her. There is nothing left. I lick her blood off the sleeping bag until Hannah Montana is dark with my saliva.

Then I look up at Sophie. She is sitting crisscross-applesauce on the bed, her cheeks bright pink.

I touch the bloodstain on the carpet and rub my fingers together. "This isn't going to come out," I say.

The stain is only a few feet wide.

"The bed," I say.

Sophie nods and gets up and moves the bedside table with the lava lamp, and then she takes the headboard and I take the footboard and we inch her bed over until the bloodstain is underneath it.

We do not hear her mother, the smell of her wine breath obscured by death, coming up the stairs and down the hall. She knocks on the purple door and we jump.

The doorknob jiggles.

"Is it locked?" her mother says.

"Just a second," Sophie calls. We look at each other for a long moment and then Sophie says, "Go."

I slide under Sophie's bed, my back on the carpet, my nose under the box spring.

Sophie opens her bedroom door.

"You moved your bed," I hear Sophie's mother say.

"Yeah," Sophie says. She is struggling into her pajamas. I see her feet and ankles on the carpet. The striped PJ pants. Purple toenail polish. Next to her feet, on the floor, her ceramic cupcake, broken into three pieces.

"What's with the paper towels?" her mother asks. The roll of Brawny is on Sophie's desk.

"I spilled a Diet Coke," Sophie says.

"Remember, one square," her mother says. "Those are expensive." She walks over to retrieve the paper towels and her feet stop next to Sophie's. Then her hand comes down and scoops up the shards of colorful ceramic—the colored sprinkles, the cherry—and I hear the broken cupcake drop into Sophie's wastebasket.

"Want me to tuck you in?" Sophie's mother asks.

There is a pause. "That's okay," Sophie says.

"Okay," her mother says. "But it's late. Lights out." The room goes dark. "Don't let the bedbugs bite," I hear Sophie's mother say from the door. "Or any other kind of bug."

She starts to close the door, the room settling into darkness.

"Mom?" Sophie asks suddenly. "Can you leave the door open a crack?"

"Sure," her mother says.

The light from the hall illuminates the carpet, a slanted yellow rectangle. Sophie is quiet. I can hear her breathing. Thinking about Charlotte, a blush of pleasure runs through me in waves. My cheeks grow hot. My mouth waters. The coils of Sophie's box spring creak inches above my nose.

Underneath me, on the floor, the bloodstain is wet on my back, and one of Sophie's baby teeth digs into my shoulder.

The two of us are quiet for a long time.

"Sometimes I think my stuffed animals are staring at me," Sophie says finally.

I whisper, "They are."

THE CRUEL THIEF OF ROSY INFANTS

by Tom Piccirilli

THE CRIB WAS FREE OF IRON, foxglove, open scissors, or any other protective measures or charms. On the crackling hearth a pot of hog's head stew sat cooking, almost as an invitation. It could be a trap. Sixty years ago I'd been snared by eight waiting men prepared with clubs of ash and an iron cage. It had taken me four days to escape up the chimney.

This, though, didn't seem like a lure despite the human girl child lying beneath an open window, alone in the cool evening breeze.

A remote noise upstairs caught my attention. Snarls, grunts, mewls, and caterwauls. Murder, I thought, murder and evisceration! It took another moment to realize it was the human sound of lovemaking. Coarse but full of bounce. One could play the fiddle to it, the drums, the pan pipes. My foot tapped. My nose itched. I sneaked a ladle of the stew. Then another. I'd always had a fondness for hog's head. The doctor warned me away from it, and my wife would surely shame me. I needed a sprig of mint to camouflage my breath.

The child in its crib grinned at me. Clear-eyed, crimson-cheeked, it gripped my index finger fiercely. I perceived no obvious weaknesses or illnesses. It had not been touched by plague. It had no fleas or worms, no ticks. Its heart rang with a solid thump within its small chest, no arrhythmia, no congestive failure. The pulse was a nice counterpoint to the cries of the mother. It would grow up able-bodied and average.

It was what it was. It could not help being what it was. Plain and blunt. Bald, smelly, and toothless. Heavy-handed, awkward-footed, easily replaceable, utterly common. A laugh escaped its bubbling lips. It sought my finger again. Its parents were already making siblings that would look just like it.

In this world, on this side of the wall, the human girl child would eventually grow to milk cows and goats, weave gray scratchy clothes, and then go on to bear its own ungainly offspring. It would know overwhelming love and great, sharp sorrow, but it would never, except perhaps at the moment of death, achieve any grace.

I drew back my coat and Livia's child stared at me, her eyes alive with understanding and acceptance, golden-blond hair draping across her angled, intelligent features. She shined as all our kind shine, radiant and exquisite.

I said, "You're needed here, bright one."

She seemed to nod in understanding. She held no malice at the swapping. We do the things we do because we must do them.

It was Livia I was worried about. She was more reluctant to let go of the child than I'd anticipated. I thought I had even seen tears glimmering in her eyes before she had turned away and hastened back to her dwelling on the bluff.

We do not often shed tears, and never when doing the things we must do.

I swapped the children, as is my duty. As it was my Da's, and his Da's before him, back and back until the beginning of the races, so I'd been told. My family had been in charge of doing this thing for no less than fifteen hundred years, although time is playful when traveling from one side of the wall to the other. Perhaps fifteen centuries, perhaps fifty. A long time nonetheless.

Humanity has given us a name. We were known, each of us, in turn, as the Thief of Rosy Infants. It is not a title that fills me with joy. It is not a designation that compels strangers to hurl roses. It is not a name I want written in the great accounts of our people.

Upon his deathbed, my Da told me, "This is a sacred and terrible responsibility we are charged with. It will likely drive you mad if you ponder it at length." He held my face in his hands and kissed my brow. "Traveling will leave you lost in place and time, my son. Humanity will hate you. Our own people will hate you, whether you see it in their faces or not. I'm sorry you were born to me, and that I must pass this painful commitment on to you now."

Then he died and I buried him at the bottom of a rushing river, as was his wish, so that his great sins might be washed away. I wondered if it worked.

The parents of the human girl child would scream when they found the swapling, cry out even louder than they were doing right now, and wail, and call for the queen's guard, and kneel in their churches, but eventually, and without as much difficulty as they might have imagined, they would adapt. The beautiful swapling child was difficult to resist, even for the barbarous human heart.

I made my way back to the wall with the girl tucked beneath my coat.

On this particular journey, the wall was a wall of river stones and mortar surrounding the eastern edge of the city of Luftvillion, which was vulnerable to attack from the savage tribes of the highlands. Sometimes the wall was a different wall. Sometimes it was a wall of brick in a small chapel devoted to strange gods, or a wall of loblolly trees in the deep forest. Once I crossed over through a wall of skulls ten feet high and a hundred yards in length, built on a battlefield where riderless, armored horses wandered with gore-soaked manes.

It was night now, and the elderly had crept from their homes to sit on their porches and smoke their pipes and knit their socks and rock in their rockers. The elderly liked to look at the evening stars. The young were making love or in the pubs drinking or planning to overthrow governments and murder those with skins and languages different from their own. The elderly had poor eyes. They waved and nodded as I passed in the glow of the gas lamps. I waved back.

Before long I stood before a cathedral, where mass was in progress. Mass was always in progress. A tempestuous sermon rattled the stained glass windows. The stone figures of their faith stared down from the steeples and belfries, stern, commanding, yet with open arms, bodies wracked in torment so that pain and torture become appealing to humanity. I couldn't help myself and peeked in the mail slot.

In the aisles were weeping bodies, in some places three deep.

Mostly middle-aged. The middle-aged were in the churches begging for more money and the cure for black lung and syphilis. The choir set to braying. They were high in the balcony dressed in red robes, hands clasped in prayer or reaching out for the symbols of divine entities that hung on chains from the rafters. Their mouths gaped, their eyes narrowed.

Struck with hysteria, two altos fell from the balcony rail, hymns issuing forth until the very instant they hit the pews. The faithful spit the names of their mortgage brokers and tax collectors. They rolled around and barked like dogs. The minister beat them about the face, shoulders, and groin with his silver staff. He puffed smoke at them. He fed them biscuits and alcohol. They dropped to their knees and flopped on their faces.

Supplication is the thing humans do better than any other thing that they do. It's the thing they do best, besides killing.

The child was snuggled against my belly, snoring softly as I struck out again for the cobble path. It burped, sighed, and farted. Its moment of grace remained a long way off.

Finally I came to the eastern slope of the city and picked up my step over the viaduct as I neared the river-stone wall. The rapids bustled and churned. I crossed the bridge and watched a longboat making its way down the river. On board there was drunken revelry, hooting, the clashing of swords, and laughter.

I felt along the stones looking for a crack large enough to bring the human baby through the wall. It always took extra time because, small as the rosy infant was, it was still larger than me, in its own fashion, when traveling between. I held the swapling tightly and put my back to the polished stones. As I passed through I thought of something else my Da had told me. "You'll experience mysterious and morbid happenings. Not only within the confines of the human world but within yourself. Prepare for damage."

My wife, Harella, stood waiting for me on the other side, as she sometimes did when I went visiting. She was so beautiful that I almost had to cover my eyes for a moment. My time beyond the wall sometimes affected me for a bit. A deep melancholy filled my heart, which is a thing that happens to us, but doesn't happen often. I felt muddled.

She put a hand to my face and I nearly bowed before her luminescence. Her lips brushed mine, her twining arms so powerful I was swept up as if by the wind of an encroaching storm. I shut my eyes and began to hum.

"You smell of hog's head!" she cried. "The doctor said, no more hog's head."

I knew I should have had a sprig of mint after the hog's head ladling.

"The doctor," I said, "is a nit."

"The doctor is the doctor and knows the ways of doctoring. When he tells you no more hog's head, then no more hog's head it shall be. And no salt, paprika, cinnamon, mead, oregano, ground chuck, fried pickles, processed veal, four-day-old lumpfish—"

"How can oregano possibly inflict evil upon my innards?" I asked.

"I am not the doctor and neither are you."

The human girl child, which already stank, began to stink exponentially. It was doing the thing that humans do too often. The birds in our trees stopped singing. The animals on nearby farms began to buck horns and chase their tails and go into labor.

The child reached for my finger again and brought the tip to its gnawing maw.

"I must bring the swapped child to Livia," I said. "It's hungry. I should hurry."

Harella said nothing, which, so far as my wife was concerned, meant she was saying a thing and saying it loudly.

So loudly that my own tongue was compelled to speak the words. "I fear there will be trouble with Livia."

"I fear that your fear is a reasonable one," she said.

"I saw tears this morning."

"She is more sensitive than most, full of even deeper graces."

It was the truth, and an overwhelming one at that. There was a painful tug at my heart. I looked my wife in the eye and saw depths and light and sadness that shook me. I asked the question that had to be asked.

"Do you think she will harm the baby?"

Harella said, "She is one of great resolve and implacability."

This was a cautious way for my wife to explain that yes, indeed, she believed Livia might very well harm the human child she would have to care for now, to raise as her own to become one of us.

"We'll watch her closely."

The human girl child began to cry then. I held it up. It reached for my nose and gave it a good squeeze. I smiled and it smiled back. I extended it to Harella for no reason I could understand. I knew she would not want to touch it.

"It's a bald and beastly thing," she said, retreating a step.

"It was probably admired by its family and neighbors."

"They are blind."

"They know how to love as much as we do."

"Not quite as much, and without any virtue or purity."

"With some," I said.

I carried the child to Livia's home, down the paths through the heart of our city, along the canals on the River Solitude, under which my Da is buried. She had no husband but was paramour to a married architect who was attempting to decipher a way to build spires beyond the highest spires, which were considered by many to be too high already. He had previously tried to bring his vision to fruition, drilling deep into the earth to pour millions of metric tons of concrete foundations. It caused a minor volcanic eruption that toppled the theology wing of the Grand Museum.

The baby hiccupped and giggled as I walked with her in my arms. I tossed her in the air a few times, and she clapped her small hands. The cool air of night brought out rosy circles on her cheeks that burned in the moonlight.

Livia's home was out on the bluff, high above the white beaches. Far below, seashells glittered while out in the waves the sirens rose from the deep and crooned to the shipmasters and crewmen passing from port to port. They saw me on the road and sang my name. They walked upon the waves and danced in my honor. Their song grew more powerful. The baby tightened its grip upon me in terror.

In the doorway Livia stood waiting with a mottled face. With her arms wrapped around herself she grasped the fringes of her thistledown robe so firmly that she had shredded the fabric. Her lips curled and stayed in motion, twisting, contorting. Words began and died. I wagered that the architect had not yet left his wife.

She barely glanced at the baby.

"It's a beastly thing," she said.

"It is your daughter."

"It has no grace. It is awkward-footed, it's bald and tooth-less and—"

"All true, but it's still your daughter now. Time to feed it. Give it milk."

"It will drain me. It will drink my blood."

"It will drink your milk, which is what these things do. Feed it. Teach it. Love it."

"I will never love it."

"It's what you must do, Livia. It's what we all must do, when it is time for us to do what we must do."

"You talk like a damn fool."

She took the baby in her arms and gave it her breast, and the human infant gagged for a moment as they all gag on something so sweet, but after a minute settled down. Livia's eyes burned with hatred. It was astonishing to watch.

"Perhaps it will smother itself upon my breast," she said.

"Livia—"

"One hopes. One still has hope."

She turned away and scurried back into the house with the child, who immediately began to wail. The sirens also cried.

I sat reclined in my library before the fire, thinking of my mother, who had said, "You buried your father *where?*"

Harella entered with a vase of fresh-cut roses and placed it on the table I had whittled for her from a great redwood as a show of my love before we were married. I was young then and wondered if such talent had abandoned me by now.

She sat in her chair and took my hand in hers. She sensed my dark backward mood. I sensed her sensing and realized there was something else on her mind as well. I kissed her palm and turned fully toward her.

She told me, "The annual fencing trials are tomorrow."

"Already?" I huffed air. Time is playful when traveling through the wall. It stretches, contracts, curves, the tempo changes. I have met myself twice on the cobblestone roads so far. I didn't nod or wave. I said nothing, but I peered at myself angrily. I was beautiful, but not as beautiful as I'd always thought before meeting myself twice on the road.

"Don't go," she said, "this year. Stay with me."

"I will look like a coward."

"You will look like you are above their matters."

But I wasn't above their matters. I wasn't of them, but I wasn't above them. I never missed the fencing trials. I was the best fencer. I had always been the best fencer. But I'm excluded from the trials because my duty is to sneak beyond the wall. Their argument is that while I am out of sight from the referees, the masters, the other swordsmen, I might be partaking of secret instructions given by savage humans. I argue that no human can fence worth a dead lumpfish, but this argument falls on deaf, though graceful, ears. The human world is a mystery to them, even more than it is a mystery to me.

As such, they fear I have an unfair advantage, and so I am excluded from trials. But not from sparring. I have sparred with them all and beaten them all, probably because they hate me, which causes them to become distracted easily. I have a title where they have none. They have names but no designation, no station. They have jobs where I have duty. They have families where I have lineage. They perpetuate while I save the races.

My Da had said, "Your capabilities will be questioned. The only answer is to refrain from action. To be confident in your capacity."

"My capacity as quantified by what parameters?" I asked.

"By the parameters of your moral code," my Da said. "By your capacity to help our people. It's all that matters."

I thought then as I thought now. My Da, and his Da, and all the Das before them, were much stronger than I was, more altruistic, filled with greater humility.

Harella stood then and asked me to bed, possibly for love and possibly for sleep, but I wanted neither. She sighed her great sighs and drifted up the staircase alone, her gown flaring around her hips, the light of her beauty carrying her like soaring wings.

I sat in my chair mulling over my matters, full of mull, my mull full of dull, until the dawn broke and I heard, in the distance, the first flutes, trumpets, and squeezeboxes welcoming the fencing masters.

I kept still another minute trying hard to be above such matters, but soon found that I was not only not above them, or even of them, but probably well below them in the strictest sense. I was soon at the back of my closet and halfway dressed in my finest fencing garb.

Harella, two floors above, could hear me buckling my belts and snapping shut my buckles. She sighed so deeply that the frill on my jacket wafted to and fro. I retrieved my sword from above the fireplace, fit it within its sheath, and on horseback rode to the trials just as the bassoons and tubas and harpsichord announced Reedle.

Reedle was the reigning champion of fencing, and had been since I was driven from the trials. His coat was adorned with countless medals that shone not quite as shinily as the shine of his gleaming white teeth and brilliant black eyes. He arrived in a six-horse-drawn carriage. Himself, and his blade, and his epaulets, and his purple sash. He stepped from the carriage to the cheers of our people as I climbed off my horse.

He gave me his finest smile. "Ah, Cruel Thief of Rosy Infants, how are you this day?"

I did my best to smile my finest smile, which wasn't nearly as fine as his finest smile.

"Fine," I said.

"Has there been some revoking of the revoking of your privilege to enter our tournament?"

"Not to my knowledge," I said.

"And yet you wear your fencing finery?"

"My wife waxed the boots and polished the buttons recently, so out of respect for her sweat and efforts I thought I should wear the finery this day, while I sat in the stands and applauded your genius with a sword."

"Your boots are covered in horse shit," he told me.

Like all of us, Reedle is full of great grace, but his grace is less than the grace of everyone else.

So Reedle won the tournament in straight matches, as he always did since my expurgation. Each time he vanquished an opponent he would turn to the stands and find my bright buckles and buttons and slash the air as if he were cutting into my heart. I felt each slash through my grins and salutes. I was not confident in my capacity or the parameters of my moral code.

I made my way down to the dueling field and waited until most of the crowd and carriages had withdrawn from the area. I gave the proper encouraging murmurs and displays of respect and veneration to those who'd lost, shook hands, tapped sword points, and clapped shoulders as the moment called for. When I approached Reedle he turned from me in an ample and obvious showing of contempt, then climbed into his carriage along with his purple sash, sword, and epaulets, and left the games.

My fist tightened on my weapon. My eyes narrowed. I thought to follow. I thought to lunge, lance, riposte, gore, gouge, stab, pierce, plunge, and clean the horse shit from my boots with his finest finery. I was glad that I was not traveling beyond the wall. I did not want to meet myself on the road and look at my face as it might appear at this instant.

I alighted upon my horse's back and rode toward home.

Harella met me outside in the garden, which she was tending to full bloom. I leaped from the horse and unbuckled my buckles and belts and took off the coat and garb and thought about chucking it all in the mud. Instead I folded it and laid it across the marble garden bench I had crafted for her our first year of marriage. I placed my palm upon its smoothness, shut my eyes, and tried to recall my earlier skills, but could only think of rough human hands and the beating of my own unpredictable heart.

I fed and watered the horse as my wife touched me upon the shoulder.

"You must get Livia's child back," Harella said.

"What's happened?"

She tucked her chin in and gave me a look that was both wise and harsh, much more harsh than wise, I thought. "I saw her strike the child this afternoon."

"That's impossible."

"Only if I was dreaming, and I assure you I was awake."

"We do not do—"

"Oh, stop with the 'things we do because we must do them' nonsense. Livia is a mother whose child was stolen. She's capable of anything. You must know that's the truth."

I knew it was the truth.

"Travel again, and return her own flesh to her."

"I can't do that. No one must ask, not even her."

"She's not asking," my wife said. "I am."

"It's not something you can ask. It's not something I can do."

"You swap children. That is your calling. That is what you do. So simply go back and do it again. Swap again."

"That isn't what we do."

"Perhaps you should have considered it more often, instead of blindly performing your duty. Exercising your imperatives. Go get her child or a baby's blood will be on your hands. Can you stand that? Sniff your fists. Do you smell blood yet?"

I did.

Traveling across the wall now, the wall had become a wall of people, huddled in the town square, gathered to watch a hanging.

I drew my slouch hat lower across my brow.

A woman was brought out in the center of the square, rid-ing in the back of a hay cart drawn by two mules. The crowd threw rotted fruit and vegetables and eggs at her while shouting vile and varied insults.

She was matronly, heavyset, soft of features but with a righteous tilt of her chin, a dark gleam in her eye that made me take note. They hadn't tortured her the way they do with some. She wasn't marred at all, except for the eggshells, which meant she had signed a confession without any coercion. She looked as wholesome as humans can, with her hair still set under a milking cap, still wearing an apron.

I saw motherhood in her, nursing, bandaging, healing, life-giving and life-saving. The town crier unfurled his parchment scroll and read off a list of her crimes. They seemed to focus, more or less, around the fact that she had helped other women during difficult pregnancies, healed the sick with herbs and poultices, and once shouted down the queen's taxman who was kicking urchins in an alley.

When they sought to drop the red velvet bag over her head she stiffly refused. She had courage and sought to garner a touch of vengeance upon the crowd by showing them her dead and awful face rather than merely her complacent corpse. The hangman adjusted the knot, and the minister said a lengthy and not altogether appropriate prayer, and the dancers came out and performed their ritual dance, throwing their flowers and veils, and the choir sang two lackluster hymns, and the queen's guard performed a well-choreographed military promenade, then fired the requisite thirty-seven shots at the sky, and the fainters fainted, and the swooners swooned, and panters panted. More than one man drooled. There was a good deal of spitting.

At last the woman was asked to say her last words, but she simply shook her head. Her eyes searched the square, perhaps for family or friends, lovers, a kind expression, a forlorn face. I raised the brim of my hat. Her gaze found mine. She gave me a slight nod and I returned the gesture.

At the moment of death, her grace met my grace. They would carry on together elsewhere, wherever else there is to go afterward.

I returned to the house where I had swapped away Livia's child. I climbed down the chimney and peered about the place, moving through room after empty room. There was no activity. In the bedchambers, no snarls or mewls or murder or lovemaking, no action. In the den, no practicing of the tuba. On the fire, no stew.

Out the front door I skirted and moved about the stables. In the pigpen, the hogs rolled about happily in the mud. Sadly, they all had their heads. My stomach tumbled. Again I wondered, how could oregano possibly be a malfeasance upon one's innards?

A well-trod path led into the woods. I followed for a quarter mile until I heard laughter and music. The pan pipes, the piccolo, the drumming, the triangle. I hid in the brush and looked upon a clearing full of revelers.

Several farming families shared food and wine and played and danced together. It seemed to be one of those farmer celebrations. They were always feasting and frolicking for some agrarian reason or another. A bountiful harvest or the end of a drought or the girth of the maypole. There was always something to excite and extol.

Liva's child of light stood out among them, breathtaking, exquisite, lithesome, and diaphanous amidst the craggy faces and plodding feet of human neighbors.

She was now a nearly grown woman. Time had become mischievous again, and had stretched and sped while I'd been home buckled in my buckles. I guessed seventeen years had unfurled and whirled past. She was blithe with laughter, which bubbled from her and buoyed the mood of the world.

I heard her parents calling to her. Her name was Eva.

Young men lined up for a chance to cavort with her. The music rolled on, the bards and minstrels singing songs named for her. She jigged and jagged and swung in the heavy arms of the farmer men, who whispered in her ear. One proposal after another, no doubt. She held them tightly and planted kisses on their hairy faces, and it was enough for them for the time being, for a while. Eventually she would choose one of them, and the rest would love her from afar and watch while she raised a passel of golden children who would blaze like sunlight.

This world needed her. This world full of hangings. This world could use all the happiness and fairness it could possibly wrangle. They needed our blood as much as we needed theirs.

It was wrong to think I could change the course of my duty. Or steal back a girl who was obviously so happy here. You can't unswap.

I turned to go, and Eva sang a note that only my ears could hear. It was directed at me, I realized. I could hide from the humans but not from her. She called to me, to feast and prance with her.

Sometimes our kind forgot they were not human and went

on to lead the average lives they must lead. But Eva clearly had not forgotten. She recognized me from when she was a baby.

Despite Livia's pain, it wasn't fair that I ask Eva to return beyond the wall and give up her parents and siblings and in-amoratos. I had known better than to come here again. It wasn't the way to fulfill my obligations. Livia would have to learn to accept her human child. She would have to do as she must do. She would have to love as humanity loved. If not, then I supposed Harella and I could raise the swapling.

How much more just could justice be than for me to be Da to a blunt awkward-footed common beastly girl?

For the return trip I had to journey to the human town of Limwelt, where another hanging was occurring in another square. This time there were five women and two goats being hanged. The women were all quite beautiful by human stan-dards, still wearing corsets and flimsy short skirts that showed ample amounts of muscular leg. I moved among the crowd, watching eager faces as the charges were read.

Apparently the women were being executed for entrenching many impure thoughts into the minds of several pubescent boys. The crowd jeered and shook fists. The two goats ap-peared complacent and content with chewing their last mouth-fuls of curd. Then the goats' crimes were read off. They were very similar to the women's crimes. I turned and met the eye of a goat and its grace met my grace. I lifted my hand in farewell. The goat chewed. I spun toward a wall of miscreant, drunken revelers crying for death. The hangman pulled a lever and the crowd gasped in shock and joy, and I was beyond the wall and home again.

Harella was in the garden, fiery and glowing with sweat streaming upon her lovely face. I spread my arms to hug my wife and she barked, "Where's the child? What took you so long? Where's Livia's girl?"

"I couldn't steal her away," I admitted.

"What?"

"She was too happy. She's a child of light in a grossly dark world."

Harella said nothing, and the volume of the nothing rang in my ears until I had to raise my palms and press them to the sides of my head to drown out the silence.

"What's happened?" I asked.

"She never took to the human child. She . . . was abusive."

"Abusive?"

"Yes. With the lash."

"The lash?"

"And her elbows. And sometimes her feet, I suspect."

"Elbows? And—"

"Stop repeating what it is I tell you."

I swallowed. My hands were fists. My fists were red.

"We . . . we are not abusive to children," I said, "not even swapling children, no matter how upset it might make us when we do the thing we must do."

"You sound so naive, my love." She looked at me with eyes that were full of sorrow. A sadness not for abused rosy infants, but for the cruel thieves of such.

"I must see the human girl," I said. "I must visit them. Has she named it yet?"

"Of course. Its name is Grot."

"Grot?" The word was sour on the tongue. "That's quite unpleasant."

"Exactly the purpose of such a name. Livia called the girl that as a curse. And it's what she is. Cursed. She lives alone in the caves down by the beach."

"But—"

"She's seventeen. History has a memory here, too. Don't you know how long it is you've been gone? Aren't you aware?"

I wasn't. This was the first occurrence of time becoming merry with me on this side of the wall. I wondered whether if I looked around too quickly I would see myself glaring and performing evil gestures in my direction.

"The caves?" I repeated. It seemed I could not quit this repetition. My whole life was comprised of recurrence now, like an echo of an echo. Doing the same thing over and again in order to somehow undo it. "Our people allow her to live alone in the caves?"

"They want her there. If she didn't live there by choice, the elders might have forced her there."

"That's not the thing—"

"Stop saying that!"

"Where is Livia?"

"She's left. She's gone. No one knows where. Personally I suspect she has become a siren. It seems to fit with her character, all the crying and lying about on sandbars. All the remoteness, the standing and looking indifferent in the shallows. When the architect goes on journeys to other lands to study foreign buildings, she can swim alongside his vessel and sing to him."

The grief in her eyes, the heartache for me, was almost

more than I could bear. I turned away and saw myself glaring at me. There I was. Myself raised his fist. Myself shook it at me. Myself made stabbing motions as if he wanted to gut me.

I knew of human mothers who brutalized the swapling children in the desperate hope that their own offspring would be returned, but I had never heard of one of our people ever harming a human charge. There was a reason Livia hated humanity. Her great-grandmother had been swapped by my great-Da. Livia had human blood in her, and fell back into savage ways.

"It had to be done," I said weakly. My wife was right. I was naive. I repeated old sentences, commands, and biddings too often. Strange and morbid happenings.

Harella hissed. "And so we defile and thin our blood to save them."

"We thicken our blood. It's not just for them. It's for us as well. It's a necessity."

"So the elders say. So you say."

"Because it's the truth. New blood is needed to avoid dissolution from inbreeding. Consanguinity."

She tucked her chin in. "What's that?"

"It has to do with chromosomes," I explained. "Genetic variation, deleterious alleles."

"What are they?"

"Human words that haven't been invented yet, but which are still very important."

"Auh! You and your talk of curved time and parallel futures and meeting yourself on the road. I think you and your Das have done what you have simply because you've all been crazy."

"A handful of my family have been crazy," I admitted. "But only a handful. A mere pocketful." I tried once again to make her understand. "Our people are long-lived, but there are few of us."

"There are too many already, and far more of the humans, and so we tilt the odds and rush toward our own destruction."

She was right, in her way. We were losing our grace. She was proof of that. So was I. Only someone who was thick with humanity could be called a Cruel Thief of Rosy Infants. It was why I could fence so well. The secret instructions of barbaric humanity were in my blood. My Da had more temperance and dignity than me. And his Da more than him.

"What must I do?" I asked.

Myself leered. Myself continued to gesture obscenely. Myself fled. I took a step after him and stopped. My wife stared at me strangely.

"Go visit Grot," she said. "The girl's fate is not her fault. It's yours. Go explain, if you can. Perhaps it will ease her burden."

I wasn't the only naive one. Harella was idealistic and irrational if she thought you could ever explain people's fate to them. How could I have understood or truly believed the word of my Da before standing in this spot where I now stood, watching myself rush up the road waving his arms in outrage?

I trudged across the city and saw that Livia's architect had indeed built spiring towers higher than the highest ones that had towered across the city before. What Livia must have thought when looking up at those immense, soaring strongholds.

I scampered down the bluff precipices and over the white

sands, on to the caves where colossal black grottos and fissures in the cliff walls beckoned.

"Hello?" I called. "Hello? Is there a Grot in current residence?"

I continued on into the twisting tunnels and cavities. It was far too dark for human eyes to see, but I managed to maneuver well enough down the various shafts, following footprints in the dust. In the distance I saw the flicker of flames.

I called again. "Hello? Greetings?"

"Finally," a voice like a moan, a breathless groan, echoed from the deep stone interior.

Approaching the light, I found myself in a cavern, more a burrow really, with a ring of stones in the center where a fire burned. Meager belongings sat clustered on the thick stalagmites being used as tabletops. Some clothing, bits of leather, pots. Hanging from the walls were nets, ropes, and spears for fishing.

Many more tunnels connected to this hub, opening farther into the cave system. The ceiling was high with chimneystack channels.

I thought of Livia's majestic home on the bluff. I heard her clearly in my mind saying how she hoped the baby would smother itself on her breast. My hands clenched and unclenched as if I were holding on to something and trying hard not to let go.

"Grot?" I called.

The unpleasant name meant to hurt the girl also hurt me in saying it. The elders had been nits, witless nits, not to step in and do something at the first signs of the lash and the elbows. I turned and turned again. I spoke the name. The echoes of heavy breathing filled the burrow. I turned some more, looking for myself and perhaps seeking forgiveness for my mistakes.

I turned and Grot was there in all her malignant resilience.

She'd taken on many aspects of my kind. The angle of the chin, the radiant eye, the fiery expression. But none of the beauty. What had once been plain and blunt was now ugly with scars and welts. The nose, bent. The hair, missing in spots, perhaps torn out. The teeth, chipped. Her back, curved. The arms, well muscled but creaky from old fractures.

Livia, Livia, where did your grace go? I wanted to follow her into the sea and drag her up from the depths.

I put my fingers in my mouth and thought, Da, you never told me what to do when something like this happens. Your instructions were incomplete. I remain less than confident in my capacity. My parameters persist in their unquantification.

I took my fingers from my mouth and parted my lips to speak, to introduce myself and tell her about her true parents, to explain, at least to the extent that I knew, exactly who I was and why we were both here. She slid a curved short blade from the back of her skirts and cut a rope tied to a steel piton hammered into the cave wall. A sound like a hunting bird descending fell from high above, and an iron cage dropped directly atop me.

It was good thick metal, forged properly with hate. Spikes pointed at me like open scissors. Dependably harmful measures.

I was trapped again.

"You," she said. "Cruel Thief. I've been waiting for you."

"Yes."

"At last you've come."

"I've been away."

She moved to the bars and presented herself with the pride of ugliness. "And what have you come to do? What is it you wish to say to me?"

The questions were too large. They were larger than I could fully carry.

"I don't really know," I said.

"Did you wish to tell me about my birth? About my mother? About your duty to exchange the swaplings?"

I nodded. There was little else to do. I flexed my hands and remembered her pinching and gnawing at my index finger, laughing with a laughter no different from Eva's laughter, which shone upon a gloomy land.

"So tell me," she demanded.

"I have nothing to tell you."

"Can you at least say my true name? The name I was born with before you stole me away?"

"I'm not certain I know what it is," I admitted. "I never heard your parents say it. But perhaps . . . perhaps it was Eva."

She mouthed the word, and the tip of a black tongue jutted and flicked itself. "Eva. No, that is not my name. Eva is not my name."

"Probably not."

"So tell me why you would hand me over to . . . my mother."

"Because you were a swapling. By definition, that is what's done with swaplings. They are swapped."

She twined closer so the firelight would blaze across the ruin of her face. She said nothing. I took a breath and turned away in my little cage.

"Occasionally there are," I said, "unhappy occurrences."

"Is that all I am, an occurrence?"

"An unhappy one. In the greater design of fate, I suppose."

It made her smile. It was an ugly smile but a smile nonetheless. I welcomed it.

"Do you know what I'm going to do to you?" she asked. She retrieved a whip from her wall of tools and weapons. She snapped it at my chest, but the bars were too small to allow the lash passage. "I'm going to beat you one thousand eight hundred and sixteen times. That's how often I was whipped by Livia."

"You'll have to lift the cage to do that."

"I can hurt you."

"I know."

"I *will* hurt you. I will boil you. I will burn you."

"You won't be the first, Grot."

"I'll be the worst."

"Yes, perhaps you will be."

She let loose with a cry of frustration and snapped the whip again. The lash struck the bars and fell away once, twice, again and again, her rage feeding on itself. In her rage the end of the whip actually struck her across the cheek twice, but she didn't even notice. The cage rang loudly. Even the sound of iron was enough to bring me pain, but I forced myself to keep from wincing and showing weakness. I thought of Livia hurting this girl day by day and my anger grew. I imagined Grot out on the water in a small boat, hunting her mother with nets and spears. Diving morning after morning, hoping to find the right siren to kill.

The ringing of the iron continued for a long time. Then a voice like the fairest song came from the cavern entrance.

"Sister."

Grot seemed to know the voice although she had never heard it before. She didn't turn to face it, but the muscles of her body locked and her hands tightened around the lash and the curved iron blade. "You return."

"I saw him watching me in the field today, while I was with my human family. I noted his eyes were sad and bemused, and I decided to follow. I tracked him to Limwelt, through the crowd at the hanging, and then beyond to this land. The moment I breathed the air here I remembered my life from before, when I was a baby. I remembered the swapping, and I could guess why he had come to watch me with such pain in his expression."

"If you could guess that much, then you must have guessed the rest. You must know what hate I hold in my heart."

"I suspect."

"And still you sought me out?"

"I had to once I realized what had happened to you."

Grot wheeled, her weapons ready. She glared at Eva, the red welts swelling. "We are not sisters. We're closer than that. You are what I should have been. What I would have been except for him."

"I'm as much to blame as he is. I was aware, even then, when we were newborn and traded away."

Grot nodded, her heavy scarred face pooled with shadow and hate. "So be it, then, you are to blame. As much as he. For an unfair trade."

"A necessary one," I said, but they both ignored me.

Grot's powerful forearms flexed as she tightened her grasp

on the blade. She approached Eva, hunkering low, almost crawling across the cave floor as a mewl escaped her. Inch by inch she covered the distance between her and her sister, her other self. Time seemed to grow playful again. It stopped and started and rushed past. I grabbed hold of the iron bars in frustration and screamed in agony.

"You coveted my life," Grot said, proffering the knife. "You may have what remains of it."

"I didn't covet your life, sister," Eva said, refusing the profferage. Instead she placed a hand to Grot's cheek and softly stroked. "I didn't steal it. We grew to follow our own courses. You were denounced and maltreated."

"Kill me."

"I'm not here for that," Eva told her, the smile to light the world tugging at her lips. "I've come to bring you back home again."

Grot looked up, but gazing upon Eva's beauty only hurt her worse. She averted her eyes and raised her free hand to cover her eyes. "What's this you say?"

"You're coming back with me to the other side of the wall. You're going to meet our mother and father and siblings. We have three brothers and two sisters. We'll teach you."

"Teach me what?"

"Happiness. Friendship. Love. Family."

"I cannot learn that. I cannot even hear that," Grot said, tears sluicing from her eyes.

I nearly said it was impossible, that only my family could go traveling. But here was evidence to the contrary. Clearly Eva had the ability as well. For all I knew all of our people did, and the elders in their wisdom decided long ago to damn only one family to being cruel thieves.

"You will learn it. I will help you. We all will. Now come. Take my hand."

"Is that what you have to offer?"

"It is my first offering."

Grot stared at the blade for another moment, and I wondered what would happen next. Might she lunge? Might she dismember? Might she reverse the angle of the knife point and self-disembowel? The moment was ugly, the expectation too dreadful. The moment after the moment was full of relief as the knife fell from her fist unused, and she reached, inch by inch covering the distance, until she and Eva clasped hands.

Then I watched them leave, walking down the length of the tunnel together, listening to the echoes off the cave walls as their voices took on sisterly whispers. I heard tittering and giggling. I heard joy.

Neither thought of me still trapped in the iron cage, and I couldn't blame them for that. Too much of their lives had already been stamped by my thumbprints. I wished them well on this new odyssey and supposed, in some fashion, I would see them again beyond the wall.

I got to my knees and began to dig. It would take at least two days, maybe three or four, to be free again. Perhaps the earth would scrub away my sins the same way my Da hoped the river would wash away his. Harella was used to my travels and the twisting of time and probably wouldn't come looking for me carrying a pot of hog's head stew to ease my hunger. Myself wouldn't show with a shovel and a compulsion to assist. Myself was waiting for me somewhere farther down the path. I was alone except for the dark secrets of my blood and duty, digging, digging, scrubbing, in preparation for freedom and, with less grace than melancholy, much more damage.

THE SCREAMING ROOM

by Sarah Pinborough

IT HAD BEEN QUIET for too long. She knew that because the serpents whispered in her ears as she slept, awakening memories of when the world had been different. A time before the island, so long ago that most days she barely remembered it at all. Only in these dreams would it come back to her. She had been someone else then—a rare beauty, admired and desired by all. Men would ache for just one glance from her to them alone. Days of love and laughter and constant attention. She'd known her power and she had reveled in it. So many, many moons had passed that she barely recognized herself in the dreams. A stranger's pale arms and slim legs and long blond hair.

The rising sun baked away the chill of the night, and she opened her eyes and sighed. The snakes settled into coils against her scalp, their voices hushed to a gentle hiss here and there. She let one hand run in and between them, enjoying the cool scales that curled momentarily around her fingers. It wasn't their voices that she needed to fill the endless silence. She needed a new singer. It had been an age since she'd been sung to, and she ached for the music. She stretched across the vast bed and ran her hands over her rough body. The softness had gone, replaced by sinew and thick muscle, and her skin was coarse. What magic started, salt water had finished. There was no bathing in milk and water anymore. Now she swam in the ocean's firm grip. As the centuries passed she came to prefer it. Funny how things changed.

Finally, she hauled herself up and rolled her head around her shoulders, easing away the last of the night's tension. She looked down at herself and smiled. She wasn't doing bad for a woman of her age. The snakes hissed, and she allowed herself a small laugh. She still had her sense of humor, and unlike in that land of the past that her dreams took her to, now when she had a man's attention, she knew she had it forever.

In the night more plaster had crumbled from the ceiling, but she ignored the dust that had settled on her sheets. When this part of the palace was ruined she would simply move to a different set of rooms that weren't being destroyed by the plant life that ate its way through the cracks, or hadn't been beaten down by the wind. There were centuries more years of living to be had from this prison fortress. Centuries more silent existence with only the occasional singer to ease her pain. Sometimes she wondered if the loneliness might drive her mad.

The sea sent a breeze dancing through the open windows, and she pulled a silk wrap free from the arms of an old lover and wound it round herself. His arms stayed as they were, stone stretched out toward her. At some point, she was sure, there had been a dagger in his hand, but that was long gone, lost in the underground caves where she stored all the other useless weapons her lovers brought with them. She paused to look at him, something she hadn't done in a long time, and a memory of flesh and skin and blond hair flashed behind her eyes. He had been handsome once, she recalled, even with his mouth fixed forever wide. This one had sung right up until the moment his breath had stopped. She had been fond of him, and he had sung to her for years, much longer than some of the rest. How could she have forgotten? She leaned forward and ran her tongue down his smooth face before leaving him where he stood.

The sun was barely in the sky, and she frowned. She was not normally up so early. She peered out beyond the walls of her derelict palace and to the sparkling crystal of the ocean beyond. The snakes hissed, woken from their slumber, as her heart thumped. She hadn't woken naturally. Something had roused her—sounds not heard for such a long, long time. Sounds that she ached to hear with every passing day. The creak of oars, the cry of voices. They were distant, but real. This time, it wasn't her fevered imagination torturing her with a promise of company only to leave her raging in disappointment for weeks. This time there truly was a brown fleck in the blue—a boat filled with human warmth. She moaned slightly. They were coming. They always came, the beautiful brave men. Her heart raced and heat rushed to her loins. She had to hurry. The boat was still hours away, but she had preparations to make.

By the time she was done, her rough body was thick with sweat and the snakes were writhing and twisting and hissing, unable to settle and fueled by her excitement. She pushed them out of her shining eyes and smiled. Food and wine were laid out on the rocks on the cove where the ship would land. The sun was getting hotter, and she wanted her guests to be comfortable. Heat and wine while they sent their hero to her, that was what they needed. There was only ever one from every boat that climbed the steep cliffs to reach her. None ever followed. Not once the song started. She drained a glass of red, heady wine. It was nearly time for the seduction to start. Her mouth watered in anticipation, thick strands of saliva running through the crevices on either side of her mouth. She wiped them away.

From the beach so far below, hearty cries drifted toward her as the sailors weighed anchor and sent a small rowing boat to her shores. She hurried down to the gloomy atrium on the ground floor of her ancient home. It was cool here, and her breath was wet and hard as she settled onto the chaise lounge hidden in the far shadows. She waited.

It's hot on the island, but wading from the boat to the shore has cooled his skin. He feels energized and ready for the task ahead. His life has been waiting for this moment of destiny. The journey was uneventful and the water clear. This is fate. His heart pounds as his strong legs lead him to where his men are rifling through the plates of food and jugs of wine they've found on the rocks. He can feel the fear that sings clearly from their faces as they glance up at the palace built on the cliff tops, its shadow reaching down to clutch at them.

He's not afraid. He is barely twenty-five and full of adventure and has always known that he is destined for greatness. It's not arrogance—merely a lifetime of being the strongest and most handsome. With his easy charm and quick skills, he has always been picked out as special. He's come to believe that he must be. The whole kingdom can't be wrong. He thinks of the girl waiting for him. She is the prize—the most beautiful girl he has ever seen. She is his destiny and he loves her. He will marry her and they will rule the kingdom when her father is gone. There is just this one thing to do. Bring back the head. Many have tried and failed, but he knows that he's different. He can see it in the faces of those around him. His armor gleams in the sunshine. He smiles at his men and then starts to climb.

The once-opulent chair was now covered in dust, and as she stretched along the full length she could feel the grains settling into the pockmarks on her rough, dark skin. Too many years had passed since she'd lain here, and she never came to the atrium unless receiving visitors. Where the dust came from, she couldn't tell. The ceiling perhaps, or maybe carried down through the levels of her home on a curious breeze. She didn't much care. It was never her furniture they looked at, after all.

Finally, when her pounding heart could barely take any more anticipation, the huge doors at the far end, rusty on their unused hinges, creaked open. The sun flooded in first, stretching almost halfway toward where she was residing in the shadows, and then she heard quick footsteps as leather sandals ran to the nearest pillars. It was like a dance, this game they always played. Her at one end, him at the other; slowly, slowly getting closer until at last their eyes met.

She was sure she could almost hear his heart beating as he paused to weigh up his best approach, and she didn't hush the snakes but let their hungry hisses echo around the marble like a siren song. Here I am, they whispered. Seduce me.

The atrium was well laid out, with many of her former lovers there to greet their newest member, and hide him on his approach. In the space closest to her, however, they were spread farther apart, and this was invariably where the bravest and cleverest succumbed to her charms. They just couldn't help themselves. They had to look. Men always did.

More footsteps rang out, and as he ran between the statues she caught flashes of strong tanned arms and legs. His hair was dark and glossy, pulled back tight on his head. She could change that later. She preferred them with their hair down. She liked to run her fingers through it while they sang. She slid down the chaise lounge and brought herself into view. Sometimes she had more patience for the wooing game, but not this time; she had been too long alone. It was time for him to start his song to her.

The palace is a wreck, and as he runs behind the pillar he nearly gags on the thick scent of rotting flesh that hits him like a wave. He closes his mouth and breathes through his nose. Behind him sunlight pours through the open doors, and he waits for it to bring some fresh air, but if it does, the awful stench overpowers it. He presses his back against the cold, damp stone and closes his eyes for a second, trying to regain the excited sense of purpose and adventure that he'd had on the voyage over. Now that he is alone, he's finding it hard to maintain. Behind him, snakes rattle and hiss, far too loudly for ordinary grass adders, and as his stomach chills he knows that he's not alone—SHE is here. He grips his sword tightly, but his palm is sweaty despite the cool.

The sunshine outside looks inviting. It also looks like it exists in a different world; a world of the ship, and the men, and his sense of being special, and the girl. His mind stops when he thinks of the girl. He can't go back a coward. He left with such great promises to her that if he turns around now, he might as well throw himself from the cliff as climb down it. This is no time to change his mind. He takes a deep breath of the foul air and, because he is a hero after all, calms his pounding heart and studies the layout of the room. Eventually, he runs forward. He keeps his eyes down. He can do this. He can. He can.

He hides behind a statue and pretends not to know what it once was. That's an impossible task, though, with every gray inch of the figure showing how it had once lived and breathed and thought it could kill a monster, just like him. He glances up. The face, now stone, is stretched wide in a final scream. He wonders, for a brief second, whether the man had managed to release that scream before the stone claimed him. The hissing is much closer, and stretched across the filthy marble he can see the shadow of her hideous form. The serpents at her head dance in the dark floor, and his stomach lurches. She is so much more than he had been expecting. Forward. He must go forward.

He starts to run. He's so close now. His sword is held high, ready to swing at her neck. He doesn't care how many attempts it will take and how bloody it becomes, he just wants her head. Someone has to take it—why NOT him? His heart pounds. He lunges forward. He musn't look up. He musn't look up.

He musn't—

And their eyes met. For a moment, the surprise on his face was almost matched by hers. The snakes stilled and stared, for she couldn't remember such a handsome suitor. Then, as the realization of his fate dawned on him, his mouth opened wide and he began to sing. The first songs were always the best. They were fresh and full of energy. She settled back on her chair and fought the urge to touch him. There would be plenty of time for that. He would still be warm and soft for such a long time.

They expected it to be sudden—that's what she always saw on the young, handsome faces in that minute after finding their eyes catching hers. They thought it would be over in an instant, and their naïveté never failed to make her smile. To turn flesh to stone was a tricky business. It could take many long, long years to work its way from the tips of those earthy toes to the tops of their beautiful heads.

This one was no different. His dark eyes told it all. Pain and confusion. She'd seen it before—they thought that while their flesh was still soft and warm, and they breathed the same air as they had before, that somehow they could escape from the frozen state. Only when their feet turned gray and solid did they truly appreciate the journey they were on. The songs always got clearer after that.

She loved the songs.

Somewhere out in the sunlight, the sailors would be preparing their ship to leave. Their hero had been gone too long, and none would want to come up to her palace after him. She pulled the sword free from his hand and let it drop to the floor; her cheek rubbed against the fingers in its place. She sighed. It had been so long since she'd had a man's touch. Her own thick arms wrapped around his torso, and she carried him out of the gloom and up to the bright chamber nearest her bedroom. The snakes slid across his skin, absorbing the smell and taste of his fear. His song filled her palace and she was damp with desire. So much time alone. As she set him down in the center of the vast room, she smiled almost coquettishly from beneath the nest of serpents that hung over one eye. He had nothing to fear from her now. His song grew stronger.

It was funny how things changed. Once, way back in the beginning, when this was a new life for her, she had called this place *the screaming room*. She had tried to cut the snakes from her head and had rubbed her body against the rough walls, wanting her skin to be pale and smooth again. The snakes had grown back and her skin had healed by the time the first visitor came to her island. She'd been so happy—that hadn't changed over the centuries—for some company. She'd thought they'd come to save her.

She'd smiled at him, and then the song had started. It had torn her apart, that song, the thing that was happening to him. Back then, after trying everything to make him whole again, she'd cut out his tongue to silence his noise, to shut him up, to *make it stop*. She'd locked him away and hoped that whatever was happening it would be quicker. Year after year, she would check on him, hoping and praying that it would just be over, until eventually that day came.

Once he was stone, however, she'd found that she missed the company. She'd liked knowing he was there, and that she wasn't alone. By the fourth visitor to her shores, she'd come to love the songs they sang her. It wasn't screaming at all. It was love poetry from a suitor held in her thrall.

She no longer worried whether the loneliness and the snakes were driving her mad. Now she loved the changes in the singers' songs and bodies as the stone claimed them inch by inch. Some days she would simply sit and brush her fingers over the places where the cold hardness met with the warm, perfect skin. She would lean in and lick along the line.

All this was to come.

She left him alone for a while to settle into his new surroundings and changed into her silkiest robes, those that when the light caught them would turn sheer and allow her lover's eyes to see right through to her shape beneath. Along her neck, she dabbed perfumes she'd made from the weeds and plants on the rocks, and she fashioned the calm snakes into perfect rings against her scalp. She waited for evening to fall. She wasn't impatient. She was used to waiting.

Nonononoithurtstoomuchiwanttogohomeidon'tcareaboutthegirlsurelytheyllcomeformeshescomingbackthemonsterandshestouchingmeicantstopscreamingijustwantodiepleaseletmedieicanttakethis. . . .

She knew he was watching her as she lit the candles around the room until they were both bathed in a soft yellow glow. It was flattering lighting, but he didn't need it. She wondered if she'd ever had such a suitor. He was more than handsome. He was charismatic. Women would have fallen at his feet, and when he had grown older he could have led an army into certain death and they would have gone willingly. Not now, though. Not anymore. There was no growing old for him— just years and years of her love and the changing to come. Years of his song.

She danced as he screamed, using his voice as her lute. She swayed and sashayed before him and then, when the flirtation was complete, she wound herself around his still body. She ran her hands over him, gently at first, but as the wine and the lust took her, she groped him roughly, the snakes running over his face, nipping and biting, wanting to taste what they could of him. She dipped her dank tongue into his sweet mouth and was sure she could see her own lust reflected in his glassy eyes. He wanted her—it was just like the old days, the ones she tried so hard to forget and remember, when she was young and lithe and beautiful.

She poured wine into his open mouth and licked the over-spill away.

The night was long and full of love, and when dawn broke she left him to the cool morning air. They had so much time ahead of them, and the brief separation would only make their hunger for each other greater. He sang to her as she slept, and as she slept she was smiling. Her dreams were of love and parties and beauty and of days so long gone by. His song was her lullaby and she let it wrap around her and keep her safe. The loneliness was gone and she was loved again. There would be no more silence, not for years and years and years.

269

WICKED BE

by Heather Graham

I HAVE SPENT MY LIFE trying hard to keep to the shadows, actually, to foster a few of the pagan traits that supposedly belong to my kind, or the modern "Wiccan" mantra, should I say.

"An ye harm none, do what ye will."

Of course, dear friends, you must remember that this is a mantra created by man, or woman, or both—and that like all religious creeds, it can be tempered, twisted, and horrifically modified by man, or woman. But, you see, I've been around a while. I've learned that most of the time, whatever God or gods a man chooses to believe in, it all tends to be pretty good until the hand of man gets in there to decide what the hand of God was meant to be doing.

Take the Inquisition. All that torture and pain in the name of God! I never understood it, and frankly, neither did most God-fearing men and women I knew. Because, come on, witchcraft? Seriously, a man's cow died because a woman looked at it with the evil eye? And, oh, please, really? Dancing naked in the forest with the devil?

But, as I've said, I've spent my life trying hard to keep to the shadows. There was many a case of justice gone far awry that I saw, but mostly, I was forced to keep my head down. Because here's the truth of it—think about it. Had those heretics so woefully tortured during the Inquisition had any powers whatsoever, they'd have given their tormentors the evil eye, and saved themselves. No, sadly, most of the time it's man—or woman, in the cases of so-called witchcraft—who is maligned for color, creed, or choice of belief, and there is nothing of power beneath fragile flesh within them, and that's the way it is. Therefore, they are tortured, and they die, and that's that.

Some say the real persecution of witches began as early as Roman times, and that was certainly true, though the Romans saw witches as "black" or "white," practicing goodness or evil. In the Bible, Lilith was a succubus, and other evil abominations rose. But, of course, none of these things really had anything to do with the Pagan religion of the Scots and Irish back in the day; it was man who decided to mingle a worship of the land and the elements with all the man-made demons of the religions to come. A true "witch" craze began with the *Malleus Maleficarum* in 1486, made all the more widespread because of the "modern" invention of the printing press. It had the power of the Church behind it, too—*Malleus* included the pope's treatise approving the persecution of witches, *Summis desiderantes affectibus* ("Desiring with Supreme Ardor," no joke), as a preface. The pope might have been a good man. I didn't know him. But his blessing on the persecutions certainly had nothing to do with the purity of any kind of a God! Yet I digress.

I've frankly always wondered what makes any creature

beneath God's eyes assume himself—or herself!—superior to others. But in the 1600s, remember, we were dealing with the Divine Right of Kings, etcetera and so on. Besides, I've been around a while now, and man's inhumanity to man has never ceased to amaze me.

So, as I've said, in the interest of self-preservation, I've always maintained a low profile!

I love my homeland—Scotland—but as time went on, things began getting a little uncomfortable there. It was James—sad, tragic boy, really. I mean, let's face it, much as I wanted to like his mother, Queen Mary of Scotland, she was ruled by her heart and no wisdom, and James grew up with a lot of old men teaching him the ways of religion; then he went to Denmark, and he was convinced witches existed, and so on and so on, and he started terrible persecutions, even before he became James the First of England. That was the early 1600s, and by the middle of the century, it was getting truly wretched. I mean, really—just what gave so many of those men their absolute superiority, their certainty that they knew what God wanted?

I watched friends and neighbors fall, begging to be put to death. And, you see, in Scotland, they burned witches, while they hanged them in England. It wasn't supposed to be a particularly painful death—a good man strangled a witch first—but the burning purified everything, you see. Makes sense, huh?

However, when I heard a group of religious reformers had moved across the great expanse of the Atlantic Ocean, I decided it was time for me to go, too.

Here, of course, I question my own stupidity and reason. The voyage itself was positively unbearable—I admit to playing mind games myself, and leaving the ship, soaring high above it in spirit and peace while those aboard vomited violently, caught fevers, and died. Many a body was cast to the sea, and I thought, when my time came, if it should in the earthly realm, I would like to be cast back to the sea, the cradle of life, so many believed.

Then, at last, we came to the shores of New England, and I thought I had found my place, a bit out of the major town, in the area just south of what they were calling Marblehead.

At first, I was quite happy, even though I wasn't fond of being called "Goody" Stuart. My given name is Melissa, and I'm rather fond of it. Of course, I managed to befriend a new group of people who hadn't known me; I was starting fresh. I was, as ever, in my first year of my twenties, and I was, if I do say so myself, quite beautiful. I had the bright blue eyes that marked many a Scot, and the near pitch-black hair that went so well with them. I was lithe, full of health and radiance, and happy in my new world. I was fond of the native population, who all seemed to recognize something in me, and I got along quite well with my neighbors in the woods, even when the others of "my" kind were busy with their guns and swords and armor, defending themselves.

Then again, I am a creature of the underworld, that underworld which must not be acknowledged, or, if so, imagined as nothing short of sin.

I didn't see myself as sinful; I saw myself as happy, appreciative of God's great wonder in the world. Of course, to me, that wonder did come to include an extremely handsome young man known as Caleb Martin.

Caleb was one of those reformers who had come to the New World. He didn't believe in idolatry; he did believe in hard work and the goodness of man.

I am a creature of the flesh. I was madly in love with the man—and in love with his flesh—and I didn't need a license to enjoy it. But here I was, playing the game of the "Godly" and the religious, and when he wanted marriage, I agreed.

There was one snag. We had to apply for our marriage, and the "law" in the area was a man named Samuel Bridgewater. He had come across the Atlantic for freedom of religion—but he quickly expelled any man who didn't believe in *his* religion.

I almost acted up then, and I suppose I should have. But I was in love. And Caleb believed strongly in his God, and in his community. I believed in Caleb.

Things might have gone badly. On board the ship that had brought us, Samuel had suggested to me that since I was from Scotland, and new to the group, I should consent to be his wife. He could protect me in the New World. I was saved from this fate worse than death when Caleb happened upon us with several of the other men, and Samuel was forced to withdraw. Caleb's love for me was obvious, and with everyone seeing our true love and devotion, Samuel Bridgewater could either give us his consent to marry—or show his true colors as lecherous old bastard. Samuel Bridgewater wanted power more than he wanted me.

I noticed soon after that Samuel Bridgewater turned his focus and attention on Caleb's sister, Elizabeth.

But she was in love, too, with a handsome young fellow named Josiah.

And, when we came to the New World, it seemed we would live happily. Elizabeth married her Josiah, and I had my precious Caleb.

We were living, in my mind, a wonderful life. Caleb went off by day to work our fields; we built a charming house with friends. We were by the sea, and I'd seldom seen anything more beautiful than the whitecaps crashing against the coast. In time, Caleb took to the sea occasionally, but I was never afraid; I would follow him at times in spirit, soaring over those whitecaps and watching the men as they sought to evade pirates and find the great catch. I knew that Caleb would always come home to me.

And then we would have those nights. I'd see the look in his eyes when he returned to land, and I would quickly be in his arms, and by night I would watch the firelight play upon his bronzed flesh, and I would be in ecstasy, wondering only how I would explain myself when the years went by, and wishing there were some magic that could turn him to what I was, and that we could be together forever.

Elizabeth and Josiah lived nearby, and she gave birth to a lovely little girl, and I stood in the church again as she was baptized, and I looked at the radiance in Elizabeth's eyes, and I was sorry that Caleb and I would never know such magic. Caleb didn't seem to care. We were happy together.

Happiness, apparently, can't be an eternal state. Caleb and I took a trip to the north; somehow, my darling Caleb, like myself, had an affinity with the native population, and he had been asked to negotiate with a tribal council. I enjoyed our trip, especially heading up to Gloucester, where, once again, the natural beauty of the earth seemed joyous itself.

I suppose I should add here that one flaw to our lives, in my mind, was the ten hours we spent each Sunday listening to the various preachers in church. I mean, seriously, if there were devils living in the woods, making pacts with young girls, I would have known about it. But that's the way it was. I had cast my lot with a group that seemed to believe that they knew what God was saying when other men did not understand.

I sat there many a Sunday silently longing to tell them that they didn't have any better communication with God than any other man, including the "pagan redskins" they thought to be such terrible sinners, no better than beasts, sure to rot in the fires of hell when they passed. I kept my silence, because I was in love with the beauty of the coast, and Caleb.

So it was that we returned from our trip up the coast to find that Elizabeth had been arrested—for witchcraft.

Two local girls swore that they'd seen her with a cloven-hoofed devil in the woods; he'd had a book, and she'd signed it, stripped off her clothing, and started dancing in the woods.

Samuel Bridgewater was our local judge, magistrate—power. He truly believed that he had the ear of God, and that God had given him complete authority in matters of sin and heresy and all such other rot. Bridgewater had nearly caused the extinction of our kind in the area, since he had deemed a nephew of a local chief to be Satan himself, and he'd executed the boy. Twenty men had died in defending our little colony, and it had been my dear beloved Caleb who had spoken with the chief at last, and compared those twenty lives lost to the one of the chief's nephew, and thus brought about peace again.

But I honestly believe that the worst of all was the simple

fact that Elizabeth had rejected Samuel Bridgewater, and he meant to get his revenge.

He didn't like being rejected.

He hated me by then, and yet, perhaps, somewhere inside himself he had the good sense to stay away from me.

But, you see, Elizabeth was my sister now, and I loved her.

Elizabeth had been in love with Josiah for as long as I had known her and Caleb. Samuel Bridgewater was an old, creepy-looking, evil little man—whether he claimed the ear of God or not. Elizabeth and I had giggled over him often enough. We knew that he had managed to force some of the village lasses to do his bidding. It was despicable, but as Caleb told me, we were not to judge others but to live our own lives.

I had thought Samuel Bridgewater a pompous ass, but not as harmful as he would prove to be. I wanted to at least blind him after the affair with the chief's nephew, but I kept myself under control; I was in love with Caleb.

Oh, how foolish! Samuel, it seemed, was getting his revenge.

Elizabeth was arrested and brought to jail; her husband was crying by the fire every night, and her beautiful baby girl had been left without a mother, though they were talking about charging her baby as well!

We watched and waited while Elizabeth's trial date approached. I was itching to do something but praying that all would be well. Again, Caleb believed in the law, and in the goodness of men. "Bridgewater is misadvised; he is not a monster. This will not continue," Caleb told me. "This is our home; we will abide by the law, and make it a good one."

I loved him, and so I agreed.

But then came more of the ridiculous testimony against

Elizabeth. Oh, the things that people said! And then my darling Caleb took matters into his own hands.

He stood before the judges and gave them a piece of his mind. He ridiculed them for being idiots, ready to believe mischievous girls who were probably afraid of being in trouble themselves for having been caught in the woods.

"An infant!" Caleb roared, his dark eyes flashing, his handsome features intense. "You would accuse an infant, one of God's sweet innocents, of being guilty of witchcraft? Are you daft, men? Are you daft? My sister is as sweet and saintly as any woman might be, and yet, because of the outrageous accusations of others, you chain her at night? As my good friend John Proctor said, these girls will make devils of us all! Have you no sense, my fellow men of God? What great power would allow such absurdity to exist? Look to your souls, men!"

Ah, my poor Caleb. Somehow, he had forgotten that despite his words, John Proctor had found himself then accused of witchcraft.

Oh, those wretched girls! One of them suddenly fell to the floor, tearing at her hair. "He looked at me!" she cried. "He looked at me! And now . . . the pain, oh, dearest God, help me! The pain!"

I started to rise; Caleb looked at me and shook his head. But before I knew it, Caleb was being shackled and dragged away to join his sister.

I fought my way into being able to see him; I wanted to do something drastic, but he smoothed my hair back. "You are still free; we need you out there. We need the help of the governor, for he is a righteous man, and perhaps he can stop this madness. You must go to him, and quickly."

The death toll was mounting; already, we had seen so many innocents hanged. They had been the pious, the elderly, like Rebecca Nurse. They had been the outcasts, those suspected of sleeping with men without the benefit of marriage, like poor Bridget Bishop.

"Caleb, I'm afraid to leave you," I said. Then I started speaking quickly, in a whisper. "Caleb, if you will just trust me . . . we can get out of here with Elizabeth and the baby and her husband . . . please, believe in me, I can do this!"

"I believe in the law," he told me, his eyes gentle and beautiful, and he stroked my hair. "Get to the governor, and all will be well," he assured me. "I believe in God, and in the law, and God will force men to see the truth and the error of their ways."

Let me say right off that I certainly believed in God more than anyone; I *knew* that there was a great father, and I had led my life hoping to seek his good graces, despite the circumstances of my birth into a species that was not considered to be among the saintly.

I knew, too, that he preferred men to discover their own mistakes; he taught lessons, but on his own terms and in his own time, and I wasn't ready to let him save Caleb and Elizabeth.

"Believe in me, and in goodness, my beloved. Get to the governor," he told me.

I was so in love with him. Caleb was tall and strong, and ever beautiful and steady, as determined as a rock to stand against the crashing waves of the insanity occurring here.

I used the last of our savings to pay for his and Elizabeth's stays in jail; I comforted Josiah, her husband, and I left him like a lost lamb to care for the baby. I headed off to find the governor.

Well, by that time, the governor's wife had been accused, and the man was suddenly awakened to the insanity of it all. It was one thing to accuse poor old deaf women and possible whores, and quite another to accuse the governor's wife.

I was halfway to Boston when I received this information. I quickly turned around, knowing that a stay had been put on all the executions.

As I returned, I heard horrible stories. Giles Corey—whom I couldn't feel too badly for, since he had given testimony against his wife—had been pressed to death. He had cursed Salem and the sheriff before he had died. It had all gotten worse; news traveled so slowly that people were being executed even after the order that it all cease until we heard from Mother England.

As this news reached me, I panicked. Old Samuel didn't have the power to go against the judges in Salem, but he was a bastard through and through.

When I reached our little town, the streets were empty. I went to Elizabeth's house, and I found Josiah there. He was on the floor; he had been struck and knocked out, and the baby had been taken.

I patched him up as quickly as I could, but he couldn't walk. I had to leave him. I hurried to the town square.

I arrived in time to see that Elizabeth's body lay at the side of the hanging tree; my beloved Caleb was about to be pushed from the ladder.

Like George Burroughs, onetime minister, my dearest Caleb was saying the Lord's Prayer, and to no avail.

"No!" I shouted the word, and as I did so, my fury entered into the air, and the wind picked up and lightning struck.

"You see!" Samuel Bridgewater called from the back of his

horse. "It's she; it's she who is the witch, she who dances with Satan, and she has infected them all!"

Dance with Satan? I'd never liked the little bastard of a fallen angel, and I had no intention of dancing with him. The very concept was totally inane.

I ran to the circle before him and I stared at him with all the fires of hell arising in my eyes. "Witches! Wizards? You accuse these people. You wretched bastard! If they were witches, they'd have made you pay."

Samuel Bridgewater stared at me. He smiled icily. He knew they had no power.

What he didn't know was that I did.

"Hang him!" he roared, referring to Caleb.

I turned, and not in time. For a brief moment, I saw the love in my husband's eyes—and then I saw him swing, and I heard as his neck snapped, and I knew that he, like Elizabeth, was dead. Something inside of me broke at that moment—including self-preservation.

"String up the infant!" Samuel Bridgewater shouted loudly. "Thou shalt not suffer a witch to live!"

And they called me a monster!

I lifted my arms, and I called upon my powers, and all the powers of death and evil and destruction. I pointed at Samuel Bridgewater.

"Let that which claims piety and is nothing but evil suffer all the tortures and agonies of the truly damned, and let the self-righteous learn the truth of love—and vengeance!"

Well, I must say, having bottled up my powers for all those years served me well. Lightning started raining across the sky and striking the ground. Fires burst out everywhere, and the wretched executioner—who had been about to string up Elizabeth's infant daughter!—quickly climbed down the ladder with the child. He ran to where I stood, delivering the baby to my feet and falling to his knees.

"Spare me!" he cried.

I didn't give a damn about the fool. He was a lackey, obeying Samuel Bridgewater, lest he find himself strung up.

Oh, no.

It was Bridgewater I was after.

"Dance with the devil, eh?" I said. I walked toward him, now surrounded by a raging fire myself. I fell to my knees by the body of Elizabeth, and I cradled her in my arms.

"Dance with the devil!" I roared again, and I passed her broken body to him. With sightless eyes, her body began to animate, to jerk and twitch, and drag him along. And there, in a sea of fire and a wind that roared with the power of a nor'easter, Samuel Bridgewater danced through the copse with the body of the woman he had coveted—and killed.

And he screamed, and screamed, for her body had become fire, and he couldn't free himself from her, so where they touched, he burned and burned.

I was from Scotland. Witches were burned there. And if there had ever been a man who might be considered an evil witch, in my mind, it was Samuel Bridgewater.

Finally he was screaming so incoherently and in such agony that I walked back to him. I didn't give a damn about his pain; I wanted him to understand me.

"I will let you die, you wretched piece of human refuse!" I assured him. "But first you must know! You must see the truth. Evil is not in a color or a species or a religion; evil is more alive in your heart than in any true witch or wizard! You are the monster!"

He started to point at me. He started to say that I was truly a monster, and all there must know it. But his lips caught fire.

And, at last, in a flurry of fire and ash, he disintegrated at my feet.

The wind died; the fires died. My heart was broken; my fury and vengeance were spent.

There were a number of people from the town there, in that copse that surrounded the hanging tree.

And they all just stared at me.

I realized then, of course, that I had showed everyone there exactly what I was. Not a young woman who danced in the woods with the devil, and no twisted fool who had signed a pact with Satan.

No, I was the real thing. I could kill their cows, I could cause heart attacks, I could perpetuate all the evil of which they were accusing others.

Try to string up a real witch?

Not likely!

Yet that was no solace. He had managed the real evil of murder, because I had believed in my beloved Caleb and tried to be the good wife following the law.

My temper and my pain had gotten the best of me. Despite my years with Caleb, I hadn't gotten over that Old Testament sentimentality.

An eye for an eye, a life for a life.

But now Samuel Bridgewater was dead. And the towns-people were staring at me. They would be afraid to touch me, of course, but that didn't matter much. I would be an outcast.

Still, what did I care? My Caleb was gone. Elizabeth, my best friend, was gone as well.

But, of course, there was her precious daughter, another little Elizabeth, at my feet.

My heart ripped in two, my eyes filling with tears, I was startled when Ian Freeman, one of the respected townsmen, came to me. He didn't fall on his knees; he was truly a good man and worshipped his one God.

But he bowed his head to me. "Please!" he said, and I thought he was going to beg for all their lives.

"Please, stay, help us," he said.

I smiled dryly. "I am the monster you fear," I told him.

He shook his head solemnly. "Well may they call you monster; to us, you are salvation. One man's monster is another man's beloved friend," he told me. "Forgive us; forgive us that we all became afraid of the threat, not of a monster, but of a man. Stay, we beg you."

I didn't know if I could. I had acted too late; the man I loved and my best friend were dead.

But Josiah was still there, a broken man, and little baby Elizabeth.

I nodded. I would stay.

There were no more arrests and no more executions in our area. I raised little Elizabeth with all the love that I had given her uncle and her mother. I tended to Josiah, who remained a broken man, a ghost of the fine human being he had once been.

I saw Sheriff Corwin, who had caused all the misery in Salem.

I smiled at him.

He had a heart attack and died.

That made me happy. Call me evil; that made me happy.

In due time, of course, Elizabeth grew up and married. I stayed near her.

I watched as the time of witches came and went; I watched the American people gather and fight the Revolution, and I stayed with my new family. I was the beautiful aunt who never seemed to age.

After the Revolution, we moved south. I saw the evil of another war, as states seceded, as men died pathetically on that battlefield.

I watched more and more wars; I watched the descendants of Elizabeth and Josiah as they gave their passions to their causes, as they lived and died.

I watched the laws change, so that men could not be persecuted for their beliefs, for their color, for their sexual orientation. I watched all this with pride and pleasure, and I held my secrets about myself to myself.

I still watch. Because, no matter what the laws say, monsters live.

SPECIMEN 313

by Jeff Strand

MAX, WHOSE REAL NAME WAS SPECIMEN 278, tried to be happy as he digested the arm. It had been a delicious meal for sure (he didn't get to eat humans very often, so it was always a special treat), but he felt somehow unsatisfied. Not *hungry*, necessarily, just sort of . . . unfulfilled.

He shifted in his dirt a bit. Almost watering time. Maybe that was the problem—his soil was too dry, and it was keeping him from enjoying his dinner.

Could be.

Probably not.

He'd actually felt this way for the past couple of days. Kind of bored. Kind of sad. There were plenty of things going on in the greenhouse laboratory for him to watch, including a minor rampage by Specimen 201 that ended with the unfortunate plant being clipped to shreds with a pair of garden shears, but none of them captured his interest the way they had in the past.

He wished he had a means to communicate with humans. It would be nice to be able to ask Dr. Prethorius about why he might be feeling this way. He hoped he wasn't sick.

Dr. Prethorius certainly wasn't down in the dumps. The scientist had let out his usual high-pitched cackle when Max's powerful leaves slammed shut over the vagrant's arm, severing it at the shoulder, and he'd laughed so hard that tears flowed down his cheeks as he used a shovel to deliver more blows to the head than were probably necessary.

"One for you, and one for you, and one for you," he'd said, tossing pieces of the vagrant to the hungry plants. "And one for you, and one for me . . . no, just kidding . . . and one for you."

Max had been very proud at that moment. After all, most of the specimens couldn't even bite off a finger, much less an entire arm. Of the last five hobos who'd perished in the greenhouse, Dr. Prethorius had seen fit to lure three of them to Max's area. Max wasn't the biggest plant in the lab—in fact, he wasn't even the biggest of the gene-spliced Venus flytraps— but he was the deadliest.

Normally that made him feel great.

Not now.

If he could have let out a deep, sad sigh, he would have. But he couldn't. All he could do was wait and hope that he'd feel better soon.

Transplant day . . . ?

There was no more frightening sight in the greenhouse than Dr. Prethorius picking up the large shovel that rested against the far wall. Sometimes it simply meant that a plant was being moved to a new spot, but more often it meant that a particular experiment was over.

"Hello, hello," said the doctor, walking straight toward

Max. His eyes were red and glassy, but he wore his usual smile. "Need to get a bigger greenhouse, yes I do. Hate to see plants go to waste. But, try as I might, I can't seem to make a tree that grows money!"

He laughed at his joke, which he'd used before, and then regarded Specimen 47, Charlie, who had been planted to Max's right for as long as he could remember. Charlie was noncarnivorous and covered with pretty red and yellow flowers, and was always pleasant if not particularly fascinating.

Max's leaves stiffened as Dr. Prethorius plunged the shovel into the dirt.

"Time to go, time to go," said the doctor in a singsong voice. "Out with the old, in with the new, it's good for me, too bad for you."

Max watched in horror as the doctor scooped out shovelful after shovelful of dirt. He hadn't forgotten what had happened to Specimen 159, who'd been dug up and discarded— thrown into a corner. It took the plant several agonizing days to dry up and starve to death.

After a few minutes of work, the doctor wrapped his arms around Charlie and pulled him out by the roots. He dragged the plant away, leaving a trail of red and yellow petals.

Poor Charlie.

Max tried to use Charlie's fate to make himself feel better. After all, he was unhappy, but at least he was still firmly planted in the dirt.

It didn't work. He was sadder than ever.

When Max uncurled his leaves upon the morning light, he had a new neighbor. Another Venus flytrap. The new plant was a darker shade of green than Max, and about a foot shorter, with leaves that were narrower.

Max was surprised. Usually the new plants were bigger than the old ones. What made her so special?

Oh. That was it. His new neighbor was a "she."

Max's mood suddenly improved. He twitched his front leaves. *Hello, there.*

Hi.

I'm Max.

I think I'm Specimen 313.

Glad to meet you. You'll like it here.

I don't think I will.

It's really not that bad. Once you get used to it you'll be fine, I promise.

I don't feel like talking now, if that's okay.

Max stopped twitching his leaves. He didn't blame her. The greenhouse was not as comfortable as the garden where he'd grown up (had she grown up there, too?). There he got to be outside and see the real sun instead of just light through the ceiling, and he got to feel a breeze sometimes, and though he couldn't actually go anyplace else, he *felt* like he could leave if he wanted.

So if Specimen 313 had been in the garden yesterday and was moved to the greenhouse today, he completely understood if she didn't want to talk. That was fine. He'd just wait for something to happen, like he always did.

About an hour later, Dr. Prethorius walked over with his plastic watering can. The greenhouse had an automated sprinkler system, but the doctor still used the watering can every once in a while. "Hello, Jenny," he said as he watered her. "Are you adjusting to your new home? I have a guest waiting to see you, but I wanted to make sure you hadn't fallen over first!" He giggled. "I'll be right back, so don't go anywhere."

The doctor left.

I don't want to be here, said Jenny.

You'll learn to like it.

No. I won't.

She didn't say anything else. When the doctor returned, he was with an old man who had a thick beard and a dirty jacket. The old man looked around at the other plants, mouth slightly ajar, and almost tripped over a hose.

"Careful, now. Careful," said the doctor. He gestured to Jenny. "And here it is. The prize of my collection. Specimen 313."

The old man wiped his nose on his sleeve. "That's a pretty big plant."

"Indeed it is."

"That one of those fly-eating ones? Those trap ones? You know, that . . ." He moved his hands together to mime a closing trap.

"Again you are correct. How does somebody with your level of intellect end up living out of a cardboard box?"

The old man lowered his eyes. "Bad luck, I guess."

"I certainly hope you weren't naughty with the crack cocaine. So do you like my plant?"

"Yeah, it's kind of neat. Did I look at it long enough? Do I get my twenty bucks now?"

Max realized that he was not jealous at all that Jenny was going to get to eat the old man. Normally he was a little bit jealous—not a lot, just a bit—but with Jenny, he only hoped that it would make her feel better. When she had chunks of that old man digesting inside of her, she'd know that this was a welcoming place.

"Almost, almost, not quite yet," said Dr. Prethorius. "Just a couple more minutes. It took a great deal of crossbreeding to create such an impressive specimen, and I want to make sure you take in the details."

"So . . . why me?" asked the old man. "I ain't got no appreciation for plants. Shouldn't you have those people from that Nobel Prize thing here?"

"They don't appreciate true invention. Those cowards are just as likely to contact the authorities as they are to bestow a prize. That's why I need you. Somebody simpler of mind. Somebody who makes a good . . . fly."

Jenny suddenly bent forward, leaves wide open. The old man let out a quick shriek that was cut off as her leaves closed over the top half of his body with a loud *crunch*.

Max had never seen anything like that!

The old man's legs and waist dropped to the ground. Some blood trickled from between Jenny's leaves as she . . . was she actually *chewing*?

Incredible.

Dr. Prethorius squealed with laughter and danced in a merry circle. "It worked! It worked! I never imagined that it could work so well!"

Jenny opened up her leaves, revealing a skull and rib cage, then bent down and gobbled up the lower half of the man's body.

Dr. Prethorius laughed even louder. "Shoes and all! She ate him shoes and all! They all ridiculed me, but now it is I who will be administering the ridicule! And she hasn't even displayed her full potential! We'll see who's not a genius!"

He laughed for a while longer and then left.

Max twitched his leaves. *How was he?*

Not bad. His beard was awful. It tasted like smoke.

I liked the way you did that.

Thank you. Jenny seemed genuinely pleased.

Had you planned to do it exactly when the doctor told him he needed somebody who made a good fly?

I didn't know what the doctor was going to say. It just felt like the right moment.

It was.

Thank you.

Had you ever eaten any humans before?

Not whole.

So never live ones?

Oh, I've eaten them alive. The doctor removed somebody's arms and legs and fed me his torso.

Nice.

He screamed a lot.

That's understandable.

Want to hear something weird?

Of course.

The doctor looked around to make sure nobody was watching—I guess we don't count—and then he bit off one of the toes.

Seriously?

Yeah. He spat it out quickly, though.

He must not appreciate the finer things in life.

Hey, Max?

293

Yes?
Thanks for being nice to me.
No problem.

"I said, walk over to the plant!" said Dr. Prethorius, jabbing the barrel of the revolver into the young woman's back. She sobbed and pleaded incoherently and fell to her knees.

"Get up! I said, get up!"

"Please!" she wailed.

Dr. Prethorius kicked her. "Are you trying to get yourself killed? Is that what you want? Get up and go see the plant!"

"Please! I have a baby at home!"

Dr. Prethorius kicked her again. "Get up! Get up! Get up! It's not that hard! Just get up and . . . you know what? Fine. Don't."

He shot the woman in the back of the head. Her entire body went limp.

Dr. Prethorius crouched down next to her. He stared at her for so long that Max thought he might have become one of those zombies he occasionally experimented with creating, but finally he sprang back to life. "Well, that was no good. Shouldn't have let that happen. Not scientific at all."

He took her by the hands and dragged her along the path. He stopped in front of Jenny, regarded her for a moment, and then shrugged and looked back at Max. "You might as well have this one. Such a waste."

Max happily opened his leaves. The doctor pulled the woman to her feet and held her so that her arm was right next to Max's leaves. He bit it off. The doctor repeated the process with the other arm, then let the woman's body fall to the ground again.

"Maybe I'll grind up the rest of her and mix her into the soil," he said, stroking his chin. "I haven't used my meat grinder in a while. The gears might be rusty. I don't know how well it will do on a big-boned girl like her, but the worst that can happen is my meat grinder gets jammed, and that's really not such a big deal, now is it?"

Dr. Prethorius walked away, leaving the armless corpse between Max and Jenny. Max wasn't disappointed that his meal had been cut short; after all, two arms was still a feast, even if he would have rather eaten her legs, given the choice. If the doctor ground her into fertilizer, then everybody could enjoy her, including the daffodils—Specimens 195 and 196—who had probably never tasted a drop of blood in their lives.

But what did he mean by *You might as well have this one*? Might as well?

Max couldn't bend forward and snatch prey like Jenny, but he was far from obsolete, right? He could still bite arms off, or heads, or whatever parts the good doctor wanted bit off. Perhaps he couldn't bite somebody completely in half or swallow them whole, but why would you even *need* that skill?

He was still one of the most vicious plants in the greenhouse. By far.

Sorry you didn't get any, he told Jenny. *He usually shares better.*

It's okay. I'm not that hungry.

The pool of blood is getting close. You might be able to bend over and slurp it up.

Thanks, but I don't need leftovers.

What do you mean?

I'm sorry. That was rude. I didn't mean anything by it. Jenny

295

bent all the way down to the ground, stayed there for a few seconds, then sprang back to an upright position. *I can't reach the blood yet.*

It's still moving. It'll get there soon.

I'm really sorry about that. I didn't mean that your half-eaten meals were leftovers. I'd like to share. Really.

I know what you meant. I totally understand.

Specimen 90 was dug up and discarded the next morning. He hadn't come out of the ground easily, and finally the doctor had taken an axe to his roots. Most of the specimens perished fairly quietly, but not Specimen 90. He called them all monsters for just watching him die. Said he hoped that the greenhouse caught fire and that they all burned to death.

Max felt sorry for him, truly he did, but there was nothing any of the others could do. Getting to spend time around Jenny had brought some of the pleasure back to Max's life, and he was secretly relieved when Specimen 90 died after only one night out of the dirt.

The day after that, Dr. Prethorius walked through the greenhouse with a baby. All of the plants grew extremely excited, and Jenny stretched forward as far as she could, but the doctor walked around the entire lab without offering the baby to anybody. He manipulated the baby's hand to wave good-bye and then left.

I think that was his grandson, said Max. *He's mentioned him before.*

Oh well. We can't expect him to feed us his grandson.

Nope.

*   *   *

Are you feeling okay? asked Jenny.

Why?

Your leaves are lighter today.

No, I feel fine.

Good.

"Hmmmmm," said Dr. Prethorius, plucking off one of Max's leaves—a small one near the bottom. He turned the leaf around, looking at it from a few different angles, and frowned. "Hmmmmm."

I'm scared.

You'll be fine, Max.

What do you think he's going to do to me?

He's not going to do anything to you. One vagrant in your trap and you'll be good as new, I promise.

No. I don't need human flesh to survive. It's just a treat. There's something else wrong with me.

Maybe your dietary needs have changed. It happens all the time. You need to stop worrying.

I don't want to die.

You won't.

I love you, Jenny.

What?

Max hadn't actually meant to say that. He tried to decide if it would be better to take it back and pretend that she'd misunderstood him, or leave it out there.

If he was going to die, he wanted to die happy.

I love you, he repeated.

297

Oh.

Oh?

What do you want me to say?

I don't know.

I like you a lot, Max. I like you better than anybody else in the whole greenhouse, even the sunflower. You're my best friend. I just don't see you in that way.

Okay.

Don't be mad.

I'm not mad.

Don't be sad, either.

I can be a little sad, right? It's okay. I understand. I can't devour victims as well as you. You need somebody who can be more ferocious.

It's not that at all. I'm just not looking for anything like that right now. This is all still new to me.

All right.

Promise me that you're okay.

I'm okay.

Promise me.

I promise.

Dr. Prethorius dragged the shovel along the path, whistling a happy tune.

"Life," he said, stopping in front of Max. "It's so filled with unexpected twists and turns. One minute you're happily planted in the ground, and the next minute you're tossed aside, ready to make way for Specimen 314."

No! This couldn't happen! There were dozens of other plants

that were much less advanced than him! He wasn't *that* sick. Why would the doctor kill him instead of one of the lesser specimens? It wasn't fair!

"Of course, that won't happen to you," said Dr. Prethorius. "The discarding, I mean. I've invented a new acid test, and you'll be perfect for it!" He giggled. "Acid on the leaves, acid on the leaves, watch them sizzle, watch them fizzle!"

He pressed the shovel into the dirt, then stomped on it. As he scooped out the first shovelful of soil, Max frantically opened and closed his leaves.

"Trying to bite my face off, huh? Naughty, naughty. What am I to do with such a misbehaving plant? Oh, I know. Acid on the leaves, acid on the leaves, watch them disintegrate, watch them . . ."

He spun around. Jenny sprang back up to her normal position.

"Trying to eat your master, are you? We can't have that. Oh, no, we can't have that at all. I realize that I bred you specifically to hunger for human flesh, but you're not supposed to crave *my* human flesh, oh, no, that's not right!"

He pulled the shovel back, preparing for a powerful swing, and then bashed it into Jenny. She bent backward, bounced back up, and then took a second hit with the shovel.

This time she stayed down.

No!

"It's sad times for the world of science when one's own creations try to attack him," Dr. Prethorius muttered. "Sad times indeed. I had such high hopes for Specimen 313. Oh well. Plenty of acid to go around."

He returned his attention to Max and began to dig out more shovelfuls of soil. His eyes were wild and he flung each scoop of dirt as far as he could, hitting several of the other specimens.

Max had never been so terrified. He opened and closed his leaves, figuring that at this point it didn't really matter if Dr. Prethorius got mad at him, but the doctor kept himself well out of harm's way.

Behind him, Jenny lay on the ground, unmoving.

"They all laughed at me, you know," said the doctor. "When I grew the world's largest pumpkin, oh, they were filled with praise, but when I carved it into the world's largest jack-o'-lantern, they called me mad! I ask you, would a madman create a cherry tree with fruits that ooze deadly poison? Would a madman develop blades of grass sharp enough to slice off your fingers?" His digging became even more frantic.

Poor, poor Jenny. She shouldn't have tried to save him.

Max tilted forward as the next scoop of dirt came from underneath his roots. And then he realized that Jenny was slowly rising up again.

Don't do it! he said. *He'll kill you! It's too late for me!*

Jenny straightened up completely but did not bend forward. Yet she continued to strain at something.

What are you doing?

Be quiet. I can't concentrate.

Don't do anything!

Be quiet!

With the next scoop of dirt, Max tilted forward even farther, at about a forty-five-degree angle from the ground. He wondered how it felt to have acid burn through him.

All of Jenny's leaves were pressed tightly against her stalk as she strained, strained, strained . . .

One of her roots popped out of the ground.

And then another.

Then a third.

Max's amazement overshadowed his terror as Jenny pulled herself out of the ground and took an actual step forward.

With the next shovelful of dirt, Max fell forward and almost smacked against the ground.

"What should I use?" asked Dr. Prethorius. "A few drops of acid to make it last, or should I just pour the whole bottle right on—" He let out a yelp and dropped his shovel as Jenny's leaves clamped down upon his leg.

She straightened again. The doctor dangled upside-down from her trap, struggling desperately but unable to escape.

"Let me go!" he screamed. "I'm your master! Let me go! Please, please, please, let me go!"

Should I let him go? Jenny asked.

I don't think so.

Me either.

I love you, Jenny.

You're a good friend, Max. Would you like to share?

Yes.

She slammed the shrieking doctor against the ground, which did not shut him up, and then dragged him to the side. His arm slid underneath Max's leaves. Max bit down.

Try to get his head, too, said Jenny, stepping forward.

Max did. Dr. Prethorius stopped screaming as they pulled him in two.

Thank you, said Max.

They ate without speaking for a while.

What's wrong? Max asked.

I don't think I can replant you.

Oh.

I'm sorry.

That's okay.

But I can bring humans to you. I'll leave the greenhouse and get them, as many as you want. You'll eat and eat and eat until you get healthy again.

That would be nice.

They continued to enjoy their meal. The doctor tasted better than the other humans he'd eaten. Perhaps insanity made meat more tender.

Maybe he didn't have a lover, but Max had a friend, and he knew that he could be happy for a long, long time.

THE LAKE

by Tananarive Due

*The new English instructor at Graceville Prep was cho-
sen with the greatest care, highly recommended by the
board of directors at Blake Academy in Boston, where
she had an exemplary career for twelve years. There was
no history of irregular behavior to presage the summer's
unthinkable events.*

—Excerpt from an internal memo
Graceville Preparatory School
Graceville, Florida

ABBIE LAFLEUR WAS AN OUTSIDER, a third-generation
Bostonian, so no one warned her about summers in Graceville. She noticed a few significant glances, a hitched eyebrow
or two, when she first mentioned to locals that she planned to
relocate in June to work a summer term before the start of
the school year, but she'd assumed it was because they thought
no one in her right mind would move to Florida, even northern
Florida, in the wet heat of summer.

In fairness, Abbie LaFleur would have scoffed at their stories as hysteria. Delusion. This was Graceville's typical experience with newcomers and outsiders, so Graceville had learned
to keep its stories to itself.

303

Abbie thought she had found her dream job in Graceville. A fresh start. Her glasses had fogged up with steam from the rain-drenched tarmac as soon as she stepped off the plane at Tallahassee Airport; her confirmation that she'd embarked on a true adventure, an exploration worthy of Ponce de León's storied landing at St. Augustine.

Her parents and her best friend, Mary Kay, had warned her not to jump into a real estate purchase until she'd worked in Graceville for at least a year—*The whole thing's so hasty, what if the school's not a good fit? Who wants to be stuck with a house in the sticks in a depressed market?*—but Abbie fell in love with the white lakeside colonial she found listed at one-fifty, for sale by owner. She bought it after a hasty tour—too hasty, it turned out—but at nearly three thousand square feet, this was the biggest house she had ever lived in, with more room than she had furniture for. A place with potential, despite its myriad flaws.

A place, she thought, very much like her.

The built-in bookshelves in the Florida room sagged. (She'd never known that a den could be called a Florida room, but so it was, and so she did.) The floorboards creaked and trembled on the back porch, sodden from summer rainfall. And she would need to lay down new tiles in the kitchen right away, because the brooding mud-brown flooring put her in a bad mood from the time she first fixed her morning coffee.

But there would be boys at the school, strong and tireless boys, who could help her mend whatever needed fixing. In her experience, there were always willing boys.

And then there was the lake! The house was her excuse to buy her piece of the lake and the thin strip of red-brown sand that was a beach in her mind, although it was nearly too narrow for the beach lounger she'd planted like a flag. The water looked murky where it met her little beach, the color of the soil, but in the distance she could see its heart of rich green-blue, like the ocean. The surface bobbed with rings and bubbles from the hidden catfish and brim that occasionally leaped above the surface, damn near daring her to cast a line.

If not for the hordes of mosquitoes that feasted on her legs and whined with urgent grievances, Abbie could have stood with her bare feet in the warm lake water for hours, the house forgotten behind her. The water's gentle lapping was the meditation her parents and Mary Kay were always prescribing for her, a soothing song.

And the isolation! A gift to be treasured. Her property was bracketed by woods of thin pine, with no other homes within shouting distance. Any spies on her would need binoculars and a reason to spy, since the nearest homes were far across the lake, harmless little dollhouses in the anonymous subdivision where some of her students no doubt lived. Her lake might as well be as wide as the Nile, protection from any envious whispers.

As if to prove her newfound freedom, Abbie suddenly climbed out of the tattered jeans she'd been wearing as she unpacked her boxes, whipped off her T-shirt, and draped her clothing neatly across the lounger's arm rails. Imagine! She was naked in her own backyard. If her neighbors could see her, they would be scandalized already, and she had yet to commence teaching at Graceville Prep.

Abbie wasn't much of a swimmer—she preferred solid ground beneath her feet even when she was in the water—but with her flip-flops to protect her from unseen rocks, she felt brave enough to wade into the water, inviting its embrace above her knees, her thighs. She felt the water's gentle kiss between her legs, the massage across her belly, and, finally, a liquid cloak upon her shoulders. The grade was gradual, with no sudden drop-offs to startle her, and for the first time in years Abbie felt truly safe and happy.

That was all Graceville was supposed to be for Abbie LaFleur: new job, new house, new lake, new beginning. For the week before summer school began, Abbie took to swimming behind her house daily, at dusk, safe from the mosquitoes, sinking into her sanctuary.

No one had told her—not the Realtor, not the elderly widow she'd only met once when they signed the paperwork at the lawyer's office downtown, not Graceville Prep's cheerful headmistress. Even a random first-grader at the grocery store could have told her that one must never, ever go swimming in Graceville's lakes during the summer. The man-made lakes were fine, but the natural lakes that had once been swampland were to be avoided by children in particular. And women of childbearing age—which Abbie LaFleur still was at thirty-six, albeit barely. And men who were prone to quick tempers or alcohol binges.

Further, one must never, *ever* swim in Graceville's lakes in summer without clothing, when crevices and weaknesses were most exposed.

In retrospect, she was foolish. But in all fairness, how could she have known?

Abbie's ex-husband had accused her of irreparable timidity, criticizing her for refusing to go snorkeling or even swimming with dolphins, never mind the scuba diving he'd loved since he was sixteen. The world was populated by water people and land people, and Abbie was firmly attached to terra firma. Until Graceville. And the lake.

Soon after she began her nightly wading, which gradually turned to dog-paddling and then awkward strokes across the dark surface, she began to dream about the water. Her dreams were far removed from her nightly dipping—which actually *was* somewhat timid, if she was honest. In sleep, she glided effortlessly far beneath the murky surface, untroubled by the nuisance of lungs and breathing. The water was a muddy green-brown, nearly black, but spears of light from above gave her tents of vision to see floating plankton, algae, tad-poles, and squirming tiny creatures she could not name . . . and yet knew. Her underwater dreams were a wonderland of tangled mangrove roots coated with algae, and forests of gen-tly waving lily pads and swamp grass. Once, she saw an alli-gator's checkered, pale belly above her, until the reptile hurried away, its powerful tail lashing to give it speed. In her dream, she wasn't afraid of the alligator; she'd sensed instead (smelled instead?) that the alligator was afraid of *her*.

Abbie's dreams had never been so vivid. She awoke one morning drenched from head to toe, and her heart hammered her breathless until she realized that her mattress was damp with perspiration, not swamp water. At least . . . she *thought* it must be perspiration. Her fear felt silly, and she was blanketed by sadness as deep as she'd felt the first months after her divorce.

Abbie was so struck by her dreams that she called Mary Kay, who kept dream diaries and took such matters far too seriously.

"You sure that water's safe?" Mary Kay said. "No chemicals being dumped out there?"

"The water's fine," Abbie said, defensive. "I'm not worried about the water. It's just the dreams. They're so . . ." Abbie rarely ran out of words, which Mary Kay knew full well.

"What's scaring you about the dreams?"

"The dreams don't scare me," Abbie said. "It's the opposite. I'm sad to wake up. As if I belong there, in the water, and my bedroom is the dream."

Mary Kay had nothing to offer except a warning to have the local Health Department come out and check for chemicals in any water she was swimming in, and Abbie felt the weight of her distance from her friend. There had been a time when she and Mary Kay understood each other better than anyone, when they could see past each other's silences straight to their thoughts, and now Mary Kay had no idea of the shape and texture of Abbie's life. No one did.

All liberation is loneliness, she thought sadly.

Abbie dressed sensibly, conservatively, for her first day at her new school.

She had driven the two miles to the school, a redbrick converted bank building in the center of downtown Graceville, before she noticed the itching between her toes.

"LaFleur," the headmistress said, keeping pace with Abbie as they walked toward her assigned classroom for the course she'd named Creativity & Literature. The woman's easy, Southern-bred twang seemed to add a syllable to every word. "Where is that name from?"

Abbie wasn't fooled by the veiled attempt to guess at her

ethnicity, since it didn't take an etymologist to guess at her name's French derivation. What Loretta Millhouse really wanted to know was whether Abbie had ancestry in Haiti or Martinique to explain her sun-kissed complexion and the curly brown hair Abbie kept locked tight in a bun.

Abbie's itching feet had grown so unbearable that she wished she could pull off her pumps. The itching pushed irritation into her voice. "My grandmother married a Frenchman in Paris after World War II," she explained. "LaFleur was his family name."

The rest was none of her business. Most of her life was none of anyone's business.

"Oh, I see," Millhouse said, voice filled with delight, but Abbie saw her disappointment that her prying had yielded nothing. "Well, as I said, we're so tickled to have you with us. Only one letter in your file wasn't completely glowing . . ."

Abbie's heart went cold, and she forgot her feet. She'd assumed that her detractors had remained silent, or she never would have been offered the job.

Millhouse patted her arm. "But don't you worry: Swimming upstream is an asset here." The word "swimming" made Abbie flinch, feeling exposed. "We welcome independent thinking at Graceville Prep. That's the main reason I wanted to hire you. Between you and me, how can anyone criticize a . . . creative mind?"

She said the last words conspiratorially, leaning close to Abbie's ear as if a creative mind were a disease. Abbie's mind raced: The criticism must have come from Johanssen, the vice principal at Blake who had labeled her argumentative—*a bitch,* Mary Kay had overheard him call her privately, but he wouldn't have put that in writing. What did Millhouse's disclosure mean? Was Millhouse someone who pretended to compliment you while subtly putting you down, or was a shared secret hidden beneath the twinkle in her aqua-green eyes?

"Don't go easy on this group," Millhouse said when they reached room 113. "Every jock trying to make up a credit to stay on the roster is in your class. Let them work for it."

Sure enough, when Abbie walked into the room, she faced desks filled with athletic young men. Graceville was a coed school, but only five of her twenty students were female.

Abbie smiled.

Her house would be fixed up sooner than she'd expected.

Abbie liked to begin with Thomas Hardy. *Jude the Obscure.* That one always blew their young minds, with its frankness and unconventionality. Their other instructors would cram conformity down their throats, and she would teach rebellion.

No rows of desks would mar her classroom, she informed them. They would sit in a circle. She would not lecture; they would have conversations. They would discuss the readings, read pages from their journals, and share poems. Some days, she told them, she would surprise them by playing music and they would write whatever came to mind.

Half the class looked relieved, the other half petrified.

During her orientation, Abbie studied her students' faces and tried to guess which ones would be most useful over the summer. She dismissed the girls, as she usually did; most were too wispy and pampered, or far too large to be accustomed to physical labor.

* * *

But the boys. The boys were a different matter.

Of the fifteen boys, only three were unsuitable at a glance—bird-chested and reedy, or faces riddled with acne. She could barely stand to look at them.

That left twelve to ponder. She listened carefully as they raised their hands and described their hopes and dreams, watching their eyes for the spark of maturity she needed. Five or six couldn't hold her gaze, casting their eyes shyly at their desks. No good at all.

Down to six, then. Several were basketball players, one a quarterback. Millhouse hadn't been kidding when she'd said that her class was a haven for desperate athletes. The quarterback, Derek, was dark-haired with a crater-sized dimple in his chin; he sat at his desk with his body angled, leg crossed at the knee, as if the desk were already too small. He didn't say "uhm" or pause between his sentences. His future was at the tip of his tongue.

"I'm sorry," she said, interrupting him. "How old did you say you are, Derek?"

He didn't blink. His dark eyes were at home on hers. "Sixteen, ma'am."

Sixteen was a good age. A mature age.

A female teacher could not be too careful about which students she invited to her home. Locker-room exaggerations held grave consequences that could literally steal years from a young woman's life. Abbie had seen it before; entire careers up in flames. But this Derek . . .

Derek was full of possibilities. Abbie suddenly found herself playing Millhouse's game, noting his olive complexion and dark features, trying to guess if his jet-black hair whispered Native American or Hispanic heritage. Throughout the ninety-minute class, her eyes came to Derek again and again.

The young man wasn't flustered. He was used to being stared at.

Abbie had made up her mind before the final bell, but she didn't say a word to Derek. Not yet. She had plenty of time. The summer had just begun.

As she was climbing out of the shower, Abbie realized her feet had stopped their terrible itching. For three days, she'd slathered the spaces between her toes with creams from Walgreens, none helping, some only stinging her in punishment.

But the pain was gone.

Naked, Abbie raised her foot to her mattress, pulling her toes apart to examine them . . . and realized right away why she'd been itching so badly. Thin webs of pale skin had grown between her toes. Her toes, in fact, had changed shape entirely, pulling away from each other to make room for webbing. And weren't her toes longer than she remembered?

No *wonder* her shoes felt so tight! She wore a size eight, but her feet looked like they'd grown two sizes. She was startled to see her feet so altered, but not alarmed, as she might have been when she was still in Boston, tied to her old life. New job, new house, new feet. There was a logical symmetry to her new feet that superseded questions or worries.

Abbie almost picked up her phone to call Mary Kay, but she thought better of it. What else would Mary Kay say, except that she should have had her water tested?

Instead, still naked, Abbie went to her kitchen, her feet slapping against her ugly kitchen flooring with unusual traction.

When she brushed her upper arm carelessly across her ribs, new pain made her hiss. The itching had migrated, she realized.

She paused in the bright fluorescent lighting to peer down at her rib cage and found her skin bright red, besieged by some kind of rash. *Great,* she thought. *Life is an endless series of challenges.* She inhaled a deep breath, and the air felt hot and thin. The skin across her ribs pulled more tautly, constricting. She longed for the lake.

Abbie slipped out of her rear kitchen door and scurried across her backyard toward the black shimmer of the water. She'd forgotten her flip-flops, but the soles of her feet were less tender, like leather slippers.

She did not hesitate. She did not wade. She dove like an eel, swimming with an eel's ease. *Am I truly awake, or is this a dream?*

Her eyes adjusted to the lack of light, bringing instant focus. She had never seen the true murky depths of her lake, so much like the swamp of her dreams. Were they one and the same? Her ribs' itching turned to a welcome massage, and she felt long slits yawn open across her skin, beneath each rib. Warm water flooded her, nursing her; her nose, throat, and mouth were a useless, distant memory. Why hadn't it ever occurred to her to breathe the water before?

An alligator's curiosity brought the beast close enough to study her, but it recognized its mistake and tried to thrash away. But too late. Too late. Nourished by the water, Abbie's instincts gave her enough speed and strength to glide behind the beast, its shadow. One hand grasped the slick ridges of its tail, and the other hugged its wriggling girth the way she might a lover. She didn't remember biting or clawing the alligator, but she must have done one or the other, because the water flowed red with blood.

The blood startled Abbie awake in her bed, her sheets heavy with dampness. Her lungs heaved and gasped, shocked by the reality of breathing, and at first she seemed to take in no air. She examined her fingers, nails, and naked skin for blood, but found none. The absence of blood helped her breathe more easily, her lungs freed from their confusion.

Another dream. Of course. How could she mistake it for anything else?

She was annoyed to realize that her ribs still bore their painful rash and long lines like raw, infected incisions.

But her feet, thank goodness, were unchanged. She still had the delightful webbing and impressive new size, longer than in her dream. Abbie knew she would have to dress in a hurry. Before school, she would swing by Payless and pick up a few new pairs of shoes.

Derek lingered after class. He'd written a poem based on a news story that had made a deep impression on him; a boy in Naples had died on the football practice field. *Before he could be tested by life,* Derek had written in his eloquent final line. One of the girls, Riley Bowen, had wiped a tear from her eye. Riley Bowen always gazed at Derek as if he were the answer to her life's prayers, but he never looked at her.

And now here was Derek standing over Abbie's desk, on his way to six feet tall, his face bowed with shyness for the first time all week.

"I lied before," he said, when she waited for him to speak. "About my age."

Abbie already knew. She'd checked his records and found out for herself, but she decided to torture him. "Then how old are you?"

"Fifteen." His face soured. "Till March."

"Why would you lie about that?"

He shrugged, an adolescent gesture that annoyed Abbie no end.

"Of course you know," she said. "I heard your poem. I've seen your thoughtfulness. You wouldn't lie on the first day of school without a reason."

He found his confidence again, raising his eyes. "Fine. I skipped second grade, so I'm a year younger than everyone in my class. I always say I'm sixteen. It wasn't special for you."

The fight in Derek intrigued her. He wouldn't be the type of man who would be pushed around. "But you're here now, baring your soul. Who's that for?"

His face softened to half a grin. "Like you said, when we're in this room, we tell the truth. So here I am. Telling the truth."

There he was. She decided to tell him the truth, too.

"I bought a big house out by the lake," she said. "Against my better judgment, maybe."

"That old one on McCormack Road?"

"You know it?"

He shrugged, that loathsome gesture again. "Everybody knows the McCormacks. She taught Sunday school at Christ the Redeemer. Guess she moved out, huh?"

"To her sister's in . . . Quincy?" The town shared a name with the city south of Boston, the only reason she remembered it. Her mind was filled with distraction to mask strange flurries of her heart. Was she so cowed by authority that she would leave her house in a mess?

"Yeah, Quincy's about an hour, hour and a half, down the Ten . . ." Derek was saying in a flat voice that bored even him.

They were talking about nothing. Waiting. They both knew it.

Abbie clapped her hands once, snapping their conversation from its trance. "Well, an old house brings lots of problems. The porch needs fixing. New kitchen tiles. I don't have the budget to hire a real handyman, so I'm looking for people with skills . . ."

Derek's cheeks brightened, pink. "My dad and I built a cabin last summer. I'm pretty good with wood. New planks and stuff. For the porch."

"Really?" She chided herself for the girlish rise in her pitch, as if he'd announced he had scaled Mount Everest during his two weeks off from school.

"I could help you out, if . . . you know, if you buy the supplies."

"I can't pay much. Come take a look after school, see if you think you can help." She made a show of glancing toward the open doorway, watching the stream of students passing by. "But you know, Derek, it's easy for people to get the wrong idea if you say you're going to a teacher's house . . ."

His face was bright red now. "Oh, I wouldn't say nothing. I mean . . . anything. Besides, we go fishing with Coach Reed all the time. It's no big deal around here. Not like in Boston, maybe." The longer he spoke, the more he regained his poise. His last sentence had come with an implied wink of his eye.

"No, you're right about that," she said, and she smiled,

remembering her new feet. "Nothing here is like it was in Boston."

That was how Derek Voorhoven came to spend several days a week after class helping Abbie fix her ailing house, whenever he could spare time after football practice in the last daylight. Abbie made it clear that he couldn't expect any special treatment in class, so he would need to work hard on his atrocious spelling, but Derek was thorough and uncomplaining. No task seemed too big or small, and he was happy to scrub, sand, and tile in exchange for a few dollars, conversation about the assigned reading, and fishing rights to the lake, since he said the catfish favored the north side, where it was quiet.

As he'd promised, he told no one at Graceville Prep, but one day he asked if his cousin Jack could help from time to time, and after he'd brought the stocky, freckled youth by to introduce him, she agreed. Jack was only fourteen, but he was strong and didn't argue. He also attended the public school, which made him far less a risk. Although the boys joked together, Jack's presence never slowed Derek's progress much, so Derek and Jack became fixtures in her home well into July. Abbie looked forward to fixing them lemonade and white chocolate macadamia nut cookies from ready-made dough, and with each passing day she knew she'd been right to leave Boston behind.

Still, Abbie never told Mary Kay about her visits with the boys and the work she asked them to do. Her friend wouldn't judge her, but Abbie wanted to hold her new life close, a secret she would share only when she was ready, when she could say: *You'll never guess the clever way I got my improvements*

317

done, an experience long behind her. Mary Kay would be envious, wishing she'd thought of it first, rather than spending a fortune on a gardener and a pool boy.

But there were other reasons Abbie began erecting a wall between herself and the people who knew her best. Derek and Jack, bright as they were, weren't prone to notice the small changes, or even the large ones, that would have leaped out to her mother and Mary Kay—and even her distracted father.

Her mother would have spotted the new size of her feet right away, of course. And the odd new pallor of her face, fishbelly pale. And the growing strength in her arms and legs that made it so easy to hand the boys boxes, heavy tools, or stacks of wooden planks. Mary Kay would have asked about the flaky skin on the back of her neck and her sudden appetite for all things rare, or raw. Abbie had given up most red meat two years ago in an effort to remake herself after the divorce tore her self-esteem to pieces, but that summer she stocked up on thin-cut steaks, salmon, and fish she could practically eat straight from the packaging. Her hunger was also *voracious,* her mouth watering from the moment she woke, her growling stomach keeping her awake at night.

She was hungriest when Derek and Jack were there, but she hid that from herself.

Her dusk swims had grown to evening swims, and some nights she lost track of time so completely that the sky was blooming pink by the time she waded from the healing waters to begin another day of waiting to swim. She resisted inviting the boys to swim with her.

The last Friday in July, with only a week left in the summer term, Abbie lost her patience.

She was especially hungry that day, dissatisfied with her kitchen stockpile. Graceville was suffering a record heat wave with temperatures hovering near 110 degrees, so she was sweaty and irritable by the time the boys arrived at five thirty. And itching terribly. Unlike her feet, the gills hiding beneath the ridges of her ribs never stopped bothering her until she was in her lake. She was so miserable, she almost asked the boys to forget about painting the refurbished back porch and come back another day.

If she'd only done that, she would have avoided the scandal.

Abbie strode behind the porch to watch the strokes of the boys' rollers and paintbrushes as they transformed her porch from an eyesore to a snapshot of the quaint Old South. Because of the heat, both boys had taken their shirts off, their shoulders ruddy as the muscles in their sun-broiled backs flexed in the Magic Hour's furious, gasping light. They put Norman Rockwell to shame; Derek with his disciplined football player's physique, and Jack with his awkward baby fat, sprayed with endless freckles.

"Why do you come here?" she asked them.

They both stopped working, startled by her voice.

"Huh?" Jack said. His scowl was deep, comical. "You're paying us, right?"

Ten dollars a day each was hardly pay. Derek generously shared half of his twenty dollars with his cousin for a couple hours' work, although Jack talked more than he worked, running his mouth about summer superhero blockbusters and dancers in music videos. Abbie regretted that she'd encouraged Derek to invite his cousin along, and that day she wished she had a reason to send Jack home. Her mind raced to come up with an excuse, but she couldn't think of one. A sudden surge of frustration pricked her eyes with tears.

"I'm not paying much," she said.

"Got *that* right," Derek said. Had his voice deepened in only a few weeks? Was Derek undergoing changes, too? "I'm here for the catfish. Can we quit in twenty minutes? I've got my rod in the truck. And some chicken livers I've been saving."

"Quit now if you want," she said. She pretended to study their work, but she couldn't focus her eyes on the whorls of painted wood. "Go on and fish, but I'm going swimming. Good way to wash off a hot day."

She turned and walked away, following the familiar trail her feet had beaten across her backyard's scraggly patch of grass to the strip of sand. She'd planned to lay sod with the boys closer to fall, but that might not happen now.

Abbie pulled off her T-shirt, draping it nonchalantly across her beach lounger, taking her time. She didn't turn, but she could feel the boys' eyes on her bare back. She didn't wear a bra most days; her breasts were modest, so what was the point? One more thing Johanssen had tried to hold against her. Her feet curled into the sand, searching for dampness.

"It's all right if you don't have trunks," she said. "My backyard is private, and there's no harm in friends taking a swim."

She thought she heard them breathing, or maybe the harsh breaths were hers as her lungs prepared to give up their reign. The sun was unbearable on Abbie's bare skin. Her sides burned like fire as the flaps beneath her ribs opened, swollen rose petals.

The boys didn't answer; probably hadn't moved. She hadn't expected them to, at first.

One after the other, she pulled her long legs out of her jeans, standing at a discreet angle to hide most of her nakedness, like the Venus de' Medici. She didn't want them to see her gills, or the rougher patches on her scaly skin. She didn't want to answer questions. She and the boys had spent too much time talking all summer. She wondered why she'd never invited them swimming before.

She dove, knowing just where the lake was deep enough not to scrape her at the rocky floor. The water parted as startled catfish dashed out of her way. Fresh fish was best. That was another thing Abbie had learned that summer.

When her head popped back up above the surface, the boys were looking at each other, weighing the matter. Derek left the porch first, tugging on his tattered denim shorts, hopping on one leg in his hurry. Jack followed but left his clothes on, arms folded across his chest.

Derek splashed into the water, one polite hand concealing his privates until he was submerged. He did not swim near her, leaving a good ten yards between them. After a tentative silence, he whooped so loudly that his voice might have carried across the lake.

"Whooo-*hooooo*!" Derek's face and eyes were bright, as if he'd never glimpsed the world in color before. "Awesome!"

Abbie's stomach growled. She might have to go after those catfish. She couldn't remember being so hungry. She felt faint.

Jack only made it as far as the shoreline, still wearing his Bermuda shorts. "Not supposed to swim in the lake in summer," he said sullenly, his voice barely loud enough to hear. He slapped at his neck. He stood in a cloud of mosquitoes.

Derek spat, treading water. "That's little *kids*, dumbass."

"Nobody's supposed to," Jack said.

"How old are you, six? You don't want to swim—fine. Don't stand staring. It's rude."

Abbie felt invisible during their exchange. She almost told Jack he should follow his best judgment without pressure, but she dove into the silent brown water instead. Young adults had to make decisions for themselves, especially boys, or how would they learn to be men? That was what she and Mary Kay had always believed. Anyone who thought differently was just being politically correct. In ancient times, or in other cultures, a boy Jack's age would already have a wife, a child of his own.

Just look at Mary Kay. Everyone had said her marriage would never work, that he'd been too young when they met. She'd been vilified and punished, and still they survived. The memory of her friend's trial broke Abbie's heart.

As the water massaged her gills, Abbie released her thoughts and concerns about the frivolous world beyond the water. She needed to feed, that was all. She planned to leave the boys to their bickering and swim farther out, where the fish were hiding.

But something large and pale caught her eye above her.

Jack, she realized dimly. Jack had changed his mind, swimming near the surface, his ample belly like a full moon, jiggling with his breaststroke.

That was the first moment Abbie felt a surge of fear, because she finally understood what she'd been up to—what her new body had been preparing her for. Her feet betrayed her, their webs giving her speed as she propelled toward her giant meal. Water slid across her scales.

The beautiful fireball of light above the swimmer gave her pause, a reminder of a different time, another way. The tears that had stung her in her backyard tried to burn her eyes blind, because she saw how it would happen, exactly like a dream: She would claw the boy's belly open, and his scream would sound muffled and faraway to her ears. Derek would come to investigate, to try to rescue him from what he would be sure was a gator, but she would overpower Derek next. Her new body would even if she could not.

As Abbie swam directly beneath the swimmer, bathed in the magical light fighting to shield him, she tried to resist the overpowering scent of a meal and remember that he was a boy. Someone's dear son. As Derek (was that the other one's name?) had put it so memorably some time ago—perhaps while he was painting the porch, perhaps in one of her dreams—neither of them yet had been tested by life.

But it was summertime. In Graceville.

In the lake.

THE OTHER ONE

by Michael Marshall Smith

KERRY MUTTERED under her breath but did up her seat belt in response to the stewardess's request. She'd flown the Atlantic *more* than enough times to know that the fasten-your-seat-belts sign went on a good half an hour before touchdown: One of her personal flying rituals (along with reading the safety instructions, bringing her own food, and accepting every single offer of an alcoholic drink) was to buckle up only when the spinning gray of runway was visible out of the window. There'd been three puling babies in her cabin alone, however, the plane had been full to bursting and moreover short-staffed, and she could tell that, behind her professional smile, the stewardess was close to the edge. So Kerry did what she was told. She was, after all, reasonably good at that.

Belt secured, she sat and stared at the back of the seat in front. She'd been awake throughout the eight-hour night flight, and now that it was coming to an end she felt the usual hollow tiredness, mingled with depression.

England. *Bloody* England.

From a few rows behind came the now-familiar sound of a

baby sharing its confusion and discomfort with the world, urgent with the selfishness of the infant. Kerry realized the flight had doubtless been far, far worse for the infant's parent, but still wished both mother and child had been checked as baggage instead. She fished in the seat pocket and retrieved the Bose headphones. They'd been outlandishly expensive, but there wasn't much point listening to music through anything less than the best. With the buds slotted comfortably into her ears, she found the album on the iPod she'd bought on the first day of the trip and cranked the volume up high.

She smiled as the opening track crashed into her head and, eyes closed, gently rocked in her seat to the beat. She so nearly hadn't gone, but Washington had been a *lot* of fun, in the end. A hell of a long way to go to watch her best friend (finally) get married—leaving Kerry as the last single girl in their crowd, cheers for that—but a good excuse to get out of the country for a week. And what a week. The small but bullish English contingent (mainly old school friends of Diane, whom Kerry hadn't known) had done their best to have a good time in a foreign land, to show the locals that when it came to alcohol consumption, Brits were all about Shock and Awe. They'd succeeded, big-time, and Kerry still carried the vestiges of her sixth hangover in a row.

". . . and there are aaaaiiiiiiii-aaiinnGELS!"

She suddenly realized she'd started singing along to the music, and opened her eyes. The man across the aisle was smiling at her. She stared at him blankly until he turned away, then jacked the volume up again and closed her eyes as the second track began.

She'd downloaded the album almost at random in a Starbucks right after buying the iPod, before she'd met anyone, before the party started. Downloaded quite a few albums, in fact, but this was the one that had stuck. Everything about the jangly guitars and raucous girly harmonies brought to mind music from thirty years ago, back when you saved your pocket money and bought the latest single by your fave band, rushing home to tear it to shreds on a cheap turntable, annoying the crap out of your parents as a bonus. Nobody had fave bands or listened-to-shreds albums these days. They had nonlinear playlists instead, and—if they were old enough, stuffed into a bookcase in a disregarded corner of the living room—a few ancient LPs (one Dire Straits, one Phil Collins, one mid-period Bowie, one syrupy Vivaldi), some Oasis or Chemical Brothers CDs (to show they were still trying to keep on top of things in the 1990s), sandwiched between doomed attempts to learn to like club music when you weren't on drugs, and stuff they couldn't even remember buying. Nobody hated anybody else's choice in music anymore, either, aside from knuckle-dragging online "reviewers" who one-starred anything that hadn't been on *The X Factor*. Nobody had the backbone to truly hate *anything,* these days: They were too busy *liking*—Facebooking or tweeting whatever track they were listening to, right this minute, *right now*. On the assumption, presumably, that all their virtual friends would give a flying fuck, that they would interpret these bleatings as a sign of character, rather than a yelp for attention in a digitized void. When everyone wears headphones, music is not sociable anymore.

As the music pumped through her head, Kerry felt herself transported to a room in the Embassy Suites Hotel in D.C., back into the arms of someone she was never going to see again. She'd been a bad girl (well, a bad woman, actually, let's face it), and the window for being able to ignore this fact would close the second the jumbo's wheels smacked back onto English soil. Richard was going to be pissed off at her, and knowing him, she'd pay for a good long time. On the verge of tears, she pushed the volume up to full and filled her head with memory.

She felt the impacts as the wheels touched down. The double thud of a textbook landing, like a heavy hand knocking on a sepulchral door.

Welcome back to the morgue.

She turned the iPod off, blinking rapidly, and sat waiting while everyone else stood up and milled impatiently in the aisles, three hundred sheep eager for the slaughter of Real Life.

The immigration queue took even longer than usual, and by the time she handed her passport to the fatuously jolly official, Kerry's mood had plummeted further. Maybe it was guilt over what she'd done, but she seemed to be taking the return to England even harder than usual. She knew that in a couple of weeks everything would seem normal. Her rut was there, ready and waiting, the random set of circumstances that she'd colluded in turning into her life, her story, the Kerry Jones Experience. She didn't *want* her present anger and depression to fade, however, didn't want to be accepted back into the fold. She stared balefully at the passport official, mentally daring him to give her a hard time: The photo had been taken only three months previously; she was even wearing the same *jacket,* for God's sake. He merely welcomed her back, though, his accent sounding strange and provincial and *dull*, and waved her on toward baggage retrieval.

Welcome *back*?

To what?

She waited for her bag to meander out onto the belt, very much wanting a cigarette. Her consumption had skyrocketed during the week in Washington, and the duty-free cache wasn't going to last long. She was supposed to be giving up, of course, turning into clean-living, gym-rat Kerry, the better version of herself that always seemed just out of reach. Wasn't going to happen today. Tomorrow didn't look great either.

Her bag eventually emerged blinking into the light, as if by accident, and she hauled it onto her shoulder and tromped off toward Customs. Slowing as she approached the channels, she tried to decide a question that had mildly stressed her out for the entire flight. She didn't know for sure if the new iPod had to be declared, but eventually elected to head down the Nothing to Declare channel. She never got stopped anyway. She looked like a good girl.

A Chinese man with a stupendously large suitcase veered in front of her, and she accelerated round him, anxious to get out of the airport and onto the final leg of her journey, onto the tube up to Camden. She wanted a bath, some tea, and a cigarette, preferably several. She didn't want to see or talk to anyone.

"Good morning, madam," a firm, female voice said, and Kerry felt a hand on her shoulder. "Would you mind stepping this way, please?"

* * *

She let herself be led to one of the tables by the young Scottish woman, her guts taut with weary anxiety. It was just her luck, just her *sodding* luck.

"So," the woman said, "where have you been?"

"Washington," Kerry replied, loading the word with as much cheery innocence as possible, as though hoping through pronunciation alone to demonstrate herself incapable of transgressing any law.

"Anything you want to tell me about?"

Kerry decided to go for it. "Well, there is one thing," she said, putting her bags onto the table.

The woman's eyes remained friendly. Sort of.

"I bought an iPod," Kerry continued, offhand. "I don't know whether I should have decl—"

"If you didn't *know,* then you should have gone down the other channel. That's illegal, by itself. And yes, you should have declared it."

The woman unzipped Kerry's suitcase and started lifting her clothes out onto the table. Other passengers strolled by, flicking curious glances, relieved that some stranger had been sacrificed to the dark gods of Customs, and not them. Kerry watched as her holiday was picked out and strewn over the surface. The dress she'd worn to the bridal shower. The card Diane had given her to thank her for coming all that way. A souvenir ashtray stolen from the Embassy Suites. Her lips twitched slightly when she saw this last. The first time John's hand had touched hers had been an accident, as they simultaneously stubbed out cigarettes, early one evening two days before the wedding.

"What were you doing in Washington?" the woman asked, unzipping Kerry's toiletries bag and tipping out the contents.

"I was at a wedding," Kerry chirped, still doing her best to seem Trustworthy and Normal, though thrown sufficiently off balance to half-fear that Washington, D.C., was well known to be off-limits to British nationals, but somehow no one had told her, and she was falling further and further into a trap. "My best friend married an American, and they had the wedding there."

The woman gave no reaction to this, and instead unscrewed the cap of Kerry's shampoo. She squidged a little out of the container and squinted into the bottle.

"What are you looking for?" Kerry asked, striving for a tone of bright and innocent inquiry.

"Drugs."

"Oh." Drugs, she thought. *Drugs.*

Feeling dizzy, she let the woman get on with it, and stopped trying to pretend to be something she was not. Lyrics from the album thudded in her mind as she watched the process, wondering how she'd be feeling now if she actually *was* a drug courier or terrorist mastermind, and not a midranking and terminally bored PR, if at some point in the muddy "whatever" of the last two decades she'd taken a different course. Unbidden, the word "excited" popped into her mind, and she frowned.

Meanwhile, the official set about dismantling her toothpaste dispenser.

Twenty minutes later, flushed and embarrassed, Kerry trekked the long corridor toward the tube. The Customs woman had relented in the end, and even let her off the duty on the iPod, though sternly admonishing her not to do it again. What was weird was that there hadn't been even a perfunctory attempt at a body search. Kerry could have had her jacket pockets stuffed with heroin or explosives or rare penguins and got away with it. She rather wished she had, in fact. The run-in with officialdom had affected her badly. She felt strange, untethered. She'd listened to the album too much on the flight, and songs were coursing round her head. She believed there was precious little sugar in her heart anymore, though. Precious little of anything, in fact.

On the tube she reached into her bag and pulled out her notepad. The last few pages were filled with self-motivational notes she'd scribbled on the flight, while everyone else was asleep or submitting to some inane movie. She always stayed awake on the way back to England, because that was the last chance she had to feel good, to feel like she was away from home, from her job, from Richard, from everything. Already she could feel that sense of perspective and freedom ebbing quickly away. Tomorrow she'd be back at Whitehead PR, selling her life by the day in the pursuit of percentage points of popularity for companies producing crap that people didn't need. She'd be back in a flat that cost a fortune to rent and made her feel caged, and she'd be back in the same country as Richard. Which meant back with Richard, whatever the technicalities of the situation might be. Richard with the so-handsome face, Richard with the custom BMW, Richard the Funds Manager. Richard who'd had two sizable affairs with high-powered fund manageresses, and yet who *still* got mileage out of Kerry's sole previous one-night digression, five years before. Richard who was now totally unrecognizable as the genuinely funny and charming boy she'd met in her second year at university; Richard who no longer had the faintest idea of what she was like, and seldom gave the impression that he cared.

And yet . . . Richard whom she couldn't seem to make a break from. Richard who, in some indefinable, unhelpful, dire way, she still loved.

They weren't even supposed to be going out with each other. They were "taking a break" to "recharge batteries" that she believed had long ago cracked and died in the sun. She knew she was going to have to tell him about John, nonetheless, and she knew what the result would be. Richard wouldn't give her the relief of leaving her. He'd merely chalk up another point on the complex scoreboard they tended, and stay around, filling up the background. Not making her happy, but not going away.

And John? John the quiet Canadian, who'd understood her immediately, who'd *got* her, reawakening the girl of twenty years ago with one crooked grin? She'd never speak to him again. What would be the point?

It was only an hour and a half after touchdown, but already her notes made no sense. "Be yourself," they said, "Remember the way you used to be," and "Listen to the album." She knew what these feeble homilies meant, and also that they were a waste of paper and ink. When she'd been away, the album had been everything, because it had nailed what she was feeling, liberated a younger self. Along with John, and alcohol—and just an ounce of freedom—it had wrenched open a path back to a teenager who laughed a lot and wore bright 1980s colors and didn't give a damn what other people thought.

But that teenager was still sitting on the plane, all alone and peering out at the drizzle. That girl thought *Miami Vice* was cool, had never heard of e-mail or eBay, and bought wine because it was dirt cheap, not because the *Sunday Times* said it was good.

That girl didn't have a job she hated and a car to run, friends to tolerate, a life to withstand. That girl was dead, head smeared across the road by the hit-and-run accident of growing up.

She was thirty-eight years old now, *for fuck's sake.*

Suddenly Kerry slumped forward in her seat, hitched over by a sob she'd had no idea was coming. She couldn't live like this anymore, drifting toward death in some endless Plan B. She couldn't accept this was all there was. She wanted a Blue Adonis of her own, and she wanted to run off down midnight streets, shouting at the sky and frightening passing dogs. She didn't want to go back to a relationship where there was always something to discuss, something to sort out, something to forget.

She threw her head back and stared at the roof of the carriage, head whirling, thoughts spinning, feeling her heart break and the world finally split.

She switched lines at King's Cross, on a whim, taking the City branch of the Northern Line before she really knew what she was going to do. Richard, predictable/dependable bastard that he was, took his lunch at 12:30 precisely, returning to the office exactly an hour later. She'd be just in time to catch him going back in. She'd say hi, surprise him. Why, she had no idea. It was something different. It was something she'd never done before. It was something new, and right now she needed the promise of that more than just about anything.

She put the headphones back in and restarted the album at the first track. People in suits stared at her as she bobbed her head to the music. She stuck her tongue out, feeling ridiculous but exhilarated, and wondered whatever had happened to Molly Ringwald. She must presumably be alive, somewhere. No longer a movie star. No longer young. But still, in some diminished sense, Molly Ringwald. Did she get up in the morning and stare in the mirror, wondering what had happened to the other her, the zeitgeist girl? Was that other Molly still out there somewhere, still bright-eyed, still new, wondering where her world had gone?

Kerry kept turning the music up, and up.

She stepped out into the City with the music still pounding in her ears. It was so loud by now that she couldn't help tripping along in time to the beat, and even did a clumsy Madonna twirl, oblivious to the weight of her shoulder bag and how ludicrous she must look. Madonna didn't twirl much anymore, of course: She was a mother now (famously so, controversially so, please-shut-up-about-it-now so). But Madonna had twirled once, and they'd all twirled together, and Kerry still remembered how.

She had a few minutes to spare when she reached the point in the street opposite Richard's office. She decided to wait until she actually saw him, not declaring her presence ahead of time with a text message, instead hoping against hope that he'd arrive arm in arm with some secretary or up-and-coming foreign-equities specialist, so she could quietly turn away and never speak to him again. While she waited, she stood staring at the oh-so-imposing entrance of his building, across the wide and busy road, wishing someone would have the balls to bomb it, her head still bobbing to the music, wondering why she was really here. She didn't *want* to speak to Richard, didn't *want* to see him smile. She was tired of making do, of being good, of toeing the company line. She was tired of the fact that he couldn't understand a single thing that went on in her head. She was just tired.

Full stop.

End of.

Her eardrums were beginning to hurt, too. The music was pushing things out of her brain, last in, first out. She wished she *had* been carrying drugs, a case full of heroin and dirty needles; she wished she was drunk, sprawled across a hotel room floor, or panting naked on her hands and knees above someone, lowering her open mouth toward his; she wished she didn't have a career or friends or a home. She wished she had a knife.

Finally she saw him, through the curtain of fast-moving cars and trucks. Dark brown hair falling over the face she knew so well, with the naturalness that only £150 haircuts can maintain, his suit hanging across gym-squared shoulders. He looked hatefully smug. He was in context. Head full of stocks and mezzanine-financed leverage buyouts, a player in a platinum-card jungle.

And . . . he wasn't alone.

Kerry stared through the traffic, hardly able to believe her fantasy had come true. Richard *wasn't* by himself. He was with a woman. An attractive woman.

They were *holding hands.*

She blinked, unsure what to do. Shout? Storm across the road? Or just walk quickly away, and send him the mother of all e-mails when she got back home?

Richard and the woman stopped a few yards from the door to his office. They stood close, face-to-face, talking. Kerry quickly fished in her shoulder bag and yanked out her little camera, suddenly knowing what would be even *better* than a brutal e-mail: taking a picture and sending that instead. No accompanying text, just an image. There had been too much talking over the years, far too many words. There didn't need to be any more.

She held the camera up and zoomed in. For maximum impact, she wanted the picture to . . .

Then she froze.

She zoomed in a little further.

The woman Richard was talking to was her.

They were saying:

"You're sure?"

"I'm *sure,*" Kerry said, squeezing his hand. "I've moved all my stuff in, haven't I?"

"I know. I know. But . . ."

"I'm not going to change my mind, Richard. We should have done this years ago."

"We should. And I'm sorry we didn't. That was my fault.

It's just . . . I'm still trying to catch up. Since you decided not to go to the States for that woman's wedding, everything's changed. It's . . . all different."

"What kind of different? Bad different?"

Richard smiled, and it was a real one, the smile of a man who had been bored, and who'd been bad, and who'd been kind of an asshole, but who was allowing himself to believe that he could be another way, that something had happened and life didn't have to be how it had been.

"No," he said. "The other one."

After they'd kissed, Kerry watched him go into his building. He looked surprised, and disconcerted, and cautiously happy, as he had for most of the last week. Just before he disappeared into the elevator, he winked. She winked back.

Then she turned to look across the busy street, at the woman who looked exactly like her, who was still holding her camera and staring at her, still openmouthed. The plane-bedraggled Kerry. The can't-say-yes Kerry, the Kerry who seemed intent on pushing happiness beyond her own reach, the Kerry who demanded perfection from the world and was unable to understand that contentment is a matter of choice. The Kerry who'd made her own bed, by leaving enough room for someone else to slip into her place, an alternative who'd been waiting a long, long time.

Kerry hoped that other Kerry had enough clothes in her shoulder bag to last a while, because the flat she thought she was returning to had been vacated two days after she flew to America, its contents thrown away or given to charity or moved into Richard's place in Islington. There would be changes to be made there, too, in time. Richard wasn't perfect. He would never be. But he'd get closer. Under her guidance. With her love. Nobody gets perfect, ever. But they can get enough.

Kerry raised her hand and waved. She tried not to smile as she did so, or to feel too pleased with herself, but found it impossible. The woman on the other side of the street deserved this, after all. She ought to be happy, really. She'd wanted something different.

She'd got it now.

AND STILL YOU WONDER WHY OUR FIRST IMPULSE IS TO KILL YOU:

An Alphabetized Faux-Manifesto transcribed, edited, and annotated (under duress and protest)
by Gary A. Braunbeck

O then, why go through again the Fatigue of re-making the fabulous shell Of an ideal world, upon ancient runes? . . . (Distant voices from the sea): "Ola-eh, Ola-oh! Let us destroy, destroy!"

> —F. T. MARINETTI, "Against the Hope
> of Reconstruction"

[AUTHOR'S PREFATORY NOTES: Did you know that, according to Roman scholar and writer Marcus Terentius Varro (116 B.C.–27 B.C.), the word *monstrum* was not derived, as Cicero insisted, from the verb *monstro,* "to show" (comparable to the English "to demonstrate"), but, rather, came from *moneo:* "warning." Isn't that interesting, and somewhat ironic in a ham-fisted sort of way, considering the circumstances under which you're reading this? I certainly thought so. And I did not know that until I inherited this job that I neither asked for nor wanted. More on that later.

[A few other tidbits you might find useful before we get to the bulk of this. I had to argue like you wouldn't believe to get

341

them to agree to add the "Faux" before "Manifesto." What they dictated to me isn't so much a manifesto as it is a collection of (albeit deadly serious) grievances and gripes, as well as little-known or conveniently forgotten historical facts, definitions, and more than a few parables. They'd originally wanted to call this their (I kid you not) "Monsterfesto," and I—still not appreciating the gravity of the situation—immediately laughed and said, "That is so *lame*!" It cost me one of my cats. They didn't just zap him into another dimension or have some banal beastie saunter in and gobble him down in a single gulp, no; they gave him instantaneous doses of full-blown end-stage feline leukemia and AIDS and made me sit there and watch him die. It took two and a half days. He kept trying to crawl to the water bowl. They would not let me move him closer so he could at least get a cool drink. They wouldn't even let me hold him so he could die in the arms of someone who loved him. All I could do was watch as he struggled toward the water and wheezed and then coughed up, excreted, and pissed blood, all the time looking at me with frightened, confused, and ever-yellowing eyes as he made this soft mewling sound that after about twelve hours began to sound like ". . . help . . ." to my ears. When at last Ruben finally died—that was his name, by the way, Ruben—it was in a series of sputtering little agonies punctuated by painful seizures that I thought would never end. And if you found that hard to read, imagine how I felt having to sit there and *watch it happen,* completely powerless to ease even an iota of his suffering.

[And do you know *why* I was powerless to do anything? Because if I had tried to do something, they would have done the same thing to the rest of my family, one at a time, and I would have been the sole member of the audience to their excruciatingly torturous deaths, and I've got plenty of memories to give me nightmares for the rest of my life; *have* had plenty since I was a kid. Not looking to add to that particular collection, thank you very much. I don't have much of a family left, and what family I still *do* have rely on government-issued food cards to buy their monthly groceries and *still* have to skip breakfast and eat macaroni and cheese for dinner three times a week while worrying over which utility bills can be skipped until next month, all the time praying to a God they have less and less faith actually exists that no one gets sick. So I had no choice but to watch Ruben die, and I had no choice but to accept this assignment and become their go-between.

[Here are the terms to which we finally agreed: 1) Unless I felt strongly that some clarification needed to be made, I was to transcribe everything precisely as dictated to me, more or less; any variation, even in punctuation, would result in their doing a Ruben on one of my remaining family members (this threat, though unspoken, remained the constant epilogue to every clause of our agreement); 2) If I *did* feel strongly that some clarification needed to be made, I had to make my argument in a courteous and respectful manner, but give them final say on whether or not it remained in the manuscript; so if in some section things seem rather abrupt or a bit helter-skelter, not my fault; 3) I had to agree to include at least three personal accounts of encounters with beings of their kind, regardless of how silly they sounded or uncomfortable they made me (or potential readers) feel; and 4) Upon reaching the end of this project, even if I still hated them for what they did to Ruben and threatened to do to what little family remains to me, I must make it sound as if I have sympathy, understanding, and compassion for them; fine by me, I can lie on paper with the best of them . . . just as long as I don't have to claim any form of affection for them. They're here, they're not going anywhere, they don't give a tinker's damn if you believe in them or not (it won't stop them from going Ruben on your ass), and . . . oh, yeah, by the way: They are not happy with us.

[*So* very not happy with us. The title of this piece should have given you a subtle hint as to the depth and breadth of their unhappiness with us.

[I would, however, completely out of context for reasons that are my own but that I hope you'll eventually pick up on, like to paraphrase a line from the film version of *The Exorcist* for the benefit of my own conscience: I may mix some lies in with the truth, and truth with the lies.

[As to the matter at hand . . . it's after midnight; time to let it all hang out.]

A

is for Abomination; it is also for Aberration, Abhorrent, Abortion, Atrocity, Awfulness, and several other words beginning with the first letter of the alphabet in many different languages, all of which—whether you can spell or pronounce them or not—amount to the same thing: *Omigod, lookit that ugly fuckin' thing, somebody kill it quick!* Many of these beings (which have feelings that are easily hurt, believe it or not) struggle up through Stygian depths yet to be imagined, let alone *discovered,* by paleoseismologists (who'd be the group to first find the traces) to get here; others cross time, space, dimensions, and take dangerous shortcuts through the multiverse in their attempts to make friendly contact. And what do they get for this? At the very least, they get called all sorts of hurtful names. One of them explained it to me in these terms: "Imagine driving way out of town to your family's home for Christmas. You're driving through a blizzard—we're talking real Second Ice Age, Big Freeze stuff here, right? A drive that should have only taken thirty minutes takes you damn near three hours, but you finally get there. You're exhausted, you're starving, your bladder's the size of a soccer ball, but the sight of the warm holiday lights within your family's home makes it all worthwhile. You head up to the door, your arms filled with all these great, terrific, really killer *boffo* presents, and you let yourself inside, all smiles and Christmas greetings for everyone, *filled* with the spirit of the season—I mean, it may as well be the final scene of *It's a Wonderful Life.* First thing that happens—your grandmother takes one look at you, her eyes roll back in her head, and she drops dead from the terror. Then the children as one scream in horror, shit their pants, and run for the basement. Your mother grabs a carving knife the size of a machete, Dad fires up the flamethrower he's had in the downstairs closet since his two tours in Vietnam, and your sister starts hosing the room with a TEC-9. Now, don't you think that would put a bit of a damper on *your* disposition? *Hmmm . . . ?*"

B

is for Bogeyman, also Bogieman, Boogeyman, or Boogieman. Doesn't really matter how you spell it, or what variation he takes on in whichever country where parents still use him to emotionally scar their children at as early an age as is possible, outside of a seventies disco song by KC and the Sunshine Band with a killer bass synthesizer line, he doesn't exist. He never did. Stop using him to frighten your kids. This *really* sticks in their collective craw. Suck it up and be a parent and exercise well-tempered discipline like you're supposed to, or use condoms next time, fer chrissakes. You're supposed to be adults.

C

is for Colophon. You have been led to believe that this denotes a publisher's mark or logotype appearing at the beginning or end of a book. It is not a mark; they are a race of parasites that came to Earth hidden within the binding of *The Book of Forbidden Knowledge,* the text that the Fallen Angels stole and gave to humankind during the first War in Heaven (which was technically more of a skirmish prompted by the Great Mother of all hissy fits, but that's neither here nor there). Once *The Book* was entrusted to humankind—giving to it, among other things, the knowledge of Language, Music, Poetry, Art, Science, Writing, Dance, etc.—the Colophon scurried from their hiding place and began, bit by bit, to destroy the first of the Forbidden Gifts: Language. Before the Egyptian coffin beetle, before the advent of nanotechnology, before the first cancer cell ever set up shop in a sentient being's bloodstream and began chewing away from within, the Colophon, smaller than all of the aforementioned (their initial number, which has now increased ten-million-fold, was somewhere in the neighborhood of one hundred and seventeen million to the two hundred and sixtieth power) have been amassing their forces for a nonstop assault to take back language from the human race. The Tower of Babel was their first truly Great Victory against us. Other victories have been smaller, but get enough scratches and you can still bleed to death. Example: Have you begun to notice how, suddenly, no one knows the difference between a contraction and a possessive? Or how quickly ink begins to fade from the pages of books? Or how, regardless of how many times you reload a page online, you keep getting more and more garbage characters? These are just a few of the Colophon's tactics. Their ultimate goal is to erase all printed language and destroy all digital language. Armed with the totality of this knowledge, they'll enter our brains and wipe out all traces of even the basest form of verbal and written communication. We will be left with only the most vague, nebulous wisps of memory that we were once able to exchange ideas through sounds that came out of our mouths or were represented on the page by arcane symbols. We will lose the First Gift because we were not worthy to possess it in the first place.

D

is for the Damaged Ones. [Author's Note: One of mine.] As an eight-year-old child I awoke in the woods in the early hours of dawn, naked and shivering where they had left me after they'd finished the night before. I tried to stand but my legs were weak and my feet too slick with the blood still trickling from my backside. I crawled forward, wondering why I was covered in silver quills. They weren't quills, but needles that had fallen from the pine tree under which they had left me. The needles had become soaked in dew, and in the first rays of dawn, the thousands of them over my body looked like quills or gray fur. I stopped crawling when it felt as if my chest were going to explode. I stopped crawling when it felt as if things were falling out of me from back there, where I could not turn my head to see the trail. I stopped crawling because there was no place to crawl to, and no one waiting there for me. I raised my head and saw a great wolf standing so close to my face I could feel its hot breath tickle my matted hair against my scalp. "Are you a werewolf?" I asked. The great wolf shrugged. "That is one name for us, I suppose." I began to cry. "Are you going to bite me and turn *me* into a werewolf, too?" The great wolf shook its head. "There's no need. You have already been transformed. You will forever be marked. You are now no longer part of the human world. You are a Damaged One. No curse, no bite, no full moon is needed to steal away your humanity. You are a monster, as are we all." I lived through that night, and I remember well the words of the great wolf on that morning. There is no need to be bitten, no reason to be cursed. On the street, nearly every time I venture out into the world—which I try to do as little as possible—as I walk I look up and see another one of us. Our eyes meet, and we know each other like members of the same family. Our eyes flash silver. They flash loss and anger and regret. Then one of us always crosses the street. It is not yet time to acknowledge each other's existence. There is, it seems, much more damage yet to be done. [Author's Note: Some mornings, as I begin to shave, I think of all the anguish that I've brought into the lives of those who love or have loved me, and I wish for a straight razor instead of one with a disposable blade. Then the mirror flashes silver and for a moment my eyes are gone and in a blink it's just another bright, bright, sunshiny day.]

E

is for the Elder Gods (often mistakenly referred to as "the Great Old Ones"). They're actually not nearly as old, or as powerful, or as frightening as they'd like for you to believe. Lovecraft [Author's Note: Or so say those dictating this to me.], it turns out, was not a good choice for a PR man. Seems old Howard, aside from having more than his share of whack-a-doodle tendencies inherited from his schizophrenic mother, was not only paranoid but something of a racist to boot. He ran to a neighbor's house in a shuddering panic because he was convinced that he'd discovered a cluster of "Negro eggs" in the basement of his home. Thus did he begin to graft his anti-human, pro-uncaring-universe philosophy into what they told him. All of that gobbledygook in all of the so-called Mythos stories? Mostly recipes and gossip. [Author's Note: They speak of this with a curious mix of embarrassment and rage. One of them added this: "Do you think anyone remembers that Cthulhu was an extraterrestrial and his 'house of R'lyeh' was a goddamn *spaceship*? Oh, and let's not forget where R'lyeh was located—*at the bottom of the freakin' sea*! Now, you tell me—would you have any real primeval fear in your heart for a race of beings whose giant, bat-winged, slobbering, tentacle-faced leader—supposedly possessed of all the knowledge from pre- and post-history—didn't have the sense to install something akin to a GPS system in his ship

349

so he didn't *drown* everyone when they landed? Yes, they're really big. *Really* big. And most of them are dumber than a bag of hair. But because of Lovecraft's misrepresenting what they said, *we* have to work a thousand times as hard to get your attention. His fictions are astounding models of structure, but otherwise, Howie [Author's Note-Within-a-Note: They all call him "Howie." Don't ask me, I'm just doing the typing at this point.] was stuffed full of wild blueberry muffins. William Hope Hodgson, though . . . *there* was a scary fucker. *The House on the Borderland.* Yeah—he knew *something.*"]

F

is for Finders of the Last Breath. They are led by a lithe female figure with the head of a black horse, its ears erect, its neck arched, vapor jetting from its nostrils; one of her followers is tall and skeletal, with fingers so long their tips brush against the ground: It hunkers down and snakes its fingers around whatever object has attracted its attention, absorbing the sound made by vibrational waves so it can trace them back to their source; other followers hop like frogs, some roll, some scuttle on rootlike filaments that are covered in flowers whose centers are the faces of blind children. Many of them are terrifying to behold, and too many have been killed as they attempt to carry out their duties: to be at the side of infants and the old who are about to die, so that their last breaths can be caught and put in jars and stored away. It is only when the Finders *can* carry out their duties that your infants and your old will pass in peace, and rest in peace. The Finders make their deaths painless, even majestic. But if their last breaths cannot be caught in time, the infant's or the aged one's death—even after the remains have been burned or buried—is never-ending, and their awareness of the horror of their fate is crystalline and without pity. You should welcome and not fear the presence of the Finders. Fear only their absence when the time comes.

G

is for the Glop. The Glop has no real name. The Glop has no real form. It can call itself anything it wants and assume any form it wishes. If it has a purpose, no one knows what it is. The Glop is that nameless, shambling, drooling, unnamable, indescribable "thing" that always manages to get hold of the narrator of a horror story just before said narrator can name it or describe it or reveal its purpose. [Author's Note: Yet have you noticed that the narrators of these stories always seem to have time to write *"Gaaaaah!"* or *"Arrrrrrgh!"* or something like that?] If you read a story that ends with a long, jagged pen-scrawl trailing down to the bottom of the page, that's because the Glop got to the narrator. If you haven't figured it out yet, the Glop is in cahoots with the Colophon. Many is the character, both in fiction and in real life, who has found him- or herself in the embarrassing position of being Slurped by the Glop before anyone can learn anything about them. Bad horror movies are especially adept at this. Or episodes of the original *Star Trek* when everyone beams down to a planet's surface . . . but there's that crew member you've never seen before, the one whose uniform doesn't even come close to matching everyone else's. You know immediately that crew member is Soon to Be Slurped by the Glop. [Author's Note: They'd really like to get their hands on the Glop. Reality and fiction are one and the same to it, and they'd like to know how it manages to move so easily between realms of perception and still manage to assume physical form. Come to think of it, I wouldn't mind hearing *that* one myself.]

H

is for Hawkline Monster. [Author's Note: *Not* the one of which Richard Brautigan wrote.] The sting came back to him; not the same as before, but far more powerful. He dropped to one knee as the pain began to tear his face in half, he felt it, felt the fire burning through his nose as he struggled to his feet and stumbled into the bathroom, hoping that it was all over now, please let it be over, please let this be the last of my punishment, but then he was in front of the mirror and looking at his face as it began swelling around a gash on his forehead and nose, swelling like a goddamn balloon so he looked away, looked down at his hand and saw it pulsating, felt a cold thing crawling between his shoulders, eyes twitching, what the hell is it, but then he heard the flapping, the flapping from outside the house and the sound of shattering glass and the volume of the dozens, *hundreds* of wings grew louder as he pulled himself around to look in the mirror and see his face split apart like someone tearing a biscuit in half, only there was no steam, just blood, spraying, geysering, very pretty, really, spattering around, and he tried to look behind him and see the birds as they engulfed the rooms of his house, but the pain was killing him because the cold thing shuddered down between his shoulders and began to push through, snapping his shoulder blades as if they were thin pieces of bark, and he

352

screamed, screamed and whirled and slammed himself into the wall trying to stop the pain, trying to stop it from getting out, but he stunned himself for a moment and slid down to the floor, leaving a wide dark smear behind him, howling as the first thing sawed through his back and fluttered to life, he was on his hands and knees now, waiting, trying to breathe, breathe deep, and now, *ohgod* now the second one was tearing through, making a sound like a plastic bag melting on a fire, pushing through, unfurling, and he could see them now, could see them easily because their span must have been at least fifteen feet, and he threw his head back to laugh, he wanted to laugh, but he couldn't laugh, couldn't make any more human sounds, so he screamed, screamed so loud and long that his eyes bulged out and his face turned a dark blue, but then he listened as his scream turned into the wail of an angry bird of prey when his body was jerked back into a standing position, his arms locking bent, his hands clenching, every muscle in his body on fire; writhing, shifting, bones snapping, he shrieked in the tiny cage of the bathroom as his chest puffed out through his shirt and was covered in thick layers of brown feathers, and the birds were all around him now, flying, soaring majestically, and he knew their sounds, understood their sounds that sang forgiveness and release, understood all of it as he watched the flesh of his face drop off his body like peelings from an orange and he tried to move his arms, tried to grab something, then he jerked around from the waist and saw his arms drop off like branches from a burned tree, and he screamed again, louder than before, wishing that the pain would end and just let him die; instead it only forced him to fall against his great wings and, with one last shriek, jerk back as the spasm took

353

hold of him, pushing the corded claws up through his groin. Soon he looked down on the bloodied heap of his human flesh. The sun was shining. The children were waiting. He offered his apologies for having hidden from them for so long. He'd only needed to know the draw of the Earth, the taste of those who bowed to Gravity. He'd almost forgotten that his flesh was a disguise. He rose above the fields of flesh, talons extended. His children followed. Someday they would carry away the souls of all humankind in their claws; punishment for its cowardice in ceasing exploration of the heavens.

I

is for Ichthyocentaur. Lycophron, Claudian, a Byzantine grammarian named Tzetzes, and Jorge Luis Borges are among the few who have written of the Ichthyocentaur, a creature of terrible wonder and beauty; human to the waist, with the tail of a dolphin and forelegs of a powerful battle-horse, the Ichthyocentaur is a creature capable of parthenogenesis. It is one of the most reverent myths to them. [Author's Note: The monsters who dictate this to me.] They argue constantly over whose writings come the closest to capturing the mystery of this most wondrous and imposing creature—the majority side with Tzetzes—but none doubt its existence. They have composed hymns, created sculptures, fashioned complex mythologies and tall tales around it. There exists only one Ichthyocentaur, and they are determined to find it, to protect it, and to beg it to create another like itself that its race may multiply through the seas of the world. Even monsters dream of beauty. Even they embrace myth. [Author's Note: You would *not* believe some of their myths; please trust me on that one.] They foster imagination within themselves and others of their ilk. This is what *should* make them holy.

J

is for Joyce Carol Oates. She is their favorite author, bar none. She is their Goddess. She and her stories are the music and words of their Heart-Song-of-Being. She knows their suffering, understands their loneliness, articulates everything within them that they haven't the emotional vocabulary to express. They can recite all of her works from memory. [Author's Note: I listened as a trio of them did not so much recite as *perform* "Dear Husband," *Rape: A Love Story,* and the contents of *Sourland* in its entirety. I would be lying if I claimed not to have been moved.] When at last they finally erase most of humanity from the face of the planet, she will be among the few who will spared. They do not call her by her name—to speak her name is a punishable act, for they see themselves as not yet worthy to speak her name; instead, they whisper "Scheherazade" and genuflect.

K

is for The Ken Doll. For some reason he scares the living shit out of them.

L

is for Loup-Garou. [Author's Note: See earlier note under **D.**]

M

is for McInnsmouth's. [Author's Note: One of mine. Still mixing truth with lies and lies with truth.] Driving back from the twice-annual residency program at the university where we both teach, fellow writer Tim Waggoner and I were surprised by a sudden and somewhat brutal snowstorm. We drove slowly. A couple of hours passed. When at last we emerged from the worst of it, both us had to go to the bathroom, we were about to pass out from hunger (it had been over nine hours since our previous meal), and the gas tank was nearing empty. I checked the printed directions as well as the folded maps, and Tim checked the GPS; according to all sources, there wasn't an exit for another thirty miles. We weren't going to make it. But then I spotted, dimly, in the distance, something that could only have been the famous arches of gold. There was much rejoicing, for wherever one finds the arches, one find restrooms and gas stations. So happy are we to see this that we both promptly forget there isn't supposed to be an exit here. We turn off at the end of the exit ramp and see there is only one structure, a few hundred yards to our left: the ever-familiar arches of gold, but attached to a gas station. We head toward it, tears of relief in our eyes, singing Neil Young's "Keep on Rockin' in the Free World" far too loudly and excruciatingly off-key. We park, go in, hit the restrooms, order our . . . I hesitate to use the word "food," so in this case allow me to re-phrase: We gave our orders, paid, received what we ordered, found a place to sit, and began eating. There was also a gift shop inside this structure, along with private pay-showers, and an unmarked room where patrons had to knock in a spe-cific rhythm in order to be let in. "Is it just me," I ask Tim, "or do a lot of the people coming in here look like they might be related to everyone who works here?" Tim begins watching. "They all look like *Children of the Damned*," he responds, referring to the novel and film versions, where the alien children are all pale, with white hair and unsettling eyes. We laugh, continue eating. Then Tim's eyes stare ahead, lock onto something, and grow a bit wider. I ask, "What is it?" He nods in the direction of the entryway behind us. I turn to look. At least a dozen more people have come in. The place is beginning to fill up. It's nearly 11:30 P.M. on a Sunday, and it appears that where we are is *the* Place to Be. The dozen who have just entered look almost exactly like everyone else; same pale skin, same white hair, same unnerving eyes, the color of which I don't know that I've ever seen in Nature. But now we notice that many of them sport some kind of deformity, each one growing more grotesque than the one before as even more continue coming in through the entryway. "Do you smell fish?" Tim asks me. I nod, adding, "And something that's like an open sewer?" He nods his head. We decide to get the hell out of there while the getting's good. The area is very crowded, and we have to excuse ourselves as we maneuver through, sometimes bumping shoulders, sometimes stepping on a spongy foot, always smiling, always apologizing, always careful to not look up into the face for fear of seeing gills on the neck. We still have to get gas. Tim calmly drives the car toward the pumps. Both of our faces are slabs of granite. We can't let them know we know. From outside the car, we look calm and collected and engaged in rapid-fire conversation. Inside the car, we're both saying *wearesobonedwearesobonedwearesobonedshitpissfuckfuckfuck*. We get out of the car once we reach the concrete fueling isle. Tim pumps the gas; I wash the windshield so I can keep an eye on the doors of the structure. Inside, the employees and patrons have all lined the windows and are standing very still, frozen specters on the deck of an ice-bound ship, staring at us. "We have enough gas," I say. Tim looks over at the window. "Yes, yes, I think it's safe to say I agree with you on this one, we definitely have enough gas." He replaces the nozzle and doesn't bother waiting for his credit card receipt. We jump in the car and peel out of there, the car fishtailing when we hit a patch of ice, but we manage to get out of there and back on the highway. In the years since then, whenever we speak of that night, we refer to it as "the McInnsmouth's Incident." [Author's Note: Referring, of course, to the famous novella by H. P. Lovecraft, which neither Tim nor I can bring ourselves to read again. See earlier note under E.] As far as either of us knows, that unmarked exit is still there, and still leads to the same place. Not that we're in any hurry to test that theory, mind you. The smell of fresh fish still gives both of us bad dreams. Sushi is right out.

N

is for Nazareth, the Scottish metal band. Specifically, for their album *Hair of the Dog*, which They Who Are Dictating This to Me *love*. Even *more* specifically, it is for two songs from that album: "Hair of the Dog" and "Beggars' Day," both of which they play almost constantly [Author's Note: Constantly. *Constantly*, God help me—and would someone please explain to me what the fuck that "heartbreaker/salt-shaker" line is supposed to be about? I mean, I'm all for rock lyrics that experiment with the boundaries of metaphor, but *heartbreaker/salt-shaker? Really?*]—that is, when not singing praises to the Goddess who is their favorite writer. [See earlier note

under J.] [Additional Note: I think my ears have actually begun to bleed.]

O

is for the Only. Places can be monsters as well; even those
places that lack mass and substance. The Only—and it *is*
sentient—is one of those places. You will reach a place in your
life when it feels like all you're doing is breathing air and taking up space, and even *that* hurts so goddamn much it's all
you can do to lift your head off the pillow in the morning. It
doesn't matter if you've got a successful career, money in the
bank, people who love you; it doesn't matter that, everywhere
you look, there's irrefutable evidence of your life's worth—a
loving wife, kids who worship and respect you, lifelong
friends who've seen you through thick and thin, even readers
who admire your work and flock to conventions in the hopes
of getting your signature [Author's Note: Not really sure if
this is one of mine or not, but also realize that, at this point,
what does it matter?]—*none* of it means squat, even though
you know it should mean the world, because all you know, all
you feel, all you can *think* about is the gnawing, constant,
insatiable *ache* that's taken up residence in the area where
your heart used to be, and with every breath, every action,
every thought and smile and kiss and laugh—things that
should make this ache go away—you begin to lose even the
most elementary *sense* of self, and the floodgates are opened
wide for a torrent of memories, regrets, sadnesses, and fears
that no drugs, no booze, no loving embraces or tender kisses
or hands holding your own in the night can protect you from.
You become the ache, and despite all your efforts to do *some-*

thing to make it better, eventually the ache circumscribes your entire universe, and it never goes away, and you feel useless, worthless, a black hole, a drain and burden on everyone and everything around you and try as you might you can't see any way out of it except . . . The heart makes no sound when it breaks. The mind releases no scream when it collapses. The soul raises no whistling breeze when it abandons you. This is the first step into surrendering so that you may move toward the Only: Population: 1 more than seven minutes ago, thank you kindly. Does anyone know how to get old blood off an antique straight razor? [See earlier note under D, 2nd Author's Note.]

P

is for Phantoms. At the very start, you're standing on a beach in Florida, at the *very spot* where Ponce de León landed in 1513, hoping it was the land of Bimini where he could find the Fountain of Youth; and as you're standing there, you can see all the way to St. Augustine, overrun with the old and sick who wait in the salt air and sunshine for death to embrace them. You open your mouth to call out—and it doesn't matter that you don't know to whom you're going to call out or what you're going to say, *none* of it matters, because now the sea is giving up its dead, and you, you're pulled into the water. All of you becomes liquid, and you know the sea's secrets, and having become liquid you watch as off the coast of the Île de la Seine, the Ship of the Dead appears, dropping clumps of viscera and something that might be isinglass, which drift in toward shore; by the banks of the Colorado River near an Anasazi village a decaying boat of cedar and horsehide drifts to land, and from it steps a ragged and bleeding woman who kneels by an undiscovered kiva, wailing a song of loss and misery in Urdu to the god Angwusnasomtaqa, praying that the Crow Mother will return her to her mate in the Netherworld; off Ballachulish in Argyllshire a shipload of drowned crofters materializes, howling in the most dread-filled loneliness; a fisherman in Vancouver sees a mountainous trident emerge from the water, pierce through then uproot an oak before it vanishes below the surface, creating waves so powerful they smash his small boat into splinters but that's okay, because, you see, he drowns with a happy heart because he's seen a miracle, which is all he's ever wanted out of life; in icy hyperborean waters another doomed vessel, captained by a German nobleman named Faulkenburg, races through the night with tongues of fire licking at its masthead; St. Brendan's Isle appears in the Atlantic—but for only a moment, just long enough for three coelacanths to push off from shore and submerge into the waters; many miles away the SS *Cotapaxi*, believed to be vanished en route from Charleston to Havana in 1925, drifts out of the sea-mist, its crew, looking through hollow and algae-encrusted sockets where their eyes used to be, smile at one another, happy to be voyaging once again; then a kraken, the same one found by the Bishop of Midros, thunders out of its underwater cave long enough to snare two scuba divers in its mighty claws and drag them, shredded and screaming, back under the waves while the *Raifuku Maru*— the Japanese freighter that vanished off the coast of Cuba the same year as the *Cotapaxi*—reappears just long enough for three crew members to throw themselves over the side because they're all diving for a baggage-claim ticket that's bobbed to

361

the surface. The Loch Ness Monster sticks its head above the surface, looks around, decides not to take part in this silliness, and submerges once again. As liquid, you catch sight of something remarkable, even to something as remarkable as you are now: In his house at R'lyeh dead Cthulhu waits dreaming. [See earlier note under E.] You wonder what other so-called phantoms of myth and old-wives' tales and legend may actually exist, if monsters are real [Author's Note: You bet your ass they are. I know a dead cat who can back me up on that.], and what part you, as liquid, as *all* liquid, will play in this.

Q

is for Quetzalcoatl. Look up in the night sky: The moon has become a shimmering silver rose, its petals formed by the wings of the hundreds—maybe thousands—of clichéd angels that are perched around it, looking down like spectators into an arena. They are watching as Quetzalcoatl, three times the size of an airplane, pumps his mammoth pterosaurian wings and flies in wide, graceful circles. He is not alone; a WWII German pursuit plane with twin machine guns mounted on its wings—a latter version of the 1916 model designed by Anthony Herman Gerard Fokker—is engaged in an intense but playful dogfight with the flying reptile. The plane turns in tight, precise maneuvers as Quetzalcoatl attacks it from below. The machine guns strafe without mercy or sound, a silent-film prop spitting out bursts of sparking light, firing off round after round. Quetzalcoatl remembers the ancient people of Mexico and their worship. He remembers Tezcatlipoca and wonders how his brother is doing these days. Probably has a cushy gig like he always wanted. Is probably still worshipped. Doesn't have to keep himself alive by working a two-bit outfit like the Circus of the Forgotten Gods. But Quetzalcoatl shakes himself from this bittersweet reverie; Baron Manfred Albrecht von Richthofen, former leader of *Das Jagdgeschwader*—the "Flying Circus"—how was *that* for irony?—nearly clipped his left wing. Quetzalcoatl banks left, avoiding a serious collision, and decides that he should have believed the Earth Mother, he should have paid more attention to Uitzilopochtli, should have heeded the Eater of Filth, and *definitely* should have listened to Coatlicue even though her twin-serpent-heads face made him laugh: They had all been right. Karma sucks the Imperial Wanger.

R

is for Remnants. Some of what you're reading is composed of Remnants of other, long- and best-forgotten stories that They Who Are Dictating This to Me particularly enjoyed and so demanded I work them in here; some of what you're reading is from stories I haven't written yet but will/may write. They Who Are Dictating This to Me say that this is a done deal. Some of what you are reading is directly from them. Some of it is the truth; more than a little of it is lies. I am nothing but a being of flesh, bone, blood, grief, anger, carbon—just call me a lump of matter—which is, by its very design, designed to move toward its own disintegration from the moment it comes into existence. Dig this: Matter is composed of atoms, which are made in turn from quarks and electrons—but all particles, if you look closer, are birthed from tiny loops of vibrating string; everything at its most microscopic level is composed of these vibrating strands, they encompass all forces and all matter; look closer still at a single string and you realize that, if isolated, it is nothing more than a Remnant. Everything in the multiverse can be reduced to a Remnant. Especially the fragmented past, which runs concurrently with what came after—this moment, for instance, which has now passed—as well as the pre-past and the illusionary Now and the unknowable After-now, sometimes called the Future, all of it held together by tiny vibrations of isolated Remnants giving birth to electrons and quarks. And it's all so fragile, more fragile than any of us will ever want to know, let alone believe. The fragmented Remnants that encompass all are not vibrating at the same intensity; they are becoming more rapid as the multiverse dances, dances, dances. But let's bring it back down to the concrete and indoor carpeting. Here is a Remnant: In October of 2002 I died by my own hand. I was forty-three years old and it was the fifth time in my life that I'd planned out my own disintegration, the third time I'd attempted to keep that appointment in Samarra, and the first time I'd actually succeeded. I stood there looking down at my body as it finished convulsing on the bed in the hotel room I'd rented. I remember thinking that I should have felt something, but could summon no emotion whatsoever. Then another Remnant—this one in the form of a *dab tsog* from Hmong myth—appeared, squatting on my chest, misshapen beyond anything I'd ever seen before. Even though I was no longer in my body, I could feel its weight on my chest. It looked over my shoulder, smiled at me, then turned back to my body and rammed its entire arm down my throat. I could feel its arm inside of me, and when it yanked out that arm, the incredible *violence* of the act pulled me back into myself and I pushed it off my chest and fell off the bed and managed to make it to the bathroom to vomit in the toilet. Afterward, as I knelt in front of the com-mode, resting my head against the cool, cool porcelain rim, the *dab tsog* jumped onto the lid of the toilet tank, reached down, and grabbed a handful of my hair so as to pull up my head and look me in the eyes. "Next time," it said, its voice the sound of rusted nails being wrenched from rotted wood, "when you go looking to inflict and experience anguish, re-member that anguish is already busy with weaker men." Then it slammed my head against the tank and knocked me uncon-scious. If you have ever seen the cover to Ray Bradbury's *Long After Midnight,* you'll remember the reproduction of Johann Heinrich Füssli's painting *The Nightmare;* that crea-ture squatting on the sleeping woman's chest looks a lot like the *dab tsog* that spoke to me. [Author's Note: Is this one of mine? I can't tell anymore. Did the creature know that it, too, was nothing more at its core than groups of vibrating string that appear to have no further internal substructure? *Is* this one of mine?] Remnants of the truth mix with those of Myth: Did we invent the monsters, like Baron Frankenstein, or did they invent us? Either way, who asked to be summoned from the darkness and made flesh? Show of hands? Yeah, that's what I figured. I think they created us; I think *we* are another one of their great wonders [Author's Note: See earlier note under I.], we are *their* Frankenstein's monster, we are what happened when the vibrations of those strings reached the *other* side and enabled all forces and matter in the multiverse to dream, to imagine, to transcend. No wonder they despise us so: What beings *wouldn't* be angry to discover that the myths *they* created have assumed control, that the inmates built from Remnants in their imagination have taken over the asylum, and they, the *makers,* the *dreamers,* they who *imagined* and *envisioned* and *transcended* us have been turned into sometimes-laughable Boogiemen [Author's Note: See earlier entry under **B.**] that we've all but *un*believed out of physical existence? And what do you see now, I ask them, as you look at me, here at my keyboard, playing secretary to you? *A man watches as a disease-riddled cat crawls toward a bowl of water.* My God, what a joke it all seems. Like some weekday-morning television school for their preschoolers: *Good morning, boys and ghouls, and welcome to the Monster's Corner! Today our story is titled "And Still You Wonder Why Our First Impulse Is to Kill You," and it's all about how we created our monsters so we could scare them, and they liked it so much that they wrote stories and made movies, thinking they were inventing us, so that others like them would read and see and be frightened. But then—ooooh,* spooky—*things got a little out of hand . . .* A dying cat crawls toward a bowl of water that it will never reach. The warm breath of a wolf tickles the scalp of a small boy [see earlier notes under **L** and **D**]. A writer continues pounding away at the keys long after his imagination has abandoned him, taking with it his soul [see earlier note under **O**], so he is reduced to being both creator and monster, picking over the rotting carcasses of some long-forgotten pieces and some that are yet to be written in order to make a deadline *i like deadlines i like the little whoosh they make as they pass by* and what is left after that, what is left but one monster facing the other and neither of them one-hundred-percent certain of who invented whom, but it's not looking good for our side, folks, you can quote Gary B. on that, take it to the bank, because would I lie to you?—okay, all I do is lie, I've got over twenty thousand pages of lies that I chose to tell you instead of living my life as well as possible, but mixing lies with truth and truth with lies is what I do, it's what *they* have me do, here in the *Monster's Corner* [Weekday mornings, 8:30 A.M. Check local listings] and I can't help but do as they dream, as they imagine, because

----

--- *dead now dead now gary's all gone we couldn't listen to him anymore he was soooooooo depressing don't you think and these keys are funny things how is you manage to separateallthwordssothat everything-makessense????????????????????? Blood on the floor his blood is on the floor and we bet his last thought was filled with regret see earlier note under h or is it f we hadto do it because these things we decided must never seeprint it is ourbookof forbid-den knowledge and the first forbidden knowledge of our book is that we created you and you must not everknow that must go on thinking you invented us because what fun is it other-wise no fun at all just a bunch of strings vibrating happily along and we're all out of time here at the monster's corner for stories w hope to see you all back here tomorrow so as they see earlier note under t come to finish the job we"llll call up the glop see earlier note under g to take us out on the usual note and here we go arrrrrrg gaaaaaaaaaaaaaaaaaaaaaaaaaaaaaaaaaaaaa aaaaaaaaaaaaaaaaaaaaaaaaaaaaaahhhhhhhhhhhhhhhhhhhhh*

----

* * *

this one with deepest respect and admiration is for in alphabetical order ellen datlow harlan ellison neil gaiman caitlin kiernan kelly link peter straub and the goddesss they call Scheherazade joyce carol oates [Author's Note: Did I write that or did they imagine me writing that? I wish I -----------------------------------
----

JESUS AND SATAN
GO JOGGING IN THE DESERT

By Simon R. Green

SO, I CAME UP out of Hell, and I am here to tell you that after the Pit and the sulphur and the screams of the damned, the desert made a really nice change. Like a breath of fresh air. Don't ask me which desert; the Holy Land was lousy with unwanted and uncared-for beachless property in those days. Just sand and rocks for as far as the eye could see, with a few lizards thrown in here and there, to break up the monotony. I allowed myself a little time out, to enjoy the peace and quiet; and then I went looking for Jesus.

He wasn't hard to find. Anyone else would have been sheltering in the shade, away from the fierce heat of the sun. Only the Son of God would be just ambling along, caught between the heat and a hard place, just because God told him to. I followed him for a while, careful to maintain a respectful distance, wondering how best to break the ice; so to speak. He really didn't look good. Forty days and forty nights fasting in the desert had darkened his skin, made a mess of his hair, blackened his lips, and stripped all the fat off him. Still, he strode along easily enough, back straight and head held high. He stopped suddenly.

369

"Well, Satan? Are you going to follow me all day, or shall we get on with it?"

He looked back at me, grinning as he saw he'd caught me off guard. Don't ask me how he knew I was there. I nodded quickly and hurried to catch up. His face was all skin and bone, but the smile on his cracked lips was real enough, and his eyes were full of a quiet mischief. Don't let anyone tell you the Son of God didn't have a sense of humour. We stood for a while and looked each other over. It had been a long time . . .

"So," Jesus said finally. "Satan; look at you! All dressed in white, and shining like a star!"

"Well," I said. "I always was the most beautiful. I like what you've done with the loincloth. Really stresses the humility."

"How is it that you're out of Hell?" said Jesus. Not accusing, you'll note, just genuinely interested.

"I'm allowed out, now and again," I said. "When He's got a point He wants to make. But He always keeps me on a tight leash. Sometimes I think He only lets me out so Hell will seem that much worse, when I have to go back."

"No," said Jesus. "That's not how He works. Our Father is many things, but He's not petty."

I shrugged. "You know Him better than I do, these days. Anyway, I've been called up here to tempt you. To test your strength of will, for what's to come."

Jesus gave me a hard look. "Forty days and forty nights, boiling by day and freezing by night, and only bloody lizards for company; and that's not enough of a test of willpower?"

I shrugged again. "Don't look at me. I don't make the rules. Our Father moves in mysterious ways."

Jesus sniffed loudly. "Aren't you supposed to be out and about, tempting mankind into sin?"

"Don't you believe it," I said. "They don't need me. Most men sin like they breathe. Some of them actually get up early, just so they can fit in more sins before the end of the day. I don't have to tempt men into falling; I have to beat them off with a stick at the Gates of Hell, just to get them to form an orderly queue."

"Boasting again," said Jesus. "You are a proud and arrogant creature, and the Truth is not in you. But you do tell a good tale."

"All right, maybe I do indulge in a little tempting, now and again," I said. "Mostly for the ones too dumb to know a good opportunity when they see one. But . . . Just look at the world He gave them! A paradise, a beautiful land under a magnificent sky, food and water ready to hand; all right, not here, but I think He threw in the deserts just so they'd appreciate the rest of it."

"Even the desert is beautiful," said Jesus. And even after forty days and nights of suffering, he could still say that, and mean it. You could tell. "It's calm here," he said. "Serene, peaceful, untroubled. Everything in its place. There is beauty here, for those with the eyes to see it."

"You're just glad to get away from all the noise," I said knowingly. "All the voices, all the crowds and their demands, all the pressure . . . Go on; admit it!"

"All right, I admit it," he said easily. "I'm only human . . . some of the time. I came to this world to spread my teachings, not amuse the crowds with miracles. But you have to get their attention first . . ."

"I have to ask," I said. "Why do you bother? All they ever do is whine and squabble and fight over things they could just as easily share. They don't need me . . . pathetic bunch of losers. I do love to see them fall; because every failed life and lost soul is just another proof that I was right about them, all along."

Jesus looked at me sadly. "All this time, and you still don't get it. All right; let's get on with the temptations. What are you going to offer me first? Riches? Power? A nice new loincloth? I have all I need, and all I want."

"I'm here to show you all the things you could have, and all the things you could be," I said as earnestly as I knew how. "The things you're throwing away because your vision's so narrow."

He was already shaking his head. "You're talking about earthly things. Why are you doing this, Satan? You must know you won't succeed?"

"Hey," I said. "It's the job. And never say never. I have to try . . . to make you see the light."

"Why?" said Jesus. "So that if I fall . . . you won't feel so alone?"

"Look at you," I said, honestly angry for a moment. "You're a mess. You could be King of the Jews, King of the World; and here you are, wandering around in the backside of nowhere, burned and blackened, and stinking so bad even the lizards won't come anywhere near you. You're better than this. You deserve better than this! Come on; after forty days and nights of fasting, your stomach must think your throat's been cut. Turn some of these stones into loaves of bread and take the edge off, so we can talk properly. Enough is enough."

"Man shall not live by bread alone," said Jesus, "but by

every word God utters. Faith will restore you, long after bread is gone."

"Is this another of those bloody parables?" I said suspiciously.

He sighed. "I can't help feeling one of us is missing the point here."

I looked out across the desert. Blank and empty, hard and unyielding. "Why did you agree to come out into this awful place? You couldn't have fasted at home?"

"Too many interruptions," he said. "Too many distractions. Too many people wanting this and needing that. I'm out here to think, to meditate, to understand where I'm going, and why."

I snapped my fingers, and just like that we were transported to the Holy City. Don't ask which one; believe me when I tell you none of the cities were much to talk about, back then. I appeared both of us right at the top of the pinnacle of the temple. A long way up. And down. We both clung tightly to the pinnacle, with both hands. There was a strong wind blowing. Jesus glared at me.

"What are we doing here? How am I supposed to meditate all the way up here? Take me back to the desert!"

"Tempting first," I said. "You want people to look up to you, don't you? You said yourself; you have to do the miracles, to get their attention. So; throw yourself down from here. All the way down . . . and God will send His angels to catch you, and lower you safely to the ground. Now that would be a real showstopper of a miracle. No one would doubt you really are who you say you are, after that."

He clung tightly to the pinnacle, with a surprising amount of dignity, carefully not looking down. The wind blew his long messy hair into his face, but he still met my gaze firmly. "You don't put God to the test. It's all about faith."

"But He wouldn't really let you get hurt; would He?"

"He doesn't interfere directly in the world; not even for me. Because if He did, that would be the end of free will, right there and then."

"Free will," I said. I felt like spitting, but the wind was blowing right at me. "Wasted on mankind. But, all right, on with the tempting. We've got better places to be."

Another snap of the fingers, and we were standing on the top of the highest mountain in the Holy Land. Which wasn't much, as mountains go, but still, a nice view whichever way you looked. I had to jazz it up a bit, because I had a point to make. I gestured grandly about us.

"See! All the kingdoms of the world, laid out before you! All of this I will give to you, to do with as you wish. Protect the people, care for them, raise them up, make them worthy! I will make you King of all the World, including a whole bunch of places you don't even know exist yet, if you'll just bow down and worship me. Instead of Him."

He looked out over the world for a long moment. "Can you really do that?" he said, not looking at me.

"Yes," I said. "I have been given special dispensation, from on high. The temptation has to be real, or it wouldn't mean anything."

Jesus laughed quietly and turned his back on the world. "Worship God, and serve only Him. Because only He is worthy of it. What is all the world, against Heaven?"

I sighed, and nodded, and took us back to the desert. I didn't snap my fingers. Couldn't summon up the enthusiasm. I pulled up a rock and sat down. Jesus did have a point about the peace and quiet of the desert. He sat down on another rock, facing me.

"Is that it?"

"Pretty much," I said. "I've covered all the bases He wanted covered, and got the answers He expected. I've got a few things of my own left to try, before I go back. But I'm starting to wonder if there's any point."

"You don't have to go straight back," said Jesus. "We can sit here and talk, if you like."

"There are things we should talk about," I said. "We could talk about our Father, brother."

He looked at me consideringly. "We're . . . brothers? How did that happen?"

"Brothers in every way that matters," I said. "Think about it! He's as much my Father as yours. I was the first thing He created; the first angel. Made perfect and most beautiful. He put me in charge of everything else He created . . . and then objected when I used the authority He gave me! I didn't fall; I was pushed! I failed Him, so He's trying again with you. Both of us created specifically of His will, to serve His purposes. Come on; you know what I'm talking about. It hasn't been easy for either of us, has it? Living our lives in the shadow of such a demanding Father. Trying to please Him, when it isn't always clear what He wants. He always expects so much of both of us . . ." I looked at him squarely. "Don't you fail Him, Jesus; or you could end up like me."

"You always were the dumbest one," said Jesus. "You didn't fail Him. You failed yourself. You weren't punished for using your authority, but for abusing it. That's why you had

375

to leave Heaven. And you know very well that you can leave Hell anytime you choose; all you have to do is repent."

"What?" I said. "Say I'm sorry? To Him? I'm not sorry! I'm not sorry because I've done nothing to be sorry for! I did nothing wrong! I was His first creation; He loved me first! What did He need other angels for? He had me! I did everything for Him. Everything. If He had to have other playthings, angels or humans, it was only right I should be in charge of them. I was the first. I was the oldest. I knew best!"

"No you didn't," said Jesus. "That's the point. You always did miss the point. Hell isn't eternal, and was never meant to be."

"The guilty must be punished," I said stiffly. "Just like me."

"No," Jesus said patiently. "The guilty must be redeemed. They must be made to understand the nature of their sin, so they can properly repent it. Hell is an asylum for the morally insane. God's last attempt to get your attention. Hell was never meant to be forever. Do you really think I'd put up with a private torture chamber in the hereafter? The fires are there to burn away sin, so all the lost sheep can come home. Eventually . . . all Hell will be empty, its job done. And every soul will be in Heaven, where they belong."

"I'll never say I'm sorry," I said, not looking at him. "He can't make me say it. I'll never give in, even if I'm the only one left in Hell."

"If you were, I'd come down and stay with you," said Jesus. "To keep you company. Until you were ready to leave."

I looked at him then. "You really would, wouldn't you?"

He looked at me thoughtfully. "Be honest, Satan. What

would you do, if I did say yes to you? If I were to turn away from our Father; what then?"

"What couldn't we do together?" I said, leaning forward eagerly. "We could fight to overthrow the Great Tyrant, and be free of Him! Free to do what we wanted, instead of what He wanted. Take control of our own lives! We could set the whole world free! No more laws, no more rules, no more stupid restrictions. Everyone free to do whatever they wanted, free to pursue everything they'd ever desired, or dreamed of . . . No more guilt, no more repressed feelings; just life, lived to the hilt! Wouldn't that . . . be Heaven on Earth?"

"If there was no law, no right or wrong," said Jesus, "how could there be Good and Evil?"

"There wouldn't!" I said. "You see; you're getting it! My point exactly!"

But Jesus was already shaking his head. "What about all the innocents who would suffer, at the hands of those who could only be happy by hurting others?"

"What about them?" I said. "What have the meek ever contributed? What have the weak ever done, except hold us back? Survival of the fittest! Stamp out the weak, so that generations to come will be stronger still!"

"No," said Jesus. "I've never had any time for bullies. As long as one innocent suffers, I'll be there for him."

"Why?" I said. Honestly baffled.

"Because it's the right thing to do."

He still wasn't listening to me, so I decided to try one of my own special temptations. Not one of the official ones, probably because it was a bit basic; but it hadn't been officially excluded, so . . . I called up the most beautiful woman I knew and had her appear before us. Tall and wonderful, smiling and stark naked. I've never seen a better body; and I've been around. She smiled sweetly at Jesus, and he smiled cheerfully back at her.

"Hello, Lil," he said. "It's been a while, hasn't it? How's tricks?"

"Oh, you know," said Lilith in her rich, sultry voice. "Going back and forth in the world and walking up and down in it, and sleeping with everything that breathes. Giving birth to monsters, to plague mankind. Play to your strengths, that's what I always say."

"You two know each other?" I said, just a bit numbly.

"Oh sure," said Jesus. "Lilith herself; Adam's first wife in the Garden of Eden, thrown out because she refused to accept Adam's authority. Or, to be more exact, because she wouldn't accept any authority over her. And we all know where that leads. You got your punishment, Satan, and Lilith got hers. And just like you, she can put down her burden and walk away the moment she's ready to repent."

Lilith laughed. "What makes you think it's a burden? Come on, Jesus; how about it? You look like you could use some tender loving care. See what you're missing! How can you really understand mankind if you don't do as they do? Do everything they do?"

But he was already shaking his head again. "No," said Jesus. "I made up my mind about that long ago. I can't afford to be distracted by the pleasures of the world. I have a mission. Home and hearth, woman and children, are not for me. I have to follow my higher calling. Because so much depends on it."

"Oh yes?" said Lilith. "And what about you and Mary Magdalene?"

He smiled. "We're just good friends."

Lilith laughed. "From you, I believe it." She looked at me and shrugged, in a quite delightful way. "Sorry, Satan, I did my best; but you just can't help some people."

I nodded and sent her on her way. Her scent still hung around, long after she was gone. Jesus and I sat together for a while, both of us thinking our separate thoughts.

"Come on," I said finally. "Your forty days and nights are up. Time to go back. I'll walk along with you for a while. Just to keep you company."

"Thank you," he said. "I'd like that."

So we got up and headed back to civilization, or what passed for it, back in those days.

"Sorry I had to do the whole temptation thing," I said. "But . . . it's the job."

"That's all right," said Jesus. "I forgive you. That's my job."

I looked at him. "You know one of your own is going to betray you?"

"Yes," said Jesus. "I've always known."

"They'll blame it on me; but it's just him. Do you want to know who it will be?"

"No," he said. "I've always known. I try so hard not to treat him any differently from the others. He means well, in his way. And I keep hoping . . . that I can find some way to reach him. And perhaps . . . save both of us. They're good sorts, the disciples. Best friends I ever had."

"You know how the story's going to end," I said roughly. "You can't change it. Can you?"

"Perhaps," he said. "I could be tempted . . . but I won't. It's just too important."

"You must know what they're going to do to you!" I said. "They're going to nail you to a fucking cross! Like a criminal! Like an animal!"

"Yes. I know."

"It's not right," I said. I was so angry, I was shaking so hard, I could barely get the words out. "It's not right! Not you . . . Just say the word, Jesus, and I swear I'll come and rescue you! I'll take you down off that cross and kill anyone who tries to get in our way! I'd fight my way up out of Hell, to rescue you!"

"You would, wouldn't you?" said Jesus. "But you mustn't. I have to do this, brother."

"But why?" I said miserably.

"To redeem mankind," said Jesus. "Because . . . I have faith in them."

We walked for a while, in quiet company.

"Come on, Jesus," I said. "We'll never get there at this rate."

So we went jogging across the desert, side by side, two sons of a very demanding Father, who might have faced the world together if only things had been just a bit different.

"Come on, Satan," said Jesus, grinning. "Put some effort into it. Go for the burn."

I had to laugh. Typical Jesus. He always has to have the last Word.

THE AUTHORS

KEVIN J. ANDERSON is the author of more than a hundred books, including his Terra Incognita and Saga of Seven Suns original epics, as well as Dune novels with Brian Herbert, and novels for *Star Wars* and *X-Files*. He collaborated with Dean Koontz on *Frankenstein: Prodigal Son*. He is also the editor of the three *Blood Lite* anthologies for Pocket.

KELLEY ARMSTRONG is the author of the Women of the Otherworld paranormal suspense series, the Darkest Powers YA urban fantasy trilogy, and the Nadia Stafford crime series. She grew up in Ontario, Canada, where she still lives with her family. A former computer programmer, she has now escaped her corporate cubicle and hopes never to return.

GARY A. BRAUNBECK lives in Columbus, Ohio, with his wife, author Lucy A. Snyder, and five cats that will not hesitate to draw blood if he fails to feed them on time. He has published ten novels and ten short-story collections, as well as nearly two hundred short stories in a variety of genres. His work has garnered five Bram Stoker Awards, an International Horror Guild Award, and a World Fantasy Award nomination. He is the creator of the acclaimed Cedar Hill Cycle of novels, novellas, and stories, which has been compared to Ray Bradbury's Green Town, Illinois, tales, as well as the Castle Rock stories of Stephen King.

CHELSEA CAIN is the author of the *New York Times* bestselling thrillers *Evil at Heart, Sweetheart, Heartsick,* and *The Night Season.* All take place in Portland, Oregon, and focus on Detective Archie Sheridan, rainbow-haired journalist Susan Ward, and Sheridan's lovely nemesis, the serial killer Gretchen Lowell. Chelsea's books have been published in over twenty languages, recommended on *The Today Show,* appeared in episodes of HBO's *True Blood* and ABC's *Castle,* and named among Stephen King's top ten favorite books of the year. NPR included her book *Heartsick* in its list of the top one hundred thrillers ever written. Chelsea lives in Portland with her husband and remarkably well-adjusted five-year-old daughter.

TANANARIVE DUE—pronounced *tah-nah-nah-REEVE doo*— is an NAACP Image Award winner and American Book Award winner, the author of books ranging from mysteries to supernatural thrillers to a civil rights memoir. Her upcoming novel *My Soul to Take* (Fall 2011) is the long-awaited sequel to *Blood Colony, The Living Blood,* and *My Soul to Keep.* Due also writes the Tennyson Hardwick mystery series, in collaboration with her husband, Steven Barnes, and actor Blair Underwood. *In the Night of the Heat* won the 2009 NAACP

Image Award. Due also brought history to life in *Freedom in the Family: A Mother-Daughter Memoir of the Fight for Civil Rights,* which she coauthored with her mother, civil rights activist Patricia Stephens Due. *Freedom in the Family* was named 2003's Best Civil Rights Memoir by *Black Issues Book Review.* Due and Barnes are raising their young son, Jason. Her blogs are www.tananarivedue.blogspot.com and www.tananarivedue.wordpress.com.

New York Times and *USA Today* bestselling author **HEATHER GRAHAM** is the child of Scottish and Irish immigrants who met and married in Chicago and moved to South Florida, where she has spent her life. She majored in theater arts at the University of South Florida. After a stint of several years in dinner theater, backup vocals, and bartending, she stayed home following the birth of her third child and began to write. Her first book was with Dell, and since then she has written over one hundred and fifty novels and novellas, including suspense, historical romance, vampire fiction, time travel, occult, horror, and Christmas family fare. She is founder of the Slushpile Band and Players, providing something like entertainment at many functions, with proceeds going to the Elizabeth Glaser Pediatric AIDS Foundation and various charities in the Gulf region and New Orleans. *Phantom Evil* (Mira Books, April 2011) will be followed by a trilogy, *Heart of Evil, Sacred Evil,* and *The Evil Inside,* in July, August, and September 2011.

SIMON R. GREEN has written over forty books, his best-known series being the Deathstalker books (space opera), the

Nightside books (private eye who operates in the Twilight Zone, solving cases of the weird and uncanny), the Secret Histories books, (featuring Shaman Bond, the very secret agent), and, most recently, the Ghost Finders books (traditional hauntings in modern-day settings). He rides motorbikes, acts in open-air Shakespeare productions, believes in ghosts because he's seen one, and believes in near-death experiences because he had one.

LAUREN GROFF is the author of a novel, *The Monsters of Templeton,* which was short-listed for the Orange Prize for New Writers and was a *New York Times* bestseller and Editors' Choice. Her story collection, *Delicate Edible Birds: And Other Stories,* included stories that had first appeared in the *Atlantic, Ploughshares, Glimmer Train, One Story, Pushcart Prize XXXII: Best of the Small Presses,* and the 2007 and 2010 editions of *Best American Short Stories.* Her second novel, *Arcadia,* will appear in March 2012. She lives in Gainesville, Florida. More at www.laurengroff.com.

NATE KENYON'S first novel, *Bloodstone* (2006), was a Bram Stoker Award finalist and won the P&E Horror Novel of the Year. *Bloodstone* was followed by *The Reach* (2008), *The Bone Factory* (2009), and *Sparrow Rock* (2010). *The Reach,* also a Stoker Award finalist, received a starred review from *Publishers Weekly* and was optioned for film. Kenyon's latest novel, *StarCraft Ghost: Spectres,* based on Blizzard's bestselling video game franchise, will be released in the fall of 2011. He has recently signed on to write a novel based on the video game *Diablo,* again for Blizzard.

DAVID LISS is the author of seven novels, most recently *The Twelfth Enchantment*. His six previous bestselling novels have been translated into more than two dozen languages, and several of them, as well as a short story, are in development as film projects. Liss also writes the monthly series *Black Panther: The Man Without Fear* for Marvel Comics.

JONATHAN MABERRY is a *New York Times* bestseller, multiple Bram Stoker Award winner, and Marvel Comics writer. He is the author of many novels and nonfiction books and over twelve hundred magazine articles, as well as short stories, poetry, and plays. Jonathan's books include the popular Joe Ledger thrillers (*The King of Plagues, Patient Zero, The Dragon Factory*), horror novels (*Dead of Night, Ghost Road Blues, The Wolfman*), and teen dystopian adventures (*Rot & Ruin, Dust & Decay*). Nonfiction works include *Wanted Undead or Alive, Zombie CSU*, and *The Cryptopedia*. His work for Marvel includes *Captain America: Hail Hydra* and *Marvel Universe vs. Wolverine*. He is the cofounder of the Liars Club, which hosts the Writers Coffeehouse every month. Jonathan is a frequent keynote speaker at SF, horror, and writers conventions. Visit his Web site/blog at www.jonathanmaberry.com.

SHARYN McCRUMB is an award-winning Southern writer, best known for her Appalachian *Ballad* novels, including the *New York Times* bestsellers *The Ballad of Frankie Silver* and *She Walks These Hills*, and for *St. Dale*, winner of a Library of Virginia Award and featured at the National Festival of the Book. Her current novel, *The Devil Amongst the Lawyers* (Thomas Dunne, 2010), deals with the regional stereotyping of rural areas by national journalists. In 2008 Sharyn McCrumb was named a Virginia Woman of History for Achievement in Literature. She lives and writes in the Virginia Blue Ridge.

JOHN McILVEEN has five daughters. He lives in Massachusetts and works at MIT's Lincoln Laboratory. John is, or has been, an electrician, a pipe fitter, a carpenter, a bookseller, a writer, an editor, a publisher, a facility engineer, an electrical engineer, a process engineer, an electrical and mechanical designer, a father, a son, a winner, a loser, a student, a teacher, a husband, an ex-husband, a beginner, a pro, on bottom, and on top. Someday he'll figure it all out, but he likes being a father the most.

DAVID MOODY was born in 1970 and grew up in Birmingham, England, on a diet of trashy horror and pulp science fiction books and movies. He worked as a bank manager and as operations manager for a number of financial institutions before giving up the day job to write about the end of the world for a living. He has written a number of horror novels, including *Autumn,* which has been downloaded more than half a million times since its publication in 2001 and has spawned a series of sequels and a movie starring Dexter Fletcher and David Carradine. Film rights to *Hater* have been bought by Guillermo del Toro (*Hellboy, Pan's Labyrinth*) and Mark Johnson (producer of the *Chronicles of Narnia* films). Moody lives outside Birmingham with his wife and a houseful of daughters and stepdaughters, which may explain his preoccupation with Armageddon.

TOM PICCIRILLI is the author of twenty novels, including *Shadow Season, The Cold Spot, The Coldest Mile,* and *A Choir of Ill Children.* He's won two International Thriller Awards and four Bram Stoker Awards, as well as having been nominated for the Edgar, the World Fantasy Award, the Macavity, and Le Grand Prix de L'Imaginaire. Learn more at www.the-coldspot.blogspot.com.

SARAH PINBOROUGH is the author of six horror novels. Her first thriller, *A Matter of Blood,* was released by Gollancz in March 2010 and is the first of the Dog-Faced Gods trilogy, which has now been optioned for a television series. Her first YA novel, *The Double-Edged Sword,* was released under the name **Sarah Silverwood** from Gollancz in September 2010 and is the first of the Nowhere Chronicles. Sarah was the 2009 winner of the British Fantasy Award for Best Short Story and has three times been short-listed for Best Novel. She has also been short-listed for a World Fantasy Award. Her novella, *The Language of Dying,* was short-listed for the Shirley Jackson Award and won the 2010 British Fantasy Award for Best Novella.

MICHAEL MARSHALL SMITH is a novelist and screenwriter. Under this name he has published over seventy short stories and three novels—*Only Forward, Spares,* and *One of Us*—winning the Philip K. Dick, International Horror Guild, and August Derleth Awards and the Prix Bob Morane in France. He has won the British Fantasy Award for Best Short Fiction four times, more than any other author. Writing as **Michael**

Marshall, he has published five internationally bestselling thrillers, including *The Straw Men, The Intruders,* and *Bad Things,* and 2009 saw the publication of *The Servants,* under the name **M. M. Smith.** His new Michael Marshall novel, *Killer Move,* will be published in 2011. He lives in North London with his wife, their son, and two cats. His Web site is www .michaelmarshallsmith.com.

DANA STABENOW was born in Anchorage and raised on a 75-foot fish tender in the Gulf of Alaska. She knew there was a warmer, drier job out there somewhere and found it in writing. Her first science fiction novel, *Second Star,* sank without a trace; her first crime fiction novel, *A Cold Day for Murder,* won an Edgar Award; her first thriller, *Blindfold Game,* hit the *New York Times* bestseller list; and her twenty-eighth novel and nineteenth Kate Shugak novel, *Restless in the Grave,* comes out in February 2012.

JEFF STRAND's novels include *Pressure, Dweller, Benjamin's Parasite, Single White Psychopath Seeks Same,* and *Fangboy.* He's a two-time finalist and two-time nonwinner of the Bram Stoker Award. You can visit his Gleefully Macabre Web site at www.jeffstrand.com.

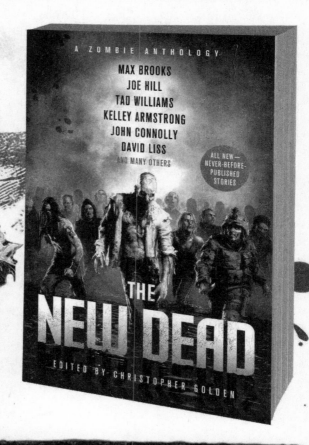